PHILIP REEVE

SCRIVENER'S MOON

SCHOLASTIC

BY PHILIP REEVE

MORTAL ENGINES QUARTET:
MORTAL ENGINES
PREDATOR'S GOLD
INFERNAL DEVICES
A DARKLING PLAIN

FEVER CRUMB TRILOGY:
FEVER CRUMB
A WEB OF AIR
SCRIVENER'S MOON

MORTAL ENGINES EXPANDED UNIVERSE:
NIGHT FLIGHTS
THE ILLUSTRATED WORLD OF MORTAL ENGINES

GOBLINS SERIES:
GOBLINS
GOBLINS VS DWARVES
GOBLIN QUEST

LARKLIGHT SERIES:
LARKLIGHT
STARCROSS
MOTHSTORM

RAILHEAD SERIES:
RAILHEAD
BLACK LIGHT EXPRESS
STATION ZERO

OTHER NOVELS:
NO SUCH THING AS DRAGONS
HERE LIES ARTHUR

BOOKS FOR YOUNGER READERS,
WRITTEN WITH SARAH MCINTYRE:
OLIVER AND THE SEAWIGS
CAKES IN SPACE
PUGS OF THE FROZEN NORTH
JINKS & O'HARE FUNFAIR REPAIR
THE LEGEND OF KEVIN

TO SARAH

Scholastic Children's Books
An imprint of Scholastic Ltd
Euston House, 24 Eversholt Street, London, NW1 1DB, UK
Registered office: Westfield Road, Southam, Warwickshire, CV47 0RA
SCHOLASTIC and associated logos are trademarks and/or
registered trademarks of Scholastic Inc.

First published in the UK by Scholastic Ltd, 2011
This edition published 2019

Text copyright © Philip Reeve, 2011
Cover artwork copyright © Ian McQue, 2019

The right of Philip Reeve to be identified as the author
of this work has been asserted.

ISBN 978 1407 18929 1

A CIP catalogue record for this book
is available from the British Library.

Printed by CPI Group (UK) Ltd, Croydon, CR0 4YY
Papers used by Scholastic Children's Books are made
from wood grown in sustainable forests.

1 3 5 7 9 10 8 6 4 2

This is a work of fiction. Names, characters, places, incidents
and dialogues are products of the author's imagination or are used
fictitiously. Any resemblance to actual people, living or dead,
events or locales is entirely coincidental.

www.scholastic.co.uk

CONTENTS

PROLOGUE

He forded the river as the daylight died and blundered into thick undergrowth between the birches on the far bank. Sobbing with fright and pain he raised his hand to his chest and felt the hard point of the arrow sticking out through his coat. He dared not look down for fear that the sight of it would make him faint, so he shut his eyes and took the bloodied wooden shaft in both hands, and snapped the head off. Pain knocked him to his knees. Groping behind him he found the feathered end of the arrow where it stuck out above his shoulder blade, braced himself, and wrenched it out. He ripped his handkerchief in half and crammed the pieces into the wounds.

He was a stranger in that country; an explorer; a scientist; a soldier of fortune. His name was Auric Godshawk. In years to come, when age had slowed him, he would be king of London, but on this night he was still in his prime; a strong Scriven male in his sixtieth year, the age hardly showing. That must be how he had survived the ambush, he thought. That must be how he

1

had managed to escape into these woods. Black trees, grey sky, the first stars showing. Cold now the light was gone. He wished he'd brought a hat with him, or gloves. He supposed he had left them behind in the inn or camp or wherever it was that he had been when the ambush happened. His memory seemed to be missing vital chunks. He felt as weak as London wine, and when he looked at his hands they did not seem to belong to him at all; frail, girlish things they seemed, turning blue where they were not crusted with his own blood.

Black trees and a starry sky and his feet crunching through the leaf-litter with sounds like someone munching on an apple. Great Scrivener, what would he not give for an apple?

Then he was lying on his side on the ground and he knew that if he did not rise and make himself go on he would lie there for ever, but he could not rise. He thought of London and his young daughter and wondered if she would ever know what had become of him and he said her name to the night, "Wavey, Wavey," until it made him start to cry.

And it was daylight, and the stink of mammoth was all about him as he opened his eyes. The animals stood around him like shaggy russet hills. Men moved between their tree-trunk legs. They were talking about him in words that he could not catch. He wondered if they were planning to save him or finish him, and he said, "Help me! I can pay you. . ."

One of the men drew a knife, but another stopped him and came and crouched at Godshawk's side. Not a man, he saw now, but a girl, with her long hair escaping in mammoth-coloured curls and tendrils from under her mammoth-fur hat. Weak as he was, Godshawk brightened. He had always had an eye for pretty girls.

"I am Auric Godshawk," he told her. "I am an important man among my people. Help me. . ."

He was lying among furs in a nomad tent, and nothing moved except the shadows on the low, curving roof. He was burning hot and he tried to push the furs off but the girl was there and she pulled them back over him and touched his forehead with her hand and held it there and it was so cool and she whispered things to him and the light of a woodstove was on her young face and in her red hair. He had seen her before. He remembered her sitting on a mammoth's back somewhere, watching as he went by.

He tried to speak to her, but she had gone, and now an ugly old man was leaning over him, chanting, singing, humming to himself as he made passes over Godshawk's face and body with a strange talisman of bones and birch-bark and scraps of age-old circuitry, jingling with little bells. He propped Godshawk on his side and scooped bitter-smelling slime out of an Ancient medicine bottle and smeared it into the wounds in his chest and his back and bound poultices of moss over them. *Your Ex-rays have come back from the Lab*, he chanted, and held up a sheet of mammoth-skin parchment so fine that the light of the fire shone through it, and Godshawk could see a childish skeleton drawn there, with red-topped pins stuck in to mark his wounds.

When he woke again the man was gone; the girl was back. He lay watching her. A tall girl, big-shouldered and broad across the hips, not a bit like the willow-slender, speckled Scriven women he liked, but her long autumn-coloured hair was lovely in the firelight and her eyes were very large and dark and she made him remember faintly a few of the pleasures of being alive. He called and she came to him and when she leaned over the bed with the loose strands of her hair falling down across his face he said, "Kiss me, mammoth-girl. You'd not deny a last kiss to a dying man?"

Her smile was sweet and quirky. She stooped and touched her warm mouth quickly to his cheek. "You are *not* a dying man," she said.

And he dozed in the warm gloom and dreamed of his daughter Wavey, but for some reason he saw her not as the little girl he'd left behind in London but as a woman nearly as old as him, and woke up weeping, and the girl was there with him again and held his hand.

"I dreamed of my daughter..." he tried to tell her. He could not explain. Everything was so strange. It was all sliding. His memories were as slippery as slabs of broken ice on a pond. Something was terribly wrong, and he had forgotten what it was. "My little girl..."

"Hush," she said. "You're feverish."

For some reason that made him laugh. "Yes! I am feverish. . . I am *Feverish*. . ."

And it was night and he was alone and he needed to pee, so he clambered out from under the fur covers and the night air was cold on his bare skin and the embers in the woodstove glowed, and as he reached under the bed for the pot he saw a movement from the corner of his eye and looked up, and there was a girl in the shadows watching him.

She was not his mammoth-girl. In his confusion he thought for a moment that she was Wavey, and he started up, and she rose too, but as they walked towards each other he saw that she was a stranger; a Scriven-looking girl, watching him with wide-set, mismatched eyes, one grey, the other brown. *Poor mite*, he thought, for she was a Blank; the Scrivener had put no markings on her flesh at all. There was an angry star-shaped scar above her breast and as she reached up to touch it he reached up too, in sympathy and understanding, and felt the same scar on his own flesh. Then lost memories started rushing past him like snow and he stretched out his fingers to the girl's face and touched only the cold surface of a looking glass.

His own numb fear looked back at him out of her widening eyes.

"No!" he shouted. They both shouted it; him and the girl in the mirror, but the only voice he heard was hers. "I am Auric Godshawk! I am *Godshawk!*"

But he wasn't. Godshawk had died a long time ago. What remained of him was just a ghost inhabiting the mind of this thin girl, his granddaughter. Her name, he suddenly recalled, was *Fever Crumb*.

And once he knew that, he could not stay. These thin young hands were not *his* hands; these eyes were not *his* eyes; this world was not *his* world any more. With a terrible sadness he let himself be folded down, like an immense and wonderful map being crumpled into an impossibly small ball, and packed away into the tiny machine that he had once planted, like a silver seed, among the roots of Fever's brain.

With his last thought, as he left her, he wondered what had brought her here, alone into the north-country with an arrow through her.

PART ONE

1

THE HOMECOMING OF FEVER CRUMB

10 Months Earlier

F ever came home to London in a summer storm, her land-barge bowling up the Great South Road beneath a sky full of rainbows.

The city of her birth had changed in the two years that she had been away. Even the lands around it looked different. The woods which once crowded close on either side of the road had been felled, leaving nothing but grey stumps. New settlements had sprung up on the hillsides; loggers' camps and waystations for the ceaseless convoys of hoys and big-wheeled land-barges which carried timber, steel and pig iron north to London. So she was prepared to find the city altered, but her first sight of it, as her barge grumbled across the Brick Marsh causeways, was still a shock. She stood at the front of the open upper deck, gripping the handrail and squinting into the stormy sunlight and the sharp north wind. She could hardly believe her watering eyes.

The London she had known was gone. On Ludgate Hill most of the old familiar buildings still stood, but they looked odd and isolated, like the last trees of a slaughtered forest. Around the hill's foot, where slums and rookeries once raised their gambrel roofs, there now stretched empty lots, and tumbled mounds of house-bricks, and rows and rows and rows of pale tents. All that remained of the vanished districts were their temples, like stony islands in a canvas sea, dwarfed by the immense new mills and factories whose chimneys filled the sky above the city with a stormcloud greater and darker than those which were gusting off Hamster's Heath. And even the factories seemed like toys compared with the new London, which squatted motionless and vast amid their smoke. Its immense chassis, broader than the biggest fleet of barges Fever had ever seen, rested on bank after bank of caterpillar tracks. Two decks or tiers of steel and timber were rising on its back, crammed with housing, bristling with cranes, stitched to the sky with scaffolding, the bright, white points of welders' torches shining amid the towering girderwork like daytime stars.

"The Lord Mayor's demolition gangs have spared the temples," said Fever's father, Dr Crumb. He stood beside her, holding an umbrella over them both and shouting to make himself heard above the hammering of the barge-engines and the hiss of the wind, which was starting to throw big, chilly raindrops in their faces. "He was afraid of stirring up religious trouble. But they will have to be torn down soon; there is wood and metal and salvage plastic in those buildings which the new city needs. . ."

Fever nodded, watching a last ray of sunlight strike the glittery thunderbolt which crowned the temple of the Thin White Duke. As an Engineer she had no time for London's silly gods and their temples, but she still felt sad that those great buildings, which had formed the skyline of her childhood, would soon be gone.

A gust blew Dr Crumb's umbrella inside out and he struggled with it for a moment, then turned away from the rail. "Come, Fever; the weather worsens; let us go inside. . ."

Reluctantly she followed him through the hatch and down the tight twist of wooden stairs. The barge was swaying and jolting as its huge wheels bumped down off the causeway's end on to London cobbles. Fever braced herself against its sudden movements without even noticing. She was used to land-barges. For two years she'd travelled as technician aboard one of them, a mobile theatre called *Persimmon's Electric Lyceum*. Right across Europa, all the way to the island city of Mayda . . . but she did not like thinking about Mayda.

Fever's mother, Wavey Godshawk, London's Chief Engineer, was waiting for them in the barge's comfortable cabin. Wavey was a Scriven; the last of that curious, mutant race, and the Scriven liked to stay inside when it was raining, like cats. "Fever," she purred, when her damp daughter came in, and she brushed Fever's face with her fingers. Fever hated being touched, but Wavey could not help herself; she loved touching the people she loved;

stroking them, caressing them, patting them like pets. She wrapped her silky arms around Dr Crumb from behind and rested her long chin on the top of his head, and Fever stood beside them, and they all three stared out through the wet portholes, watching the water droplets wriggle this way and that like blind glass beetles, watching the new city shift and twist behind the rain.

The barge pulled past Ox-fart Circus, where Godshawk's Head had once stood: the giant sculpture of Fever's Scriven grandfather, whose hollow interior had been home to Dr Crumb and London's other Engineers; the calm, safe home of Fever's childhood. Now there were only tents, and ranks of those crude, wheeled shelters which the northern nomads called *campavans*. But even with its buildings gone, London looked more orderly than it had when Fever saw it last. There was fresh lime scattered in the gutters, and wagons were ferrying waste and sewage to pits on the city's edge. Policemen wearing leather caps with big copper badges strolled in pairs between the tents, or stood directing traffic at the intersections.

They were needed, for on the rubble-paved roads which ran between the camps huge wagons and motorized drays were moving, and at one point the barge passed a line of laden mammoths, which distracted even Fever from staring at the new city for a moment. She had often heard of *Mammuthus novii*; the mighty Hairyphants of northern legend. Ancient texts spoke of mammoths as extinct, but there were whole herds of them in the north-country, so either the Ancients had been wrong, or they had found some way to make the creatures *un*-extinct again, or the mammoths of modern times were a mutation; a tribe of normal elephants in whom some old genetic switch had been tripped by the traumas of the Downsizing, causing them to grow once more those coats of shaggy auburn wool.

"Traders from the nomad lands, come south with tech or copper," her mother said, as Fever watched the animals go by. "London is like a newborn star; it draws in matter from all around. . ."

The barge went lumbering on up Ludgate Hill until it reached the summit, where the old mothballed fortress called the Barbican had once stood. A ramshackle, temporary-looking building made from wood and plastic sheeting sprawled in its place, thrusting out odd wings and annexes in all directions.

"What has happened to the Barbican?" asked Fever.

"Gone," said her mother cheerfully. "It forms part of the new city's Base Tier now."

"So is that big shed the Lord Mayor's palace?"

"Oh no. Quercus lives aboard the new London. That big shed is the new Engineerium."

"And is that where you and Dr Crumb live?"

"Good gods, no! Really, Fever, there would hardly be any point in my being Chief Engineer if I had to live in a *shed*, would there? I have requisitioned quarters for us nearby. . ."

The land-barge turned left on to the street called Bishopsgate and stopped there outside a tall, thin mansion which had once belonged to one of London's richest merchants. A Stalker on duty outside its red front door came smartly to attention as the barge ran out its gangplank and the Chief Engineer and her family disembarked. Servants came out with umbrellas to usher them inside and fetch their trunks and baggage from the barge. Fever found herself in a hexagonal hallway paved with Ancient eye-pods. Carpeted stairs ascended into the rain-coloured light from high windows.

"Welcome, Fever!" said her mother. "Welcome to your new home!"

Unlike London, Fever had hardly changed at all. She was a little tanned by the southern sun, but that was already fading. She had grown her honey-coloured hair, but it was pulled back into a bun as hard as a fist at the nape of her neck, so it did nothing to soften that bony, alien beauty. Her eyes, one brown and one grey, had seen foreign lands; her mouth had been kissed; her heart had been broken; but none of those things showed. Apart from the hair, the girl who stared out at her from the antique mirror in her new room was the same girl who had left London two years before. She was back where she had started, and not at all sure that she had the energy to start again.

Outside her window, despite the rain and fading light, the salvage gangs kept working. She studied the gaps between the buildings, half hoping to snatch another glimpse of the mammoths she had seen on the road, but they must be long gone by now; on their way home to their chilly northern hills. She watched a row of townhouses in Clerkenwell collapse into smudges of dust. From the new city came the sound of hammers, and from the door of her bedroom a sudden knocking. Too dazed to say, "Come in," she turned as the door was booted open. A boy in the white coat of an apprentice Engineer entered, carrying a pile of towels.

"Sorry," he said, seeing her there. "I thought you was downstairs, I never meant. . ."

His voice trailed away. He stared at her over the towels, and she remembered him staring at her once before, in a fogbound garden, a gun between them and him holding it. She did not know his name. He was the Skinner's boy. The last time they met, he had killed her.

"Go away!" she said loudly. She was not afraid of him exactly, but she was startled by how much he startled her. The boy took a step back, still holding the towels. There were footsteps on the stairs and Dr Crumb appeared in the doorway behind him, nervous as a bird.

"Oh, Fever, I should have warned you. This is Charley Shallow, my apprentice. I know, I, erm, well, that you two have met. . ."

"I was just bringing her some towels, like you asked," said Charley, turning to Dr Crumb as if he'd been accused of something.

"Yes, Charley, quite. Thank you. I thought Fever was still downstairs with her mother. I'll take those. . ."

Fever felt her ears turn red. She had been irrational. A glance at Charley Shallow should have told her that he had changed almost as much as London since she last saw him. He looked less like a boy, more like a young man. His hair was cropped as short as Dr Crumb's. He had probably been trained in the ways of calmness and rational thought by the Guild of Engineers. "I was taken by surprise. . ." she said, waiting for her heartbeat to return to normal.

"My fault," Dr Crumb said, manoeuvring Charley awkwardly out of the room. "I should have said something, I am sure I meant to, but. . ."

But how did you tell someone that the lad you'd taken on as your apprentice was the same one who had chased her through the Brick Marsh and shot her with a magnetic pistol? He bustled Charley down to the next landing and said again, "My fault, Charley, mine entirely. Even so, it might be best if we found you some duties in the Engineerium. Fever has had a troubling time, and I don't wish to upset her. . ."

"You mean I have to move out?" asked Charley, looking as if he had just been slapped.

For a horrid moment Dr Crumb thought that the boy was going to burst into tears. He was an Engineer. He was not used to dealing with emotions. It had not occurred to him that Fever might be unhappy if she knew that Charley was living in the same house. It did not occur to him now

16

that Charley might feel hard done by at being thrown out and made to go and share a draughty dormitory in the Engineerium with a half-dozen other apprentices. "Yes," he decided. "That would be best, I think. Gather your stuff, Charley; Fever can take over your duties here as soon as she has settled in."

And so, on the day that Fever came to her new home, Charley Shallow was cast out of it. Carrying his small trunk of belongings, he set off through the lashing grey rain, while the Stalker that guarded Wavey Godshawk's door watched him go with its unthinking, lamp-like eyes.

2

ENGINEERIUM

From apprentice Skinner to apprentice Engineer was a strange leap to make, but Charley had managed it. It had been kind of Dr Crumb, he realized, to take him on as his apprentice, back in the first days of Quercus's lord mayorship, when it would have been just as easy to abandon him, or have him hanged for trying to do away with Fever. So he had worked hard at his lessons (he had not been able to read or write before that summer) and done everything that Dr Crumb told him. Nobody had ever bothered trying to educate him before, but he was a bright lad and he quickly made up the lost time, learning all the things an apprentice Engineer was meant to know.

He'd never got the hang of Wavey Godshawk, though. She was a Scriven and he was a Skinner's boy, so it had never been likely that they'd hit it off, but at least in those first few months after the nomad takeover he had not seen much of her. Injured by a rogue Stalker, she had stayed aboard Quercus's traction fortress, where Dr Crumb visited her, sometimes shamefacedly clutching a handful of flowers. When she finally emerged and announced that she was going to marry Dr Crumb, Charley felt sure that he was doomed. She must know that Charley had been an apprentice Skinner, and she would not have forgotten the way the Skinners of old had butchered her people. The very best that Charley could hope for was that she would forbid Dr Crumb to keep him on. It was more likely that he'd just vanish, like other enemies of the new regime, and be found in the Brick Marsh months later with a pistol ball rattling around inside his skull like a ball bearing in a puzzle.

But Wavey Godshawk seemed untroubled by his presence. Sometimes she was kind to him in a distant way, sometimes she just ordered him about. When she and Dr Crumb first moved into the house on Bishopsgate she still could not walk, but lay all day upon a sofa, calling for Charley to bring her books or cake or glasses of wine. At first Charley thought that it must give her pleasure to have such power over a former Skinner, and because of her beauty and her flashes of kindness he felt almost inclined to forgive her for her Scriven-ness and arrogance. But soon he came to understand that he was just so unimpressive that he meant nothing to her at all. And that, of course, was unforgivable.

So he hated her, and she fascinated him. He had never met anybody who was so certain of herself. It was there in the way she spoke, the way she moved, the haughty tilt of her chin. She never doubted for an instant that she was the most beautiful woman in London and that it was her absolute right to impose her wishes on all those around her, and because she believed it, Charley found himself believing it too.

Trudging away from her house through the swaying curtains of the rain, he realized that he was going to miss her. Why had Fever had to come home? That spindly, odd-eyed girl had ruined everything for him. He clenched his fists, ashamed and angry, remembering how she'd once saved his life, and how he'd tried to put an end to hers.

There was a sign pinned up next to the doors of the new Engineerium that read *No Gods Allowed*; some apprentice's notion of a joke. Someone else had defaced the wall with a big circle of red paint, a blue stripe slashed across its centre. Charley ignored both, knocked, and showed the note that Dr Crumb had given him to the bored apprentice on duty in the lobby. Rain rattled on the plastic roof. The building had been put up by Engineers, so it was weathertight and sturdy, but it had not been built to last; it was just a stopgap, to house the Guild till they could move into smart new quarters on the base tier of the new city. It had a dank, shabby, temporary feel, like a fairground tent left up too long. The dormitory, which was not much bigger than the room Charley had had all to himself in Wavey's house, contained seven iron beds and a smell of armpits. He started unpacking his stuff, telling himself that an Engineer did not care about physical comfort. The rusty bed-springs gave a dispirited *squoink* as he threw himself down on them to think. All the beds at Wavey's place had been perfect; imported from a master-bedmaker in Hamsterdam. Everything there had been expensive, even the hinges on the doors and the catches on the cabinets; they hadn't been made of gold or anything, you could just tell they were pricey because they worked so perfectly.

He was still thinking about that when his new dorm-mates came in. They gathered round his bed and stood staring down at him as if he was something nasty which they were viewing through a microscope.

"What's that?" asked one.

"That's Crumb's apprentice, the old Skinner's boy. Didn't you hear? Crumb's thrown him out."

"What for? Did he try to skin Wavey?"

"No, you nit. Crumb's girl's come home. *She'll* be his apprentice now."

"What's she like? Pretty?"

"Pretty ugly. Half Scriven."

"Well, Crumb's cast-off can't stay here. He's just a commoner! He'll lower the tone."

The Guild of Engineers had altered more than just its name since Charley joined it. Back when it was merely the Order of Engineers it had been a bit of a joke; a gaggle of monkish baldies living in an old head. The men who became Engineers in those days had been the poor-but-brainy ones, like Gideon Crumb. Now, with the new

London rising and making ready to move, the wealthy families on Ludgate Hill were starting to realize that in future they would be living aboard a huge machine, and that the people who would grow rich and powerful there would be the ones who knew how to run it. Boys who would once have gone into their fathers' businesses and become merchants or priests were now being apprenticed to the Guild instead. They did not much like finding a commoner in their quarters.

"We should turf him out," said the oldest of them, a tall boy of about Charley's age whose name was Ronnie Coldharbour. "He reeks like an old wet dog. I bet he's lousy, too. I say we make him sleep in the corridor."

Charley kept his eyes shut, pretending that he wasn't listening. He had a nasty idea that this was what his future was going to be like. After all, this was what his past had mostly been like. Growing up in Ted Swiney's pub on Ditch Street he had spent his days being ignored, jeered at and occasionally hit. He had barely understood that life could hold anything different until Bagman Creech came and took him away. Bagman had been good to him. Bagman would not have cast him off just because some long-lost daughter came home and didn't like him.

Remembering the old Skinner, he felt his eyes fill with tears. He knew he must not cry; not in front of these preening, sniggering boys. Bagman would have told him not to. Bagman would have said, "You may be low-born, Charley boy, but you're worth ten of these cloots." Bagman had been low-born himself, but he'd walked tall in the eyes of all London. Nobody would have dared to jeer at Bagman and say that he smelled (even though he did).

Charley opened his eyelids just a crack, not enough to let the tears out, but enough to show him the faces of his enemies. Ronnie Coldharbour reached down and prodded him. In a moment, the name-calling would turn to blows.

What would Bagman have done? he wondered. How would he have turned this round?

Coldharbour jabbed him again, harder. "Hey, Skinner's boy. I'm talking to you."

Charley came off the bed like a lit firecracker. Before the ring of boys could do more than gasp he was on his feet, and the iron jug from the washstand was in his hand. He brought it down hard on Coldharbour's long nose, once, twice, three times, then he flung it at the nearest of the other boys in case they were thinking of coming to Coldharbour's rescue. Coldharbour whinnied, both hands to his face, blood between his fingers. Charley wrenched him round, and reached inside his own coat. In an inner pocket, next to his Engineer's slide rule, he kept his one souvenir of his time as Bagman's 'prentice.

It was a Skinner's knife. The long, curved, mammoth-ivory handle made it look like a gigantic penknife. Along one side in crude brown letters Bagman had carved *This Ain't Genocide!* Along the other, completing the old Skinner war cry, were the words *This is Rock 'n' Roll!* The letters felt rough under Charley's fingers as he flipped the knife open. All the light in the room seemed to gather in that blade.

"You're right, Coldharbour," he said, and his voice slid from the careful, high-London accent he'd learned from Dr Crumb back into the guttural mockney growl of Ditch Street. "I *am* a Skinner's boy. That makes me better than you an' all yer mates, no matter 'ow smart you fink you are, nor 'ow much money yer dad made selling scents and old-tech to the Dapplejacks. So there's not gonna be no more o' your lip. Understand?"

He pressed the blade against Coldharbour's throat until Coldharbour screamed in a high, girlish voice that he did. Then Charley gave him one hard kick for luck and casually put the knife away. The other boys watched him from the corners of the room. The door opened and an old Engineer called Griffin Whyre peered in to ask what all the noise was.

"Coldharbour tripped, Dr Whyre," said Charley. He looked at the others to see if any of them wanted to disagree. If they told Whyre what had happened he knew he would be out of the Guild by nightfall, back to begging for scraps in the ruins of Ditch Street. But none of the boys said anything. Two came to help Coldharbour to his feet and lead him off to the infirmary. The rest just watched Charley. He thought how proud Bagman Creech would have been of him, of the way he'd grown up. He didn't reckon those others would give him any more trouble now. They could all see what kind of person Charley Shallow was.

3

THE FUTURE SIGHTS OF LONDON

Wavey had talked all the way from Mayda about how much she was looking forward to giving Fever a guided tour of the new city, but now that she was home she was far too busy seeing friends and attending parties, so it was Dr Crumb who first showed Fever around the strange thing that London was becoming.

She had seen it before. At least, she had glimpsed what it was meant to be. Auric Godshawk's vision of a mobile city was one of the memories that had seeped into her mind from the machine he'd implanted in her brain when she was little. In his imagination it had been a towering, gleaming thing; a proud tower of buildings on a wheeled base. In reality, the new city was much, much broader than it was high, and its upper levels were still mostly girders and emptiness, like a diagram drawn on the sky. Beneath the skirts of the Base Tier Fever could see the big, tracked wheels, rank upon rank of them, with gangs of men creeping over them like ants. Could wheels that big possibly *turn*? she wondered. Could there be power enough in the world to drive them? Would even tracks that broad spread the new city's weight enough to stop it sinking axle-deep into the earth as soon as it rolled off the plinth of compressed rubble where it was being built?

Dr Crumb seemed untroubled by such questions as he led Fever up one of the temporary wooden stairways into the city's Base Tier. They emerged in the Engine District, which looked at first a little like an ordinary district in an ordinary city, except that those weren't buildings which rose on each side of the streets but the housings for gigantic Godshawk engines, and that was not a lowering, pigeon-haunted sky that stretched above them but the steel and timber underbelly of the tier above.

The scale was dizzying, but Fever tried not to let it impress her as she followed her father along planked pavements, past ducts and furnaces, through forests of pistons and fog-banks of drifting smoke. However wonderful it was that such things had been built, it counted for nothing if they were not rational.

Dr Crumb showed her aboard a clumsy freight elevator, and led her off it again on Tier One, where the Housing Committee was erecting blocks of workers' flats: lightweight buildings made from balsa wood and panels of lacquered paper, each block hexagonal and fitted in among its neighbours like the cells of a wasps' nest. "We have calculated the exact volume of space which each person requires," explained Dr Crumb, with modest pride. "The apartments are all based on that; not a cubic inch is wasted. The streets which radiate out from the hub are known by letter while the cross-streets have numbers, and each is preceded by its tier-number, so all the streets on this level have the preface 1. We are walking down 1:E, and just about to cross 1:12. It is a most rational system. Unfortunately the workers seem to find it hard to remember; they keep trying to give the streets old London names. Look there!" He pointed to a cardboard sign, tacked crudely to a wall, on which someone had written, *Eel Pie Lane*. "We must educate them," muttered Dr Crumb.

Fever's Engineerish heart leapt at the sight of so much reason on display, but the pigeons which flew confusedly between the tier-supports reminded her of the angels of Mayda, and the angels reminded her of Arlo Thursday, the young Maydan inventor whom she had helped to build a machine so delicate that it made all the wonders of the new London seem crude and clumsy. It had been a flying machine; the first true, heavier-than-air flying machine since Ancient times. She had *flown*. She watched the pigeons swoop overhead and the memories of her flight came back to her, and mingled with the memory of her first kiss; her one kiss. *Arlo...*

"Fever?" called Dr Crumb.

"Coming," she said.

They crossed 1:15 and reached an unfinished section where a spindly platform of wooden scaffolding poked out from the city's flank. All around them, like trees on a steep hillside, cranes towered up, hoisting fresh loads of steel and timber from the marshalling yards below and swinging them aboard the half-built higher tiers.

"So!" said Dr Crumb, turning to Fever as if he could no longer wait to hear what she thought of it all. His eyes were shining. His whole face seemed to shine. "So, what do you make of it?"

What did she make of it? Fever looked down past cranes and foundry smoke at the fields of tents planted around Ludgate Hill. Teams of mammoths and heavy horses were dragging logs in from the cleared woodlands west of the Brick Marsh. The city that her grandfather had dreamed of had been a crazy, glorious thing. This reality, all creaking timbers bolted to a swaying cage of steel, was far less grand. Still crazy, though.

"I know what you're going to say," said Dr Crumb. "You're going to say that it is irrational. I thought so myself, at first. But look at it, Fever! Just look at what we have built here! It is the most ambitious project that mankind has undertaken in all the millennia since the Downsizing. Even before that! Even the Ancients never constructed anything like this!"

"Why should they have wanted to?" asked Fever. "What good reason is there to build a city on wheels?"

"Because London cannot stay where it is for much longer," said Dr Crumb, who had had that same question answered for him by Wavey two years before. "Because the glaciers may soon push further south. Because there are

28

new volcanoes growing in the north, and who knows what savage tribes will be driven from their hunting grounds up there? And because it would be wasteful to leave London's fabric behind us when we seek new lands to live in. So we shall carry it with us, like the humble snail. . ."

Only a bit slower than the humble snail, thought Fever, but she did not say so. Instead, she said, "Londoners are angry, irrational people. Don't they complain that Quercus has torn their homes down?"

Dr Crumb shook his head. "We have both had bad experiences of the London mob," he admitted. "But it seems they are not entirely deaf to reason. They know that these tents in which they are forced to live are a temporary measure. Soon they will be rehoused in the buildings we just saw: clean, healthy, efficient buildings, far better than their slums and hovels in the old London. And there are lot of new Londoners now; people who came south with Quercus, or who have flooded in since to help with the building, knowing that there are good wages to be had here, and a rational government to guard and guide them."

"Rational?" exclaimed Fever, remembering her meeting with Quercus and the Movement, fierce northern warriors aboard their trundling traction castle.

"Oh yes, Fever. The Movement has always been one of the smallest of the nomad nations, and it has survived by being more modern and forward-thinking than its rivals. Nikola Quercus is a deeply rational man, and he is advised by rational men. For instance, I suggested to him that free workers are more efficient and humane than slaves, and he agreed. Not only has he freed all the slaves which the Movement brought south, he has purchased whole regiments of slaves from the southlands, and freed them all as soon as they arrived in London."

"And did they not just return to their own homes?"

"A few did, but most saw that it was more rational to stay. They earn good money here, and live in tents provided by the council, which also provides schooling for their children and doctors for the sick and pensions for the old."

"How can Quercus afford all that?"

"Oh, the workers pay a portion of their wages back to him as tax. We all do. It funds our welfare, and helps to pay for this new city on which we shall soon live. Of course, better paid people like myself and Wavey pay a larger proportion of our earnings than the humble labourers."

"I suppose that is a rational system," admitted Fever.

"It is good for everyone," said Dr Crumb. "It means that it is in the interests of the commoners to support Quercus and what he is doing here. All down the centuries kings and councils have tried to tame the London mob with guns and soldiers, and Quercus has achieved it through the application of reason. Soon all the junk and clutter of the bad old London will be gone. In its place will be a shining new city of science and progress, not tied to one place but free to roam and grow as reason demands..."

Fever reached out and fondled the taut rope which formed a handrail at the platform's edge. She could feel it quivering; throbbing like a live thing with the beat of the work being done in the heart of the new city. *It is rational*, she told herself. *If Dr Crumb sees it, why can't I? It is rational, and the changes that Quercus is making here are* good. And she knew that she should be grateful to have a chance to help. She should feel happy to be home.

4

ANCESTRAL VOICES

F ar, far, far to the north, where the ground was ice and the night skies filled with shifting light, the rolling empire of Arkhangelsk was on the move again. Centuries had passed since its founders abandoned the deep-frozen harbour on the White Sea that had given it its name. Peoples from all over the north had joined their caravan as it journeyed on and on, creeping across the world's steep face in endless search of fuel and pasturage. Their fighting men and landships were away battling the Movement's northern army in the Fuel Country, but still the empire rolled, the huge heart-fortress of the Great Carn grinding along amid a ring of smaller traction-houses, and behind them the *Kometsvansen*, a tail of barges and wagons and mammoths and reindeer herds which stretched for eighty miles across the tundra.

If there had still been people in the Ancients' legendary skycastles, thought Cluny Morvish, they would have been able to look down from space and wonder at the *Kometsvansen* as it went creeping across the snows of

Heklasrand like a line of ants; the biggest parade the world had ever seen. How astonished they would be at the power and glory of Arkhangelsk! It made her feel proud as she stood upon the balcony of her family's rolling fort and watched the other vehicles spread out astern in the light of the First Frost Moon; all those campavans and wanigans, with a few spiky landships snarling up and down the fringes of the convoy, keeping watch for raiders.

Where was it going? The little people back there in the Great Carn's wake did not care; they followed his heart-fort without question, as their fathers and their fathers' fathers had. But Cluny's family had a fort of their own to steer, and Cluny's father was a Carn, and privy to the decisions that the Great Carn made in his high council chamber. Cluny was only a maiden, seventeen winters old, but since her older brother Doran died her father had taken her more and more into his confidence, so she knew how hard such decisions had become.

To Cluny, her empire's travels felt like the aimless pacing of a trapped animal in a cage. In the north the new volcanoes were spewing ash across the empire's former pastures. In the east the Iron-horde of the Novaya-Khazak barred the way. In the west there was nothing but cold sea and cold, hard, hopeless, nightwight-haunted hills. And to the south there was the Movement; a small empire, but fierce in its defence of the Fuel Country, and greedy for material since it had conquered London. Just that day a merchant had brought word of the city that Quercus was remaking there. There had been a tattered pamphlet with a woodcut of the great tiers rising. Crude and unbelievable, yet it had unsettled Cluny, like a fingernail drawn across the blackboard of her mind; like a memory of some childhood nightmare. That was why she was up on the sterncastle that night instead of in her nice warm bed below. That was why she was watching the lights of the *Kometsvansen* through the veils of her freezing breath.

"We must move south soon, or perish," she had heard her father say, when the Carns of the other traction-houses came aboard to talk over the merchant's news. "Perhaps this mad moving city notion will draw the Movement's strength away to London."

"It will need oil," said gloomy Carn Masgard. "A whole moving city? It will drink oil like I drink vodka, Carn Morvish. It will eat coal like a child eats cloudberries. The Movement will fight harder than ever to keep hold of the Fuel Country now."

"We will defeat them," said Carn Persinger. "These new electric guns our technomancers have contrived, these Tesla weapons. . ."

"They are not enough," said Cluny's father. "We lost twelve forts this past year alone. Twelve forts, a hundred landships, thousands of good men. . ." He did not need to remind them that he had lost a son as well.

Above Cluny's head the northern sky fluttered its magic lights. In the far south-west the clouds flashed with gun-light as another assault got under way against the Movement mechanized divisions dug in around Hill 60. *All this fighting*, she thought, remembering how she had longed to go south with Doran the previous summer, and how it had not been allowed because she was a girl, and how Doran had not returned. He had fought bravely, the survivors said, but then the Movement had unleashed its Stalkers, and who could fight against the armoured dead? *How stupid it all is*, she thought. *If only there could be peace.*

But there was never peace; not among the nomad empires. The best you could hope for was a gap between one war and the next. Cluny turned from the rail and went below. She thought that she was tired enough now to fall asleep. Tomorrow, she would hunt. Rise early and ride hard, following the belling of the hounds till she had left all thought of wars and mobile cities behind.

She lay in bed and at last the familiar sound of the fort's engines soothed her to sleep like a lullaby. Then the bad dream that had been sniffing around the edges of her mind ever since she heard that merchant's tale saw its chance, and found its way in. It came at her like a boar out of a thicket and smashed her awake with a scream that brought guards and servants and the Carn himself all pounding on her chamber door.

She had not had such a nightmare since she was a little child. It left her whimpering like a baby. It was some minutes before she was able to tell them all what it was that the night had shown her.

"It was the city ... Quercus's new city. It is coming. It will devour us all!"

Four days later, when she had the same dream twenty times and was afraid to even close her eyes, they made her go across to the heart-fortress to tell it to old Nintendo Tharp, the Great Carn's technomancer. In Tharp's sanctum, down among the fort's engines, candles flickered behind the screens of Ancient *tellies* and puddles of oil burned in Set-a-light dishes and a thousand talismans of wire and circuitry swung from the carved beams. Cluny's father was there, and the Great Carn himself. They stood and watched while the technomancer circled Cluny, muttering his sacred runes and apps. Tharp had a long face like the face of an aged lizard and a long beard with bones and bits of circuit-board plaited into it. On his head he wore a thick leather cap with a steaming metal stove mounted on top; a samovar-hat in which he was brewing cloudberry tea for the Ancestors. The hot coals inside it shifted and rattled as he shuffled round the chair where Cluny sat with fragments of Ancient power-machines balanced on her head and wrists. He waved his hands in ritual movements, then reached up and turned the handle of the hat's tap to fill three little glasses, which he set on the deck at Cluny's feet.

Cluny had never liked Tharp. As a little girl she had always been secretly afraid that he might pick her or Doran or little Marten when he went looking for a sacrifice to

36

blood the heart-fort's wheels for Winterdeep. But Tharp was the only one who could say whether Cluny's dream was just a dream, or something more, so she told it again, sitting statue-still for fear the magic machines would tumble off her head, while he waved rusty devices in front of her face, and her father waited in the background, scared for her and trying not to show it.

"I saw the new city," she explained, struggling to keep her voice steady as she recalled the terrible vividness of her dream. "I saw Quercus's new city finished, rolling across the earth. It was ten times bigger than this fortress. It was like a mountain, but with houses instead of rocks, and factories instead of crags, and wheels instead of foothills. And it had *jaws*. They opened, and there were furnaces and smithies inside. They closed, and dragged whole forts like this one into London's belly. And I knew that nothing can stop it, and that if we let it, it will eat up all the world."

In the light from behind the dead screens Tharp's face was as impassive as a leather mask. Steam leaked from his hat. He held an Ancient talking-box against his ear, listening to spirit-voices that only he could hear.

"This dream was sent by the Ancestors," he said at last. "It is a warning."

Cluny let out a shaky sigh, and one of Tharp's devices fell off her head and clattered on the deck. She had been hoping and hoping that the dreams were just dreams, and that the technomancer would have some potion that could stop them coming. She did not want to be the medium for messages from Arkhangelsk's honoured dead. Why had the Ancestors picked on *her*? she wondered. Why her, of all people? She did not want to be important...

"This is a warning, Great Carn," Tharp was saying. "The Ancestors have spoken to us from the World Without Time. They have shown this maiden a vision of the future. We must not ignore it."

"But what can we do?" asked the Great Carn, fingering his beard. He was a soldier: technomancy gave him the jitters.

Tharp looked briefly blank. It was Cluny's father who answered in the end. "We should ask Cluny, shouldn't we?" he said. "It is her dream. What do you think we should do about it, Cluny-my-daughter?"

Cluny laughed nervously. She thought it was one of her father's jokes. She knew nothing about politics and tactics. She was just a maiden. She'd have been given in marriage and busy with babies by now if she hadn't been her father's favourite. Yet they were all looking at her, even the Great Carn himself, waiting for her to tell them what should be done.

She remembered the thoughts that had come to her three nights before, up on the sterncastle. She said, "We must start telling people what the new London means. Not just our own people. Everyone. We must send envoys to the Suomi, the Novaya-Khazak, even to the Movement."

"We are at *war* with the Suomi and the Novaya-Khazak!"

roared the Great Carn. "It is the Movement who are *building* this crazy city!"

"Those wars must cease," said Cluny. "This is more important. And not *everyone* in the Movement can *want* this new thing. They cannot *all* be crazy."

Both the Carn and Cluny's father looked outraged. They had not got where they were today by imagining that the enemies of Arkhangelsk could be anything but crazy. Talk of ending wars was womanish.

But Nintendo Tharp raised his bony hands, as if to warm them in front of Cluny's wisdom. "It is the will of our Ancestors!" he said. "Let it be done! Let Cluny herself go to the Suomi, and the Novaya-Khazak, and the Movement. Let her tell them in her own voice of this thing the Ancestors have shown to her!"

5

VICTORY BALL

I n London the year went on its way, down into the cold and dark of winter. Construction work continued by night and by day, the noise so ceaseless that Fever had quickly stopped noticing it. She worked with her father, drawing up plans, designing things, telling herself that this was what she liked doing best; it was like being small again, and back in Godshawk's Head. Sometimes when she looked at the new city it seemed wonderful that human beings could build such things. Sometimes it looked like a madman's nightmare coming to life. She still did not know what to feel about it, so she settled for feeling nothing.

From the north came word of battles and volcanoes. New fire-mountains were sprouting in Heklasrand, and their upflung ashes painted the sunsets gold and carmine. Up in the Fuel Country the Movement's northern army was warring with the Arkhangelsk; there had been huge battles at a place they called Hill 60, and the reports said that the enemy had found a new type of weapon, an electric gun which scrambled the brains of the Movement's

Stalkers, destroying them or sending them flailing back in mindless fury through their own ranks. Twice, Hill 60 had almost been overrun; if it fell, the way would lie open for the Arkhangelsk to pour south across the dry North Sea to London.

So the militias trained each morning at the edge of town, target-shooting with their new Bugharin rifles. Wavey took Fever to watch them one chilly morning. They sat in her sedan chair at the edge of Hamster's Heath and watched the lines of men marching and wheeling on the snowy commons as if it were all a display which Wavey had laid on for her daughter's entertainment. After the things she must have seen, Fever wondered how her mother could be so light-hearted about the prospect of another war. But when she mentioned it Wavey just laughed and said, "Your grandfather used to say that there is no end to war among the nomad empires. He always said, 'The best you can hope for is a gap between one war and the next.'"

Wavey was trying to befriend her daughter. She had been in exile when Fever was growing up, and although it had not exactly been her fault, she still felt guilty that she had missed her child's childhood. She meant to make up for it now, but she had no idea how to be a mother, so she tried to treat Fever like the best friend she wished she had had when she was Fever's age (instead of all the catty, treacherous Scriven princesses who had been her actual friends). She confided in Fever about her new-found happiness with Dr Crumb. "I know he seems boring, but

41

after the life I've led a little boredom is quite a change. And have you noticed how, when we snuggle, he is just the right height for me to rest my chin upon his head? I think there is a lot to be said for a husband who can be used as a chin-rest."

Fever just winced with embarrassment.

Wavey gave her presents; whole trunks of dresses ordered from her own dressmaker and from dressmakers in Paris and Hamsterdam too, so that Fever would cut a dash at the Winter Festival parties. Even Wavey had to admit that she was herself a little old to wear some of the latest fashions, but it pleased her to imagine Fever dressed in them; she knew just the colours that would bring out her daughter's striking looks.

But Fever would not go to parties, and she never opened her overstuffed wardrobes. Instead, each morning, she dressed in a grey shirt, black trousers, twenty-eyelet boots and a plain white Engineer's coat. She agreed to an appointment with Wavey's expensive hairdresser, but only let him trim her hair, then tied it back again in that hard, unflattering bun.

So Wavey tried to interest her in the mysteries of her own past; the curious operation which Godshawk had performed on her when she was just a sickly baby. The technomancers whom Quercus had recruited from the north had brought an Electric Microscope with them. In its chamber at the Engineerium, while burly apprentices worked the treadmill which powered it, mother and daughter sat side by side and peered at a drop of Fever's blood, magnified many hundreds of times. For the first time Fever glimpsed the tiny machines which twitched and fidgeted there.

"Mechanimalculae," murmured Wavey, entranced, leaning forward for a closer look. "I guessed as much. Stalkers have them, but I didn't think Godshawk had ever found a way to keep them working in a living person... No wonder that gash on your face healed so beautifully when we were coming home from Mayda. All these busy little things inside you, mending damage, protecting you from germs. I don't suppose you've had so much as a cold in your whole life, have you?"

"I don't remember," said Fever, remembering times when everyone aboard the *Lyceum* had been sneezing and coughing and only she had escaped the infection. At Godshawk's Head, too, in the flu season, she'd sometimes had to nurse Dr Crumb and the other Engineers, and never caught their illnesses herself.

On the screen the mechanimalculae frisked and jiggled, each no bigger than a corpuscle. "How are they *powered*?" she asked.

"Molecular Clockwork," said Wavey airily, as if she knew what that meant. "It doesn't matter, Fever. Don't trouble over details."

But the things were in her daughter's blood, not hers. Fever could not *help* but be troubled.

*

Down amid the gloom and snow the old year ended and a new one began. The weather did not get better, but it stopped getting worse. In springtime when the roads were open again the convoys bringing fuel and timber from the north brought good news too, from Quercus's old comrade Rufus Raven, who commanded the army there. The war was won: the Great Carn of Arkhangelsk had made peace, and his forces had withdrawn into their old hunting grounds further north. The clap of victory fireworks was added to the din of the construction work, and portraits of Raven appeared in shop windows and on huge banners which hung from the girders of the half-finished city, honouring his triumph.

By early summer Wavey had a triumph of her own to celebrate. She had persuaded Fever to attend Quercus's victory ball, which was to be held aboard the new city, in the echoing, metal cavern called the Great Under Tier. Realizing that it would be futile to suggest a gown, she dressed her daughter in a new white coat, longer and better tailored than her others, with mother-of-pearl buttons. In the light of paper lanterns suspended from the vaulting roof all the fashionable people of London danced and chattered, bright as birds. Musicians played on one of the bridges that spanned the enormous space, while drinks and dainties were served in the landship hangars, which opened off it on each side. Wavey took time out from the waltzes and hip-hops to point out eligible men among the crowds. "That dashing young officer is Bjorn

Somersby, Fever. I do believe that he admires you! And look, there is good Captain Andringa, one of Quercus's most promising young men. . ."

Fever looked at the couples on the dancefloor, the way they held each other. She did not like being touched. The only person she wanted to hold her like that was Arlo Thursday, and she would never see him again.

Wavey seemed to sense what she was thinking. Afterwards, when they were heading home up Cripplegate in their big, Stalker-drawn rickshaw, she said, "Fever, we really *must* find you a new boyfriend. I was never short of boyfriends at your age. Can it be that you are *still* moping about that boy in Mayda? That wretched Thursday boy?"

Fever just rubbed a gloved finger over the steamed-up window. She thought of Arlo's little ship, alone on the face of the ocean, sailing into the west. She had lied to save him from Wavey's agent Dr Teal, who would have killed him to suppress the secret of his flying machine. She had lied, and Arlo had thought that she'd betrayed him. He had sailed away alone. She had stood on the end of the harbour wall, calling and calling his name, but he had not heard her, or had not cared.

"He is not the only boy in the world," insisted Wavey.

"I expect you miss the children, Fever?" said her father, hoping to change the subject.

Fever kept rubbing the window, making a square hole in the condensation. "Fern and Ruan are much better off without me," she said. "I had a letter a few weeks ago. The

45

Lyceum is travelling among the Italian city-states. Fern is becoming quite an experienced actress. Ruan talks of becoming apprenticed to a painter. And I had a parcel from Mayda containing something that I believe was once a piece of cake; wedding cake, from the wedding of Dymphna Persimmon and Jonathan Hazell. . ."

"But what about Arlo Thursday?" Wavey pestered. "Is there any news of him? You still think about him. I can tell you do. Look, you've gone bright red!"

Fever looked away angrily. (People who are prone to blushing do not need anyone to *tell* them when they do it.) She wondered if Wavey knew that she scanned the travellers' tales in London's newspapers each week in the hope that there might be word of a boy arriving on the shores of Nuevo Maya; a boy who talked to birds and knew the ancient mysteries of flight. She said, "It is unlikely that he survived on that wide ocean, in such a small boat, and with one arm injured before he even set out. . ."

"Poor Fever," Wavey said, laying her hand on Fever's cheek. "It passes, you know. There will be other boys. But it's no help, is it, my telling you that? Oh *look*!" she added, suddenly leaning across her to see out through the clear patch she had rubbed on the window. "Borglum is here!"

The chair was crossing a region of waste ground where buildings had lately stood and which tents had not yet had time to colonize. A travelling show had set up there, a spiky black barge with a big tent pitched beside it and torches burning at the entrance. For a moment

46

Fever wondered if it might be old friends of hers from Summertown, but no; this was a raggedy northern show; the sort of show which opened when respectable people were heading home to bed. Along the side of the barge, in big red letters made to look as if they had been painted recently in blood, it wore the name *The Amazing Borglum's Carnival of Knives!*

Wavey rapped on the wall of the chair to make the bearers stop. "Oh, my dears, we *must* see the Carnival of Knives!"

"A Carnival of Knives?" said Dr Crumb. It was already past his bedtime, and he yawned as he spoke. "Wavey, it sounds somewhat irrational. . ."

"Nonsense," said his wife. "It is the very thing to cheer poor Fever up!"

There were a lot of showmen in the world who styled themselves Amazing, but in Jasper Borglum's case it was the simple truth. He even felt amazed at himself, as he stood on the roof of his land-barge watching his audience gather. He had not visited London since the Movement took it, and he felt hopeful about the place. It reminded him of huge nomad encampments that he had known up in the Birkenmark. And here he was, with his circus ready like a net to gather in the shoals of shiny little coins that swam in this canvas sea.

He was about the same age as Dr Crumb, and in some ways he was rather like him, for he was intelligent, cautious and neat, although when necessary he could show a certain reckless daring. Like Dr Crumb he cropped his hair down to a fuzz, but it was a blond fuzz in Borglum's case, and he left one long lock at the front to dangle down over his forehead and half hide one of his eyes, which were as bright as chips of feldspar. For clothing he favoured the furs and 'broidery waistcoats of a nomad nobleman, and he wore a jewelled dagger in his belt that was just for show and a plain one in his boot that was not. When he drew himself up to his full height he stood just a half-inch under three feet tall.

Quite early in his life the Amazing Borglum had understood that he was an oddity, and that people were going to try to exploit him. Travelling shows stopped most summers at the village where he grew up, and there were whole barges packed with freaks and misshapes for the paying public to google at. Once the silky gent who ran a barge called the *Knuckle Sandwich* tried to persuade Borglum's ma and da to sell him their little dwarfish boy for twelve gold coins. They wouldn't sell, for they loved their son, even if there was a little less of him than they might have hoped. But they wouldn't be around for ever, would they? And even while they were, what was to stop some big neighbour from picking Borglum up and selling him to the shows without their permission? It was a burden to a young man to be worth a dozen of gold.

So the following summer, when the *Knuckle Sandwich* reappeared, Borglum went and made his own deal with the silky gentleman. He gave the money to his ma and da, wished them a loving farewell, and set off upon his travels. If people wanted to exploit him it seemed to him that he'd best beat them to it and exploit himself.

He missed his parents, but otherwise life on a travelling show suited him well. It was better than village life, with all those towering lads who'd scoffed and bullied and the girls who would never even notice him. Aboard the *Knuckle Sandwich* he made friends who'd been born with the same lopsided luck as himself; the Stone Faced Man and the Bearded Lady, pretty Liv the Human Lemur with her covering of pale gold fur, who taught him to juggle and walk stilts, savage Quatch who made rich ladies faint when he roared at them and rattled the bars of his cage, but who wasn't really savage at all, and who, on quiet nights between stops, would entertain the company with lovely songs and play to them upon a balalaika. Pretty soon young Borglum found that the only thing he didn't like about this new life was the way that all the work of performing and roaring and being gaped and googled at was done by him and his friends, while all the money went to the silky gentleman and his wife and grown-up sons, who styled themselves the proprietors of the troupe. Borglum's friends often grumbled about it, and he felt sure that they were right, but it was not in Borglum's nature to be a grumbler.

So he made himself useful to the silky gentlemen; helped him count his money and make up his accounts.

From the grown-up sons he learned how the barge's big old engines ran. And when the silky gentleman and all his family met with a terrible accident it was discovered, amazingly, that he had left the *Knuckle Sandwich* and all it held to Borglum.

At this long remove of years it was hard for Borglum to recall the exact details of the accident. "It was a tragic business" was all he'd usually say, if ever anyone asked about it. Sometimes, if they pressed him, he would bare his little yellow teeth and his feldspar eyes would glitter and he'd say, "It involved *knives*. . ."

By coincidence, "It involves knives" was more or less what people had been saying about Borglum's carnival that night, as word of its arrival spread excitingly through all the flapping canvas streets and cardboard cul-de-sacs of Tent Town. For too long the workers of London had been forced to make their own entertainment, which mostly meant dog-fights and cock-fights and knife-fights. Now the professionals had arrived! Young men stood in the light of the flaming torches and stared up at the gory paintings on the barge's sides. Children scampered off to tell their parents what was taking shape. Tired workers coming down from shifts on the new city and drunken young noblemen stumbling home from Quercus's ball were all revived by the sight of Borglum's blood-red banners licking at the evening sky. From all over Tent Town, groups of people made their wondering way towards the carnival, drawn by its powerful promises of violence and glamour.

Amongst them, unnoticed in his drab off-duty clothes, came apprentice Charley Shallow, as eager as anyone to see what the Carnival had in store. He had been out that evening with a girl called Milly Floater, and had decided that this might be a good way to round the night off. From what he'd heard in Tent Town it was meant to be quite horrifying, and he knew that girls, when horrified, liked a protective arm around them, and that one thing might lead to another.

He was fond of Milly, but as they joined the end of the queue he glanced around to make sure that none of his fellow apprentices was there. Round, good-natured, cheaply dressed Milly was exactly the sort of girl you would expect to see with a boy of Charley Shallow's sort, and for that reason he did not want to be seen with her. Ronnie Coldharbour and his friends still didn't like Charley, but they had learned to respect him, and he liked to drop hints to them about all the girls he knew in Tent Town. If they saw that he could do no better for himself than Milly Floater it could dent his reputation badly.

Sure enough, there was Coldharbour with a couple of the others, a few yards further up the queue. Before he could look back and notice Charley, Charley took Milly's arm and dragged her into the slipstream of a passing Movement officer and his lady; rich folks from Ludgate Hill who thought that queues were not for them. Hurrying behind these nobles, they quickly reached the front of the crowd, where an entrance painted like a fanged mouth opened into the carnival tent. "Roll up, roll up!" the men who guarded it were shouting, while a girl with green eyes sold tickets in a canvas booth. A pretty girl, thought Charley, as he fumbled for his purse, and then saw as he proffered his bronze half-quid that she had no hands for him to put it in, only a sort of mechanized lobster-claw strapped to the stump where each hand should be. She laughed at his confusion and showed him the brass bowl where the coins went, and Milly laughed too. Charley thought, *Stupid tarts*, but he grinned as he took the ticket from her pincers, and turned to go in through the painted mouth.

They entered a dim-lit, awninged space. Blocks of steep-raked benches had been erected round an oiled canvas groundsheet mapped and marbled with alarming stains. The seats were filling fast. As he squeezed in next to Milly, Charley heard the barkers outside changing their message. "That's all! Come back tomorrow. Another show tomorrow. . ."

A hush fell over the crowd on the benches. Even the rich people stopped talking about themselves in such loud voices and used whispers instead. Charley could hear moths battering their wings against the big lanterns, which swung on chains from the timber props that helped hold up the roof. Milly giggled nervously, squeezing herself against him. He looked across the canvas arena, checking for Coldharbour and the others. He could not see them, but he did notice three latecomers making their way into a space opposite: two white coats and an expensive fur cloak.

"What is it, Charley?" Milly asked, noticing the way he stared at them.

Charley didn't answer. He was too surprised. What were Wavey and those Crumbs doing at a thing like this? He studied them, confident that they would not notice him among so many other faces – they'd probably forgotten he had ever existed, he thought bitterly. Wavey was talking, smiling, but Doc Crumb looked bewildered, while Fever sat so stiff and straight that you could almost see the disapproval crackling off her. Charley looked at her long white neck, the subtle shape of her under that crisp, buttoned-up coat, and he felt angry again at the girl who sat beside him. If Milly Floater had looked more like Fever Crumb he would not have minded showing her off to Coldharbour or anyone else. . .

Then the music started, so sudden and so deafening that all the thoughts flew out of his head like scared birds rising from a tree. He jumped. Everybody jumped, all along those rows of hard, uncomfortable benches. The music sounded like tin pans and bicycle chains, like bad plumbing and xylophone bones and the murder of elderly dustbins. Into the arena marched a bizarre army with a fur-clad dwarf strutting at its head.

"Welcome!" shouted the dwarf, into the silence that

came down when the music stopped. He had the voice of a much bigger man, and a manner that commanded you to watch him. Nimble as a tumbler, he vaulted up on to the armoured hand of a massive Stalker that stood just behind him; a man-shaped hulk that looked ready to leap into the crowd and start ripping heads off, but was restrained by a blindfolded African woman holding tight to a leash fastened around its neck. Charley had seen plenty of these armoured zombies since the Movement seized power, but never one like this: barnacled with studs and spikes, it wore as a headpiece two massive, curving mammoth tusks. Above the glowing green slot which served as its eyes the silver figure of a winged woman jutted from its forehead; the hood ornament from an Ancient motor-carriage.

Who would decorate a Stalker like that? Charley wondered. How could this ramshackle circus even *own* a Stalker? Surely only powerful warlords and their technomancers were able to control those weird old war machines, and even they were starting to run short of them as stocks of mechanical brains wore out. Maybe this was one of those crazy ones you heard about that went rogue and struck out on their own?

It started to dawn on him that being a spectator at the Carnival of Knives might not be altogether *safe*...

The dwarfish ringmaster ran up the monster's armoured trunk like a squirrel up a tree and perched grinning on its head, holding on to those tusks to steady himself as the thing started to lumber around the edge of the arena. "I'm Borglum," he announced. "A travelling man. My legs are short, but long leagues lie behind me. All over the wild northlands this circus of mine has rolled, and everywhere we go there we find war. Little wars and big, my friends, old wars and new. Those nomad empires are forever a-squabbling, sending forth their landships and their valiant soldier-boys. And people ask, 'Why? How is it that these wars keep happening?' Like wars are freaks of nature that fall all unbidden on poor human beans."

The audience shifted, fidgeting, wondering when Borglum would come to the point. The freaks of nature they wanted to hear about were the grisly crew lined up behind him; a hairy giant and an armoured dwarf, a bone-white snowmad sword-boy, that night-black, blindfolded amazon. The points they were interested in were on the racks of swords and nameless spiky things which his mutant roadies were setting up at each end of the ring like vicious fences.

But Borglum knew the value of a good build-up. "Well, my dearies," he went on, "I've looked hard at war. Looked at it from outside, mind, since I don't quite make the height requirement for any army I've yet met. And I can tell you why war keeps on thriving. It's because men love it so. They do! Deep in the darklymost ventricles of all their secret hearts, blade, bone and bloodshed is what thrills 'em best. The Ancients understood. The showmen who ran their coliseums and their multiplexes knew how even the peaceablest man does long to see a little carnage now and then. So here it is, O my ladies and my gentlemen of London Town. The Amazing Borglum has prepared you a little taste of War that you can savour from the safety of your seats. . ."

The silence of the crowd had thickened. The awning flapped heavily. Moth-wings pinged and ticked against the lantern-panes.

"Without further ado," cried Borglum, "we give you: The Carnival of Knives!"

6

THE CARNIVAL OF KNIVES

They'd practised long and hard, those mis-formed fighters Borglum had gathered to his carnival. They never did each other lasting harm, but that was not how it looked as they went at one another with cutlasses and clubs, bare hands and bladed flails. They fought one against one to begin with, and interspersed their duels with other tricks: tumbling through flaming hoops, juggling with knives. Then more fights, in larger groups, each melee choreographed like a brutal dance to the music of dinged armour and clashing blades. They knew just where to place a shallow, harmless cut to draw the most blood, and in the spiny racks of blades and maces at each end of the arena they knew where to find theatrical weapons with foldaway blades that could be used to simulate a mortal blow. The entrails which splattered the canvas floor had been bought that afternoon from a butcher's shop, and the fallen fighters who were dragged off groaning down paths of what appeared to be their own gore would all make miraculous recoveries before the next night's show. But the audience didn't know that. They saw only the blood and the glinting metal; fights with nets, with fists, with flaming torches; knives buried in bellies; clubs slammed against heads, strangling chains pulled taut on straining throats.

Fever, who knew a thing or two about theatre, guessed quickly that the blood was fake, and kept leaning across Wavey to tell her father so. Dr Crumb was appalled by the spectacle, and still more appalled by the people around him, who whooped and cheered at every blow. "Kill him!" they yelled, men and women, rich and poor, as if they were all eager to live up to Borglum's low opinion of their appetites. "Gouge his eyes out!" they hollered, making trumpets of their hands to help the fighters hear them. "Rip her head off!" "Spill his lights!"

Wavey laughed and clapped and shouted with the rest of them.

Charley Shallow watched her. Milly was agreeably thrilled and clung to him in just the way that he had hoped, but he ignored her, for he had noticed something far more interesting. At the last lull in the action, when the dwarf Borglum came riding round the arena on his tame Stalker, introducing the next pair of fighters, he had spotted Wavey in the crowd, and their eyes had met. She had given the faintest little smile, and just for an instant the showman had lost the thread of what he was saying. It had been only a tiny hesitation, and it was only because he was watching Wavey instead of the show that Charley had noticed it at all. Now he was trying to think what it might mean. What possible connection could there be between the Chief Engineer and this disreputable out-country dwarf?

After a long time, when most of the fighters had fallen, a young albino snowmad was left battling against the Stalker. Everyone was rooting for him. Fever almost joined the chant herself, but remembered just in time that she was an Engineer and immune to the crowd's gusts of emotion. Still, she could not help but admire the young man. There was real skill in the way he parried the Stalker's blows with that cleaver-like snowmad sword. But surely, she thought, as she watched him twirl through the lamplight, it was irrational for him to wear his white hair so long?

She was right. The Stalker grabbed him by his flying ponytail and yanked back his head, bearing his throat to one of its rusty blades. The watching Londoners all gasped together. Fever felt herself gasp too, afraid for the boy even though the fight was fake. For an instant she thought that he really was about to die; that maybe Borglum's carnival must end with real blood before the audience could go home satisfied. She felt disgusted, and underneath the disgust was an undertow of something worse: a dark excitement.

Then Blind Lady Midnight – who had been swiped aside by the Stalker earlier in the fight and flung across the ring with such violence that half the crowd thought she was dead and the rest had forgotten her – recovered suddenly and came to the boy's rescue. She was immensely tall and strong but earlier, when Borglum introduced her, she had torn off her blindfold to show everyone her spooky white eyes, without iris or pupil. The audience gasped again as she crossed the arena in a series of handsprings and vaulted up to sit astride the Stalker's huge head.

"Lady Midnight is not really blind," said Wavey. "Those misshape eyes of hers see heat instead of light."

"She can perceive the infrared end of the spectrum?" asked Dr Crumb, intrigued despite himself.

"Hush!" laughed his wife. "It is much more dramatic if people think she has no sight at all."

The Stalker had let go of the snowmad and was flailing its claws at Lady Midnight, but its shoulders were so massive that it couldn't reach her. While it was trying, she drew a bodkin and drove it through the green eye-slit, which spewed a satisfying cloud of sparks and vapour and went dark. The snowmad boy, meanwhile, picked up his sword, found a chink in the Stalker's armour and drove it in, letting out more sparks, more smoke, and a spew of ichor. The Stalker groaned like rusty brakes and toppled backwards, Lady Midnight jumping clear as it crashed to the canvas. She reached out to the snowmad boy, who took her hand, and together they made their bow while the boneyard music started up again. The show was over.

"What a horrible spectacle!" complained Dr Crumb.

"But so exciting!" said Wavey. She shifted uncomfortably,

and Fever knew that she was in pain. Her pelvis had been broken by the rogue Stalker Shrike years before, and although the injury had healed well, a night of dancing and an hour on Borglum's hard bleachers was enough to set it hurting again. Of course Wavey would never mention it; she hated anyone to think that she was weak. She kept her smile and said, "It reminded me of the old days, the fights Godshawk staged at Pickled Eel Circus. Except that no one is ever really killed in Borglum's shows. Well, barely ever... Come, we'll wait until the crowd is gone, and then I shall take you to meet him; you shall meet them all."

Neither Fever nor Dr Crumb was keen to meet the dwarf showman or his frightening friends, but they knew that it was futile to argue with Wavey, so they waited meekly, yawning from time to time, while the rest of the audience filed out.

On the far side of the arena, among the crowd around the exit, Charley Shallow waited too, and watched. He had this vague idea forming that there was something shady about Wavey and that dwarf, and that if he could learn the secret of it, well, he might use it to his own advantage.

Milly pulled at his hand. "You'll walk me home, Charley, won't you? Ooh, I should be scared to walk home all alone, after seeing all that..."

Charley barely heard her. "You run along then," he said. "I'll catch you later."

"But Charley!"

"I said 'op it," he said, his voice sliding down to the Bagmanish growl which the other apprentices had all learned to fear. "I got *business*."

She said something bitter which he did not catch and flounced off. Charley kept his eyes on Wavey and the Crumbs and moved himself sideways, behind the back rows of benches, into a tight and shadowed space where he could watch unseen.

Borglum was watching too, while the last of his audience drained out of the arena, their chatter fading. Then, while the girl with the lobster-claws went round snuffing the lanterns one by one he crossed the stained canvas to the bench where Wavey sat, flanked by the white coats of her family.

"Jasper," she said, with a smile in her voice. She knelt down, and they embraced, the dwarf's big head resting for a moment on her shoulder. "Duchess!" he said, and stepped back, still holding Wavey, his eyes darting over her face, as if he were taking stock of all the ways in which she'd changed since last they met. Only then did he spare a glance for Dr Crumb and Fever.

"My husband and daughter," said Wavey.

Borglum beamed. "Dr Crumb. It's good to meet you, sir. And little Fever. . . Not so little now! The Duchess used to talk about you often. 'Course, she wasn't even sure you were alive back then. Now look at you. Grown up, and pretty as your mother."

He held out his hand.

"You have upset them with your display," said Wavey.

"Then I'm sorry to hear it," Borglum said. He did look sorry, too, just for a moment. Then he turned to Wavey again, as if he could not stop looking at her for long.

"So what brings you to London?" she asked slyly.

"How do you know it's not just business?" asked Borglum. "All these workers Quercus has dragged here, hanging around bored and in need of entertainment. I'm on a humani-bloomin'-tarian mission to bring some excitement to their lives." He chuckled. "Anyway, 'tis but a fleety visit. We'll pass a fortnight here, then we're for the north again. I was planning to come and find you in the morning. I thought you'd be too posh now to come and watch the carny. I got some news from the north I thought would interest you. About the tower up there. But come; come aboard the barge, my dearie-os. I'll tell it to you all in comfort. . ."

"It is very late," said Dr Crumb uncertainly. "Perhaps we should go home, and save this news for tomorrow. . ." But it was no use, for the dwarf had reached up to take Wavey's arm and they were walking together towards the side exit, which hung half-open, revealing the hatchway of the *Knuckle Sandwich* waiting just outside. Fever gave her father an encouraging smile. She was tired too, but she was curious to find out who these strange friends of her mother were, and how she knew them. She was relieved when her father shrugged, and shook his head, and started following Wavey out of the tent.

Charley Shallow watched them go from his hiding place in the shadows between the back row of the seats and the tent wall. It was a good hiding place, but he was too far away from Wavey and the dwarf to catch what they were talking about. "*News for you. . .*" Borglum had said, hadn't he? ". . .*about the power up there. . .*" Something like that. As they all started to leave he squirmed quietly sideways, hoping to get closer, but his foot came down on a loose plank beneath the seats which croaked like a bullfrog. Borglum, standing at the exit to hold the tent-flap open for his guests, looked round. There was a slinking sound and a flash of quicksilver reflections as he drew his dagger.

"Is someone there?" asked Dr Crumb, who was still jittery after the night's display of violence.

"Prob'ly just some low-life come sneakin' round to try an' steal our fuel or catch a peek at Lady Midnight in her undiewear," said Borglum. "Quatch! Stick!" he shouted. "Get out here!"

Charley heard the footsteps thudding down the gangplanks as the misshapes came scrambling out of the barge. He didn't see them, though, since he was busy struggling his way out through the tent's side by then; wrenching apart the ties that held two panels closed and forcing himself out through the gap he'd made.

Tent Town seemed quiet. He set off running, drawn by the faint sound of fiddle music and a raucous laugh from one of the canvas pubs. But behind him he could hear those 'shapes yelling to one another as they came out through the Carnival's hungry mouth.

"There he goes!"

"Get him!"

Charley regretted running. If he'd just walked away casually the 'shapes might have taken him for a passer-by. He could have called out to them and said, "I seen the man you want; big fellow; he went that way!" But ideas like that always came to Charley just too late, and so he ran, and the misshapes ran after him. Along an alleyway between two rows of tents he went, leaping guy-lines like a hurdler. The pub he'd been aiming for loomed up ahead, but when he got close he saw it was a Movement place, with a northern name outside the door and northern songs spilling out. He couldn't be sure how the folks in there would take it if a London boy came asking them to save him from angry 'shapes. They might help, but then again, they might stand back and watch the misshapes murdering him like a free show.

So he swerved around the pub, stumbled over a drunk in the shadows behind it and ran on, flagging now, wondering if any of the empty-looking tents around him would make a hiding place. But when he looked back he could see the misshapes behind him; big hairy Quatch and that snowmad boy, and if he could see them then they could see him and they'd follow him into any tent he chose like ferrets down a rabbit-hole.

On his left now something dark rose, like a sea-cliff

rearing up out of a surf of tent-tops. It was the old temple of St Kylie. Till lately it had stood huddled round with houses at the heart of a busy web of streets, but the salvage gangs had taken all the houses now and left it lone and lorn. For the moment, fear of St Kylie had made them spare the temple, and Charley offered up a heartfelt prayer of thanks to her as he scampered round a corner, up the steps and into the shadows of the portico.

He could hear the voices of the misshapes coming closer, but they weren't in sight yet, so he nipped through into the temple precinct; a space as big as their arena, open to the sky, where a statue of St Kylie towered behind a broad stone altar. He ran behind her, hoping the misshapes might be too superstitious to search there. Above him dozens of broken kites rustled and whispered on strings stretched between the temple's eaves. The gods and goddesses of London seldom saw eye to eye on anything, but this past year they had all united to forbid their worshippers from making anything that flew, and most of the city's temples now sported these swags of torn kites, like ugly bunting. On the wall behind the statue something glistened: a red circle with a blue line slashed through its centre. Charley had been seeing that symbol on walls all over London lately, or at least, in all the bits of London where walls still stood. It was the mark of the London Underground, and this particular one was still wet. He reached out quickly and touched it and his fingers came away smeared with fresh paint.

Voices echoed under the portico. He turned, hearing the crunch of the misshapes' boots as they came down the steps into the precinct and started towards the altar. So they weren't superstitious after all. Charley started to realize what a poor bolt-hole he had chosen. He pulled out Bagman's old knife and unfolded the blade, and the feel of the rough handle in his hand gave him some comfort, although he knew he wouldn't be able to win a knife-fight with those 'shapes. If one of them came round one side of the statue and one round the other he'd be caught between them with nowhere to run. . .

All of a sudden a hand came from behind him and went over his mouth, while another seized him by his knife-arm and dragged him backwards. He didn't even have time to struggle; it all happened too quickly. It turned out there was a little secret doorway in the base of the wall, and someone pulled him through it and shut it tight behind him, so that when Borglum's misshapes came around St Kylie's skirts they saw no sign of him at all.

"I *told* you he wouldn't come in here, Quatch!" said the young snowmad. "It's a dead end, isn't it? Only an idiot would hide in here."

"Well, I heard something," said his hairy friend, and sniffed the air suspiciously, but any trace of Charley's scent was buried under the fresh-paint smell of that sign on the wall. He shrugged, and the two of them turned away and went to continue their hunt among the maze of tents.

7

NEWS FROM THE NORTH

The main cabin of the *Knuckle Sandwich* was a cosy place, warmed by a big iron stove, where the carnival's fighters and musicians sat about drinking from tin mugs and helping themselves to slices of pie. It was all so neat and small and cosy, and so rational in the clever way that so many cupboards and lockers and fold-down seats fitted into the tight space, that Fever could almost have imagined herself back aboard the *Lyceum*, except that the occupants were so strange, and so many of them wore bandages and sticking-plasters over fresh wounds, and there was such a smell of sweat and liniment mingling with the odours of the pie. Also, weapons hung on the walls instead of plates or pictures, and items of spiked and studded armour dangled from a line above the stove, steaming gently where the blood had been sponged off them. The Stalker stood motionless in a corner, draped with damp laundry.

Even though she had worked out that most of the wounds the fighters had suffered were pretend, Fever was still startled to see just how unharmed they were. That small, dark man, the Knave of Knives – she was *sure* she'd seen him torn across the face with Lady Midnight's flail, but there wasn't a scratch on him anywhere now.

"Look who's here!" said Borglum loudly, showing his guests in.

Some of the misshapes cheered as Wavey entered, some just smiled, but they all looked happy to see her. These people were a family for each other, and Wavey was a part of it. It seemed that Fever and her father could be part of it too, if they wanted, for the misshapes greeted them both with huge kindness when Borglum explained who they were. But they could not join in the conversations which were flowering around Wavey, the "how have you been"s and "how you've changed"s of old friends meeting. They stood uneasily at the edge of the gathering, listening without really understanding while Wavey joked with Borglum's bowler-hatted bargemaster Ned Fenster about some adventure they'd shared out in the Birkenmark, and admired the claws of the lobster-girl, whose name was Lucy.

"Your mum made me my first pair when I was little," Lucy said, grinning shyly at Fever. "Borglum and Master Fenster copied her design to make me these."

At last Dr Crumb found a chance to say, "But Wavey, how do you *know* these good people?"

"You mean she didn't tell you?" asked several of the misshapes all together. "You mean she never told you

about the Carnival of Knives? Oh, Wavey! Oh, Duchess!"
And Lady Midnight, who had swapped her armour for
a fluffy pink cardigan, said chidingly, "Is it that you're
ashamed of us, Wavey?"

"Of course not, Agnes, dear," said Wavey, caught out,
and blushing a little.

"Of course she is," said Borglum. He clambered on to
a leather armchair near the stove and pulled out his pipe.
"When *you* become a fine lady, Agnes Ndende, and marry
a good gent like Dr Crumb, I don't expect you'll tell him
about how you used to trundle round the north-country
with a rough 'n' tumble carny crew. But that's what Wavey
did, Doc, for a couple o' years. And mighty good at it she
was, too, and much we miss her. So sit down, sit down,
and grab a bit o' pie, and Borglum will tell you all about it."

Fever and her father sat. There seemed to be no choice.
The misshapes were all sitting down too, apparently
looking forward to Borglum's tale. One of the musicians
teased gentle music from a harp with her seven-fingered
hands. Wavey said protestingly again, "I am not ashamed
of you, of course I'm not," and took a seat beside her
husband.

Borglum lit his pipe and looked at his little audience
through its smoke.

"Well, here's the thing," he said, "and some of you has
heard it before, and some of you maybe hasn't, having
joined our merry band after the Duchess left us. But this
here is the story of how she came to join us in the first

70

place, and I don't blame her a jot for never having told it to the doc and Fever here, for there's parts of it as must be hurtful to her to think of.

"We was up in the Birkenmark that summer," he remembered. "It was the year the Scriven were overthrown in London, and news of it had just reached the north. We was setting up the show in the old caravanserai at Ulm when we heard of some travelling Londoners who'd captured a Scriven maid. *Skinners*, these bozos called theirselves, and they was bragging about how they'd drag this girl home with them to London Town an' flay the hide off her in Barbican Square. The last of the Scriven, that's what they said she was.

"Well, we didn't like that sort of talk. You see, Dr Crumb, we've got a sympathy for misshapes and outlandish folk, as you can imagine. And while the Scriven had always been a bit too high-and-mighty for my liking, I found I didn't much care for the idea of this one losing her skin. It was about all she had left at that point, except for her bones, which poked out through it like sticks in a bag.

"Well, the Carnival of Knives can always use an extra freak, and it seemed to me that if this poor quail was really the last of the Scriven, that made her valuable to a showman like myself. So I made those Skinner boys an offer. Give us the girl and they'd get a purse of silver and free tickets to the show. Mighty generous, I thought. But those boys weren't interested in money (which is a sure sign of danger in a man). So Quatch and Lady Midnight made them a different sort of offer, namely, give us the girl and they'd get to keep on breathing. Even that they turned down. It's funny how blokes like them will always think they're sharper and quicker than poor mis-formed folk like us, and how often they are wrong. When negotiations closed there were a few less Skinners in the world and your mother had become a carny girl.

"And do you know what was the first thing she said, when we brought her aboard the Sandwich and took off the gag those Skinners had put on her? Why, she just looked around, cool as a cucumber, calm as a courgette, and she says, 'I expect you could use a technomancer.' Turned out she wasn't just the Last Living Dapplejack, but a machine-wrangler too, and soon she was rigging up murdering machines to thrill our punters, as fierce as any that ever spilled a fighter's blood at Pickled Eel Circus. Halved the coal our engines ate, to boot. Even made herself a boiler-plate bikini and took turns in the fighting pit herself sometimes, though we had to paint some extra speckles on her, since the Scrivener had been so parsimonious with her pigmentation."

He sighed, and a smoke ring wobbled up out of his pipe and hung in the air above his head like a fading halo. "She was our wonder girl," he said. "Near broke my black old heart when we stopped among the Movement's forts one time and she chose to up and leave us and become technomancer to Quercus. Not that I blame her for it. She's a lady, and made for better things than this old carnival."

He fell silent, watching the flames in the stove. Was that a *tear* glinting in the crease beneath his eye?

"You said you had news for me, Jasper," Wavey reminded him, after a little while.

Borglum looked up. "That's right. I 'spect it's nothing, but you told me once how old Godshawk went expeditioning up into the edges of the ice, and how he found an old tower there, a pirrie-mid sorta thing, up in Caledon."

Wavey nodded. "A place the snowmads call Skrevanastuut. That's right. Godshawk thought it might be important, but he had a terrible time getting there. When he finally reached the pyramid, he found that there was no way in. He came home knowing nothing more about its origins than when he left London. It was long ago. I was just a little girl."

"Well, I remember you telling me that story," said Borglum. "And I heard something else just recently that brought it to mind. I was talking to a scavenger named Duergar, who'd been up in them hills last summer, and lingered too long, and got caught by the first snow. Struggling south again he'd lost his way, and fetched up at this pirrie-mid of yours, which most folks in the north know to avoid, because it's the haunt of ghosts and nightwights and the walking dead. He told me that there's a way in now. Those earth-storms we've had up north these past few years have opened a crack or a fissure or something, and he reckoned that somebody could get inside, if they wanted to. Which he didn't, on account of how haunted and unlucky the place is. He was dying when I talked with him, and he blamed his sickness on having spent just one night in the shadow of that pirrie-mid. Though given how much he drank, I 'spect it was booze that killed him, not a curse."

Wavey said nothing. Dr Crumb looked at her inquiringly and said, "I have heard of these pyramids. There are several of them, far to the north, on the High Ice. It is where Stalker brains are supposed to have come from. I did not know that there were any so far south as Caledon. . ."

"There aren't," said Wavey. "All the pyramids that we know of on the ice were looted long ago. This one at Skrevanastuut is different. It is smaller, and Godshawk believed that it might be even older."

"Perhaps the first Stalker-builders made it and then moved north to construct the others," reasoned Dr Crumb. "The world may have been warmer then."

Wavey was looking at the fire. She said, "Godshawk believed that the Skrevanastuut structure might hold . . . oh, all *sorts* of secrets."

"If there is really a way in, we shall soon hear all about them," said Dr Crumb. "Some scavenger or archaeologist will have penetrated its mysteries by now."

"Not likely," said Borglum. "The passes have all been closed by winter since old Duergar came by. Even if they weren't, the place is cursed."

"My dear sir, there is no such thing as a curse."

"Maybe not. But the snowmads believe there is, and they're the only people likely to go a-roaming in those lonely hills. They'll steer clear of that old pirrie-mid, be it open or shut."

Wavey laughed her silvery laugh. "Dear Jasper! And you came all this way just to tell me of it."

"Not just that, Duchess." Borglum blushed a deep red. "We're here on business, like I said."

The barge shook with footsteps. The cabin door opened to let in Quatch and the snowmad boy. Borglum jumped up, saying, "You remember Quatch, Duchess, and here is one of our new recruits, Harrison Stickle. We call him Stick."

It seemed that Wavey did remember Quatch, for she was already hugging him, snuggling her head against his hairy shoulder, while Dr Crumb looked on and worried about fleas. Fever made a neat, Engineerish bow to Harrison Stickle, who looked away from her and said to Borglum, "We chased that snooper far into the tents, chief, but there we lost him. . ."

In the chamber behind the altar Charley had struggled with his captors, uncertain how many they were or what they meant to do with him. In the confusion he imagined that they must be some of Borglum's people, and bit desperately at the hand which was gagging him.

"Ow! Keep still, kid!" said a gruff voice. "Do you want those northish 'shapes to find us all?"

Charley went still. He heard other people round him keeping still too: their breathing; the sounds their clothes made as they shifted. Outside, the voices of his hunters moved away.

"They've gone," a woman's voice said.

Someone opened the shade of a dark-lantern and yellow light washed over wall paintings of scenes from the Life of St Kylie. The place was a robing room where the priestesses of the cult changed into their mitres and ceremonial hot-pants on festival days. The woman who had spoken looked like a priestess herself; dark robes, and the saffron mark of the saint on her high white forehead. Two men stood with her; ordinary men, with ordinary faces attached to ordinary bodies, clad in the overalls of workers on the new city. One held a pair of paint pots, so it seemed safe to assume that these were the people who had just finished painting the roundel of the London Underground on the temple wall when Charley blundered in.

He supposed that he should feel afraid of them. Everyone knew that the London Underground were terrorists. But they seemed so much less frightening than the fighters from the Carnival of Knives that it was hard to feel anything but relieved.

"Why were they after you?" the woman asked.

"Saw me nosing round their circus," said Charley.

"I told you we should let them take him," said one of the men, the older one, whose cropped white hair glittered like hoar frost in the lantern light. "They'd probably just have given him a good hiding and let him go. Now he's seen us."

"We'll have to kill him," said the other man, but he didn't sound very convinced, and neither of his friends took any notice.

The priestess moved closer to Charley, studying the knife they'd taken from him. She was a tall, plain-featured woman with a stale, sweetish smell of incense coming off her clothes each time she moved. She read the legend on the knife's handle and then looked hard into Charley's face. "He's the Skinner's boy!" she said. She shut the knife and turned to her friends. "Don't you remember the upsets before the Movement came? He's Bagman Creech's boy, I'd swear to it!"

Charley felt grateful to her for remembering. There'd be no question of harming him now that they knew who he was. He smiled his friendliest smile.

The older man turned away in disgust. "Some Skinner's boy! He works for that Dapplejack slut who Quercus made Chief Engineer."

"That's not true!" said Charley. "I mean, it is, but I never *asked* to work for her. It's no fault of mine she got set up over the whole Guild. I hate her. That's what got me in trouble tonight. I was spying on her. Her and her Scriven-loving husband, and that scrawny brat of theirs..."

"I thought you said you was at the Carnival of Knives?" the young man growled.

"I was! An' so was they!"

All three of them looked sharply at him. The white-haired man said, "Wavey Godshawk was there?"

Charley nodded. "She knows that dwarf showman. I heard them talk. He brought news for her from the north. Something about some *power*."

Both men looked at the priestess.

"Which power?" she said. "Arkhangelsk?"

"I dunno. I couldn't hear much. Then I had to scarper."

Charley didn't know why, but what he'd said had made his three new friends tense like spooked dogs. They kept glancing at each other, asking questions with their eyes that they didn't want to voice in Charley's presence. He felt pleased.

"I can find out," he said. "I'll find out what she's up to, if you want, and come and tell you."

The older man sniffed. "You know who we are, kid?"

Charley nodded eagerly. "I saw that sign you painted. You're the Underground, ain't you?"

The man nodded. "We're the only ones in London with the guts to stand up to Quercus and stop him stealing our city away."

"Well, I can help," said Charley earnestly. "You just have to let me know where I can find you again. . ."

8

PLANS

"No, Snow Leopard. You are Chief Engineer, and we have a city to move. We cannot afford to lose you."

Not many people dared say no to Wavey Godshawk, but Nikola Quercus, Lord Mayor of London, Land-Admiral of the Movement, was one of them. He was a mild-looking man, no taller than Dr Crumb, pale-complexioned, dressed in a simple grey tunic with none of the braid or jewellery that Movement warriors usually favoured. He did not look like a man who had conquered and looted half the cities of the Birkenmark, or fought off the Suomi horde at Hill of Skulls, or won himself an empire that stretched all the way north from the Anglish Sea into the Fuel Country. Yet he had done all of those things, and many more, and now he sat at the Crumbs' breakfast table in the watery sunlight of a London summer, looking at the map of the north which Wavey had spread out there.

"Where did you say this black pyramid lies?"

"Just here, Lord Mayor..." The map had been rolled, and showed a tendency to curl up at the edges. Wavey walked around the table, weighting the corners down with three cups and a jam-pot. She leaned over her lord mayor's shoulder and pointed to a spot among the busy contour lines of the old Scottish mountains. "The pyramid is not marked. Godshawk knew where it lay; I remember him pointing it out to me on his charts. Alas, those perished with him in the Skinners' Riots."

"That is beyond the edges of the ice."

"Not quite. Not at present. Not in the summertime."

Wavey had been thinking all night about Borglum's news, and she had come down to breakfast determined to set off for Skrevanastuut at once. None of the sensible, rational objections which Fever or Dr Crumb raised could stop her from summoning the Lord Mayor and explaining her scheme to him. Now they sat mutely watching while Quercus raised all the same arguments that they had tried.

"It's savage country north of London. The brigand-kings of Leeds and Lincoln have no love for Londoners."

Wavey chuckled. "I am not proposing to go *alone*. I hoped I could borrow one of your landships, and a few of your soldiers. We'll take your excellent new roads north over the old sea, and avoid all the savages. We shall meet no brigand-kings when we reach Caledon; no one lives there at all."

"Only nightwights," said Quercus darkly.

"*Nightwights?*" Wavey laughed again. "Bogey men for nomad nursemaids to frighten little children with. Surely you do not still believe in *nightwights*, my Lord Mayor?"

Quercus said, "If you really think there is valuable old-tech in this pyramid, we could send another Engineer. Steepleton, or Lark."

"Lord Mayor, did I not explain? This place may have been made by the first Stalker builders. We might find Stalker brains there, which would be useful enough, since we have no spares left, and our Stalkers are wearing out at a frightening rate. Or we may find something better: the secret of making Stalker brains for ourselves; the answer to the mystery of how the Stalkers are powered. You think the new London is mighty now? Imagine how much mightier it would be if you could power it by Molecular Clockwork!"

Quercus said nothing.

"How many Stalkers do we have left now?" asked Wavey. "Fifty, is it?"

"Fifty-six. Another sixty in the north with Rufus Raven's Lazarus Brigade."

"Well there you go. You could do with some more, I'm sure. Steepleton and Lark know nothing about Stalkers. I am the only one qualified to investigate this site. If you lend me a landship I could be there and back in a few weeks and bring home all sorts of wonders. Dr Crumb and his colleagues are perfectly capable of continuing the work on London while I am away."

Quercus scratched his chin and studied the map.

"If I don't go there, someone else will," Wavey warned. "Native taboos may keep nomads and snowmads away, but news that the tower is open is sure to spread. When it does, adventurers from Paris and Hamsterdam and Bremen will set off, hoping to secure its secrets for *their* cities."

Those three cities were London's main rivals. They had scoffed at Quercus's plan when it was first announced, but now they were growing worried; in the past year they had all stopped selling steel and other raw materials to London. Paris was rumoured to be building a huge chassis of its own.

"Very well," said Quercus suddenly. That was his way; he considered things deeply, made decisions swiftly, and stuck to them. "Take a landship, and my blessing. Dr Crumb will serve as Acting Chief Engineer in your absence. We shall tell no one your real reason for going."

Wavey smiled in the calm, contented way she always did when she had just got something that she wanted. "I shall set out with Master Borglum. We can tell people that I am going to visit friends in the north."

Dr Crumb started to protest again. He had never been further north of London than his old childhood home at Lesser Wintermire, and Lesser Wintermire had been quite bad enough. The far north was a wild place, where science and reason were unknown. But he had never been able to get his own way with Wavey, not since that first long-ago day when she decided that he was to be her lover, and he didn't now: she hushed him, and she and Quercus began discussing arrangements and the best route north.

Fever went to the window. The rain was still falling. Out in the sodden street a passing apprentice Engineer paused to peer at the house, probably wondering why the Lord Mayor's chair and bodyguards were waiting outside. She caught his glance, his eyes dark as charcoal smudges. *Charley Shallow...* Why did that boy always make her feel guilty? she wondered. It wasn't as if *she* had tried to murder *him*...

He saw her watching him and went hurrying on his way, trying to pretend that he had not been looking at the house at all.

It wasn't his fault, Fever decided. It was just London, so dingy and crowded, so full of upsetting memories. She felt caged here; had felt it ever since they brought her home from Mayda. A view opened in her mind of worldwide moors under a high sky; curlews calling, ice on the skyline like a long white wave, curtains of light dancing in the dusk. She could almost see Skrevanastuut itself; a black pyramid on a bare hill. *North.* Even the word sounded clean and free.

She turned, and her mother stopped talking and looked up expectantly at her.

"Wavey," she said, "when you go north – can I come with you?"

"Oh, that would really not be—" Dr Crumb began.

But Wavey bared all her many teeth in a brilliant smile and said, "Fever, I was *hoping* you would say that!"

9

PIES, SPIES AND LITTLE WHITE LIES

On the lower slopes of Ludgate Hill, round on the St Kylie side where the houses already wore white crosses to show that they were marked for demolition, there was a long, low, salvage-plastic eatery called Nye's Pies. Who Nye was, and whether he existed at all or had just been dreamed up by some former owner looking for a name that rhymed with "pie", nobody knew and nobody cared. All that mattered about the place was this: it had a long counter, at which labourers queued to buy their pies, and fourteen greasy tables where they sat to eat them.

"The table nearest the window," that was what Charley had been told by the London Underground before they booted him out of the robing room behind the temple of St Kylie and let him find his own way home. "Someone will be waiting." So here he was, scurrying through the chill, half-hearted rain, shoving the pie-shop door open and stepping inside, blinking at the steam and warmth. The place smelled of damp overalls and unwashed bodies, which at least served to mask the smell of the pies.

Big, grimy men sat at every table except the one by the window, which was occupied only by a girl in worker's gear, dark hair escaping in random curls from under her orange headscarf.

Even from the doorway Charley could tell she was a looker, and he grinned, congratulating himself on the way his luck had turned. He watched another man approach the table and the girl send him away. "I'm waiting for a friend," he saw her say, reading her lips. Then she looked at Charley and nodded. "There he is."

Charley squeezed his way between the chairs and tables. The girl had already bought two pies. She slid one to him as he sat down. "You're Charley Shallow," she said, not smiling, black eyes flicking across his face and clothes. A gypsy-looking girl with a long nose and rosy cheeks and a small, red, serious mouth. Older than Charley, but not too much older.

As if she had caught his thoughts she said, "How old are you, Charles Shallow?"

"Eighteen," said Charley.

"Never."

"Seventeen then. I don't properly know, to tell the truth. I was brung up at the old Mott and Hoople on Ditch Street, back before they knocked it down. I dunno when my birthday is nor how many I've had or nothing."

"Fifteen, more like," the girl said. Charley could tell she was his sort of person, a good London guttersnipe, not some posh bit from the top of the hill. He leaned back in the rickety chair and grinned easily at her and said, "If you want to hear what I know you'd better get listening quick, before I get any younger."

The girl frowned. "I don't want to hear nothing. Not here. How do I know I can trust you? How do I know you wasn't followed? Eat your pie, then we'll go somewhere we can talk." She picked up her own pie and took a big bite from it, and the grease of its nameless filling ran down her pointed chin.

Charley blushed, angry at himself for being stupid and at her for pointing it out. Spies and terrorists didn't just discuss their secrets in pie shops. She'd met him here so it would look natural, just a girl meeting her boyfriend for a bite of dinner. Then she'd lead him off somewhere secret, where the rest of her gang would be waiting. He liked the idea that all the people in the pie shop would imagine she was his sweetheart. It cheered him up. He said, "Don't I even get to know your name? Since you know mine an' all?"

The girl took a second bite while she thought this over. "Gwen Natsworthy," she said with her mouth full.

"Then I'm pleased to meet you, Gwen."

"Eat your pie."

So he ate his pie and when he was done he followed Gwen Natsworthy through some of the mean little alleys that were still standing in that quarter of the city until she was satisfied that they were not being followed, and then out across the endless, windswept, empty lots which had once been Whitechapel and Shadwell, until they came to a hole. There were steps leading down into it and a brick-lined portal at the bottom. Weeds grew round it. It gave Charley the creeps. Reminded him of that nasty tunnel he'd slunk along once in search of Fever Crumb, the day the Movement came. Still, he wasn't going to let Gwen Natsworthy see that he was scared, so he went down the steps and she followed, and in a little maze of forgotten cellars down there her friends were waiting for him.

There were five of them. One was the priestess-like woman he had met before, but he did not know the others. They were men, and they all wore workers' slops, those stiff garments of blue and blue-grey hemp that had become the unofficial uniform of London these past few years. One man was smoking a pipe and the fug from it hung between their faces and Charley's so that it was hard to see them clearly, and he wondered if that was deliberate.

Gwen Natsworthy followed him in and kicked a door shut behind her. The lantern flames wavered, throwing odd shadows up the walls, and for a moment he felt uneasy again 'cos they could kill him down here and who'd ever know. Who'd come looking for Charley Shallow? No one, that was who.

"This is the boy," said the priestess (though Charley wasn't sure she was a priestess now; the mark had gone off her forehead and she was in normal clothes like all the rest).

"The Skinner's boy, as was," said one of the men.

"Still am, master," said Charley. He had got the impression at his first meeting that these Undergrounders had it in for Wavey Godshawk, and he thought he could use his background as a Skinner to impress them. "I work for the northerners, but I'm a Londoner through and through: a proper Mockney, born within earshot of Bowie Bells. I just been biding my time, waiting for a chance to bring some harm to that speckled witch."

"Good lad," a man said.

"No." It was the pipe-smoker who had spoken. He had a posher way of talking than the rest. He took the pipe out of his mouth and pointed at Charley with its stem. "That sort of talk is no good. It's not Wavey Godshawk that we hate. Her speckled skin does not concern us. Quercus and his northerners don't offend us because of their northern-ness. You mustn't get the idea that we are crackpot London-for-the-Londoners fanatics, peddling hate for hate's sake. The only thing that we are against, the thing that we are sworn to destroy, is the new city."

The others muttered their agreement. Even the man who'd called Charley a good lad said, "Sorry, Doc, yeah."

"Doc's tellin' it right," said Gwen Natsworthy. "My old street got cleared away to make that new city. It's nothing but waste and lunacy and wickedness."

"My street too," said one of the men. "All our homes are gone. Quercus promises new homes for all aboard that monstrosity of his, but who'd want to live in them? Eh? Who?"

"Nobody," said Charley obediently, although secretly he was thinking that quite a lot of people would, given how airy and neat the houses on the new city were compared with the slums that Quercus had cleared. But he wasn't going to risk offending these people. This was the most interesting thing that had happened to him for months. He was looking forward to seeing where it would lead.

"We want this new city stopped, see?" said a third man; an old plastic-smith judging by the way he wheezed, his lungs ruined by the fierce fumes from the blending vats. He reminded Charley a bit of Bagman Creech; same phlegmy whine; same mad light in his eyes. "We want it stopped, and London put back the way we liked it; the way it always was."

"The way it was but *better*," insisted Gwen Natsworthy. "With trees and stuff, and good homes for all, and parks where the kids can play."

Yeah, and fountains of wine and gingerbread houses and pavements made of gold, thought Charley, but he didn't say it.

"Now, Charley," said the one called Doc, with an air of someone calling things to order. "Now then, you spied on Wavey Godshawk's meeting with this short chappie, this Borglum. Is that so?"

"'Tis," said Charley, peering at the old man through his haze of pipe smoke. His face seemed familiar. Take off that greying beard, that shock of hair, and. . . Who had he been? Someone used to better things than brewing bitter plots in basements, that was for sure.

"I heard the dwarf say he had some news from the north," he explained. "News about a power. That's all."

"I am thinking Arkhangelsk," said the priestess. "Arkhangelsk is the chief power in that region."

"Could mean trouble," said Doc, and sucked thoughtfully at his pipe so that an ember glowed bright red inside its bowl.

"All depends who the dwarf works for," said the plastic-smith. "We can't be sure he's Quercus's creature."

"But we know the Godshawk woman is," said the priestess. "So if the dwarf brings news to her it must surely be news that helps Quercus, or can harm our friends."

"Could mean trouble," said Doc again.

"I'll tell you something else," said Charley. "Whatever this news is, it's got Wavey all fired up. She's sent a note to Quercus himself asking for leave of absence. I heard a couple of the Guildsmen talk about it at the Engineerium. They say she's going north herself."

"The Chief Engineer?" Doc said. "Going north?"

They all stared at Charley and he thought, *They ain't much of a conspiracy if they didn't know that!* Well, that was all right with him. If they weren't much good it only made it easier for him to impress them, and he liked to impress people, specially when it was easy and some of them looked like Gwen Natsworthy.

"She's taking her daughter with her," he said. "I don't know what it's about. She says it's a holiday, but everyone knows she's got some hush-hush business going on up there."

One of his listeners turned to Doc and said, "Our friends must be warned! Great gods, do you think she knows about the alliance?"

"Quiet, you flap-jawed cloot!" growled the plastic-smith, his eyes on Charley.

"It's all right," said Doc. He stepped forward and put a hand on Charley's shoulder, and Charley looked up into his big, kindly face and suddenly knew where he had seen him before. Take off the beard and that shock of steel-wool hair and he'd be Dr Stayling, the one who was Chief Engineer until Quercus dismissed him and gave his job to Wavey Godshawk. So *this* was where he'd ended up!

"It's all right," he said again, looking seriously at Charley. "I think we can trust Charles. I think this a great day for our movement. At last we have a friend, an *operative* indeed, inside the Guild of Engineers." He paused, looking rather pleased with himself; he had been waiting for a chance to use the word "operative". "The information that he has already shared with us may prove vital to our friends in the north. We shall send word at once to warn them of this new development. And Charles, we shall ask you to keep listening. You are close to Dr Crumb, and Dr Crumb is close to Quercus. Keep your ears wide, and tell us everything that you hear."

"Oh, I will, sir," Charley said, "I will!" Nobody had placed such trust in him since old Bagman died, and he felt a little bit guilty about letting them think he was as fired up as them over this moving city business, when in truth he didn't care tuppence whether London moved or not so long as he was safe and prospering. He told himself it was only a white lie. He'd just said what they wanted to hear. It pleased him to see the smiles that he'd put on their faces as they came crowding round to congratulate him.

"Welcome," they said.

"Welcome, Charles!"

"Welcome, mate."

"Good to have yer with us."

"Welcome to the London Underground!"

10

NORTHWARD HO!

The Guild of Engineers had rescued many odd and interesting books from houses that were being demolished by the salvage gangs; in one of them, Dr Crumb had found a few meandering notes which had enabled him to rediscover the Ancient art of Photography. He had built an experimental camera, and constructed a darkroom in a former closet at Number One Bishopsgate. There, by the light of lanterns with red glass panes, he patiently dipped the plates he had exposed into vats of pungent chemicals. He had made several portraits of Fever in shades of grey and silver, staring at the camera lens with hawkish concentration. He had tried a few of Wavey, too, but Wavey was not good at sitting still. His photographs of her always came out blurred; a shadow-woman with uncertain eyes and other faces peering around the corners of her own, her restless hands transforming into fans of light.

He made one last picture of them both on the day of their departure, setting up his camera outside the Movement landship which would be carrying them north, and hiding beneath a black cloth to open and close the aperture while they posed stiffly in their new cold-weather clothes; their fleece-lined boots and catskin hats, Wavey's ermine cloak. Then they went aboard the landship, and Dr Crumb followed it as far as the foot of Ludgate Hill, waving to them as they stood on the open upper deck, sometimes calling out last-minute advice: "Shallow breathing is recommended in very cold regions!" or, "The savages of the high north may be pacified by gifts of fat or salt!"

He had been arguing hard against the trip all week, sure that the north was far too dangerous, even after Rufus Raven's victories. But that morning he had changed his mind. He could see how eager Fever was to go. He had been worried about his sad and beautiful daughter. Perhaps he had been wrong to make her leave her friends on their irrational theatre barge and bring her home. This expedition of Wavey's would do her good, he thought, and he stood at the end of Bishopsgate watching the landship pull away into the haze, waving and waving until he could see it no more.

Then he went home to develop his photograph, which he would keep by his bedside to help him remember them until they came home again. Fever peering at him all solemn and owlish from between the fur flaps of her hat; Wavey, as usual, a blur.

The new London took much longer than the old to disappear. All morning the landship and Borglum's barge travelled across the low, dun-coloured hills of Hamster's Heath, past Slugg's Pottage and on into the Wintermires, and still when the passengers looked back they could make out the upper levels of the new city rising faint and hazy in the distance. No wonder the people of the roadside villages seemed nervous and oppressed. This had been a country of small independent market towns and farmsteads that had gone on unchanging through generation after generation. Now it was part of the territory of the Movement. The New North Road sliced through farm and town alike, cobbled with the rubble of old London and forever busy with the Movement's traffic. The strong young men who should have been working the fields had gone south to join the construction teams, leaving their elders to sow and reap the corn that fed London. By night the lights of the new city peered at them over the shoulders of the land. Fever thought that it must be like living under the gaze of a newborn monster.

The landship was called the *Heart of Glass*. It was an unprepossessing vehicle; an armoured barge painted in dirty white dazzle patterns, rolling on big, clawed wheels. Movement landships were faster than most, but it still could not keep pace with Borglum's speedy *Knuckle Sandwich*, which kept running on ahead and pausing to wait impatiently for it to catch up, like a thoroughbred in the company of a carthorse.

Wavey had helped herself to the captain's cabin and covered its whitewashed wooden walls with tapestries and fine hangings to make it feel more homely. "After all," she told Fever, during the first afternoon of the journey, "what is the point in being Chief Engineer if I cannot travel in comfort? I had a hard struggle to get where I am now. When you were a baby I had to flee London like a common criminal, pursued by those mad Skinners, hunted everywhere, till Master Borglum took me in. I lived like an animal, forever frightened, lurking in culverts and reed beds by day, moving on each night, trusting no one. My shoes fell apart, my clothes went to rags, my poor starved ribs looked like a toast rack. Don't you think I deserve a little luxury now that I am old?"

Fever, who had been standing at the window to look back at London, turned. Wavey was sprawling lazily on a cushioned bench beside the stove, eating Turkish Delight with a little silver fork. Fever had never heard her speak before about the dreadful things she had endured after the Skinners' Riots. It made her feel suddenly protective. "You're not old, Wavey," she said.

"Oh, but I am," said Wavey. She altered her position on the bench and plumped a cushion, inviting Fever to sit down beside her. It was true, she *was* beginning to look a little gaunt; the skin stretched taut across the fine bones of her face. "We Scriven live far longer than the common human herd," she said, "and we do not suffer so much from the diseases of old age, but even by Scriven standards I am no longer a young woman. It is starting to show, I fear. These creases around my eyes – *crow's feet*, people call them; isn't that horrible? You are so lucky to be young, Fever. You should make the most of your body, my dear, before it starts to let you down. Speaking of which, have you noticed young Harrison Stickle? I'm sure he fancies you. I think he's rather handsome, in his curious way. . ."

Fever wasn't listening. She was busy wondering why the Scriven aged differently. What was it about their bodies that had made them less susceptible than other people to the trials of time? She wished that her father were there so that she could discuss it with him.

Turning back to the window, she saw that London had finally sunk behind the hills.

Sometimes the snow lay year-round on those hills, leading Londoners to believe that they could see the snouts of glaciers when they looked north from their city's borders. But that year was warm, and the ice and snow were gone, leaving the land dotted with meltwater meres. The convoy rattled past them, swinging eastward through heaths and scrub woods and showers of cold grey rain. It crossed Kingsbath marshes and entered Doggerland, a foggy, fenny place, so flat and so full of still, reflecting waters that there seemed to be nothing there except the sky. That country had all been beneath the North Sea until a few centuries ago, and in the mist that met the convoy it looked as if it still was. Borglum said that it must have been cheerier when it had little fishes swimming about it. Still, there was a good road there; a Movement road that ran north-east as straight as a ruler, low hills rising into cloud on its left-hand side, the old seabed stretching out for ever on the right.

Towards sundown a long, low ridge appeared ahead, rising like an island from the marshes, with the road leading over it. This was Dryships Hill, and at its foot on the northern side lay Three Dry Ships, a settlement built around the hulks of some freighters abandoned there when the sea drained away. Their timber hulls had been much built-upon, and sheds and shanties sprawled all around them, for this was an important way-station now on the roads that linked London to the Fuel Country. Filthy children came running and shouting behind the *Heart of Glass* as it pulled in, and for a moment Fever was reminded of other arrivals in other towns, when she had travelled aboard *Persimmon's Electric Lyceum*. But those journeys had been in southern lands, nothing like the damp plains of Doggerland, and Ambrose Persimmon would never have brought his theatre to a place as grimy and desperate as Three Dry Ships.

There were not enough people there to warrant setting up the arena and staging a proper show, but the carnival fighters sparred with one another in the light of the campfire while Borglum's cook prepared the evening meal, and the people of the place gathered round to watch.

Fever watched too, for a little while. She had not meant to, for she was alarmed by the carnival people, with their strange looks and costumes and their easy laughter and all the memories they lit in her of her old life in Summertown. At first she stayed in her own small cabin aboard the *Heart of Glass* and tried to read Wintervale's *History of the Northern Peoples,* because she wanted to learn something about the places that she would soon be seeing. But trying to follow the alliances and fallings-out between those ever-shifting nomad empires was like trying to map smoke, and the clang of weaponry from outside was distracting, so at last she put the book aside and stepped out into the chilly night air, which was filled with the smell of the gorse-root fire and the grunts and war cries of the sparring fighters. The huge, hairy one they called Quatch was crossing blades with the Knave of Knives. Fever watched them, trying not to disapprove, and ate stew from a wooden bowl that someone handed her. She looked across the fire at the lad called Stick and remembered what Wavey had said about him, and he *did* look handsome in the firelight, but he was sitting beside Lucy the lobster-girl and it was it was quite obvious that he was her boy or her sweetheart or whatever the silly expression was, and that made her feel suddenly very lonely.

Quatch gave a great roar, swinging his cleaver in a blow that should have lopped off his opponent's head, but the Knave ducked under it, tripped him, somersaulted over him as he fell and ended up astride him with his knife at Quatch's throat. The onlookers clapped and cheered. They knew it was a friendly bout so there was no need for fakery and butcher's shop blood. The fighters stood up, bowed, and went to find their own bowls of stew.

Next came something special: a new act that Borglum was trying out. Lady Midnight swaggered out on to the fighting-ground. She chose a long blade from the weapons rack and stood there swinging it, splashing glints of firelight over Borglum's face as he warned the audience to keep quiet, so that the blind woman could hear her foe approaching. Then he left her and hurried into the knot of fighters and crewmen waiting by the barges, grinning at Fever as he came. "This'll be good!" he said. "This is something special! Oh, but it's grand to have your mother back. . ."

Fever looked around and saw that her mother was no longer watching the fight. She must have gone back aboard the barge. . . Or aboard *Borglum*'s barge. For a moment she had a horrible feeling that Wavey was going to emerge in the boiler-plate bikini of which the dwarf had spoken so fondly. But what actually came down the ramp of the *Knuckle Sandwich* and stepped out into the firelight was something far, far worse. For a moment nobody could work out what it was. When they did, a murmur of surprise ran through the watchers.

"'Tis a paper dolly. . ."

"A cut-out man. . ."

"But how's it *moving* then?"

Flat as an outline chalked around a corpse, blank face flickering with firelight and shadow, the paper boy stood and looked around, turning its flat white head from side to side, until it saw Lady Midnight waiting on the far side of the fire.

"Oh!" said Fever, and put a hand up to her face. She was well able to control her emotions usually, but the paper boy was so unexpected, and it reminded her with such awful clarity of the time when she and Dr Crumb and poor Dr Isbister had battled things like that in the library at Godshawk's Head; *really* battled them, not just in play. For a moment she was afraid that she would faint.

"It is all right," said a voice beside her, and there was Borglum, looking up at her all kindly and concerned. "You're wondering how we make him move, the mannikin? 'Tis all done with technomancy, my dear. There is a machine aboard the *Sandwich* which talks somehow to a little wafer of a brain that's slipped inside the paper of him. Your mother's operating it now; what he sees, she sees, and she tells him where to move. It's a marvellous engine."

"I did not think there were any such things left," said Fever, who had burned the last of London's paper boys herself.

"We picked it up from an antiquarian in Hamsterdam who didn't know how to make it work, and in truth we didn't know neither, but your mother came aboard today, opened it up, tinkered a while inside with wires and such, and our little papery friend sprang straight to life."

The paper boy tensed, then started to shuffle forward, mincing along on the edges of his cut-out feet. He moved so silently that Lady Midnight seemed not to have heard him.

"Behind you!" shouted someone in the crowd, forgetting that they were not supposed to speak.

Lady Midnight swung round with her sword ready. The paper boy raised one paper hand, and from his fingertips five tiny claws emerged.

"Poisoned needles!" Borglum shouted importantly. "Envenomed with the ichor of the deadly Zagwan centipede, a vicious reptile from Lady Midnight's mother country!" He nudged Fever and muttered, "There ain't no such creature really, so don't worry; it won't give our Agnes no more than a scratch. . ."

Lady Midnight had sensed the thing's approach, perhaps by the small scritching sounds its feet made in the grass. She swept her sword at it, and it bent backwards with inhuman suppleness so that the blade swished through empty air. Lady Midnight hesitated, looking confused. No doubt she knew what she was facing; no doubt she and Wavey and Borglum had planned out every step. But Fever did not feel that she could watch any more. She turned and walked away from the fire, away from Three Dry Ships, into the quiet and the dusk. She climbed the hill behind the town and stood on its summit looking east across the marshes at dozens of distant points of fire which burned like red stars, far away behind the mist. The Ancients had dug oil wells out there, and the Movement had reopened some of them, and found others in places which must have been too difficult or too expensive for even the Ancients to reach when they lay deep under water.

Deep under water. . . How strange it was to think that

the sea had once covered all this land. At Fever's feet, in bald patches between the grass, scatterings of tiny white seashells glowed in the twilight. She sat down and picked up a handful and let them trickle through her fingers, and thought about the seas of the south, and Arlo. If only she had gone with him. If only she had stayed with the *Lyceum*. Ever since Wavey reclaimed her she had felt like a doll or a pet. She had thought this journey to the north would change things, but she was as listless as ever. She wished something would happen to her.

It was a wish that she would come to regret.

11

THE REVOLUTIONISTS

Dr Crumb was a punctual man. If you wanted to bump into him it was not difficult. You just had to station yourself between Bishopsgate and the Engineerium when the six a.m. bells were ringing to summon the day shift to the factories and there he would be, hastening along with his case full of plans and papers on his way to start his morning's work.

So that was where Charley Shallow stood, in the grey of a drizzling Monday morning, a few days after Fever and Wavey departed for the north. "Good morning, Dr Crumb!" he called, and tried to sound surprised to see him there.

"Oh … Shallow…" Dr Crumb blinked at him. He had always had a vague feeling that Charley might have been unhappy at the way he'd been dismissed when Fever returned home, but he was glad to see that the boy seemed friendly enough. Not only that, but he was carrying a large umbrella, and since Dr Crumb had left his at home as usual it was only rational that he agree to

Charley's suggestion that they walk together and share the shelter of it.

"You are quite sure I am not taking you out of your way?" he insisted, as they started down Ludgate Hill. "I am working aboard the new city this morning. . ."

"Oh, that's all right, Dr Crumb," said Charley. "I'm going there myself. Me and Coldharbour are helping Dr Steepleton with the new boarding ramps in the Gut."

Dr Crumb sighed. "It is the *Great Under Tier*, Charley. I do wish people would call things by their proper designations, instead of all these silly nicknames. Say 'G.U.T.' if you must, but not 'Gut'."

"Sorry, Dr Crumb."

"That is all right, Charley. I did not mean to snap. . ."

"I expect you're under a lot of pressure," said Charley kindly. "I mean, it must be a worry and all, with Mistress Crumb and young Miss Crumb going off with that circus. . ."

"They have not *'gone off with a circus'*, Charley; they are undertaking a scientific expedition. There is no rational cause for worry."

"Still, you're lonely without them, I expect?"

"A rational man need never be lonely, Charley. I have my work and my books and my own thoughts to keep me company."

Liar, thought Charley to himself. But all he said was, "That's so true, ain't it, Dr Crumb?"

The rain was passing. Splashes of sunlight lit the roofs

of Tent Town. The flanks of the new city were wreathed in rainbows. Afraid that Dr Crumb would decide he no longer needed Charley's umbrella and hurry on without him, Charley looked for a new peg to hang their conversation on. He was determined not to let the old blogger escape until he had steered it round to the subject that he really wanted to talk about.

"Rainbows!" he said. "I always wondered what they were. Bridges to fairyland, the girls at the Mott and Hoople used to tell me when I was a nipper, but I know now there must be a more scientific explanation. . ."

"Oh, there is indeed!" said Dr Crumb, and he was off, describing the way that water droplets split the sun's rays like a prism, revealing all the colours of the visible spectrum. Charley put a look of deep interest on his face while he screamed with boredom inside. *This is the sort of smart-arse lecture Fever must have had to listen to the whole time, growing up with him,* he thought. *No wonder she turned into such a stuck-up little know-all icicle. . .*

"I expect you miss Miss Crumb?" he said, when the lecture ended. "Miss her as an assistant, I mean. It seems irrational somehow for a man as learned as you to have nobody to do the little chores for you while you turn your mind to more important stuff."

"Oh, there is a maid who does the dusting, and so forth," said Dr Crumb. He had been about to recommend a good book on optics, and was surprised that the discussion of rainbows had ended so abruptly.

"No, I mean a scientific assistant," Charley explained. "Someone to draw up plans and keep papers in order and do small bits of research for you and stuff." He had thought that Dr Crumb would have caught his drift by now, but he hadn't, so Charley ploughed on. "You know, I wouldn't mind moving back in with you if you wanted. Just till Mistress Crumb and Miss Crumb get home again, I mean. Not that I don't *like* living in the Engineerium, but it's hardly rational, is it, for my old room at Bishopsgate to be empty and a man of your learning labouring away without anyone to help him?"

Dr Crumb stopped and blinked at him again. They had come to the foot of Ludgate Hill and the place where their ways divided; Dr Crumb's road curved away through Tent Town to the stairs which led up into the Engine District, Charley's ran straight to the new city's prow, where the huge outer doors of the Gut stood open like enormous jaws. "Well, Charley," said the Engineer, "that is an interesting idea. Most interesting. I shall certainly consider it. Yes, indeed."

Which wasn't really the answer that Charley Shallow had been hoping for. *Still, better than nothing*, he thought, as Dr Crumb went scurrying away. *He'll come round.* He had a feeling that he understood Gideon Crumb. A clever man, he was, but weak; he needed somebody to tell him what to do, and with Wavey gone, why shouldn't that somebody be Charley Shallow?

It was all very well helping the Underground start their

revolution, but he wasn't at all sure they could deliver. While he was waiting he'd much rather live in his cosy little room at No.1 Bishopsgate than in the Engineerium.

He spent that day in the Gut, doing as little actual work as possible while Ronnie Coldharbour and old Dr Steepleton fussed about with tape measures and theodolites. Once London got moving the Gut would be a garage where land-barges and other vehicles could be housed. When the doors were opened ramps would extend so that they could drive in and out, and Steepleton said it was vital that the ramps and the hydraulic systems which would move them be positioned just so. All very interesting, no doubt, but Charley had his mind on other things. Two rival versions of his future hung in his mind, and each made for pleasant daydreams. In one he was Dr Crumb's trusted assistant, living in the big guest bedroom at Bishopsgate, eating meals cooked for him by Wavey's Parisian chef and a great favourite with the maidservants. In the other he was on the barricades, leading the uprising against Quercus, with Gwen Natsworthy fighting at his side. Well, maybe not actually *fighting*, maybe just waving a banner or something, urging the others on. . .

He couldn't decide yet which of these futures he preferred, but either of them would be a step up.

When his shift ended he strolled round to the south side of Ludgate Hill. There was a digger's pit there where a flaky archaeologist named Vimto Grebe had been busy since long before Charley was born, excavating the remains of some old temple. He claimed he'd found the legendary St Paul's Cathedral, and he had written many letters to Quercus about it, inviting him to come and see the heap of filthy old stones and suggesting that the thing should be reconstructed on the new city's topmost tier as a symbol of London's continuity. Quercus had ignored them all, and so Master Grebe had become a friend of the Underground, and let them hold meetings sometimes in the big tarpaper sheds that protected his diggings.

There were more than a dozen of them there that night, including Dr Stayling, Gwen, and the priestess from the temple of St Kylie, whose name was Margaret Shamflower. They were all waiting to hear what Charley had to tell them, about what he'd learned among the Guild and in the Engine District.

Generally when he met the would-be rebels he told them what he thought they wanted to hear. That worked with most people, in his experience. It made them like you. But he didn't want this lot just to like him; he wanted them to look up to him. So he had decided to try a new approach.

"It ain't going to work," he said. "That's what I reckon. I been asking around, quiet like, trying to tell if any of the other Engineers might be on our side, or any of the skilled men working the high steel and that. And you know what? They're all solid for Quercus. You can print as many leaflets as you like and paint your symbol on the walls till there's no walls left to paint on, but you're never going to turn people against the Lord Mayor and his plans. They don't care about the London that's gone, and when they think about the London that's coming it's Quercus's London they see, not yours."

Gwen could not have looked more shocked or indignant if he had pinched her, but Dr Stayling nodded amiably, and Mistress Shamflower said, "Thank you for your candour, Charley."

"My what?"

"You have thought rationally about this," said Dr Stayling. "And you have spoken the truth as you see it. But there is one factor that you do not know. "

"What's that then?" asked Charley.

Gwen laughed. "Don't look so clever now, does he?"

"As you know," said Dr Stayling, "Quercus has only a small army here in London. Most of the Movement's forces are in the north, under the command of Rufus Raven. And Rufus Raven feels as we do, Charley. A grand alliance is forming among the powers of the north. We do not need to be ready to start an uprising; we just need to be ready to help Raven when he comes south with his legions to free us from the madness of Quercus."

That was a shock, all right. Charley thought about what it might mean. Civil war inside the Movement, most likely, and he didn't like the sound of that. He would have to take care that he got himself on the right side.

He said, "So that was why you lot were so worried when I let on about Wavey going north?"

Dr Stayling nodded. "You did well, Charley. We sent word to Raven at once. His patrols will intercept her convoy."

"And what will they do to her?" asked Charley. He felt, just for an instant, a little uneasy about what he'd set in motion. "Her and Fever. . . Will they be. . .?"

Dr Stayling looked at the floor. "They'll be captured or. . . Well. . ."

Mistress Shamflower said, "May St Kylie have mercy on them both."

"I didn't think St Kylie cared for Dapplejacks," said Charley.

"Please, Charley," Dr Stayling warned. "This is a serious matter."

"No, he's right," said Gwen, and Charley saw that she was looking at him and her face was kind of lit up, the same way that Milly Floater's lit up when he said something that pleased her, only Gwen was so much prettier than Milly that it was quite a thing to have her look at him that way. "Charley's right," she said firmly. "That's the attitude we need, if this is to be a revolution and not just a talking shop. We mustn't care what happens to Wavey Godshawk and her like. They're the ones what tore old London down, and designed this new monstrosity. We ought to be pleased if Raven takes her hostage, and pleased-er still if he cuts her speckled throat. *I'm* pleased.

You know why? 'Cos it's begun. And I pray that soon Raven will come south and kill Quercus and the rest of his shower and then London will belong to Londoners again. In fact, I don't know why we don't do for Quercus ourselves, so there isn't even anyone to lead his army when Raven comes."

Some people cheered her, others disagreed, and the evening wore itself out in long arguments about the best way to proceed and the rights and wrongs of murdering people, even people like Quercus. Charley didn't join in, just sat half listening. He couldn't stand all this talking and talking. But he liked the way Gwen Natsworthy's rosy cheeks grew even rosier when she was arguing some point or other, and he liked the way her eyes shone, and how they sometimes seemed to seek him out, as if she wanted to make sure that he was watching. And later, when they were all leaving Grebe's dig in ones and twos and heading homeward, she waited for him outside.

"Walk me home, then, Charley Shallow?" she said, with a look that seemed to be daring him to say no. And her hand was small and hot as it slipped into his.

12

ACROSS THE DRY SEA

The *Knuckle Sandwich* and the *Heart of Glass* had continued their northing, from Three Dry Ships to Wamethyst, from Wamethyst to Ravensburn. There the road divided. The main spur ran on northward, but Wavey and Borglum turned north-west along a lesser road, following the line of the old coast which lay off to their left with mist growing on its lonely hills like mould on old loaves. Each time they stopped, the fighters sparred, and even if they were far from settlements or oil wells people still appeared out of the wet countryside to watch, and sling coppers into the hat that Lucy carried round. But Fever stayed in her cabin, reading Wintervale and trying to ignore the noises from outside. She did not want to see Borglum's paper boy again.

Then one morning, in the grey borderlands between sleep and wakefulness, she dreamed of Skrevanastuut. A squat, flat-topped pyramid, it crouched on a plain of windswept heather and bare stones, striped with drifts of snow. She thought that she could see the ruins of other buildings around it, but they were so low and eroded that they might have been nothing but reefs of bedrock. So might the tower itself, wind-worn and weathered as it was, except that its geometry seemed too precise. Beyond it in the near distance lay mountains of snow and cold black rock. Above it, the stars were out, but the sky was not dark: it flickered with banners of feathered light, green and gold and rose, the colours reflecting faintly from the tower's walls.

Fever woke. She had slept late, and the landship was already moving. She lay a moment thinking back over her dream, wondering, *What is that thing made of? Slate? Obsidian?* No: she could remember the feel of those walls under her fingers and they had been none of those things. . .

With a soggy sense of dread she started to realize that the dream had been too vivid to be simply a dream.

Wavey Godshawk, dressed in her fur-trimmed nightgown, was just sitting down to breakfast when Fever stormed into her cabin. "Oh, Fever," she said, looking up from her kippers and kedgeree. "I do hope you'll try some of this. . ."

But Fever had not come for breakfast. "I saw it," she said. "I touched the tower, and it felt like . . . like *pottery*, like *china*, but it was so hard it wouldn't break, and it had no door, so the journey had all been for nothing. I dreamed it all! Except it wasn't a dream, was it? I've had dreams like that before, about the laboratory under Nonesuch Hill. They aren't dreams at all. They're memories; *his* memories."

She slumped down on a bench, feeling shivery and sorry for herself, wondering if it were all about to start again, that rising fog of Godshawk's memories which had once threatened to blot out her own personality entirely. Her hand went to the back of her head, feeling under her hair for the scar where he had inserted his machine. "That's why I've come with you on this stupid journey," she said sullenly. "I thought I was here because I wanted to be, but it's that machine of his, still at work inside me, making me want to go to places where he went."

"Oh, Fever," said her mother, hurt, "I thought that we were having *fun*..." She stood up and came around the table to take her daughter's hands in hers. "And the fact that Godshawk's memories are still in there..." She looked deep into Fever's eyes, as if trying to catch a glimpse of the Stalker device which had spread its spiderwebs through her daughter's brain. "Fever, I think it's *wonderful*. Don't you realize how *lucky* you are? Most of us, the closest we can get to your grandfather's genius is by reading his books, and most of those are lost. Even I have only memories of the things he told me, and they are such old and fading memories now that I cannot really trust them. But you, oh, you have his own thoughts in you, like books you can take down whenever you wish from the library of your mind..."

Fever broke away from her and ran out of the cabin, along the wobbling passageways of the barge to a place where iron rungs went up the wall like the stitches on a cartoon scar. She climbed out through a roof-hatch on to the open upper deck behind the main gun turret. Wavey didn't understand a thing. Godshawk's memories weren't like a book that she could take down when she needed to. They were like an illness; a frightening seizure that came on her unawares while she was sleepy or distracted and made her doubt whether any of her thoughts were really hers. And what if they started to come at other times? What if the machine in her head had recovered from the blast of Charley Shallow's magnetic gun?

She climbed the rope ladder which led to a crow's nest halfway up the landship's flag-mast. There she sat down in the lee of a swivel-mounted carronade and rested, her chin on her knees. The vibrations of the barge engines and the shudder of its wheels over the rough ground came up through her body and rattled her teeth. What was she doing here? Why hadn't she listened to her father? It was ridiculous to come travelling in the north-country. She felt as if she had kidnapped herself.

A snarl of sound drifted across the flatlands, and she glanced ahead and saw a squadron of the Movement's monowheels emerge from the morning mist, bowling down the road like dropped tin plates, engines moaning, fumes spurting from their exhaust flutes. The *Heart of Glass* and Borglum's barge started to pull aside to let them past, for the road was narrow here, much of it running on causeways across damp saltings.

Instead of speeding by the 'wheels slowed and stopped, some blocking the way ahead, some rolling past the convoy to take up positions across the road behind. Men jumped down from their cabins, and Fever saw the flash of sunlight on gun barrels. Wondering what the matter could be, she climbed quickly back down through the barge to the main hatch, where her mother and the *Heart of Glass*'s commander were already climbing out to welcome the newcomers.

A tall young officer strode over from the idling monos and saluted. "Chief Engineer, I have been sent to escort to you to Marshal Raven at Hill 60."

Wavey smiled indulgently. She was annoyed at having her journey interrupted for no good reason, but she was always prepared to indulge handsome young men. She said, "That is kind of dear Marshal Raven, I'm sure, but I do not have time to visit Hill 60! I am bound for Caledon, on a private matter. Move your vehicles out of the way."

"My orders are that you are to be brought to Hill 60, you and your daughter. It is for your own good. This area is unsafe for travellers."

"Unsafe?" Wavey sounded astonished. "I thought the Marshal had established peace and sent all enemies of the Movement packing?"

Borglum joined them, jumping down from the forward hatch of the *Knuckle Sandwich* and waddling angrily up to where the captain stood. "What's this, then?" he demanded. "Rufus Raven owns this road now, does he?

Honest travellers can't go about their business in peace? She's travelling with us, this lady and her girl, and she hasn't time for detours, and hobnobbing with Rufus Raven."

Instead of answering, the young officer struck him hard across the face, the sound echoing flatly off the flanks of the barges. Borglum stumbled backwards and sat down, one hand going to his bloody nose, the other reaching for something in his boot. The soldiers from the monowheels raised their guns.

"I must insist that you come with us," said the officer.

"Captain, are you *arresting* us?' asked Wavey.

The captain bowed. "Marshal Raven wishes to speak with you," was all that he would say.

13

THE RAVEN'S NEST

So the *Heart of Glass* went on its way without Borglum's carnival, the monowheels rolling ahead and behind. Wavey, angry at the treatment of her friends, sulked in her cabin, playing something red and spicy on her scent-lantern. But Fever felt too uneasy to remain below. She braved the cold and stood watching on the upper deck, which was now manned by silent, serious men from the monowheels.

They joined a broad troop road again, striking north-east between the bogs and lakes which filled the centre of that empty seabed. They passed the gaunt, ghostly stumps of Ancient oil rigs, and stranded hulks converted into houses, whose owners stopped digging in the salt pans and stood watching as the landship and its escorts thundered past. The further north and east they went, the more the land was dotted with the Movement's vehicle parks and fuel-dumps. They stopped the night at one: Wavey silent and furious at supper, a ring of sentries around the landship. Before dawn they were moving again, and late in the afternoon of that day they came in sight of the wide, wedge-shaped hill where Rufus Raven had held out for so long against the Arkhangelsk. Dozens of Movement landships and a few small mobile forts slumbered among the gorse bushes on its lower slopes. Further up there were big brown tents, thickets of standards, and a surprising number of tethered mammoths. On the summit, red and sullen-looking, squatted Raven's famous traction castle, Jotungard.

As the *Heart of Glass* drew near to the encampments a group of mammoths passed, and one of them shied a little at the noise from the monowheels. The girl who rode it pressed her heels hard against its neck to steady it and looked at Fever as the barge went by, making a wry shape with her eyebrows. Fever supposed she was commenting on the accidents of birth which had brought them both to this place, one riding on a mammoth and the other on a motorized gun-emplacement. An attractive girl, but savage-looking, with masses of rust-coloured hair, and a rusty clutter of ancient circuitry and clockworks hanging round her neck. She was not a girl of the Movement, Fever thought, watching her with a strange feeling she could not quite name, and feeling sorry when she passed out of sight. She had looked more like the drawings of the Arkhangelsk in Wintervale's book. Perhaps her presence here in Raven's camp had something to do with the new peace. But somehow the mood of the place did not *feel* like peace; more like the calm before a dreadful storm.

Fever tried to remember what she knew about Raven. She had seen him once, on one of his brief visits to London, but only from a distance; she had not spoken with him. A big man, strong but kindly; that was the idea she had of him. He liked the old ways, so the Movement had been surprised when he threw in his lot with the great modernizer Quercus, but he had been a staunch ally to him down the years; loyal as a hound. Not the sort of man who would arrest the Chief Engineer and her daughter. Wavey was right; this was all a mistake...

The *Heart of Glass* was herded into an open area between a pair of small traction forts. Soon a soldier came to tell Fever that she and her mother were to wait upon the Marshal. She went below, and found Wavey in her cabin, busy changing into a gorgeous new fur-trimmed robe of white silicon-silk embroidered with swallows and dragons.

"Fever," she said, "you can help me with the ruff. It fastens at the back, do you see?" She held her white hair aside while Fever fumbled with the catch, securing the ruff of stiff red lace around her mother's throat. Wavey's mood had not improved. "It is an outrage," she said. "First to drag us here like captives, and then to demand that we go aboard his stinking castle, when he should be coming here to beg *our* forgiveness and welcome us as honoured guests. Oh, Quercus shall hear of this! By the time I'm finished with him, Rufus Raven will be lucky if he can get a job sweeping up the dung of his drabble-tailed mammoths..."

"Wavey," said Fever, "it will be all right, won't it?" *What an irrational thing to ask*, she thought. How could Wavey know? But she was growing scared, and needed reassurance.

Wavey smiled and stroked her cheek. "You are not used to these north-country barbarians and their ways. They win a little power, and it goes straight to their silly heads and they start ordering everyone around and making a nuisance of themselves. We shall soon sort Rufus Raven out, and be on our way again."

It was late, and the long northern day was fast fading, the sky above the hill purpling like a bruise as Fever and her mother climbed out of the barge to join the escort of troopers waiting in the mud beside it. The young officer from the monowheel squadron had been replaced by another, just as polite, just as firm. They followed him along boarded walkways between landship-parks and mammoth-lines, through the drifting smoke from cooking fires, until they reached the rocky, battle-scarred hilltop and stood at last beside the clawed wheels of Jotungard.

Now that she was close to it Fever could see that it was smaller than the traction castle which had brought Quercus to London, but its armour was heavier, and it had even more guns mounted on its upperworks and poking out from ports on its sloping sides. Stalkers stood guard outside its huge main hatchway, clanking mechanically to attention as Wavey and Fever approached. They had been painted red to match the castle and each carried a massive, broad-bladed sword, cut from the armour of some defeated enemy fort. Stalkers had blades of their own, of course, so it was pointless to give them swords, but the sentries of Jotungard had carried such weapons since long before the Movement had any Stalkers, and Raven had kept up the tradition. That was the sort of man he was.

Fever glanced at the names on the Stalkers' face-shields as she passed them. Neither of them was Shrike. She was glad. She hoped that particular Stalker had been destroyed on the battlefields last year, before the fighting stopped.

Their escort pounded on the main hatch and it heaved open with a squawk of hinges. Just before she followed Wavey inside, Fever looked up and saw, high above her in the evening sky, the scarlet banner of the Marshal in the North rippling from the castle's topmost turret like a ribbon of blood.

Inside there was gloom, and oil-flames burning in cressets. Warriors welcomed the newcomers and guided them up the long companionways of the castle's central drum to the heart-chamber. There they found tapestries on the walls; flames roaring in a big stove; the timbers curving overhead like the ribs of a wooden whale. There they found the Marshal waiting.

Other Movement lords whom Fever had met dressed in all sorts of finery; in feathered hats and fancy uniforms they had designed for themselves. Not Raven. He was even plainer in his clothes than Quercus: an old black tunic, scuffed boots and shiny breeches, his short hair finger-combed, a holstered pistol hanging from his broad belt where normal nomad lords would wear a sword. Scars snaked like snail-trails over the worn crag of his face, mementoes of countless fights against the Arkhangelsk, the Suomi, and the Rus.

"Snow Leopard!" he said, when Wavey was shown into his presence. "Welcome to the Raven's Nest. . ." He had a rough way of speaking. He'd started out as a common mechanic, and he still loved to tinker with his castle's engines in his spare time. The grooves of his big hands were engrained with oil.

Wavey ignored his smile, lifting her chin in that way she had, Scrivenish, unable to conceal her contempt for normal men and for this man in particular. "What is the meaning of these insults, Marshal? I was stopped upon the road, my friends insulted, my daughter and myself dragged here like captives. . ."

"You are not captives, Snow Lepoard," said the Marshal. "You are my honoured guests." His eyes found Fever and narrowed, watching her as intently as he might watch a wing of enemy armour advance across a battlefield. "Your daughter too. I heard a rumour that the Snow Leopard had a cub. She was brought up in London?"

"I am not here to chat about Fever's upbringing," snapped Wavey. "I am bound for the hills of Caledon on private business. Your louts have dragged me leagues out of my way. I insist that you let me continue my journey."

"Impossible," said Raven. He glanced at his servants, waiting in the corners of the cabin, and clapped his hands. "Wine! Food! Snow Leopard, please, be seated. You too, leopard-cub."

That meant Fever. She sat down carefully on a padded settle, wondering what was happening. Something had changed in her mother's face. The Scriven arrogance had drained away, to be replaced by . . . well, if it was not fear, it was something akin to it.

"It seems to me," said Wavey softly, "that there has been a misunderstanding. I came to the north honestly enough, on a private matter. If I have intruded. . . Raven, if you are doing something here that you do not want Quercus to know about, then forgive me. That is no concern of mine."

"What do you mean?" asked Raven.

Wavey looked demurely at the deck. "There are an awful lot of mammoths outside. Far more than I recall the Movement ever using in the past."

"I have made alliances with some other groups."

The servants, who had scattered through various curtained doorways when Raven clapped his hands, came back quietly, bringing cups of warm spiced wine and plates of pastries. Fever took a cup, although she did not normally drink wine. She liked the spiced smell of it, the warmth of the cup in her hands. Sipping it, she watched the Marshal watch them, and saw the troubled look on his face. The little pastry he picked up looked too small in his big fingers. His duties as a host seemed to make him

125

nervous. She wondered where his wife was. If Wavey was really his guest, why had he not called Mistress Raven to welcome her?

"But what is the purpose of these alliances?" wondered Wavey, in a voice that seemed to say, *I am just a poor silly woman, I know nothing of warfare and the ways of men.* "I thought the Arkhangelsk were defeated?"

"That fight is finished," agreed Raven. He drank his wine quickly, set the cup down on a tray that a servant held out for him, and looked hard at Wavey. "What do you think of it, I wonder? What do you really think of this city that Quercus is building?"

Wavey started to chuckle; a soft bubbling sound, low and irresistible. "So that is it! You are making a grab for power! You are gathering an army of your own here, and you mean to set yourself up as Land Admiral over the Movement in Quercus's place..."

"That's not how it is..."

"And you think that by capturing me..."

"You don't understand!"

"Really, Marshal! I'm surprised at you! You were always the most trusted of Quercus's people. So plain and unimaginative..."

"It is not power that I want," said Raven. "It is just... It's this new city. It's *wrong*. It is the beginning of something terrible. I can't explain it..." He stood up again. His boots squeaked as he started to pace to and fro in front of Wavey's seat. "We are the Movement. We should travel as we have always travelled, free and fast. Going where we will in our campavans and track-houses. Not crammed aboard one single giant machine. The new city will alter everything. It will drain our nomad spirit. It will weaken us. The idea is not even *human*, is it? It is some crazy Scriven notion that *you* sowed in Quercus's mind, Snow Leopard. . ."

Wavey laughed, and Raven stopped, looking angry. He was not used to being laughed at. She said, "Where are you getting this stuff? 'Drain our nomad spirit'? That's not you talking! Who has been filling your head with such trash, Raven?"

"There is a new prophet in the north," he replied. "A lass named Morvish. She has seen it all. Her ancestors have shown her what it will lead to, this new city. She is in the camp now, as it happens, with some of her own people; she has been far abroad, carrying her message to the Suomi and the Samoyed, and she is resting here on her way back to her own people. I shall call for her if you like. . ."

"A prophet?" Wavey giggled. "Oh, Raven, really! There is always some new hedge-prophet springing up in the north. Why would I want to listen to such a person?"

"Because she'll explain it better than I can," Raven said. "I'm a simple man, Snow Leopard, I can't twist words around the way you smart folk do. Maybe if you talk to Cluny Morvish she'll make you see that this isn't treachery I'm planning. I'm trying to save the Movement, not take it for my own. . ."

He stumbled over his words, and blushed. Fever, who blushed so easily herself, felt sorry for him, but Wavey just laughed even more. "Even *you* can hear you're talking nonsense, Rufus. You have gone bright red! Pretty is she, this Morvish slut? She certainly seems to have turned *your* head. . ."

Raven glared at her, started to say something, then turned to the men who stood by the door. "Take her. Take both of them."

The men had been prepared for this. Before Fever understood what was happening one of them had seized her, wrenching one arm behind her back, and was shoving her ahead of him to the door, through which his friend was already pushing Wavey. "This is intolerable!" Wavey shouted. "When Quercus hears of how you're treating us. . ."

"Quercus will have better things to fret about than you, madam," Raven shouted behind them, as his men started to drive them down the long, dark throat of a stairwell to the lower decks. "The whole of the north is roused against him! Together we shall sweep him and his new city away!"

14

A SWORD AT SUNSET

The door of the heart-chamber slammed behind them. Their footsteps echoed on the stairs, the two men pushing them hastily down to a silent gun-deck, across it to another stairway, down again. Fever tried to be calm and rational, but she was shaking with fright. The last time she had been manhandled like this she had ended up tied to the rails of Arlo's house...

Below her, she heard Wavey ask, "Where are you taking us? If I am to be Raven's hostage I would give a great deal for comfortable quarters..."

Her captor let out a snorting laugh. "Hostage? Marshal Raven doesn't need hostages."

Wavey started to laugh with him as if he had made a joke that tickled her, and while she laughed she suddenly wrenched herself away from him and twisted and made a hard movement with her hand across his neck, and he flopped back against the stairwell wall with a gurgling shout, his hands to his throat and blood spewing and squirting through the gaps between his fingers. Wavey snatched the pistol from his belt and spun to point it at Fever's captor, who had let go of Fever and was cursing steadily as he groped for his own gun. Fever felt the pistol-ball flick past her face; the crash of the pistol came an instant later. The cursing stopped suddenly, and the man collapsed and started to slither down the stairs, almost knocking her over. Wavey came up to meet him, stopping him with one foot. The pistol was still in her hand, and in the other Fever saw a little red spike shining, the sharpened hairpin which she'd used to slash the first man's throat. She must have slipped it into her hair before she came aboard Jotungard, for fear that she was stepping into danger. Or perhaps, after the life she'd led, she was careful to have some small, deadly thing like that about her always.

She dropped the pin and tugged the sword out of the scabbard that trailed from the belt of the man she'd shot. It flashed in the dim stairwell light, and her eyes flashed too, glancing up at Fever. "They were going to kill us," she said. "Taking us outside to be shot like dogs. I expect the only reason they didn't do for us upstairs was that Mistress Raven would complain about the mess on her carpets. Raven is terribly hen-pecked. Come on."

"Where?"

"Outside, quickly, before these charmers' friends come looking for them." She dragged Fever after her down the stairs, past the man whose throat she'd cut, down through shadows to a bay on the castle's bottom level where red evening sunlight came in through the eye-slit in an armoured door. "Open it," she commanded, and with shaking fingers Fever undid the bolts and pushed it open. Outside a steep wooden gangway led down between two of the castle's wheels on to the hilltop. At its foot a Stalker stood, its back to the castle, sunset bloodying the huge scrap-metal blade it held. Fever quailed backwards into the shadows of the doorway, but Wavey shoved her forward. They went down the gangway and past the Stalker and he stood unmoving.

"Stupid creatures really," Wavey said. "He's been ordered to stop strangers coming in, not out. Now, where are we?"

They were on the narrow margin of land between the castle and the hill's brink. Heather grew there, and a few sparse pines which had survived the battles of the year before and had not been chopped down for firewood because Raven's wife felt they improved the view. Behind them in the castle they could hear the shouting of angry men. Someone had found Wavey's handiwork.

"We must get off this hill and find Borglum," said Wavey. "He'll help us." She set off quickly uphill through the blowing grass, the long, slanting rays of the low sun. The ground sloped steeply, pocked with old shell-holes; pines stuck their roots across the path. Fever saw that her mother was limping again. Behind, the shouts grew louder. She looked back. The castle was leaking armed men. A bullet smacked splinters from a pine-trunk.

Wavey turned and raised the pistol, urging Fever on past her as she fired. Two shots; three; a howl from one of their pursuers. Fever scrambled up between the trees and suddenly the ground in front of her dropped away and she was looking down the long scarp of Hill 60 to the scarred old battlefields and tangled woods at its foot. The drop looked almost sheer at first, but then she started to see outcroppings, tussocks, small bushes growing out horizontally from the steeps; handholds which someone in desperate straits might use to clamber down. She thought she could make it, but could Wavey?

Behind her now the clash and ring of blades. Her mother had started up the slope to join her and men from the castle had caught her halfway. Luckily most were only crewmen from Jotungard's lowest deck and did not seem to carry guns. Wavey faced them in the space between three trees. Even with her old wound slowing her she was quicker than any of the men. She drove her sword through one, hacked down another as he aimed a crossbow at her. There was a pause then and she glanced back at Fever, and her face was beautiful and pale and proud.

"Wavey, we can climb down!" Fever shouted.

"Not me," said Wavey. "Too old. Too slow. Find Borglum. He'll help you. Tell him if he won't I'll haunt him..."

Another enemy was coming at her now, striding uphill through the slanting light with his vast sword raised. The Stalker they had run past earlier had finally understood that they were its enemies.

Wavey looked back once more at Fever. "Run!" she commanded.

But Fever couldn't; she could only crouch there, staring, while Wavey cast her sword aside and raised the pistol again. There was one last shot in it, and she waited until the Stalker was almost upon her and then fired it in his face. The ricochet shrieked, rebounding from his face-plate in a spurt of sparks. She turned to run but the Stalker was already swinging his sword, and he cut her in half and kicked aside the tumbling pieces of her and came on, all splashed and steaming with her blood.

"Mother!" shouted Fever. "Mummy. . .?"

She had never called Wavey either of those things, and now it was too late, because there was no way in the world that Wavey could be anything but dead. Yet still she crouched there; still she stared, and still she could not run.

The Stalker stopped in front of her. She heard machinery inside him whirr as he raised that sword again. She looked up. The red blade hung over her, but did not fall. There was a notch in its edge where it had severed Wavey's spine. She moved her eyes from the sword to the Stalker's face; to its witch-light eyes. Wavey's shot had set its visor smouldering. The blistered paint was flaking off in little burning curls. She could not read the name which had once been written on its brow.

"Shrike?" she said.

She could not be sure. It might have been any Stalker standing there, but she felt certain it was Shrike, and for some reason of his own he did not kill her but just waited like a red statue, until the men who had been hanging back to watch grew restless and started yelling for him to strike. In Fever's numb brain echoed Wavey's voice, nagging her to run.

She ran, fighting down the feeling that it was wrong to leave her mother there alone, knowing that she would feel the guilt of it always. She ran, and the men behind her bayed. She ran, and crossbow bolts flew past her, filling the air with their quick, feathery hiss, and as she reached the brink of the hill one punched her so hard in the back that its fierce little beak stuck out through her chest.

Knocked forward by the force of the blow, she felt the grassy overhang at the hill's edge give way beneath her. Then she was rolling over and over in a rising rattle of stones, reaching for a bush and feeling that come loose too, growing aware, as she went tumbling down the scree, of a chill and fearsome pain.

She hit an outcropping of rock that stopped her slide, while stones she'd dislodged went scattering and rattling on past her and down into the trees at the hill's foot. Fearfully she put a hand up to her chest, and felt the hard cold point of the bolt jutting out there. "No! No! No!" she mewed, shuddering there on the scree, the pain and the panic rising, rising. Each breath burned. She could taste blood in her mouth. Behind and above her men came shouting along the brow of the hill and fingers of light from 'lectric lanterns went groping through the dusk.

The scree was still settling, a few last stones bounding past her and setting off little secondary slides. Before it all fell silent she made herself move, kicking away from her holdfast and slithering on down, gritting her teeth against the astonishing pain. She was barely conscious when she reached the tumble of bigger boulders at the foot of the cliff. She just wanted to lie there. She just wanted to cry.

Ahead of her the ground sloped down to the banks of a river. The river clattered, running shallow over stones, and on the far bank stands of birches showed like white railings in the dusk, with the darkness of pines beyond them. Fever knew that she had to cross the river and get in among those trees, but she couldn't make herself move. She was cold and she wanted her mother. Breathing hurt and made awful bubbling noises. Blood was running down inside her clothes. Her throat filled and she choked. Memories, her own and Godshawk's, flared in her fading mind. She saw her mother as a little girl, a young woman. She saw the pieces of her flung aside. "Wavey, Wavey, Wavey," she sobbed, crawling forward, bent double round the pain. And as she slid down into nothingness she saw very clearly for a moment the strange pyramid at Skrevanastuut, black against a rippling sky.

Far above her, men went searching along the hilltop, shining their lanterns down across the scree.

PART TWO

15

NOMADS' LAND

In the pink light of the next day's dawn Cluny Morvish stood beside Raven in the shadow of his traction castle and watched them pile the last faggots up around the pyre they'd built for Wavey Godshawk. A priest waited with a burning brand, and a boy was on hand to scare away the crows, which were already showing an interest in the remains.

"She should not have died," Cluny said.

She had not heard that Raven had captured the Movement's chief technomancer until she heard that she'd been killed. She wished that she had had a chance to talk to her. The dead woman's face seemed hauntingly familiar, although Cluny knew that she could never have seen her before. "She would have made a useful hostage. . ."

"Not that one." Raven looked grim. He was tired of talking about the rights and wrongs of killing the Snow Leopard. It was not as if talk could bring her back to life. "Not that Scriven witch. She'd have found some way to stab us in the back if we'd let her live. As it was, she killed five of my men. Anyway, I thought you Arkhangelsk didn't mind a bit of killing. I hope you don't, for there'll be a fair few more must die before we reach London."

Cluny looked at him. "What of the girl?"

"Shot by one of my crossbowmen as she tried to escape. She went over the crag there. We've not yet found the body."

"It is a bad start," said Cluny. "When the Ancestors sent me the dream they did not mean us to start killing women and innocent girls."

"Well, like it or not, it's done," said Raven. "And sooner or later Quercus will learn of it. I'll send word it was an accident; reckon he might swallow that for a while. But sooner or later the truth'll reach him, and by the time it does we'd best be ready to move."

"I shall ride back to my people and tell them to make ready," Cluny promised. "I had hoped to go south and see this London for myself, but. . ."

"No time for that," said Raven.

"No, indeed."

Wavey's pyre was ready. The priest stepped forward and thrust his torch into the faggots at the base with no more ceremony than a gardener burning rubbish on a bonfire. The flames rushed up crackling, and men who had been standing nearby stepped backwards, shielding their faces from the fierce heat.

"The last of the Scriven," said Rufus Raven. "The world's well rid of them, don't you think?"

Cluny Morvish watched for a moment longer, then turned without a word and went away.

Strange lass, Raven thought. Six months before, when he had first had word of a prophet among the Arkhangelsk, he had thought she would be just another mad messiah of the sort the northlands seemed to breed. But when the fighting stopped and the young woman came across the silent battlefields to tell him her terrible vision of London, well, it had shaken him. Cluny Morvish was no crazy priest but a proper north-country warrior girl, a hunting girl; a shield-maiden from a good fighting clan. Her dream seemed to confirm all Raven's private fears about the new city. It had been so compelling that it had made him start to think the unthinkable: an alliance with the Arkhangelsk, against Quercus.

The wind changed, blowing pyre-smoke and the stench of Wavey's burning hair into his face. He turned, covering his nose, and stomped back aboard his castle.

Cluny Morvish had not travelled to Hill 60 in a fortress or a land-barge but on mammoth-back, as befitted a prophet. Just Cluny herself and her younger half-brother Marten, a half-dozen Morvish warriors and the old technomancer Tharp, who was there to interpret Cluny's vision and make sure she did not engage in any hunting or fighting or flirting, which would not have been fitting for the Vessel of the Ancestors.

"They could not find the girl they shot," Cluny told

them, as they set about striking the tents and loading the mammoths.

"Maybe they did not really shoot her, then," said one of her warriors.

"They have no skill at tracking, these Movement men," said Tharp. He leant on his staff and spat into the grass. "It's because they travel only aboard these engines and great carts and wanigans. They have no reindeer, no mammoth. They're losing their sense of the earth beneath them. A child of Arkhangelsk could track better."

"If you want me to, Cluny-my-sister," said Marten, "I'll soon pick up this girl's trail."

"I want you to," said Cluny, calling to her mammoth to make it kneel for her, and climbing easily up to sit astride its neck.

"Why?" the technomancer asked suspiciously. He did not like to hear her giving orders. That was *his* job. It galled him that Cluny had a better connection to the Ancestors than he did, and he did not like the way the men had started looking to her for their orders before they looked to him. "Why should we want to find this southron girl?" he demanded.

"Because if she is alive, she will need healing, and if she is dead, she will need burial," said Cluny Morvish.

Only eight mammoths and nine people, but it still took hours to get them on the road, by the time the beasts were loaded and the tents were struck. They left Hill 60 in the height of the morning with the last thin smoke of Wavey's pyre going up into the sky behind them. Soon they were among the old war zones to the north-east, where the earth was full of the bones of men and Stalkers and many of the trees were blackened by the discharges of strange old weapons. Marten ran ahead on foot. He was twelve winters old, tireless, and a good tracker. The trail that Raven's men had missed was as clear as a story to him, written in pressed grasses and broken twigs, in drops of blood like red dew on leaves of hart's tongue fern. He found the girl lying close to their path, and called the others.

"She's funny-looking," he said. "Like an elf, or a nightwight."

"Her mother was Scriven," said Cluny.

"That's just as bad."

The girl was more than halfway dead, and all the Morvishmen agreed it would be kindest to finish her. Especially when she started telling them that she was Auric Godshawk. "We should kill her and bury her and be on our way," said Marten. But Cluny insisted that they take her with them.

"Why?" Tharp asked sharply. "Did you have another dream? Do the Ancestors think she is important?"

"Yes," said Cluny, because she knew he would not argue with the Ancestors.

"Godshawk was the name of the old Scriven king in London," said one of the warriors, an older man named Munt. "He was lord there in the lean years, when me and your father the Carn were sell-swords in the south."

"Godshawk was her mother's name too," said Cluny. "Auric Godshawk must be one of her Ancestors. Perhaps he is speaking to us through her from the World Without Time."

The men looked even more warily at Fever after that, but they rigged a travois and hitched it to one of the mammoths and dragged her with them, north and east and north again by marsh tracks and the ancient mammoth-ways. By night she stayed in the technomancer's tent while Tharp worked the medicine-magic on her and Cluny helped to nurse her. To the surprise of them all she began to get better. By the time they reached the *Kometsvansen* her wounds looked months old and her fever was fading, but she still clung unwaveringly to the belief that she was Auric Godshawk.

Tharp said that she was mad. He said that seeing her mother killed and being half-killed herself had broken her mind. He suggested slyly that, having Scriven blood, she would make a powerful sacrifice when the time came to bless the fortresses before they rolled to war. But Cluny had the men carry the girl aboard her father's traction fort. The technomancer grumbled, of course. "I have worked the medicine-magic on her again and again, and yet she is not cured. I am the wisest technomancer of Arkhangelsk, and if I cannot cure her, no one can!"

"Let her cure herself, then," Cluny said, and she sent him away. She had found that she liked caring for Fever Crumb. It helped her to forget her own fears, having someone even worse off to look after. She made the servants bring a bright tin mirror and hang it carefully on the wall near the sick girl's bed, angled so that she'd be sure to see it when she woke.

In the middle of that night, in the middle of another dream of London, she was woken by a terrible cry. It was coming from the sick girl's chamber.

"No! I am Auric Godshawk! I am *Godshawk*!"

When Fever woke next morning, she was herself again. She lay under the heaped furs, trying not to think about what had happened and how she had come there. Godshawk had had his own adventures in the north. When she blacked out at the foot of Hill 60 his memories must have flooded her unconscious mind and driven her onwards like a sleepwalker until the Arkhangelsk found her. She remembered it, some of it, but it didn't seem to mean anything. All she could think of was Wavey's awful death, and the things about Wavey that she would now never know, and the things that Wavey would never be able to tell her.

And I just ran, thought Fever. *I just ran and left her.*

It had been the rational thing to do. She knew that. But that did not make it feel *right*.

Someone heard her weeping. Someone came and touched her face and looked down at her, and she recognized the girl she'd seen on mammoth-back at Raven's camp. She'd not realized then how tall she was;

how big-boned, beautiful and strong. *A daughter of the frost giants*, Borglum would have billed her, if she'd joined his Carnival of Knives. *My mammoth-girl*, the ghost of Godshawk whispered wistfully, somewhere in the deeps of Fever's mind.

The mammoth-girl knelt beside the bed and said gently, "Auric?"

"My name is Fever Crumb," said Fever.

"Good."

"Auric was someone who I. . . He's gone now."

"Pity," said the girl, accepting this quite easily, with a smile. "He seemed interesting."

Fever blushed, remembering how enticing Godshawk had found those smiles. *Kiss me*, she'd said, when she thought she was him. *You'd not deny a last kiss to a dying man*. And the girl had said, "You're not a dying *man*. . ." Fever blushed at the memory of it. Of course, now that she was herself again she was repelled by the girl's musky odour and old-tech trinkets and that wild cloud of rust-coloured hair. But her smile was kind, and her lilting northern voice was lovely; she didn't just roll her Rs, she *bowled* them, pausing mid-word to take a little run-up: *in-terrrrresting*. Some lingering Godshawkish instinct still made Fever want to kiss her.

She sat up, holding the covers round her and telling herself sternly to be rational. She realized now that she was in one of the cabins of a traction fortress; she could feel the faint vibration of its engines. There were rugs on the deck, hangings on the walls. Bits of rusty old-tech dangled as charms or ornaments from the thick oaken beams of the ceiling. There was that mirror where she'd met herself last night. Some of her things lay on a table near the bed: her penknife, her slide rule and her torch. She remembered faintly her arrival here. Before that; the awful journey on that juddering travois; looking up at the branches as she passed through belts of forest. Before that...

"My mother is dead," she said.

The mammoth-girl nodded, and reached out, and moved a strand of hair from Fever's forehead. Usually Fever hated it when people touched her, but at that moment and with that girl she did not mind. "My mother died when I was small," the girl said. "I don't remember how it felt. But my brother fell at Hill 60 and that felt horrible, and it still does. I'm sorry for you."

"What is this place?" Fever asked.

"You're in the traction fort of the Morvish," said the girl. (*The t-rrraction forrrt of the Mo-rrrvish...* It was like music.) "I'm Cluny."

"Raven spoke of you. You're a prophet..."

"I'm not," said Cluny. She frowned; a shadow came into her hazel eyes. "I don't *think* I am... The Ancestors sent me a dream, and now we have made peace with the Movement and we are making ready to roll on London."

"With Raven's help," said Fever.

Cluny Morvish nodded. "We have not told him that

you are here. Nor will we. The Arkhangelsk do not kill women and girls."

"I must get to London!" said Fever. "I have to tell Dr Crumb. . ." She started to get out of bed, and was halfway before she remembered how weak she was.

"You are not well enough to travel," said Cluny Morvish, easing her back. "Even if you were, it would not be allowed. You must wait. Soon we will all be in London. We will crush the new city under our tracks, destroy its warriors, and make prisoners of its women." It sounded quite a gentle business, spoken in that thrilling voice: *c-rrrush, dest-rrroy, make p-rrriss-onairrss. . .*

"Am I a prrris . . . a prisoner?" Fever asked.

"No," said Cluny Morvish. "You are my guest."

"A guest who cannot leave."

Cluny smiled mischievously. "A prisoner-y kind of guest."

Fever needed to tell Dr Crumb about what had happened to Wavey. She hated to think of him going about his work in London not knowing what had befallen his wife and daughter. But *what we can't change, we must accept*. That was what Dr Crumb had always taught her. She was at the mercy of this Cluny Morvish, and at least Cluny Morvish seemed more merciful than Raven's crossbowmen. She tied a little charm around Fever's neck: a bird's skull and some blue glass beads wired to an old shard of circuit-board. "I had Tharp make this for you. It will protect you from bad spirits while you heal."

"There are no such things as. . ." Fever started to say, but she knew Cluny was only being kind.

"I never really trusted our technomancer," Cluny said confidingly. She looked shy for a moment, despite her savage looks. "I thought it was mostly just conjuring tricks, his medicine-magic. When I saw your wounds I thought you would die. We all did. But you lived. So Tharp must be all right at it, mustn't he?"

Fever said nothing. She knew it was not that mad old man's potions and witch-doctoring that had healed her. The secret machines with which her grandfather had injected her when she was just a baby had been at work inside her again, remaking damaged tissue and battling infection. It was Godshawk who had saved her life.

For a while after that, all her days were the same. She slept a lot. Servants brought meals for her, and helped her wash herself. Her own clothes had all been ruined, and she was given Arkhangelsk clothes instead: a brown linen dress, a stiff felt tunic embroidered with copper wire, soft deerskin slippers. Her reflection in the mirror looked shockingly thin. Shadows sat in the hollows under her cheekbones. The angry scars on her chest and back ached, seeping thin yellow tears. Each time she shut her eyes she saw Wavey hacked in half again. Each time she slept she dreamed of Arlo Thursday in his little cutter, lost on the hungry, grey-and-silver sea.

Sometimes Cluny Morvish came to see her, and those

were the best times. She liked it when Cluny settled herself on the end of the bed and talked about her family, or her animals, or the boy she'd been a bit in love with, who had grown afraid of her now and gone off with Carn Kubin's daughter. "Do you have a boy, back in London?" she asked, and Fever found herself telling her all about Arlo, whom she had never spoken of to anyone before.

This was how most people behaved, she thought; most girls, at least; talking; sharing feelings and small secrets with their friends. She had never really had a friend before; she'd never seen the point, till Cluny. She knew that if they had met a year before she would have loathed her, for she could tell what a spoiled, swaggering young noblewoman Cluny must have been. She couldn't read, she believed in all sorts of garbled magic, and seemed to think the best thing you could do in life was to ride the shaggy horses of the Arkhangelsk at absurd speeds over rough country, hunting innocent deer or foxes. But that had all been stripped from her by these dreams, which she claimed came from her ancestors. They wrecked her sleep and left her nervous and shaky, and the mad old technomancer whose word was law here had forbidden her to hunt. Now she was like a little girl again, almost as lost as Fever, trying to relearn her life just when it should all have been clear to her. And she was beautiful, too – at least, *Godshawk* would have thought her beautiful.

"I wish I could send some message to Dr Crumb," Fever said again, when she had finished talking about Arlo. "It is so sad to think of him in London, still waiting for Wavey and me to come home."

"It is a war," said Cluny. "Sad things happen." But the next day when she came to Fever's chamber she brought her father with her; a plump, bald, white-bearded man who seemed too shy and softly spoken to be a barbarian warlord. He welcomed Fever to his house and asked her if there was anything she needed, and Cluny told him that Fever had to send word to her father in London.

"Ah, now, ah, now," said Carn Morvish, tugging at his whiskers. "Now that is difficult, Miss Crumb. We are massing our forces to make war on London. We cannot have you warning the Londoners of our plans."

"They'll find out about your plans anyway," said Fever. "How secret can you keep an army of mobile castles? All I want to do is tell my father that I am still alive. And that my mother . . . *isn't*."

"That would do no harm, would it, Carn-Morvish-my-father?" asked Cluny.

The Carn was a kind man, and felt sorry for Fever's father. If Cluny had been lost somewhere he would have wanted word of her. He said, "I shall send a scribe to write down your words, Miss Crumb. Several of our people can read, so don't try to put in any clever codes or secret messages. A few trusted merchants still go south from Arkhangelsk to London. One of them will carry your letter."

16

A RATIONAL MAN

"Ah, Dr Crumb. I'm sorry to call you from your work, but I have some bad news. You'd best sit down. But no, you're a rational man, aren't you; not much troubled by life's little reversals. . ."

"Which reversals, Lord Mayor?"

They were in Quercus's private chambers at the heart of the new city. A big clock ticking, paintings of the Movement's glorious past on the walls, and on a central table a model of its glorious future: the new London. The Lord Mayor wore bedroom slippers and a silken dressing gown. Dr Crumb was in his third-best lab-coat, hot and weary after another night's work in the engine district. More than a month had passed since Wavey and Fever went away. The first full test of the city's engines was planned for the following day, and there was still much to be done. He could not imagine why Quercus had summoned him from his work. Bad news? He assumed that there must be some new hitch in the supply chain: perhaps the copper that he needed had been delayed again.

But Quercus said, "A messenger has arrived from one of Raven's garrisons in the Fuel Country. It is about Wavey and that girl of yours. It seems there has been an incident. Savages attacked their landship. It was destroyed with all hands."

"Destroyed with all. . ." Dr Crumb stood blinking at him.

"They are both dead, Dr Crumb."

"Oh. . ."

A woman who had been sitting in the shadows – one of Quercus's senior wives – now rose silently and came to lay her hand upon the engineer's arm. He looked at her in surprise. Quercus said, "It is all right, Mree. The good doctor is a rational man. He does not need comforting. It is a terrible thing. But accidents will happen, won't they, Dr Crumb? I'm sure that as a rational man you must accept that accidents will happen."

He watched Dr Crumb with interest. He had always found them curious, these London Engineers, with their faith in reason and experiment and their careful avoidance of feelings. He was glad of this chance to conduct a small experiment of his own. He noticed that Dr Crumb appeared to be trembling.

"You are certain, Lord Mayor? There can be no mistake?"

"It seems not. We don't yet know who the attackers were. Raven is moving some of his forces west to deal with them. But there is no hope for Wavey and Fever. Both dead."

"I see," said Dr Crumb, very quietly.

"I had thought of keeping this information to myself until the tests were complete," Quercus said. "I would not want your grief to put you off your work at such a vital time. But then I thought, Dr Crumb is a rational man; he will feel no grief at all, or, if he does, he will be able to suppress it. *Are* you able to suppress it, Dr Crumb?"

"Indeed, Lord Mayor," said Dr Crumb, distracted for a moment by a memory of Fever as a tiny girl, playing with a pile of cogs under his desk at Godshawk's Head.

"Excellent. Take the rest of the day off, Crumb, if you wish. And if there is anything I can do, anything you need... But of course, there isn't, and you don't. You are a rational man."

"Yes, Lord Mayor," said Dr Crumb. And, "With your permission, Lord Mayor, I shall return to my work. There is still much to be done."

"Of course, Dr Crumb. Oh, and by the way, I should like you to take over your late wife's post as Chief Engineer. She will be missed, of course, but her role was always a symbolic one; you and your fellow Engineers have always been the brains behind our work here, am I right?"

Charley Shallow was sitting on an empty crate in the Engine District, eating a cheese and pickle sandwich. He was supposed to be at work, but he found it easy enough these days to persuade the other apprentices to cover for him. If he had known that you could win people over so easily by knocking them down and poking knives in their faces, he would have started doing it years ago. But of course it hadn't just been that; lately, since he'd started walking out with pretty Gwen Natsworthy, he'd become a kind of rebel hero to them – he smiled to himself, remembering the way their wide eyes had followed her when she came into the Engine District that morning to bring him these very sarnies. Lately they'd started coming to him to ask what the best places to buy cheap wine and tobacco were, and whether he could put in a good word for them with the bar girls at the Laughing Nomad. It was like they were kittens and he was a wily old stray, wise in the ways of the backstreets of Tent Town...

So he lounged on his upturned crate in the snick between two of London's huge new engines and ate his sandwiches while they did his work for him, and doodled in his notebook until he was distracted by the sight of Dr Crumb coming back from his meeting with the Lord Mayor. He'd been feeling angry at Crumb for the past few weeks, still having had no answer to his kind offer of moving back in to Bishopsgate. He'd been trying not to think of him, reckoning his best hopes lay with Gwen and her friends. But something about the way that Dr Crumb was moving struck Charley as odd, and when he came close enough for Charley to get a look at his face and see the expression there, well, that was odder still. Dr Crumb usually looked pretty vague as he wandered among the engines, because he was always thinking about work rather than where he was going, but today he was shuffling along like a sleepwalker. Like he'd been emptied out, thought Charley, and there was nothing behind those eyes at all...

He stuffed the remainder of the sandwiches into his pocket, snapped shut the notebook and swaggered out into the man's path, trying to look as if he was a hard-working young 'prentice, making his way from one job to the next. "Morning, Dr Crumb."

"Ah," said the Engineer, pausing and blinking at him in that irritating way he had. His face was just about the colour of the cheese in Charley's sandwiches.

"Any word from Mistress Crumb and Miss Fever?" asked Charley brightly, for he had a pretty good idea what might have led his old master to look like that. He was right, too, he could tell at once, because Dr Crumb flinched at the sound of their names as if Charley had just slapped him.

"No, Charley," he said softly. "There isn't. I do not yet have all the data but... It appears they are *dead*..."

"Dead?" said Charley, like an echo. "Blimey, I'm sorry to hear that, Doctor Crumb."

Dr Crumb said nothing at all.

"If there's anything I can do," said Charley earnestly, "any help you need, like. Sorting things out, and so forth..."

"Thank you, Charley," Dr Crumb mumbled. "You are most thoughtful. I shall bear it in mind..."

Charley felt pleased. After all, with Fever gone, the Doc would need a new apprentice, wouldn't he? No harm in reminding him that Charley Shallow was ready and willing. He'd make himself useful at this difficult time. He liked that phrase; it sounded sincere and serious, like something in a letter of condolence. "Anything at all, Doctor!" he said. "Anything I can do to help *at this difficult time.*"

He watched as the Engineer went on his way to the little tarpaper hut that served as his office. Another apprentice ran up to him with a question, but Dr Crumb did not even seem to notice him. The streets of the Engine District were always littered with straw, which spilled out of the crates in which new components were brought from the factories. The wind that gusted through the unfinished city blew the straw in clumps around Dr Crumb's feet, and it looked for a moment to Charley as if he had been stuffed with straw all along, like a scarecrow, and now some vital seam had split and all the stuffing was spilling out of him and blowing away.

Half of Charley felt sorry, remembering the kindness that Dr Crumb had shown him once, and sad at seeing him so low. The other half felt a sort of awe at his own power that slowly turned into something rather like glee. *I did that,* he thought. *It was me told Stayling, and Stayling sent word north, and now Rufus Raven has murdered the Snow Leopard and her half-breed daughter...* The thought of Fever and her mother killed checked him for a moment. *Of course, I mustn't blame myself,* he thought. *Raven would have got to hear that they were in his country anyway. I thought he'd just capture them, not kill 'em. Not both of 'em.* He wondered what Raven's men had done to them, and wished he had been there to see it. *Course, it's a terrible thing; a terrible thing. . .*

But he didn't really think it was a terrible thing. Charley was starting to realize that he didn't *feel* things as much as other people did. He'd found it with Gwen, these past few days. Part of him was thrilled that she was his girl, and he strolled around the Engine District with a new confidence when he'd been to see her, everything round him seeming brighter and more interesting. Then he'd look at her sometimes while they were kissing or whatever and realize that he wouldn't mind all *that* much if he never saw her again. Oh, he'd *pretend* he did, but he knew there'd be other girls; he wouldn't really *care.* He was starting to sense how that gave him an edge over people; because if you didn't care about anything except yourself, then there were fewer ways they could have power over you.

All them old Engineers, training themselves up to be free of feelings, and look what one bit of bad news does to them, he thought scornfully, watching Dr Crumb stumble into his office with the straw blowing round his feet. *He looks like he's aged twenty years in one morning.* No, if you wanted to free yourself of feelings you didn't want to be an Engineer. Growing up parentless on Ditch Street, though; that would really do the trick.

*

Dr Crumb called a sedan chair and went back to his house; to the silence of his house. It had been peculiarly quiet ever since Wavey and Fever went away, as if it were waiting for them to return. It would wait for ever now, and the silence seemed to have deepened, muffling the sounds of the city outside, muting his footsteps as he paced through the empty rooms. From the wall of his office his photographs of Wavey and Fever gazed at him, pale and silvery as ghosts. Upset by the feelings that they aroused, he thrust the stupid thought away, took down the pictures, turned them to the wall.

He had always known that Wavey would not stay with him for long. She needed excitement, and he was not an exciting man. Ever since her return he had felt as if he was flotsam and she was the sea, and known that she would one day abandon him on some strange shore. But not Fever. Not Fever, whom he had carried back to Godshawk's Head that evening in her basket when she was so small and helpless. Even when she had run away with those theatre people he had always been sure that her rational nature would bring her back to London, and he had been proved right. But reason could not return her to him now; nothing could do that. Dimly, he began to understand why simple people sought consolation in fairy tales of gods and afterlives.

Well, there was no consolation there for him. He would find his consolation where he had found it years ago, after the Skinners' Riots, when he had first thought

Wavey dead. He would find it in rationality and hard, productive work. There was tomorrow's test to think of, and it was sure to reveal a thousand faults and glitches which would need correction. . . He began gathering files and papers from the shelves behind his desk. He could not concentrate in this house, with its unsettling smells and memories. He would move the things he needed to the Engine District, and let the demolition gangs take this place; it was high time anyway that they made a start on Ludgate Hill.

He found a box and started filling it with papers, notebooks, card folders full of blueprints. He would need things from Wavey's office too; her scrappy, eccentric plans and drawings. It would be a long job, sorting it all out. He would need help, but not from his fellow Engineers. He did not think he could face their condolences and knowing looks.

He thought of Charley Shallow. The boy showed promise as an Engineer, and he seemed eager to help. Certainly he could fetch and carry well enough. The only reason Dr Crumb had dismissed him was that he had upset Fever, and Fever was beyond upsetting now. *I shall send someone to fetch Charley Shallow here at once*, he decided.

There was much to be done: boxes of papers to be manhandled downstairs to the street door, a wagon to be arranged for transferring them across Tent Town to the new city. It fell to Charley to do all of it, for Dr Crumb seemed only half there, moving slowly, taking ages to hear anything that Charley asked him, as if time was solidifying around him. "It's so *quiet* without them, Charley," he complained. In the end it even fell to Charley to give the servants their final wages, and lock up the abandoned house. He did it angrily, twisting the key in the lock like a knife, as if he hoped to hurt the old place. He'd got to be Crumb's assistant, at last, but he'd lost his chance of living at Bishopsgate; the old cloot was intent on moving into one of those little modern cells aboard new London, and Charley hadn't enough hold over him yet to change his mind.

But that'll change, he promised himself. *That'll change.*

He turned from the door and found a boy standing in the street, watching him. For an instant he felt afraid, as if the lad could have somehow guessed what he was thinking. Indeed, in the twilight, it seemed to him for an instant that this was his younger self, a ragged Ditch Street urchin, come to gawp at the new and grown-up Charley.

But it was just some merchant's boy off a land-barge, who stepped forward holding up a sealed and folded letter. "Looking for Dr Crumb," he said. "I got this for him."

"I'm Dr Crumb's private secretary," said Charley importantly, and took it from him. "Brought in by Master van Cleef, the northland merchant," said the boy, waiting expectantly while Charley studied the address. That prim, cramped handwriting looked awfully familiar. Frowning, he tipped the boy a half-quid coin. (It was a generous tip, but Charley was determined to be generous now that he was a man of substance; he'd not forget his humble roots.) That handwriting kept nagging at him, and as the boy scampered happily away he suddenly thought, *Well, if I'm Crumb's private secretary, I ought to read his mail for him, oughtn't I? See if it's important or just someone wasting his time...*

He broke the seal with his thumbnail, reasoning that he could tell Dr Crumb it had already been broken when the boy gave it to him. *Wavey is dead*, he read. *I was injured, but I am recovering...* He skimmed down the page to the signature: *yr daughter, Fever Crumb.*

"Blogging Hell!" he said aloud. Would he never be rid of Fever Crumb? Once her father read this he'd mobilize half London to bring her back, and as soon as she came home it would be goodbye Charley all over again.

Then he remembered that he was the only person who had seen this letter; the only one in London who knew that she still lived. This was the only proof, fluttering in his hand as the breeze gusted off the Brick Marsh. If Dr Crumb never read it, he would never know, and perhaps with all the dangers in the north Fever would never make her own way home. "You keep this to yourself, Charley," he said, and ripped the letter in half across the middle. He was about to throw it away when he changed his mind and slipped the torn halves carefully into his pocket, next to Bagman's knife. It was a trophy; a sweet little reminder of Fever's misfortunes and his own power over Dr Crumb.

17

RUNNING TRUE

Charley had a special place of his own aboard the new London. He had found it soon after he moved into the Engineerium, when he needed somewhere to go that was away from the other apprentices. A steel cage had been raised right up through the planks of Tier Two, up into the giant's climbing-frame of girders and scaffolding that would one day be Tier Three. It was meant to hold one of the new funicular elevators, but there had been a change of priorities, and so the cage had been capped with a wooden platform and left standing there while the men who had built it busied themselves completing the Engine District and the housing on the lower levels.

Charley had found out that you could reach that platform, and that if you did you could look down on the new city like a king; like a god.

In early sunlight on the day of the test he met Gwen outside the shack she shared with her family and went with her aboard the new city and up the freight elevators to Tier Two, flashing his Guild of Engineers badge at anyone who questioned him, confident that on that particular morning, with so many Engineers hurrying about on so many different errands, they would not be stopped. Then it was across a few work-platforms, up some scaffolding, a long climb up a ladder, and they were in his eyrie, with all London spread out beneath them.

"Look at that, Charley!" said Gwen, peeking over the edge. "Look at all them people!"

Far below, among the factories and the tight-packed tents, thousands and thousands of tiny specks showed in the growing light. Charley couldn't think what they were at first. Then he understood. The whole of London had turned out to watch the trial.

"Are you sure it's safe, Charley?" Gwen asked. "Dr Stayling says that when the engines are turned on this whole city will shake itself to pieces. He says the noise will deafen everyone aboard, and drive people mad."

"We'll be all right up here," said Charley.

"What if something goes wrong?"

"It won't. Not with Crumb in charge. He's been working all night, like a man possessed. Like he thinks if he works hard enough it'll stop him thinking about that wife and kid of his."

"We mustn't feel sorry for him, Charley."

"I didn't say I did, did I? Anyway, he's driving everybody hard, making last checks, making sure everything's clean and shiny and ready to run true. You know how picky Engineers can be."

"What about you? Won't you be missed?"

"I told Ronnie Coldharbour to tell anyone who asks I'm on an errand for Dr Mainbrace. Unless it's ol' Mainbrace who asks, in which case I'm on an errand for Dr Whyre. . ."

He took off his coat and spread it on the platform so that they could sit down. There they waited, while the sun rose higher. Gwen lay on her back and let the light fall across her face. She lay on her front and peeked over the edge of the platform and tried to pick out her family's shack, and told Charley where all the parks and playgrounds would go once the real London was built again. He watched her talk, and tried to imagine what she would be like after the revolution. Tried to imagine what they would both be like; young heroes of London, him standing beside her while she cut the ribbon which opened some new public garden. Who'd take charge once Quercus was gone? Old Stayling was too dull. Mistress Shamflower was only a woman, and anyway, the followers of other gods would never allow a priestess of St Kylie to run London. Maybe they'd want someone young and lively. He recalled that old fairy tale about the geezer who'd heard a voice say, "Turn again, Livingstone, Thrice Mayor of London," and thought, *Mayor of London . . . I quite fancy that.*

Far below him, in a circular chamber at the heart of the Engine District on Base Tier, fifty burly Mechanics stepped up to fifty long brass levers. Behind them Dr Crumb and some of his fellow Engineers checked their pocket-watches, made notes on clipboards, or gnawed worriedly at their fingernails. Behind *them*, the Lord Mayor took his seat in a padded chair positioned at the exact centre of the chamber, the exact centre of the city. He waved aside his aides and wives and beckoned Dr Crumb to him.

"What do I say, Crumb?"

What *did* you say, to start a city moving? Dr Crumb looked blank, and for a moment, no one spoke.

"What about, 'Proceed'?" Dr Crumb suggested.

Quercus nodded, smoothed the front of his tunic, looked around to make sure that everyone was paying attention and said, "Proceed!"

With a single movement, all the waiting Mechanics pulled their levers back.

Up on Charley Shallow's secret eyrie it felt like an earthquake had begun. The first lurch almost rolled Gwen off the edge. Charley caught her and she clung to him and they stared at each other, shocked to feel the solid steel girders beneath them trembling and throbbing with the vibrations rising from the Engine District. There was noise too – they could hear it drumming away across Tent Town and hammering back at them from the hills. A flicker of movement spread like a ripple through the watching crowds as everyone down there put their hands over their ears, but up where Gwen and Charley were it seemed just distant thunder. No, it was the vibrations that Charley would remember. He had not realized until now – how could he have been so stupid? – he had not realized what a moving city really *meant*. What *power* was in it! Like a big animal waking and stirring, getting ready to move...

All through the Engine District his fellow apprentices were running to holler their reports to the Engineers who waited in the control chamber. "Full power on all the engines in Group A, sir!"

"Group B running true, sir!"

"Pressure steady..."

"Brakes are holding, chief."

"Ninety per cent on Group D, Dr Crumb!"

"Oh, Wavey," said Dr Crumb, certain that no one would hear him beneath the din of the engines. She should have been here to see this, he thought. The engines that her father had designed, and that she had perfected – with a little guidance from himself. "Oh, Fever..." Then he thought, *It does not matter. It does not matter that they are gone. Their work survives. This city; this rational city; this is what matters.* He must ignore these foolish emotions, the way he had been taught as a young Engineer. He must make himself as unfeeling as a machine, so that he could better serve this greater machine.

Quercus was signalling to him again. He glanced at his fellow Engineers, making sure that all were satisfied. Then raised a hand. Fifty levers were eased forward.

Slowly, with a dying fall, the song of the Godshawk engines ceased.

High above, Charley felt the complex tremors subside until the city was still again. Rags of smoke flew past him, wind-blown from the exhaust stacks in the west. Over on the eastern rim, above the big doors of the Gut, a crane collapsed. Up from Tent Town, far below, came the sound of cheering, or screaming, or something. Charley didn't much care what.

"...horrible! It's horrible!" Gwen was saying. "Doc Stayling was right. People won't stand for this! Who'd want to live aboard this clanking contraption?"

Charley didn't reply. He was thinking, *How could I not have understood? The power of the thing... ! If a man could command power like that, he could do anything... He could remake the world...*

He looked at Gwen, and her mouth was moving, but he didn't know or care what she was yapping about any more. They'd picked the wrong side, him and Gwen. Those others, Stayling and Shamflower, they were the old world, doomed to pass and fail and be replaced. What place had there ever been for Charley Shallow in *their* London? A blanket on the floor at the Mott and Hoople, that was all. In Quercus's London it would all be different. There had never been a city like this before, not even back in Ancient days. In a city like this there'd be new rules, and no telling how high a Ditch Street boy might rise...

As soon as they came down from aloft, Charley rid himself of Gwen, telling her he needed to show his face among the

168

other 'prentices. Once she was gone he climbed back up to Tier One.

Quercus had returned to his old traction fortress, which, stripped of its wheels and engines, had been built into the fabric of the new city at the tier's centre. Drinks were being served in there; Movement bigwigs clustered at the door. A guard stopped Charley as he hurried up the ramp. "I've got a message for the Lord Mayor," he said, showing his badge again.

"I'll give it to him."

"Dr Crumb said I was to deliver it in person."

The man looked doubtful, but an officer stepped out of the clump of men in the doorway and said, "You're Crumb's boy, aren't you? I remember you," and, to the soldier, "Let him pass."

The guard searched him thoroughly, and let him through. *No going back now*, thought Charley, as he went along the carven corridors, past hangings and statues and rooms where women talked and giggled. But the thought of going back had not really occurred to him; the moment he felt the song of the city rippling through him he had known what he had to do.

"Message for the Lord Mayor. Message from Dr Crumb..."

He had to explain himself half a dozen times before at last he stood face to face with Quercus, a surprisingly small, surprisingly ordinary man who raised one eyebrow, questioning.

"Well, boy? What does Crumb want?"

"Nothing, sir." No one was watching him; no one was interested in a scrawny apprentice delivering a message from the Engineers. All around him the talk and laughter and chink of wine glasses seemed to fade until it was just him and Quercus, eye to eye.

"I'm Charley Shallow, sir. I've got information. There's treachery brewing in London, sir. In the north too. I was almost part of it; there's this girl, sir, and she drew me into it. But I'm London through and through, sir, and I won't be part of it any more. I can give you the traitors' names, addresses, everything."

18

FEVER IN THE COMET'S TAIL

In the strange waiting time that had followed the end of their war against the Movement, the Arkhangelsk had gathered on the plains of Heklasrand. To the south and west the woods and marshes stretched away in mist; to the north and east the bony hills of what had once been Norway hunched themselves up in snow, and the sky was stained with the ash of young volcanoes. When the wind was in the north you could smell ice on the air, but here in the brief summer there was grazing for the empire's herds, and clear water flowing in a hundred rivers, and a place for the beaten-up war-wagons to repair themselves in readiness for the storm that was to come.

"We call it the *Kometsvansen*," said Cluny Morvish, walking with her guest, or captive, or whatever she was, up on the roof of the Morvish traction fort. "It means the comet's tail. The Great Carn's castle is the comet, you see, and all the other vehicles follow it, like the tail of the comet stretching across the sky."

Fever leant on the bulwark in the lee of a cannon, glad

of the chance to rest. She was well enough now to leave her room and eat with the Morvish in their big communal dining hall on the ground-deck, and to walk around the vehicle's upperworks with Cluny when the meal was over, but her wounds still ached badly sometimes. Trying to ignore the pain, she looked out across the rolling land, dappled with grazing herds, cluttered with forts, half-timbered barges, landships, and little clusters of campavans and hide-roofed rolling houses. How primitive it all was! Like something from the Black Centuries. And yet she could smell the pleasant smell of woodsmoke, and hear children playing around the nearest barges, and down at the river women were doing laundry, and all around her life was going on. In a strange way it helped her to better understand Quercus and his urge to build a moving city. Because was this sprawl of vehicles, this comet's tail, not a moving city of a sort? This was how Quercus and his people had lived too, before Wavey Godshawk lured them to London.

"In the north we call this month the Foxglove Moon," said Cluny, stooping to watch a bee bustle into one of the foxgloves that had seeded itself on the traction fort's mossy parapet. "After this comes Scrivener's Moon, the First and Second Frost Moons, Ice Moon, Brass Monkey Moon. . ." She stopped; looked serious. "The Scrivener's Moon will rise a few days from now. When it is full, we shall roll south to London and destroy Quercus's new city."

Fever watched Carn Morvish's landship *Fury* go

rumbling around the fort to test its engines, covered in spines and fluttering banners and barnacle gun-turrets. She said, "I still don't understand why you are so afraid of London. What harm can it do to you, when you have things like the *Fury* to defend you?"

"You haven't seen London," replied Cluny Morvish. "Not finished, I mean. The size of it, and its horrible jaws..."

"London does not have *jaws*," said Fever. Cluny kept on mentioning those jaws, as if, of all the details of her dream, that was the one that horrified her most. Fever could only imagine that she'd seen a picture of the serrated hangar doors of the Great Under Tier, and that it had triggered some private phobia. Patiently, she started trying to explain what Dr Crumb had once explained to her; all the good, rational reasons for making London move. "It will be safer, and cleaner, and fairer. Everyone will pay their share to provide good housing, and hospitals for the sick, and schooling for children, and pensions for the old..."

But such ideas were shocking to the Arkhangelsk. "Then none of you will be free!" said Cluny, quite appalled. "If you aren't responsible for yourselves, if you expect your leaders to provide everything, you will be no better than their pets..."

She broke off with a little whimper. She was trembling, and as Fever turned to her she swayed, and put a hand on the cannon's flank for support. Some of her bodyguards, who had been standing at a distance watching her talk with the London girl, came hurrying forward. Cluny waved them away. "I'm all right!" she said to them, and to Fever, "It is the dream again. . ."

"But you're awake," Fever pointed out.

"It comes in daylight too now." Cluny's eyes were fixed on her, but she was not looking at her; she was studying the immense, hungry face of the new city, visible only in her mind.

"Then it's not a dream," said Fever helpfully. "It's a hallucination."

Whatever it was, it seemed to be passing. Cluny ran a hand over her face and blinked. "Oh," she said, and grinned unhappily. "When Tharp first said I was the Vessel of the Ancestors and wasn't allowed to fight or hunt any more, I felt like it was a stupid punishment. But I couldn't fight now even if it was allowed. I tried sparring with Marten last week, and the dream kept rising up between us; I could hardly see him."

Fever felt sorry for her. She was ill, that was what it had to be. People's ancestors did not send them dreams; there was no way that this young woman could *really* be seeing the future. She was mad. But why had her madness seized on the image of London? And why, when she described her dream, were so many of the details correct?

"You are quite certain that you've never seen London?" she asked.

"Not the new city, no. I was in London when I was a

174

baby – things were different in the empire then, and my father the Carn was in exile; he lived in London for a time. That was back when the Scriven were in charge. There was no talk then of setting it on wheels."

That felt like a clue, but Fever could not see where it led. "Have you ever had dreams like this before?" she asked. "When you were little, perhaps?"

Cluny shook her head. "There was one that came to me often when I was a little girl, but it was nice, not scary. . ."

"Cluny! Cluny-my-sister!" shouted Marten, scrambling out of a nearby hatch. "The Kubin's old war-lamp has arrived! Tharp is going to make it work!"

Cluny shook herself. She seemed recovered. She turned to follow her brother, then looked back and said, "Come, Fever. Come and see. . ."

On the close-cropped grass beside the fort a crowd had gathered around an enormous old-tech lamp which mammoths had dragged all the way from the slow-rolling fort of Carn Kubin, at the rear of the *Kometsvansen*. This was the Kubins' contribution to the war against London, if only it could be made to work. Nintendo Tharp was dancing slowly round it, wearing what looked to Fever like a small stove on his head. He struck odd, one-legged poses like a heron, and called in sing-song voices on the Ancestors and the Repair Spirits.

Here was the reason why the Movement had been

able to hold off Arkhangelsk for so long, thought Fever, as Cluny led her to the front of the watching crowd. Quercus's technomancers were men of science; primitive, to be sure, but always ready to learn from new discoveries. Tharp and the other technomancers of Arkhangelsk had closed their minds, and still treated knowledge as their ancestors had done; a mystery to be passed down in whispers from one ignorant generation to the next. When one of the Movement's engines failed there would be a spare waiting ready in some storeroom, probably an improved model too. But when an engine failed among the vehicles of the *Kometsvansen* Tharp and his smiths might take weeks dismantling it and forging copies of the damaged parts; copies that grew cruder with each passing generation of technomancers.

Rattling a staff bedecked with ancient mobile 'phones, Tharp finished his ceremony and marched over to open the carved wooden housing of the lamp. A young Kubin warrior brought him the giant bulb, wrapped in mammoth wool and nestled in a special casket. Tharp examined it carefully before fitting it into place. Fever could tell that he had no idea how the lamp worked or what had gone wrong with it, but everyone else seemed confident in him, and when he stepped back the lamp's crew ran forward eagerly to wind the mammoth-ivory handle which was supposed to light it.

Nothing happened. A sigh of disappointment ran through the watchers.

"It is beyond even my power to mend this machine," declared Tharp, shaking his head dramatically and showering drops of scalding water from the spigot of his steaming hat. "It shall be broken up. Its wood will feed our furnaces when we roll on London."

He walked away towards the waiting bulk of the heart-fortress. Fever, who could never resist the mysteries of machinery, said as he passed her, "What is wrong with it? How is it powered?"

The technomancer started. He was not used to being spoken to like that. He pretended that he had not heard, but Cluny said, "It works by 'lectric, of course. Like most old things."

"But where does the electricity come from?" asked Fever. "There must be a generator inside. Probably a series of armature coils wound around an iron rotor. The coils are connected to the output terminals with a commutator. If one of the connections has been damaged. . ."

"What is she saying?" called a man from the crowd.

"She should not be here at all!" yelled another. "Spying on our weapons. . ."

"It's only a *lamp*!" said Fever. Their anger startled her. She was only trying to help. She waved a hand at their lamp and said, "If it was a gun or a bomb then of course I would not help you, but what harm do you think a *lamp* can do?"

Some of the Arkhangelsk called out angrily that they had long used war-lamps to dazzle ice-corsairs and nightwights. What did she know of the ways of warriors? She was just a southron! A mossy witch!

But Cluny Morvish said, "Let her try."

"Pointless," said Tharp. "The device is dead."

"Then we have nothing to lose," said Cluny. "The Ancestors sent Fever to us for a reason. If she wants to help us, let her try."

The technomancer shot a look of loathing at Fever, but he could not be seen to defy the Ancestors, so he let her step past him to the lamp. It took her a moment to find the inspection panel on its housing – it was covered with carved gods and animals like every other part of the lamp, and the bolts which held it in place were disguised as the heads of griffins – but once she had located it it came free easily enough, and behind it, just as she had expected, sat a big, crude dynamo.

Her accusers fell silent, watching. Tharp, who had never even noticed that inspection panel, came to peer critically over her shoulder as she checked the copper coils. She had seen dynamos like this in London, back in childhood days; people used to bring them to the Engineers for repair. It wasn't always easy to see where the break was, but . . . there, she had it!

"Do you have a solder?" she asked. "Spare wire?"

"No," said Tharp.

"They are in the pouch at your belt, Master Tharp," said Cluny helpfully. "Remember?"

Tharp glowered, and pressed into Fever's hand a

crude soldering device and a roll of copper wire. "Your London ways won't work on our machinery," he said in a threatening voice as he watched her work. "Our devices are protected by powerful apps."

He was trying to put her off, but Fever never felt calmer than when she had machinery to work with. Electricity had no moods or feelings; it would always run down a copper wire, and if the wire was broken then she knew just how to mend it. The thin smoke from the soldering iron tickled her nose. Tharp's voice was just a noise behind her; she paid it no more heed than the cawing of the crows or the murmurs of the watching crowd.

When she had finished, the lamp-crew tried winding their handle again. This time the bulb lit, shining like a small sun behind its faceted lens.

"Wait till the Londoners get an eyeful of that!" a woman in the crowd yelled. "They'll run like rabbits!"

Fever gave Tharp back his gear and returned to Cluny, feeling pleased with herself. Cluny looked pleased too, laughing at Tharp's loss of face. But as Fever reached her, her laughter stopped; she swayed and almost fell. Someone caught her. She looked at Fever in confusion, said, "It is the dream again. . . Worse than ever."

"Perhaps the magnetic field from that dynamo has affected it. . ." said Fever, thinking aloud.

"Nonsense!" said Tharp, barging past her in a flutter of ridiculous robes. "The lamp works by 'lectric fluxions, not magnets. This girl knows nothing. What are the Ancestors showing you, Cluny Morvish?"

Cluny turned her face to the sound of his voice like a blind girl. Her eyes were full of visions of other times. "London again," she said. "And Fever's mother, when she was young and beautiful. And – oh, Fever, it is the other dream, the one I told you of, the nice one from when I was little. The lanterns floating above the pools... Ow, my *head*..."

"*Pools?*" said Fever. "*Lanterns?*"

She remembered the headaches that she had had when Godshawk's device started firing its memories into her brain. But it couldn't be that ... could it?

Women were gathering round Cluny, cooing with sympathy and wise advice. Unable to reach her, Fever turned and found Marten waiting nervously nearby. "Does your sister have a scar?" she asked him urgently. "A small scar, on the back of... Like this." She grabbed the boy's hand and put it to the back of her own head, to the base of her skull where he could feel that tiny scar beneath her hair.

"I don't know," said Marten, snatching his hand back.

Fever turned away, thinking hard. Was it possible that when Cluny was a child in London, Godshawk had performed the same experiment on her that he had on Fever? Perhaps up here in the wilds, without the sights and smells of London to trigger it, the Stalker implant had never worked. Only now, as word of the new city spread across the north, was it starting to release a few of Godshawk's memories; and in particular, the memory of the rolling city he had dreamed of building. . .

It was not impossible. The evidence fitted. Fever remembered how frightened she had been when those memories that were not memories began surfacing. At least she had been able to understand a little, when she learned the truth. Poor Cluny, brought up in ignorance, among these savages who did not even know that electricity and magnetism were aspects of the same force! It was small wonder she thought the memories were magic visions. . .

Marten Morvish was looking at her quite fearfully. She said, "Listen, I must explain something. I know what is wrong with your sister!"

Before she could say any more she was pulled away. Two men held her while Tharp rattled his 'phone-staff in her face and shouted, "What magic have you worked on Cluny Morvish?"

"I have done nothing to. . ."

"Lies! You are a powerful technomancer! We all saw how you lit that dead lamp. And now the Vessel of the Ancestors is unwell. . ."

"I am all right now," said Cluny, from behind him.

"There is something wrong with her," said Fever, wondering how on earth she could explain it to these ignorant people. "It's not my doing. It is like an illness. That is why she has been having these hallucinations. . ."

"Visions!" shouted Tharp. "Visions, sent by the Ancestors!"

"No. I think there is a machine embedded in Cluny's brain. That is where her dreams come from. . ."

"Madness!" said one of the men who held her, sounding truly amazed that she could expect them to believe such stuff.

"There is no machine in my head!" said Cluny Morvish, touching it. "I think I'd know, wouldn't I? The dreams come from our Ancestors in the World Without Time."

"Even the one about the lanterns drifting off across the lagoons in the twilight?" Fever said. "All that orange and blue? I liked that one too. And the one about kissing that person in the park, in the snow. . . Have you had that one yet?"

Cluny looked scared, then angry, then scared again.

"We will kill her," Tharp declared. "Kill her, and offer her blood up to the Ancestors, and ask them to forgive us for ever having let her walk free among us."

"No!" said Cluny. "It is not their wish that she be killed."

"Well, we cannot let her walk around free," said Carn Morvish. He looked as shocked as his daughter by what Fever had said. "We cannot, Cluny-my-daughter."

Cluny wouldn't look at Fever. "Keep her under lock and key then," she said. "Keep her prisoner. But keep her. I don't understand it yet, but . . . she has a part to play."

So that was what they did. They took Fever back

aboard Carn Morvish's house, back to the room where she'd been staying since she got there, but this time they locked the door, and set a guard outside, and hammered fast the shutters on the windows. And there in the dark alone they left her, a captive in the comet's tail.

19

CHARLEY'S GAME

I n London, they were tearing down the temple of St Kylie. They were climbing up on scaffolding and peeling off its copper dome in segments which clanged like cracked bells when they hit the ground below. They were ripping out the panelling, and kicking down the doors, and levering the hasps and hinges and the handles off, and carting statues and reliquaries and altar decorations away for melting down. The poor saint's followers stood in the Tent Town rain and watched, and some wept, and some raged, but there was nothing that any of them could do. Their own High Priestess, Mistress Shamflower, had been found out as a traitor, and as punishment Quercus had ordered every trace of Kylie-worship to be wiped from the face of London, and the stuff of her temple sent to feed the new city.

Charley Shallow watched too, feeling a jittery sort of satisfaction as the door behind the altar which had once hidden him from Borglum's misshapes was kicked in and men went through into the hidden chamber behind and started to chuck out the temple's silver chalices and age-old plastic plates, the priestess's priceless vestments with their embroidery of copper wire. *I did that*, he told himself. But so much had changed in London, and so much of it was down to him, that it only gave him the ghost of a thrill: he was getting used to the idea of himself as someone who could make a difference to the world.

Within a few hours of his audience with Quercus, London had started to prepare for war. Stacks of timber which had been intended as the deck of Tier Three were being hammered up around the city's skirts in a crude stockade, thick enough to stop a shot from Raven's cannons. From their garages in the walls of the Great Under Tier, squadrons of landships went roaring north and east into the Fuel Country. Meanwhile, people of all sorts were flocking to join the defence force, especially the low-class labourers and the slaves whom Quercus had freed. The crackle of gunfire echoed daily across Tent Town as they trained with their new Bugharin rifles. It was a good thing, really, that Dr Stayling and his Underground couldn't see it, Charley thought. There was no sign of the popular uprising that they had thought would welcome Rufus Raven. Rather, Londoners were rushing to defend their new city.

Walking back from St Kylie's temple in the rain, he watched a convoy of land-barges rumbling in over the Brick Marsh causeways. They were carrying strange, boxy, tarpaulin-draped cargoes, and as they drew nearer to the new city and people stopped to watch, the word went round that these were naval guns, stripped from the ships of Quercus's fleet and dragged north to defend London. On the skirts of the new city, cranes were being made ready to lift the weapons into positions on the higher tiers where they would command the northern approaches.

"Those'll settle Raven's hash," shouted a plastic-smith, running past on his way to the training-grounds with his shiny new Bugharin on his shoulder.

Charley certainly hoped so. Then, as he looked up at the cranes, his gaze was caught by another of the new sights of London. From some bare girders at the edge of the base tier the carcasses of his former comrades dangled like overripe fruit, done up in little cages and swinging listlessly in the breeze. They were much squabbled over by crows, and it was hard to tell who was who, though it was still easy enough to spot Gwen Natsworthy, whose dark hair flapped on the breeze like a tattered flag. It had given Charley a funny, empty feeling in his stomach when he first saw her there. He'd told himself angrily that it weren't no fault of *his* she'd chosen to start playing at revolutions. She only had herself to blame, when you thought about it. They all did.

He no longer lived in the Engineerium with the other apprentices. He had quarters of his own now, next door to Dr Crumb's in one of the new blocks, Building 18, on Street 1:D (already known to everyone as Engineer's Row).

It was a rational little apartment, hexagonal in shape and designed according to some Engineer's calculations of exactly how much space one person needed to live in. It had papier mâché walls and a built-in bunk, and this morning it had an official note pinned to the front door ordering Charley to report to the Lord Mayor's chambers.

He wondered at once if he was in trouble. No; if he were, there'd have been a couple of coppertops waiting for him, not just a note. He told himself as he went inside to put on his best white coat and brush his damp hair flat that this summons was a good thing. It showed that Quercus hadn't forgotten him. Maybe he was going to be given a bigger apartment, better than this pokey little hutch. He set out for the city's heart, nodding importantly at the other Engineers and apprentices who called greetings as he passed them. He wished that one of them would ask him where he was going. He would have liked to say, "Quercus wants me. . ." or, "The Lord Mayor needs my advice on something. Big meeting of the council. . ."

When the official busybodies finally showed him into the council chamber he found just two men there: Quercus and Dr Crumb. They were talking, and Charley waited listening by the door until they found time to notice him. Quercus was saying, ". . .so the time it will take to complete the new city is still. . ."

"At least another year," Dr Crumb replied, his eyes on the papers which were spread out before him on the conference table. "Even if we remove the more irrational and *decorative* aspects of Wavey's plans, a year is still the minimum period in which we can hope to complete two more tiers. And during that time, the population of London will continue to grow; we may need to build *three* more tiers, and expand the Engine District again, if we are to carry them all."

Quercus shook his head. "Impossible. We are having enough trouble acquiring materials to complete even this first phase. Raven and his allies will not wait years to make their move. Dr Crumb, what would you say if I told you that it may be necessary to move London in months rather than years? Perhaps even in weeks? Either that, or abandon all this to our enemies."

Dr Crumb said nothing. The clock on the wall ticked slowly, heavily.

"Master Shallow," said Quercus, taking advantage of the pause to notice Charley and call him to the table. "I have just appointed Dr Crumb here London's new Chief Engineer."

"Congratulations, sir," said Charley. Dr Crumb looked blankly at him, still thinking about the problem Quercus had set him.

"He will need an assistant," the Lord Mayor went on. "Dr Crumb tells me that you have been helping him arrange his affairs, but it would be beneath Dr Crumb's dignity to be assisted by a mere apprentice. So I shall be promoting you to full membership of the Guild of Engineers."

"But I haven't passed the exam, sir. . ."

Quercus waved his words aside. "You can sit it when we have time to spare. Congratulations, Dr Shallow."

Charley bowed, trying not to laugh with pleasure.

"Don't thank me," Quercus warned. "It will be hard work; harder than you can probably imagine. We are entering a desperate time. Our enemies are powerful, and they wish to destroy what we have built here. You've already done your bit to stop them, but now you must do more. We all must."

"It may be possible, Lord Mayor," said Dr Crumb suddenly.

Had he heard anything of what had just been said? Had he even noticed Charley's promotion? His thin hands fiddled with the papers. He said, "It might be possible to move the city almost immediately if we were to admit that much of the present population is surplus to our requirements. When the building is done we will no longer need all these labourers. Why take them with us, expending fuel and space for no gain? Perhaps we should admit that we can make room aboard this rational new city only for rational people: Engineers, Mechanics; skilled workers who can keep things running. And their families, I suppose. The rest. . ."

"My gods, man!" Quercus said. "You are talking about leaving half the population of London behind!"

Dr Crumb winced at the Lord Mayor's shoddy mental arithmetic. "Oh, far more than half, Lord Mayor. But they are of no importance."

Quercus shook his head. "You don't understand, Crumb. A man in my position, I'm judged by the number of followers I have; the number of people in my *Kometsvansen*. The more followers, the greater the leader; that's how it's always been in the north."

"But you are not in the north any longer," said Dr Crumb. "You are no longer a nomad; at least, not in the sense that you are used to. You have built a new city, and it must have new rules. Individuals do not matter, you see; that is what we Engineers have always understood, although I'm afraid I forgot it for a time. It is only the survival and improvement of our society that is important. If you wish, I will start drawing up lists of those persons who will be needed aboard the new city."

"My gods," said Quercus again, more thoughtfully. "And they call us nomads ruthless."

"Not ruthless, Lord Mayor," said Dr Crumb. "Rational."

"And *if* we reduced our population in this way," said Quercus, "then, you think, we would be able to move sooner rather than later?"

"Lord Mayor," said the Engineer, "the engines are almost ready. There is enough space in the present structure to carry everyone we really need."

Quercus turned his pale grey eyes on Charley. "Needless to say," he said, "this discussion must remain absolutely secret. If word of what Dr Crumb has just proposed reached Tent Town, we would have riots on our hands."

"Of course, sir," said Charley earnestly. "You can rely on me, sir."

They left the Lord Mayor's quarters in silence, Charley carrying Dr Crumb's attache case with its bundled piles of Wavey's beautiful, fanciful plans. Instead of descending straight to the Engine District, as Charley had expected, they walked to the tier's edge. "A slight headache," mumbled Dr Crumb. "A little fresh air would be..." At the intersection of streets 1:17 and 1:K the workers had put up more of their cardboard signs; Ball's Pond Road and Shoe Lane. Dr Crumb pulled them down and walked on, tearing the signs into smaller and smaller pieces until he reached the tier's edge, where he threw them over the handrail like confetti.

"People are irrational, Charley Shallow," he said. He clenched his fists. "The world will never be put to rights until we cure them of that. They must be *guided*. They must be *controlled*."

"It's *Dr* Shallow, sir," said Charley. "*Dr* Shallow now, if you don't mind, sir."

A ship's gun rose creaking past them in its cradle of hawsers. Beyond it, through the thinning rain, Charley saw that the temple of St Kylie was all but gone.

191

20

PRISONER OF THE MORVISH

It was both dull and frightening to be a prisoner. Nobody had bothered to bind Fever's hands or feet so she was free to wander around her small chamber, but apart from eating the food that her guards shoved in at her sometimes there was nothing to do but sit and think, and her thoughts were all unhappy ones.

When she had been ill, and while she had Cluny to distract her, she had been able to keep her fear and grief shut away. Now they crowded into her prison with her and there was no escaping them. *Emotions are but useless relics of our animal past*, she reminded herself. She lay on her back in the dark of the night and set herself problems in differential calculus to give her busy brain something sensible to do, while the fort creaked and the wind howled and the tears ran down the sides of her face and went trickling into her ears.

When she woke the wind had blown itself out and the house was still and the silence was scratched by small noises. Low voices murmured outside her door. She sat up, noticing the cold blue light that slid its fingers in around the edges of the window-shutter. Not yet dawn, and at least two people outside her chamber.

The door opened. She saw light in the passageway and three dim human shapes outlined against it. For a moment she imagined Tharp had sent someone to murder her. Then a lantern was unshuttered and she saw that her visitor was Carn Morvish. Marten was with him, and Cluny too. She thought that she had never been so glad to see anyone in her life as she was to see Cluny.

"Talk quietly," said Carn Morvish, waiting by the door. "If Tharp finds out we came to see you he'll be furious. You showed him up over that lamp, girl. That was a mistake."

Cluny hushed him. She came to Fever and stopped and stood looking at her in the lantern light and said, "Fever Crumb, you said that you knew what was wrong with me."

"I do," said Fever. "I think I do," she said, tucking her hair behind her ears and trying to gather her thoughts. She explained, as quickly as she could, and in the simplest words that she could find, about Godshawk and his experiments.

As she spoke, Cluny's hand went up behind her own head, feeling beneath her hair for the scar that Fever described. Then she reached out and felt for Fever's scar, comparing.

"I didn't know," said the Carn suddenly. "Cluny-my-daughter, I truly did not know. I was a young man then, fortless. It was a bad time for the empire. I washed up in

London, a penniless sell-sword with a young wife to keep. The Scriven were still in charge there. I captained their mercenaries for a time. When you were born this fellow Godshawk came to me. He said that there was surgery he could perform, quite harmless, that would make you brighter, healthier... Curse it, I believed him! They knew so much, those Scriven, and Godshawk was supposed to be a mighty technomancer. He offered me money too; enough to leave his service and come north and set up my own house. It seemed such a little risk, compared with the risks all infants run, with colds and chills and things. And afterwards, oh, Cluny-my-daughter, you showed no sign of harm; just one little small scar. . ."

"This Godshawk put his memories in my *mind*?" said Cluny.

"He tried to," Fever said. "He tried many times, with many people, but the machines didn't work. My mother told me that all the living subjects he experimented on had died. Perhaps she didn't know about you. Or perhaps she just didn't want to tell me that he'd done the operation on other babies besides me. . ."

"I thought it couldn't really be the Ancestors," said Carn Morvish. "Not the Ancestors, I thought; not talking to our Cluny. We are soldiers, we Morvish; we don't have visions. I always feared it might be connected with what I let that Scriven do to her. . ."

"I don't think the machine in Cluny's head is working very well," said Fever. "She is only experiencing a few of his memories. One of them is of the city Godshawk dreamed of building."

"The city that they *are* building," Marten said. "It makes no difference where your vision came from, Cluny-my-sister. You have still seen what London will become. What we must roll south and *stop* it from becoming."

"I know," said Cluny. Her fingers were still tracing and retracing the line of the scar under her hair. "I know that what I saw was true, this changes nothing. But I would very much like to *stop* seeing it now, do you see? Before it sends me completely mad. Fever, can it be turned off, this mind-machine?"

"I don't know," said Fever. "My own machine was stopped by a magneto pistol – or at least quietened… But it would be so risky. We know so little about these things. Yours may be different to mine. The magneto pistol might not stop it. Or it might kill you, or harm your brain somehow. And Godshawk put other Stalker-stuff in me, mechanimalculae to help me heal. Do you have them too? Do you heal more quickly than other people? Do you catch colds and things as normal people do?"

"My fair share," said Cluny. "And I heal the same as anybody else, I think…"

"Then we must assume you don't have the mechanimalculae in you, and without them we don't know if you would survive the blasting of the machine…" Fever walked in small circles, thinking hard. "I wish I knew more. If only Wavey were here… But even she did not know much. That's half the reason she came north, to try and learn more about Stalkers."

"How?" asked Carn Morvish.

"There is a site somewhere west of here where she thought we might find something." Fever stopped walking and looked at him. The pyramid had not been in her thoughts for weeks, but now in her mind she saw it clear again; black slanting walls beneath a sky of light. Wavey would not have approved of her sharing the secret with this barbarian lord, but it did not seem to matter now. She said, "Sir, if you would let me go there, I might find out something. If we had some real idea how Stalker brains worked, we might be able to safely *stop* them working. . ."

"It's a trick, Carn-Morvish-my-father," said Marten uneasily. "She just wants you to let her complete the journey she and her mother were on. I expect this site is full of old-tech that Quercus needs for his new city."

"What site is it?" Carn Morvish asked.

"It is a pyramid," said Fever. "At least, the part that is still standing. . ."

Cluny looked at her father. "Skrevanastuut."

"It is shut," said the Carn. "The *Kometsvansen* swung that way once. There is a curse upon that pyramid, so I did not go near, but men who did said there was no way in."

"There is now," said Fever. "Earthstorms have *opened* a way in. It would be a long journey, but. . ."

Cluny smiled. "Mammoths move fast, when we need them to. We could be there and back within a fortnight, in time to rendezvous with Raven and the rest of the alliance."

"It is bad country," said her father doubtfully. "No roads. And anyway, Nintendo Tharp would not allow it."

"Tharp need not know, until we're gone," said Cluny. "You know what the worst of this has been, Carn-Morvish-my-father? Being locked away; not being allowed to ride, or hunt. So to take mammoths and go into those hills, before this war breaks over me... To do *something*, and not sit here in the house like a woman..."

"But you are a woman!" Marten complained.

"She was always a tomboy, this sister of yours," said Carn Morvish. "But I'd rather have my brave shield-maiden than some fragile little princess."

"I would be scared to go to Skrevanastuut," said Marten. "Scared of nightwights, and of the place itself. Skrevanastuut is a place of the dead."

"I'd be scared too," said Cluny. "But fear is slavery; to be free we must ignore fear. If you won't come with me, Marten, then Fever and I will go alone."

"That would be unwise," her father warned. "To go alone into that country, with only an enemy for company..."

"Fever Crumb is not our enemy," said Cluny. "Anyway, I want to see this place. If there is something there that could stop these nightmares... Carn-Morvish-my-father, you don't know what it feels like, having this thing in my head."

"All right," said Carn Morvish. He didn't like it, but

he didn't like having a prophet for a daughter either. He didn't like watching his brave girl turn into a shaky stranger who was afraid to go to sleep, and knowing that it was all his fault. He said, "All right, I'll think on it. But we must leave Fever alone now. If Tharp finds out what we are planning. . ."

Cluny gasped and put a hand over her eyes, and Fever knew that she had just been granted another glimpse of London. It passed quickly this time, and she looked up and smiled, and said to Fever, "We'll prepare in secret."

"I haven't agreed that you are going yet, Cluny-my-daughter," said the Carn.

"But you will," said Cluny, and hugged him. "You always do. Tomorrow night or the next we'll come for you, Fever. We'll go to Skrevanastuut together."

21

THE LONG SHORE AND
THE LONELY HILLS

I n silence they crossed the dew-wet grass between the sleeping vehicles of the *Kometsvansen*. The Morvish fort reared up black behind them on its big clawed wheels. The waning Foxglove Moon had set, but there were so many stars that their light was bright enough to see by; sometimes, as she went after Cluny and Marten, Fever thought that she glimpsed their star-cast shadows on the ground.

They had come for her after midnight; Marten relieving the guard at her door, Cluny waiting hidden below until he reckoned it safe to bring Fever down to her. The fort was asleep; the guards on the hatch they left by were Carn Morvish's chosen men who would say nothing of what they'd seen. Among the patchy birchwoods west of the *Kometsvansen* mammoths were waiting, two huge shaggy shapes that steamed in the starlight, like haystacks on a summer's morning, except that Fever had never met a haystack that breathed, or snorted, or snuffled at her clothes and face with a wet, inquisitive trunk.

"Don't be afraid," whispered Cluny. "That smaller one is Marten's mammoth, Lump. This one is Carpet, who has carried me on ever so many journeys." She stroked the beast's long, hairy nose. A small eye glittered, half veiled in hair. "We call her Carpet because she's a pet, and she looks like a carpet."

Fever thought any carpet that looked and smelled like that ought to have been burned long ago. She did not approve of carpets: irrational, insanitary objects which were home to mites and moths. She did not trust animals at all, and could never understand why people grew sentimental over dogs and horses and pretended that they could be the friends of humans. She stood beside Cluny and watched while Marten, with various clicking and cooing noises, persuaded the larger mammoth to kneel. She had to admit that the creature seemed well-trained, and that in the chill of the northern night there was much to be said for riding on something so big and so warm. Even so, she felt scared as Cluny helped her up between the bags and bundles on Carpet's back, and more scared when the mammoth rose ponderously to its feet, a shuddering, uncertain rise that made her grab handfuls of its coarse coat to save herself from tumbling straight off the other side.

Away in the night somewhere another mammoth bellowed. Carpet's trunk went up swaying like a snake and she let off an answering hoot, a plume of vapour under the stars. Marten, scrambling nimbly up on to his own mount's neck, said, "Hush, girl, hush!" It must have been strange for the mammoths, Fever thought, being singled out from their herd and led away like this with only people for company. Cluny slid herself into the coll between Carpet's shoulders and the tall, domed head, dug in her heels behind the big, flapping ears, and did something which made Carpet turn and start to move, swinging her head from time to time, those long tusks swishing through the bracken. Lump followed. The mammoths now ignored the trumpetings coming from behind them, but they communicated with each other by means of snorts and low, sub-vocal rumblings which Fever felt rather than heard.

She arranged herself on the massive, swaying back, letting go of Carpet's hair and finding better handholds in the mesh of hempen straps to which the baggage was attached. When she felt safe enough to look back, she saw that the sky above the *Kometsvansen* was already growing paler, the stars fading. Even in that twilight she could see the path that Lump and Carpet left; the crushed bracken; the big footprints across patches of bog. "They will know where we have gone," said Fever. She had been hunted before. She did not relish the thought of the Arkhangelsk tracking her with dogs and bowmen.

"Of course they'll know," said Marten, glancing across at her from his perch on Lump's broad neck. "Father will tell them we've gone hunting. I've been trying to get Cluny to come hunting with me for weeks."

"Tharp will be furious when he finds I'm gone," said Cluny.

"And when he hears I'm gone too. . ." murmured Fever.

"We'll be halfway to Skrevanastuut by then," Cluny said.

"And what if the empire rolls south before we're back?" Marten asked.

"Then they'll have to find someone else to be their Vessel of the Ancestors, won't they?" Cluny said. "Tharp can do it himself, maybe." And Fever could hear it in her voice, how glad she was to be leaving her people behind and shrugging off for a while the burden she had been carrying.

They kept moving through the dawn until the trees thinned, and the sun rose behind them and showed them a grey sea and a strand of ochre shingle that curved away from them into the mists of the west. It was the poor shrunk remnant of the North Sea, lapping against a four-hundred-mile-long beach which ran all the way from Heklasrand to Caledon. Dozens of icebergs had washed ashore there like the bones of drowned giants.

"The Longshore," said Cluny, twisting round on Carpet's neck to look back at her passenger. "We'll follow it for a few days, and then beyond it lie the hills, and among the hills is Skrevanastuut."

It was a strange place. That endless beach, the dunes behind, the stranded icebergs and the tangled stunty woods. Northward over the grey sea a pale light reflected on the clouds, for they were close to the margins of the ice and latitudes where even summer could not thaw the frozen sea. The rare fisher-villages they passed were huddles of low, domed huts with birch-bark boats drawn up on the strand in front. They slept each night around a driftwood fire. It felt timeless. It felt prehistoric. The fact that they were riding mammoths didn't help.

And yet, somewhere on that shore, Fever began to feel the first stirring of feelings she had not known for a long time. Not happiness, not quite, but a sort of contentment; a springtime feeling, as if she had been buried deep and was now stretching up shy fingers to the sun. Wavey was dead; she had not forgotten that. Wavey was dead, but the world went on without her, and Fever went with it. It felt good to be travelling with the Morvish. She sat in the sunlight and smiled at the silly, pleasant conversations which they tossed between them as they rode. Hail-showers came at them over the ice-strewn sea, and Cluny showed her how to rig the hide awning on Carpet's back to keep herself and all the baggage dry. The driven hail fell sideways. Tiny white hailstones danced madly in the grass behind the beach.

They passed a stranded whale.

They passed a long-dead ship.

They watched a houseberg sail past a mile offshore; a huge ice-floe motorized and turned into a floating home by northern fisherfolk, who could be seen hauling their nets in on its blue-white skirts. "Floemads," explained Cluny, as if Fever was a child who knew nothing of the north. "Like in the nursery rhyme: '*Nomads on the tundra, Snowmads on the ice-wastes, Floemads on the cold sea's swells. . .*'"

"'. . .*Moss-folk in the old towns, Elf-folk in the forest, Nightwights in the dark beneath the fells,*'" chanted Marten.

They forded the shallow rivers which seeped out of marshes further south.

They scattered up huge flocks of birds from saltings and lagoons, and one evening Cluny took a short horn bow from Carpet's panniers and said to Fever, "Come," and the two of them went creeping away through the alders and the birch-clumps in search of supper.

Fever had come to think herself very superior to the Arkhangelsk, but she could not move as quietly as Cluny did through the tanglewoods. She could not have plucked an arrow, set it to the string, aimed, and loosed it all in one brisk, graceful, unthinking movement, as Cluny did when she had watched the ducks upon the water for a while. She would not have thought to wait, as Cluny waited, until the scared ducks had wheeled and settled and she had a chance to shoot another.

Tramping back to camp behind her friend, carrying the brace of birds, she wondered if that was why she'd been invited on this hunting trip; for Cluny to make clear to Fever that she was not stupid, that she was as far beyond Fever in some things as Fever was beyond her in others. Then, as they hiked through the sliding dunes towards the glow of the fire which Marten had lit on the beach,

Cluny stopped and turned and said, "It's getting worse. The dreams. They breed in me."

"It was like that once for me," said Fever. "I know how you feel," she said, and it was true. *I know how you feel.* She had never really known how anybody felt about anything before.

"Were you frightened?" asked Cluny.

"Yes."

"Are you sure there'll be something at Skrevanastuut that will help?"

"No. But the more we can find out about these Stalker-brains. . ."

"I saw those lamps again," said Cluny. "Flying away across the water."

"Those were float lanterns from a party at Nonesuch House, a long time ago," said Fever. "It was Godshawk's home. He loved it."

"I see your mother sometimes," said Cluny, looking towards the fire, so that two tiny fires lit in her eyes.

Fever looked quickly away. She saw Wavey too, all the time. Whenever she thought of her she saw the Stalker cut her down, so she did not want to think of her at all.

Cluny said, "In my mind she is young and very beautiful. She has a new dress."

"Wavey always had a new dress," said Fever, and felt herself smile.

Cluny touched her shoulder. "You know, here in the north we believe that there is no such thing as time. It is an illusion. While we live we must accept it, but when we die our souls will be freed from time and we will be able to see it all as one huge pattern of unchanging moments: the past; the present; the future; all one. Your mother's life was made of many moments, and her death was only one of them. In the World Without Time, her soul is young again."

"There is no such thing as a soul," said Fever, and stepped away, startled by how much she wanted Cluny Morvish to hold her. She was glad it was nearly dark and Cluny could not see her blush. This too was Godshawk's fault, she thought, squashing the irrational yearning down. It was only because she had first seen Cluny through Godshawk's eyes. . .

Except she hadn't, of course. She had seen her first at Hill 60, watching as the *Heart of Glass* went by, and even then she had felt attracted to her, although she had not admitted it to herself.

"Fever? What is the matter?" asked Cluny.

"Nothing," said Fever, and as Cluny turned away and walked on she suddenly understood why this feeling was called *falling* in love. It was as dizzying as dropping down a hole. *We must find you a new boyfriend*, Wavey had kept telling her, but what if a *girlfriend* was what Fever needed? She felt as if she had opened the door to a room she had never noticed in a house where she'd lived all her life.

"What's happening?" called Marten, from the fireside. "Are we going to eat those ducks, or what?"

*

They passed a crumbled tower, left over from some forgotten northern war.

They passed a sandbar where hundreds of seals basked, and the scent of the seals scared the mammoths, and the scent of the mammoths scared the seals, and the day filled with trumpeting and honking and roaring and the raucous, easy laughter of the Morvish.

Fever no longer tried to stop herself from admiring the graceful sway of Cluny's back as she steered Carpet through the dunes. She waited hopefully for glimpses of Cluny's face when she turned her head to call to Marten or looked over her shoulder to smile at Fever. Her smiles were like little gifts. Was it possible, Fever wondered secretly, that Cluny felt the same things for her as she did for Cluny? She had never been any good at understanding other people's feelings. She'd had no idea that Arlo was in love with her until he'd told her so. So should she tell Cluny? But tell her what?

One afternoon, trembling with shyness, she managed to mumble, "You are very beautiful."

Cluny just laughed. "Why, thank you, London girl," she said. "You're beautiful too." She didn't mean it though; not the way Fever did. For her it was just a thing friends said to one another. Fever could not think of any other way to explain herself. Should she say, *I am in love with you*? Some mimsy, flimsy form of words borrowed from Master Persimmon's playscripts? It made her blush to even *think* of saying things like that. . .

"Marten!" Cluny called to her brother. "Fever thinks I am beautiful. Like a sunset, or a nice tree. We are both beautiful! You should think yourself lucky to be travelling with two such beautiful ladies!"

Gusts of wind came at them across the sea like skimmed stones. Fever watched Cluny tie back her hair to stop it blowing in her face; the glory of her long neck bare in the sunlight. *I should just kiss her*, she thought, *then she would know.* But would she? Would she understand? Cluny liked boys; the manly young men of Arkhangelsk. She was a nomad, with a nomad's old-fashioned notions. She probably didn't even imagine that a girl *could* feel about her the way that Fever felt. To be rejected would be horrible.

So Fever held tight to her secret and was simply grateful for Cluny's smiles, while the jokes and laughter of the Morvish flew past her like swifts on the wind.

At last the beach curved north and the wilderness of old Scotland came down to meet it in black cliffs. The air grew cold. Summer was already ending. There was frost in shady places, and inland the white hills slumbered under their icing like disastrous cakes. A broad meltwater river coiled out of the uplands, flowing clear and shallow over beds of golden gravel. Marten and Cluny used it like a road, the two mammoths wading patiently through the water, mile after mile. They camped that night in the lee of some rocks on the bank. In the darkness, above the noise of the river, Fever heard the creaking of glaciers in the valleys further north.

"We could probably walk to the North Pole from here," she said.

"Let's not," said Cluny sleepily. "Skrevanastuut is far enough for me. Anyway, we don't have time. Look."

Above the snowy shoulders of the hills across the river the young Scrivener's Moon was climbing the sky. In another ten days it would be full, and the war on London would begin.

When they moved on next day the river grew steeper, spilling down out of the high country in a long chain of rapids and stony falls which the mammoths could not climb. They kept to the bank, and the going there was easier than it had been on the day before, because they had left the woods behind and the only trees they saw were lonely pines which stood in ones and twos among the crags. This was old country; old rock. Once or twice they passed overgrown forms which might have been ruins; a cleft in a hillside too straight to be natural.

"What do you think it was?" asked Cluny. "The Downsizing, I mean; the thing that did the Ancients in. They were so powerful, and now this is all that's left. If you don't believe in gods or spirits or magic, what do you think it *was* that wrecked the world?"

"There are many theories," said Fever. "A natural upheaval, probably. An earthstorm or volcano-swarm far worse than those that trouble us these days. Some people believe it was a war, but that seems hardly likely." She was thinking of the crater of Mayda and other craters she had seen; craters so big you could sometimes barely see across them. "The Ancients were wise. They would not have done that to the world."

That afternoon they heard wolves howling, which made the mammoths nervous, and Fever too, but Cluny said they were nothing to be scared of. "They will not attack us, not when we have Lump and Carpet with us, and not at this time of the year. The wolves of the west aren't true wolves anyway; they mingled so much with dog-kind back in the Downsizing that they are half dog. We take and tame the young ones sometimes, and they are our friends."

Fever recalled the brindled creatures she had seen prowling around the *Kometsvansen*. They had not looked friendly to her. But Cluny knew far more about this place than she did, and if Cluny was not afraid then it would be irrational for her to be.

"Nightwights," called Marten, who'd steered Lump close alongside Carpet and had been listening to what his sister said. "It's nightwights we should be worrying about, in these parts."

"Don't worry about nightwights, Marten," said Cluny.

"But everybody knows they live in old caves and tunnels and things, up here near the ice! '*Nightwights in the dark beneath the fells.*' They capture travellers and drag them underground and sacrifice them to their weird old gods and *eat* them!"

Cluny said, "Marten-my-brother, nobody has seen a nightwight for years."

"The Guild of Engineers does not accept the existence of nightwights," said Fever. "It is possible that there was once some kind of nocturnal mutant strain that has given rise to legends, but there is no evidence that they survive. Proof would have reached London, if they did."

"Guild of Engineers doesn't know much then," said Marten, giving her a pitying look. "It's a big place, the north. There are all sorts of things up here, I think."

"Master Tharp says he treated a man for a nightwight bite once," said Cluny.

"It was probably a wolf that bit him," said Fever.

Up in the cold hills somewhere a wolf howled, and others echoed it, and her words did not sound quite so comforting as she had hoped.

Near nightfall they came to a sheltered place beside a spine of rocks on a hilltop where stunted thorn bushes grew up between the boulders and there was wood enough to light a fire. Cluny had shot a hare along the way, and while it cooked Marten led Fever up on to the summit of the rock-spine and pointed north. There, after much peering, she made out the tower of Skrevanastuut, tiny and dark above the blue folds of the hills like a flint arrowhead balanced on the horizon.

"There it is," said the boy, sounding sullen that Fever had dragged them here yet proud that they had made it. "It's still further than it looks, with all those ridges to cross, but if we start early we'll be there by this time tomorrow."

"Thank you, Marten," she said. "Thank you for bringing me here."

"Did it for her, not you," said Marten, looking away across the valleys where the mist was rising.

Fever took first watch that night, sitting by the fire with a rug wrapped round her and Cluny's arquebus across her knees, trying to ignore the way Cluny moaned and stirred as Godshawk's memories seeped through her dreams. Marten curled up and went to sleep as easily as a dog. Fever sat listening hard for movements out there beyond the reach of the firelight. There were plenty, but none seemed threatening, and when the Scrivener's Moon had sunk behind the hills she gently woke Cluny and snuggled down under all the furs and blankets she could find.

She lay waiting for sleep, watching Cluny cut a new length of match-cord for the arquebus, light it at the fire's edge and clamp it in the gun's dog-head. Sleepily she imagined settling in this lonely, lovely land. Building a little cabin, with a garden round it, and a turbine in one of those fast-flowing streams to generate power. Cluny would live there with her. She would teach Fever to hunt. Her nightmares of London would fade in the high silence of the hills, and Fever would build a flying machine better than the one that she and Arlo had made, and launch it from the snow-flecked crags. One day she would take Cluny's face between her hands and kiss her. . .

Only she wouldn't. She knew that she wouldn't ever be able to tell Cluny how she felt. This love would have to be her secret. Well, she thought, perhaps it was enough just to be near her. There must be lots of people in the world who loved someone without ever being loved back; the way that Borglum had loved Wavey.

It was a wistful feeling, but a sweet one. It warmed her while she fell asleep. It gave her pleasant dreams, which ended suddenly as she woke to a dying fire and a terrible screech.

She sprang up, not even knowing where she was at first. The mammoths were bellowing way down among the scrub in the valley; the fire threw smoke in her face; the night seemed full of dark and furtive movements. "Cluny!" she screamed. "Cluny! Marten!"

A hand touched her shoulder and she turned, feeling relieved until she saw whose hand it was. It was not one of the Morvish who stood behind her but a bony, ragged figure, pale eyes gleaming at her through a fall of lank hair. She stumbled backwards, shouting, "Cluny!" In the shadows beyond the fire a red ember glinted like a ruby; it was the lit end of the slow-match, still clamped in the dog-head of the abandoned arquebus. Fever crouched and picked the weapon up, turned, screamed at the black shape which leapt at her across the fire, pulled the trigger, and saw by the flash of white light which exploded from the muzzle a wide, filthy, scarcely human face, shrieking in rage and surprise as the ball smashed into him and dropped him in the embers.

That was the first time that she thought, *Nightwights...*

So much for the Guild of Engineers, then. If she ever got back alive to London she would have to set them straight on the anthropology of the north.

Another nightwight came at her out of the dark, snatching the gun, dragging her sideways with it until she overbalanced and let go of it and fell, hitting her head hard on the frosted ground. The nightwight stood over her with a grin full of dirty teeth. Then it rolled up its bulging eyes till they looked like two hard-boiled eggs and flopped down lifeless beside her.

Cluny wrenched her hunting knife out of its back and said, "Where's Marten?"

"I don't ... I don't ... I don't..." said Fever, between gulps of the chilly air. The horrible stink of burnt nightwight was in her nostrils, and her Scriven senses coloured it the nastiest grey she'd ever smelled.

Cluny left her to shiver there and strode off across the hillside shouting, "Marten! Marten-my-brother!" The only answer was the panicked trumpeting of Lump and Carpet, sounding very far away. She came back and flung her knife into the ground a foot from where Fever crouched. She dropped on her knees, as floppy as the nightwight she'd just killed, and her face in the last of the firelight shone with tears.

"He's gone," she said. "It's your grandfather's fault. That machine of his. I was meant to keep guard, but London got into my head again, and that's when the nightwights jumped me from behind. I hadn't even the wits to use the gun. Oh, Marten-my-brother. . ."

Fever wanted to hold her, to comfort her, but she hung back. She was too much of an Engineer; Cluny's grief was too raw and unsettling. She had to do *something,* though, so she pulled out the pocket torch which she had carried all the way from London. She flicked it on and started to trail its pale, moon-coloured beam across the slopes around them, walking first one way, then the other.

Cluny pushed the tears from her face with one hand, leaving it smeared with soot and grease. After watching for a moment she stood up and came and took the light from Fever. "Let me. You're only messing up the tracks. . ." She stooped low and shone the beam on broken grasses, turned-over stones. "I don't see any blood," she said. "I think they've taken him alive, down into their nest. . ."

"Oh no," said Fever.

"No, it's good," said Cluny, glancing up at her. Her despair had passed; she looked like a huntress now. "It means he might still be alive, and we can rescue him."

"How?" said Fever. "Cluny, you must try to be rational. We don't know where their nest is, or how many they are. . ."

Cluny ignored her and went downhill, sweeping the

215

light over the ground ahead. "They're supposed to live in old mine workings," she said. "Or natural caverns. Or just holes in the ground if they can find nothing better."

Fever watched her, feeling helpless. Reason told her that Marten was probably dead already, sacrificed to some weird old nightwight god inside the hill. The rational thing to do would be to leave; go in search of the mammoths and put as much space between themselves and this place as they could. But she knew she could not make Cluny see that, and slowly, as she watched her scout to and fro among the rocks, she started to realize that Cluny was right; not rational, but right. If there was any hope of saving Marten, they had to try.

22

THE DARK BENEATH THE FELLS

C luny was thorough in her tracking. Clues that Fever
would have missed even in daylight were plain to her;
she knelt to shine the torch at the print of a narrow, shoeless
foot; at fresh scratches on a lichened rock. It was really quite
scientific, the way she gathered and weighed her evidence.

The summer night was short that far north. A grey
light was seeping into the sky by the time they found the
low, arched entrance to an old mine working. There were
tracks going into it and coming out. Bones were scattered
among the rocks on the slope below, but they were old,
and not the bones of people.

"They have left no one on guard," said Fever.

"That's because they know no one's stupid enough to
go into a nightwight's nest," said Cluny.

She stepped cautiously into the tunnel. The blackness
was so complete that she might as well have stuck her
head in a bag. She turned on the torch and saw that the
tunnel sloped gently downwards as it reached into the
hill, a ribbon of water trickling along the middle of the

stony floor. Something lay there, and for a moment Cluny thought it was a body, awfully ripped and dismembered and somehow *flattened*. . . When she reached it, it was only her brother's coat.

She went back to the entrance. Night was draining quickly from the sky. "This is the place," she said.

Fever had been afraid it might be. Her deepest, most irrational instincts screamed at her not to go into that darkness, and for once the rational part of her agreed with them. But she could not let Cluny go alone, or let Cluny think she was a coward. To reassure herself, she said, "They are savages, and probably there are just a few of them. A family group. Three or four; maybe a dozen. They live in the dark and shun the day, which tells us they do not like light. Well, we have light. You have the arquebus. It is possible we may survive."

"You're such a comfort," Cluny said. She passed Fever the torch and unslung the arquebus from her shoulder. The blue smell of the slow-match tickled Fever's nostrils. The imminence of danger made her see everything with great intensity; the rocks on the hillside, the tussocks and wind-writhen thorn trees, all seemed haloed with a silver light, and Cluny looked more beautiful than ever: tall, grim, her heavy hair pulled back. *I would follow her anywhere*, Fever realized.

Just before they stepped together into the tunnel mouth Cluny looked back at her quickly and smiled. "Ancestors keep watch over us both, Fever-Crumb-my-sister."

Fever did not believe in ancestors, not the sort who kept watch over you, but she found herself thinking of her father as they went along the tunnel. "What is your plan, Fever?" Dr Crumb would have asked her if he'd been there. And she would have had to say, "Get in, find Marten, get out again." Which she knew was not the sort of plan Dr Crumb would approve of. He would be expecting something with diagrams.

They walked for what seemed a long time, stopping every now and then so that Fever could switch on her torch and check the way ahead for turns or pitfalls. Once the pale cone of light revealed a broken-up skeleton stuffed into a cleft in the wall; bones like gnawed sticks and a grinning skull. But the bones were old, and not quite human. Those wide-spaced eye sockets and the too-many teeth reminded Fever of Scriven skulls which she had seen in London, but more likely it was the remains of a nightwight. Perhaps this was how they buried their dead.

The stale air in the passage stirred, bringing an unpleasant smell to her, and a faint noise, like the far-off muttering of many voices. They moved on slowly, Cluny with the gun up to her shoulder, Fever switching the torch on at briefer and briefer intervals, lightning-blinks just long enough to reassure them that they were not about to step into an abyss. The sound ahead grew louder. It was definitely the sound of voices, mingled with shuffling movement. The passage twisted, plunging downhill more steeply. Now, even between torch-glimpses, Fever could still make out the rocky roof, illuminated by the faintest, pale grey light.

"Daylight," said Cluny, in the softest whisper. "We must've come clean through the hill. . ."

They turned a corner, and looked out over a broad gallery, hollowed by miners in some lost time, with a rugged pillar left in the centre of it to hold up the roof. It was full of nightwights.

"A dozen?" hissed Cluny accusingly. "There must be fifty of them!" Then she went quiet, for fear the nightwights would hear her. But they didn't. The cavern was too full of the scratch and hiss of their own voices. She hunkered down, pulling Fever with her, and there they waited for what seemed an age, afraid to move again in case their movements drew the nightwight's dark-adapted eyes, wondering what to do next, suspecting that they could do nothing. *There are too many of them,* Fever thought. *Too many. . .*

The ledge where they crouched was raised six or seven feet above the level of the cavern floor. Opposite it, perhaps fifty feet away, there was an opening like a long window in the rocky wall. The ghost-light of the pre-dawn sky seeped in there, filling the cavern with a grainy dusk. Even that was too much for the nightwights, who were shielding their eyes with their hands as if they feared the dingy light would blind them. Some were carrying horrid totems made of bone and hair; some wore headdresses of buzzards' wings. All were gesturing at the window, lowing and grunting and mumbling. *Religion*, Fever thought disgustedly. *They have forgotten all the things that made them human, but they still cling to religion. They are making ready to worship the sun when it rises. . .* Yet the window faced north, not east. She could see the distant red embers of volcanoes out there on the far horizon, and closer, in the centre of the view, sharp and black against the mists that lifted from the valleys, the pyramid at Skrevanastuut.

It is not the sun that they worship, she thought. *It is the pyramid!*

"Where's Marten?" Cluny whispered.

"I don't know," breathed Fever. A certain sense of expectation in the cavern made her think that the 'wights were awaiting something, and that it might have something to do with the catch their hunters had made up on the hill. Despite the tales, the nightwights probably had few opportunities to capture human beings. Prisoners were rare, and rituals would surround their slaughter. . .

Cluny was whispering again, but too softly to hear, and after a moment Fever realized she was praying. She prayed too: *Please let him be alive. Please let him be all right.* But she knew that nobody was listening.

The light slowly increased. The outline of the far-off pyramid became sharper. Suddenly a chorus of shrieks broke out on the far side of the cavern. Cluny jerked with shock, and Fever actually cried out, terrified that the nightwights had seen them, but her voice was drowned in the noise from below. Strange tides were stirring that sea of filthy bodies. Another group of feathered priests was shoving its way towards the window, carrying a mysterious shape which turned out, as it passed beneath the place where Fever and Cluny crouched, to be Marten Morvish. The boy's eyes stared out through his matted hair so fixed and unseeing that Fever was sure that he was dead. Then he blinked, and she understood that he had just sunk down into some hiding place very deep within himself where the nightwights could not reach him.

She felt Cluny tensing beside her. The light was growing steadily brighter, and she did not think the 'wights could bear it for much longer. Their ceremony was about to reach its climax. They clustered round poor Marten, reaching out grimy hands, wheedling and roaring, but the priests who carried him beat them back with clubs of mammoth bone. They dragged and fumbled him up on to the long rock sill beneath the window, where a figure dressed in a rattling vest of human vertebrae brandished a big, dull-edged knife, and then began to sharpen it, with awful scrapes and grating sounds, against the rock face beside him.

"Now!" whispered Cluny.

"But—" Fever started to say. She did not finish, for Cluny let off the arquebus with a sound like a slap round the eardrums and a spurt of sparks as fierce and ginger as a vixen.

They never knew if the shot hit anyone. It probably went into the ceiling. But the gun's bark and its belch of light were enough to stun the nightwights, and while they were still reeling Cluny jumped down from the ledge, calling for Fever to follow, and started to run towards the window and the priests and Marten. She swung the arquebus like a club, clearing a path for herself through the panic she had made, until a nightwight wrenched it from her, and another caught her by the hair, but Fever was close behind her and she shone the torch into his eyes and then into the faces of those behind him and they fell back dazzled and screeling, shocked that anyone could command such brightness. Fever laughed, and found her fear was gone, obliterated by a kind of wild elation that she had not felt since she launched herself from the cliffs in Arlo's air machine.

They came to Marten, who had already kicked his way free of the 'wights who held him and stood there looking dazed but ready, waiting for Cluny to tell him what they would do next. The nightwights were starting to recover from their surprise. Now that the dreadful torch was no longer shining in their eyes they could see that this was not an army attacking them, just two young women. The bone-clad priests urged them forward with hooting cries. While Cluny ran to her brother's side, Fever turned to face them, pointing the torch.

The nightwights stopped, but it was not the light that stopped them; the battery was failing, and the torch beam was no brighter now than the gathering daylight that flooded through the window behind her. They were staring at Fever. There was a look in their faces that she could not read, and something else; a sort of echo of a face she knew. Her own, or maybe Wavey's. Those wide cheekbones like spread wings; those too-big eyes set too far apart. The nightwights saw it too, that whisper of resemblance. It made them hesitate and wonder.

"Fever!" shouted Cluny, standing on the window's brink, hand-in-hand with Marten. Fever left the nightwights to their gawping and went to join her, wondering why she did not just run outside into the light. When she reached her, she understood. Instead of the gentle slopes she had imagined, the window opened on to a sheer drop; fifty or sixty feet into the dark waters of a river.

"Jump!" said Cluny.

"No," said Fever. "We don't know how deep that water is. . ."

"Who cares?" shouted Marten.

"Wait!" said Fever. "If our average weight is around eight stone, and we accelerate at . . . well, if $U = mgh$ where U is our potential gravitational energy and m is our altitude, we should hit the water at a velocity of, er, so the depth of the water will need to be at least . . ."

"Fever, sometimes you just have to *jump!*" screamed Cluny, shoving her forward, and there was a long moment of nothing but her panicked heartbeat and the whoosh of the air rushing past her ears at approximately thirty-two feet per second and a scream that might have been

Cluny or Marten or some angry nightwight far above, complaining at being cheated of its breakfast.

Then the water took them, dissipating some of that gravitational energy in a rackety splash and a burst of white spray, and they went down deep beneath it, but not quite deep enough to do more than bump their feet against the smooth black rocks which slept beneath the surface. As they rose the current took hold of them, and the river carried them swiftly around a spur of the hills and the nightwight lair was lost behind them. *We did it, we did it*, thought Fever, elated, joyful, and then, as the water closed over her head again, *Now, I suppose we shall drown...*

23

THE PLACE OF THE DEAD

For she had never learned to swim; not properly. When she lived with the Persimmons she had had the chance, for the theatre had stopped often at seaside towns and next to lakes and rivers, but it would have meant taking off her white coat and putting on a flimsy, floaty bathing dress, which she thought irrational. On Thursday Island she had done her best to teach herself, but she had never gone far out of her depth, and the best she had achieved was a few dozen strokes of frantic doggy-paddle in the sheltered waters of the bay where Arlo's family home once stood. In the fierce, cold current of that northern river she felt as helpless as a twig.

But Cluny could swim like a bear, and after the river had carried them a good way from the lair of the nightwights she dragged Fever through frail, splintering panes of ice to the shore, a beach of grey shingle under tall cliffs. Marten had already scrambled out. While Fever lay shuddering there he and Cluny went furiously to and fro collecting the dead branches which spring floods had abandoned in nooks of the rocks behind the beach, and ripping up tufts of pale dead grass for kindling. "Don't go to sleep!" Cluny kept shouting at Fever, who was curled around her cold self on the shingle and feeling inclined to slide away into a dream of warmer beaches.

Luckily Cluny carried her tinderbox in a plastic purse which had kept it dry. Shaking with the cold, she took it out, and dropped it, and picked it up again (her hands felt more like paws) and at last by concentrating very hard she managed to strike a few sparks and shed them into the nest of grass which Marten made. As the fire caught and grew they pulled their wet clothes off, and then Cluny undressed Fever like a doll and dragged her closer to the flames, saying all the time, "Stay awake, stay awake..."

Marten hung their sodden clothes on a dead tree which he dragged close to the fire, and Cluny knelt there in their wet-dog smell, trying to rub some warmth back into Fever's limbs and thanking the Ancestors that there was no wind to chill them. The wet clothes steamed, the fire grew scorching hot, the risen sun peeked down at their little beach. They huddled in their nakedness around the fire like three cave-people in the morning of the world, and slowly they started to remember what it had felt like to be warm.

"You were brave, Cluny-my-sister," Marten kept saying. "I was foolish to let myself be taken. I made you go into danger for my sake."

"Pooh, it was hardly danger, they were only

nightwights," said Cluny, with a laugh. Grey with the cold, blue-mouthed, bedraggled, she still looked beautiful. She caught Fever watching her and said, "Besides, I was not alone; I had Fever with me; I could not have done it without Fever-my-sister."

Fever blushed with pride, but Marten only grunted. Fever was no sister of his, and he knew that she would have abandoned him if Cluny had not been there.

"I was so afraid," said Cluny. "I thought they'd eaten you."

"I thought they were going to," said Marten. "They stuck me in a nasty little hole deep underground. Their pantry, I suppose. All bones and stink it was, and darkness, and I could hear their voices as they came gathering from all their caves and hidey-holes, and when they came to fetch me I was sure. . ."

He stopped and watched the river. He was a warrior of the Arkhangelsk: it would be shameful to admit how terrified and helpless he had been.

"It is over," said Fever, who was trying to put away her own memories of the nightwight lair and that strange resemblance she had seen in their savage faces. "It is unhelpful to keep thinking about it."

Marten glanced at her and nodded, grateful for that, at least.

They kept adding fuel to the fire until it had eaten up all the wood that was on the beach and their hot, damp clothes were dry enough to be put on again. The morning wore on. Shadows began to fill the bottom of the gorge. The beach, which had never really been a warm place to start with, grew colder and colder.

"What will become of Lump and Carpet?" asked Fever.

"They'll be all right," said Cluny. "There's nothing in these hills that could harm a mammoth. Maybe they'll make their way back to the *Kometsvansen*."

"Maybe they're still around here," said Marten. "We could shout and see if they come."

"The nightwights might come first," Cluny said.

"The nightwights might come anyway, once it gets dark," said Fever. "We should get out of here." She had been studying the cliff behind them, and she thought that she had found a way up. Perhaps if they climbed to the top of the gorge, she thought, they would be able to see where they were, and how far they had come from last night's campsite.

They climbed, and looking back across the gorge saw half a dozen different fins of rock which might have been the summit of the hill they'd camped upon. There was no sign of mammoths, not even after Cluny had made herself hoarse giving the special hooting cry she used to summon Carpet. Small flakes of snow blew past them on the breeze like sky-gods' dandruff. Fever, who believed in looking at the world straight on, did so, and could not help noticing that they were lost, with no food, no weapons, no transport; nothing, in fact, except the damp clothes they stood in. The day was waning, and sundown would bring the nightwights out again, hungry for revenge (although just plain hungry would be bad enough).

"We need to find shelter," she said.

"Shelter?" said Marten. "Here? What sort of shelter?"

But Fever had already thought of that. They climbed to the top of the next ridge and there it was, just two more valleys away, black against the whiteness of the hills beyond: Skrevanastuut.

It had been a big place once. Long before they came to the tower itself they began to pass the walls of outlying buildings; not real walls any more, of course, just hummocks in the earth, banks and knolls that looked too regular to be natural. "There was a whole town here once," said Fever. "In Ancient times, before the Downsizing. . ."

"Tharp says the Downsizing was a thousand years ago," Cluny objected.

"Oh, much, much longer than that! Nobody knows how long. All records were lost. Our modern calendars are just a guess."

"The pyramid could not have been here all that time," said Cluny.

Fever knew that she should agree; it seemed unreasonable that any building could have survived through so many ages of the earth. And yet the pyramid, rising now upon the slopes ahead of them, black and angular as an obsidian blade pushed up through the ground, did not look like anything the people of her time could make, nor the people of any other time she'd heard of since the Downsizing.

They went uphill past a low wall that seemed made of the same black substance as the tower itself, and the evening sun raking across the wall's surface picked out Ancient letters, some of which were still readable:

SCRIV N R   S TUT

"Skrevanastuut," said Fever.

"At least we have got the *right* mysterious pyramid then," said Cluny.

Fever said nothing. Those first few letters looked too familiar for her comfort. The Scrivener was the name of her mother's god; the god from whom all Scriven took their name; the dark god who wrote in secret script upon their skins to show that they were superior to common humans.

Splinters of Godshawk's memories shifted in her mind. He'd stood here once. She wished she could call on him and make him explain what he knew of this place and what he had hoped to find here, but the memories darted out of reach. *Skrevanastuut; Scrivener's-tuut...* Perhaps this place was just some old temple to the Scrivener, and that was the only reason why Godshawk had thought it so important.

But even a temple might give them shelter. Tired and hungry though she was, Fever hurried over the last few hundred yards to the pyramid. It was smaller than it had looked from a distance, and it did not quite come to a point but was flat at the top. When she placed her hands against its side she still could not tell what it was made of. Not stone. Not glass. Porcelain would be the closest thing to it, she thought. How could a tower of porcelain have lasted so long?

The sun was dipping. The hills behind her were all in shadow now, the snow in the high corries turning to the colour of bluebells. From among them suddenly a cry went up, colder than wolf-song, harsh and shrill. She looked at Cluny. Cluny looked back at her. Marten reached for his sister's hand. None of them needed to ask what the sound had been. It was the call of nightwights on the hunting-path.

"If we can find a way in we might be safe," said Fever. "I think this place is sacred to the nightwights. They may not dare to go in after us."

"They might be angry if we trespass," said Marten, who was keeping well back from the tower, alarmed by its strangeness and its sense of age.

"They're going to eat us anyway," Cluny reasoned, "so it doesn't much matter whether we make them angry or not. I hope we do; perhaps we'll give them indigestion."

They walked around the tower, and Fever discovered something that had not been obvious from her visions of it: it had only three sides. "Who would build a three-sided pyramid?" she wondered aloud. "Four would be more usual."

"Perhaps they ran out of money," said Cluny.

At the eastern corner, on the edge which faced the sunset, they found the opening that Borglum had been told of. A narrow crack in the blackness of the tower, turned down at either end like a glum mouth. Where one end of the crack met the ground there had been a cave-in, an opening the size of a manhole, across which someone, perhaps Borglum's friend Duergar, had dragged a large, flat stone.

"We can't go in there," said Marten, as Fever heaved the stone aside.

"We have to."

"If the nightwights come here they will follow us in. Cluny-my-sister, you're not going in there, are you?"

Cluny shook her head. "I'd rather die in the open."

"*Freeze* in the open, more like," said Fever. She knew that what scared Marten was the darkness; after what had happened last night, Marten might always be scared of the darkness now. She pulled out her torch and tried it, but the river-water had got inside it and it was dead. She looked into the hole. It seemed to open into a small passage, with floors and walls of the black porcelain stuff. Perhaps it had been a duct or crawl-way leading into the tower from one of those other buildings?

She swung herself over the hole's edge and lowered herself in until her feet touched the floor and only her head and shoulders poked out into the sunset. "Be careful!" said Marten behind her. He sounded very fearful; very young. "There could be nightwights *inside*. . ."

Fever crouched and peered into the gloom under the pyramid. She sniffed. "I don't think so..." The air in the passage had a curious, silvery smell, and it seemed slightly warm. She edged forward, rubble from the burst roof crunching underfoot. In the faint light coming from behind her she could see wires running along the walls; in places they had corroded away, leaving smudges of rust and verdigris. She pressed on until the light was gone and she guessed she was directly beneath the centre of the building. There the passage ended in a blind wall. She felt her way over it, wondering if this was another secret door like that one she had opened once to let her mother into Godshawk's old laboratory. It was only when her fingers had explored every inch of it that she admitted it was just a wall. She looked up.

"Fever-my-sister?" came Cluny's anxious voice, from outside.

"I'm all right," she called.

Was that light above her? Impossible; there could be no light inside that windowless pyramid. Unless there had been openings which she had not seen, up in the flat roof, perhaps... There was definitely a faint, greenish glow. She stood up slowly. There was no passage roof above her, just a square opening.

She felt around some more, and found metal rungs sticking out of the wall beside her.

Almost as frightened now as Cluny, she climbed up them, into the pyramid.

*

She emerged into a dark space, echoey, with a feeling of height to it. Grit beneath her hands on the smooth floor as she pushed herself upright. No windows, but light from somewhere caught a green jewel on the wall and made it glow like a little eye.

She went towards it, aware of dim shapes in the shadows round her. The jewel was not a jewel. It was a tiny lamp, set into a panel on the wall; the sort of panel she had often seen, rusty and ruined, dug out of some pit in London and presented to the Engineers for study. And as she stared at the panel, wondering if it could be true, and where it drew its power from, she saw her own shadow appear on the wall and realized that other lamps were coming on behind her, as if Skrevanastuut knew that she was there, and was giving her the light to see it by.

She turned. She was shaking. It all felt too much like magic, and she thought, *It is a good thing that I am rational, and know that there is no such thing.* Magic was the name unthinking people gave to phenomena they could not explain. A rational person looked closely at such things, and found an explanation. *There must be a computer-brain here. It has sensed me, and turned on the lights* ... but the idea that a computer-brain might still exist seemed almost as spooky as magic. Anyway, where did the power come from? Thermal energy from deep beneath the earth? Something in that strange black substance that the place was made of? She imagined mechanimalculae by countless millions busy in the walls themselves, drinking sunlight.

The sunlight falling on those black walls all day. Little mills and engines turning, all too small to see. That phrase Wavey used to use: "Molecular Clockwork"... Oh, Wavey, if you were only here; together we might be able to understand...

"Fever?" Cluny's voice came echoing along the tunnel again. She remembered her friends, went back to the square hole in the floor that she had come in by and called, "It's all right. It's safe..."

Cluny had already ventured halfway along the passage, and now she came quickly the rest of the way, with Marten behind her. Fever helped them up into the room. Blinking in the strange light, they stared about them at the metal cabinets which lined the walls, and the metal shelves where things lay which must have once been books, or folders full of notes, but which years and time and snails and insects had reduced to shapeless papery hulks, not much different from the old wasps' nests which hung in corners of the ceiling or lay broken on the floor.

A lot of wasps' nests, and a lot of nibbling, Fever thought; but not *that* much. Ten summers' worth, maybe. As if this place had stayed sealed tight for centuries, and ten summers ago a few cracks had opened somewhere, just big enough for insects to get in, and the cracks had slowly widened until one was big enough for Borglum's friend Duergar to notice...

She went to the nearest shelf and picked up something that looked like an intact book, but turned out to be just a plastic cover, filled with more wasps'-nest flakes. Even the plastic was brittle, crazing and crumbling as she lifted it, but on the front, in letters which had once been red, she could make out words: *The Scrivener Institute.*

"Fever, what was this place?" asked Cluny.

"I don't know. . ."

"I don't like it," said Marten. "There's strong magic here."

Fever crossed the room to a metal door that was set into the wall not far from that panel she had first noticed. She touched it, tried to prise it open. It would not move, but an odd metallic throbbing sound drew her attention back to the panel where the green light glowed. The light had turned red. On a black square of plastic below it, which she was sure had been blank before, a stylized, life-sized picture of a hand had appeared.

She looked on either side of the door for some way to open it; for a keypad like the one on Godshawk's laboratory door. There was nothing. The red light flashed; the metallic throbbing noise rang out again. Gingerly, Fever reached out and set her hand over the hand on the picture, then drew it back with a yelp. "It stung me!"

"I don't like this place; we would be better outside," said Cluny, and Fever could tell that she was trying very, very hard not to be afraid, and failing. Fever looked at her hand, and there on the pad of her middle finger was a little black speck of blood, like a sesame seed.

"It pricked me. . ." she said. Sure enough, when she looked more closely at the panel with the hand on it, there was a tiny, tiny hole in the plastic over the middle finger, where the thinnest of needles must have darted out and jabbed her.

The door opened with a fierce hiss, sliding aside into the wall so suddenly that it seemed to have simply disappeared. Fever and Marten skittered backwards; Cluny screamed. They stood poised, ready to scramble back down the ladder, but nothing came at them through the open doorway. A breeze from the passageway blew past them into the newly opened room, smelling of heather and the wide moors outside. It was as if Skrevanastuut had been holding its breath for a long time and was now inhaling deeply.

In the new room they could see metal chairs; low tables; more shelves. Fever calmed herself and edged carefully through the doorway. As soon as she was inside she grabbed one of the chairs and wedged it so that the door could not slam shut again and trap her. She beckoned the Morvish to follow her, and thought as they came to join her that they looked like animals, so wide-eyed and alert, looking so warily at everything, reaching out to touch things and then drawing their hands back so quickly, shocked at the strange feel of them.

She knew that she was behaving in just the same way.

There was not so much grit on the floor of this room; no wasps' nests on the ceiling. A thin, brightly coloured book that lay on the table looked untouched, with an uncannily realistic picture of a pretty woman grinning at them from the front cover. *Some sort of coloured photograph?* Fever wondered. It crumbled into flakes when Marten touched it. A mug stood next to it. On its side were those same three words in the same red lettering: *The Scrivener Institute*. Fever read them aloud. How many centuries had it taken for that name to be smoothed into "Skrevanastuut"?

"The Scrivener?" asked Marten. "He's a *god*. . ."

"He was the god of my mother's people," said Fever. "The Scriven believed that he was born in the fires of the Downsizing. They said he created the Scriven to replace ordinary human beings. This must be an old Scriven site; a temple or a monastery dedicated to him. . ." No: that did not make sense. If the Scriven had been able to build a place like this they would have conquered the whole world, not just London.

There were stairs in one corner of that room; a spiral of them, leading up to another metal door. They creaked slightly under the three intruders' weight, but did not shift, and the door at the top whisked open without Fever needing to have her hand pricked again. The upstairs room was triangular and seemed to fill the whole mid-section of the pyramid. There were oblong transparent panels on the wall which Fever thought at first were windows looking out on to a grey and softly glowing sky. Then she thought that they were lamps; then some sort of pictures. Finally she realized that they were screens.

All her life she had been seeing screens – they were

dug up in such huge numbers from the soils of London that some archaeologists had taken to calling the last era of the Ancient world "the Screen Age" – but she had never seen one working before. Beneath each screen there was a kind of plastic tray with square white tiles on, and on each tile a printed letter or a figure or a sign. "Keyboards," she said. She had seen houses floored with such tiles, back in London. She blew the dust from one of them, and reached out and touched a key – the letter H, which was almost in the middle. Instantly the screen above her changed colour, and showed her *The Scrivener Institute* again.

She did not know what else to do. She knew that the screen and the keyboard should be connected to one of the Ancients' legendary computer-brains. How could she contact it? H-E-L-L-O, she typed carefully. "Hello?" she said loudly. She bent down and said it to the keyboard. "Hello?"

The screens hummed softly. A few were dead. Only to be expected in such an old place. It was astonishing that any worked at all. She tried pressing more keys at random. Nothing happened. Behind her, Marten and Cluny had already grown bored and were climbing another helix of white stairs which went up through the middle of the ceiling. Fever ignored them, trying to remember everything she had ever read or heard about computer-brains. None of it helped. All the knowledge of the Ancient world might be contained in these machines, but she had no idea how to get at it.

Above her she heard another door open. Then, after a heartbeat's pause, Cluny began screaming, and did not stop.

Fever ran up the stairs to their top, where her friends stood scrunched against the handrail just outside the open door. "What is it?" she asked, but Cluny would only scream, while Marten pointed dumbly into the room they had just opened.

It was full of Stalkers.

24

IN THE UPPER ROOM

For what seemed a long time they stood there together, barely breathing, staring at the seated shapes which lined the room. Each propped on its own big throne-like chair, and each unmistakably a Stalker, its head an outsize helmet, its face a metal mask, its eyes twin lamps. Most of the lamps were dead and blank, and some of the Stalkers had disintegrated with age into heaps of machinery and a scatter of dead-stick bones, but in the eyes of a few a faint green light still played, like wills-o'-the-wisp trapped in the armoured heads. From their metal skull-pieces tangles of wire trailed, plugged into sockets on the walls behind.

"I think it is all right," Fever said, after a little time. "These are not *Stalkerish* Stalkers. . ."

If they had been Stalkerish Stalkers, she reasoned, she and Cluny and Marten would already be dead. But the figures all stayed seated, and the hands that clasped the armrests of their chairs were not gauntlets full of knives but more like mummies' hands; brittle armatures of twigs papered in ancient skin.

Fever went into the room, and stopped as one of the Stalkers raised its head to focus on her. She heard the mechanisms inside its eyes creak and grate. Behind the mouth-slit of its mask, dry, yellow teeth moved. A voice like the whisper of the air stirring dead leaves in a tomb came out at her. Words poured from it as if it had been interrupted long ago in the middle of a speech and now Fever was here it was continuing where it had left off. What was it saying? What language was that, so quick and guttural, so full of hisses and odd, half-familiar sounds?

She looked back at Cluny. "Is it speaking Arkhangelsk? Suomi?"

"I think it's Anglish," said Marten, listening hard.

It was. Fever was beginning to catch words now herself. "*Remember . . . war . . . it was decided . . . Scrivener Institute. . .*" It was Anglish, but Anglish as it had not been spoken for whole ages of the earth; Anglish as it must have sounded in the Screen Age, on the eve of the Downsizing. Fever went closer, straining her ears, snatching at every word. Now another of the ancient Stalkers had begun to speak, and its voice blended with the first, making it even harder to catch what either of them said.

"*Sixty minutes . . . all major cities . . . survivors. . .*"

"*I remember. . .*"

"*. . .then the Slow Bombs. . .*"

"*. . .it was decided. . .*"

"*. . .revenge weapons of the Barefoot States. . .*"

"*I remember. . .*"

243

". . .rushed into production. . ."

". . .base pairs . . . improved resistance . . . patented sequences. . ."

"The inheritors. . ."

"Stop!" cried Fever.

There was a moment's quiet. The Stalkers seemed to look at her inquisitively. "Who are you?" she asked. "What is this place?"

"This is the Scrivener Institute," whispered the first Stalker. "Scrivener is a registered trademark of the Scrivener group of companies. This facility has been designed to withstand an impact of up to fifty megatons. Genetic material held at this facility is the property of the Scrivener group of companies. I remember the foundation of this facility. Since war seemed inevitable it was decided that the new genome would be rushed into production. . ."

"What does it mean?" whispered Cluny.

Fever shook her head. "They're talking about a war. Something long ago."

The second Stalker was speaking again now, but all that came from it was a string of difficult-sounding words: ". . .reduced senescence . . . haem-oxygenase regulators within the mitochondrial DNA. . . Coenzyme Q – cytochrome c reductase complex three MT-CYB cytochrome c oxidase complex four. . ."

The only term Fever recognized in all that was "DNA". Certain Ancient texts spoke about a mystical-sounding spiral of matter which somehow passed down information from parents to their offspring. That was what "genes" did, too. And "reduced senescence" was about aging, about *slowing* aging. . .

Had this been a medical facility? The Scriven aged more slowly than normal humans. Perhaps they had benefitted in some way from what was done here?

"Have you heard of the Scriven?" she asked.

The Stalker paused, then said patiently, "*Scrivener is a trademark of the Scrivener group of companies. This facility has been designed to withstand an impact of. . .*"

"They aren't talking to you, Fever," Cluny said, taking her by the arm and pulling her gently away. "They're just talking *at* you." She could still hardly bear to look at the Stalkers. She held her hand up in front of her face as she spoke, trying to keep out their musty, chemical reek. "Great Ancestors!" she muttered. "Do you think *I* will end up like them? Those extra brains inside their heads. . . They aren't people; just tailors' dummies stuffed with old memories. . ."

"*The S-197 cranial implant facilitates the backing up, storage, downloading and sharing of biological memory,*" began one of the Stalkers unhelpfully.

"*In the present emergency, cranial implants have been used to preserve and retrieve information from post-functional brains. . .*" whispered another.

"*Information from post-functional brains will be downloaded to the mainframe as soon as conditions improve. . .*"

Cluny started to lead Fever towards the door. Marten

had already backed right out of the room and waited at the top of the stairs, looking ready to bolt. Fever wanted to hear more, but she let herself be led. It was good to feel Cluny's warm hand in hers in this room of the whispering dead.

"They can't tell us anything," Cluny said. "The things they're talking about were forgotten a thousand years ago."

"Longer. *Much* longer," said Fever.

"So are they going to tell us the cure?" asked Marten. "For this thing in Cluny's brain?"

"The answer's here," said Fever. "I just don't know how to find it. I might not understand it if I did. All this *stuff*..."

They went back down to the bottom floor. They barred the entrance with a cabinet and then, because they were very hungry and had nothing to eat, they lay down to rest instead, in nests which they made from the crumbling foam cushions of the chairs.

Cluny and her brother both fell asleep easily, exhausted by the terrors of the day and their long trek. Fever, although she felt as tired as she had ever felt, lay awake for a long time, thinking back over the things the Stalkers had said to her. She was sure they had been giving her the pieces of a puzzle, but she could not see how to put it together. She wondered if they were still whispering up there at the top of the tower. *Cytochrome. Oxidase. War. Inheritors*... For the first time in her life she felt stupid. She had often dreamed of discovering a place like this; the technology of the Ancients, preserved and functioning.

It had never occurred to her that she might not be clever enough to understand it.

In the morning, woken by his empty belly, Marten left Fever and his sister sleeping and crept out of the tower and went downhill with some wire he had prised from one of the cabinets. He was nervous of the nightwights, but snow had fallen in the night and the sun lay bright upon it, and he did not think that they would venture out. The snow showed him rabbit tracks on the little paths between the heather and he twisted the wire into snares which he set across them. Then he went on down into the valley, to where the river ran, and spent an hour trying to catch fish in the shallows, without luck. He did not mind. It was good to be out under the wide sky again, after being shut up in that weird old place on the hill. He was sorry that Cluny had come here. It was all the fault of Fever Crumb, he thought. The London girl was brave, but she was a bad influence on his sister.

When he returned to his snares he found that he had trapped two rabbits. He dressed the carcasses and carried them back up the hill, feeling pleased with himself for reading the tracks so well and making such good snares.

The feeling faded when he reached the pyramid. The snow around it was melting quickly, revealing footprints in the damp earth near the mouth of the tunnel. His own were there, and Cluny's, and the prints of Fever's boots too, but trampled over them were many others, the marks of bare feet with clawed and horny nails. You didn't have to be a hunter to read *those* tracks. In the night, while he and Cluny and the London girl were sleeping, the nightwights had followed their trail, and come to slink and sniff around the walls of Skrevanastuut.

Fever walked through the empty tower in silence. On the ground floor she had found three more rooms: one a sort of kitchen, another a storeroom with a toilet cubicle opening off it, the third a place that she thought might be the Resurrectory where the Stalkers in the upper room had been made; there was a metal table in the middle, and more screens, all dead, and cabinets of tarnished metal dishes and things that could have been surgeons' tools or instruments of torture. There was a plastic casket with grey dust inside, and three egg-shaped depressions in the dust, a Stalker brain nestling in each.

She was rich. A digger in London who had found just one room like that would have been set up for life. But she could think of no way to get more than the smallest of her finds home, and she did not much care about that anyway. What she wanted more than anything was just to understand this stuff.

She climbed the stairs again to the upper room, and again the Stalkers began whispering to her. Of course, they were not really Stalkers. To Stalk you had to be able to stand up and move about, and there was no sign that these creatures had been intended to do anything but sit here in their big chairs, remembering. Perhaps things like these had just been the beginning of true Stalkers. Somebody had taken the same technology, gone north, built more pyramids, and developed Stalkers that didn't just sit and remember things but could walk and fight. Then they had decided that the remembering bit wasn't so important any more...

She tried to assemble what she knew. The Stalkers kept whispering of a war. Some historians believed that the Downsizing had been caused by a war between two Ancient empires, although Fever had never really believed it. How could a society as advanced and scientific as theirs have had wars? But say they had. Just before the war, and just afterwards, the people here had *done* something, rushed *something* into production...

She thought of the way the outer door had pricked her and then let her in, the tiny needle no doubt sampling her blood somehow. If she had not been part Scriven, would the door have opened for her? She thought of speckled skins and trademarks, of legends and the birth of gods.

"What am I?" she asked.

Several of the memory-Stalkers answered her at once.

"*You are Homo superior...*"

"*You are Humanity 2.0...*"

"*You are female, between sixteen and fifty years of age...*"

"*Your genome and nanotech upgrades remain the intellectual property of the Scrivener group of companies...*"

"*Your DNA is contaminated with a standard* Homo sapiens *strain...*"

"*Sequences encoding for pigmentation have been damaged...*"

"Stop!" said Fever. The whispering ceased. The Stalkers watched her. She said, "You *bred people* here? Is that what it was for, this place?"

One of the Stalkers said, "*The survival of Homo sapiens is unlikely. The exchange of nuclear and particle-energy weaponry between the US and Greater China resulted in the loss of all major cities. It is believed that Slow Bombs will begin to arrive over the next ten to twelve years.*"

"Stop!" said Fever. "What's a 'Slow Bomb'?"

One of the other Stalkers said, "*Slow Bombs are a revenge weapon of the Barefoot States. They are small asteroids boosted on to Earth-impact trajectories. It is assumed that a number were triggered remotely during the final minutes of the recent nuclear/particle energy exchange. Estimated time to impact varies from three to six years.*"

"No, no, no," said Fever. "They've been and gone; this war you're talking about, it must have been thousands of years ago..."

But the Stalkers did not seem to understand her; they knew of only one time: after the war, before the arrival of the Slow Bombs.

"*It has been decided that the improved genome will be rushed into production to create Humanity 2.0, a new sub-species with increased resistance to radiation, fully adapted for survival in conditions of low light and sub-zero temperature ranges. Adjustments to mitochondrial DNA sequences encode for reduced senescence, ensuring a longer reproductive life, aiding spread of the upgraded population. Brain functions are compatible with current mnemonic harvesting technology to aid the exchange and retention of group knowledge. The following genetic sequences are the intellectual property of the Scrivener group of companies. . ."*

Then they were off again, all joining in, listing long chains of numbers and letters, whispering at her about haem-oxygenase and transport chains. Fever went and sat on the stairs, looking down into the room of screens.

When Cluny came upstairs a few moments later she said, "I have found out what I am."

"What?"

"The people who built this place could make *people*. I don't know how, but they could. There was a war – only they called it an 'exchange' – they must have known it was coming. I suppose that's why they built this place so strong and far from anywhere. They thought ordinary people were going to die out, so they tried to breed a better sort. I suppose those other buildings outside were nurseries . . . or . . . hatcheries. . ."

"And that's you?" Cluny climbed the stairs to her and sat down next to her. "You're one of these better people?'

"They were all speckled to start with," said Fever. "So they'd know not to mate with the old sort of people, I suppose. But it didn't work out. Something went wrong. This place was abandoned, and the new people forgot what they were, and moved away into other lands, and they only remembered the Scrivener Institute as a silly god. And the years went by, and the old sort of people didn't die out after all, and the things that had been done to make the new sort better stopped working, or got changed, and some found that they couldn't have enough babies, and their speckles started to fade, and they went south and conquered London and got wiped out by the Skinners. And some changed in other ways and started living underground, and they became the nightwights. That's why the 'wights worship this place. That's why I look like them."

"You don't look like a nightwight!"

"Yes I do. Same bone structure."

"Mmm, fair enough," said Cluny, looking at her critically. "I was thinking of their teeth and hats and things."

"I was *made*," said Fever. "I always knew I wasn't standard human, but . . . Cluny, I'm just an artefact. I'm the last bit of data in an experiment that didn't work."

Cluny shrugged. None of it meant anything to her. How could people make other people, except in the usual way? And what was the point of worrying about it anyway? She lifted Fever's chin, and kissed her gently between the eyebrows.

"You're Fever Crumb," she said. "And you're lovely."

Fever drew back and felt her ears burning. She wished those Scrivener Institute people had done something about the blush response when they had set about designing their new race. . .

252

She heard something below her. Marten was standing at the foot of the stairs. His eyes met hers, and she guessed that *he* understood how she felt about his sister, even if Cluny didn't. Maybe he had sensed it all along, and that was why he'd never liked her.

"The nightwights have been sniffing round," he said, switching his gaze very carefully from Fever's face to Cluny's. Then he held up the two skinned rabbits that he carried and said, "But look, I got breakfast, if you want it."

The kitchen that Fever had found earlier had glass-fronted cabinets with knobs and dials, but nothing that any of them could recognize as a stove. So once the rabbits were jointed they carried them up through the room of screens and the room of Stalkers, and levered open a sealed hatchway there that led out on to a flat, triangular roof with a little low wall around it. There they squatted amid the rust-stains of an old communications array and roasted the meat over a fire made out of heather twigs and the unreadable records from the shelves downstairs. They had water fetched in Scrivener Institute mugs from a nearby rill to wash it down, and the meat tasted good; better than any meal that Fever could remember, even though she had to eat it with her fingers in a most un-Engineerish way.

When her belly was full she sat beside Marten on the warm porcelain roof listening while Cluny told a story, and watching the way the sun lit Cluny's profile and the cloud of her hair. It seemed impossible that anything bad was going to befall them. So the nightwights had reached Skrevanastuut. Well, what of it? They had not come inside; they dared not; perhaps they had already given up and gone back to their lairs. Even if they hadn't, she and Cluny and Marten would be safe as long as they stayed inside the pyramid. Perhaps Skrevanastuut itself would show her a way that the 'wights could be defeated.

But even as she thought that, the smoke of their little fire was going up like a pencil mark upon the still, blue sky and, from caves and shady corries in the hills around, the nightwight hunters squinted out into the hurtful sunlight, and watched that smoke, and waited for the dark.

25

BESIEGED

For the rest of that day Fever tried and failed to make the pyramid give up its secrets. The Stalkers contented themselves with reciting lists of enzymes and molecules, and in the room below the screens just glowed and fizzed. She went downstairs to search the papers in the lower rooms, thinking that at least paper was a thing she understood, but most of what was written there was illegible, and the rest meant no more to her than the ramblings of the Stalkers. There were printed rows of numbers and what looked like lists of children's heights and weights; perhaps the vital statistics of the first generation of Scriven. On one sheet someone had scribbled, *Pearson has decided to head north...* The answers to questions which had been forgotten millennia ago.

She took one of the little silver Stalker brains she'd found and showed it to Cluny. It lay in her cupped palms like a tiny silver egg. She pointed out ports, no bigger than the pores of her own skin, from which thin cilia would emerge when it was inserted in a human being, stretching out along the nerve pathways, twining into the roots of the brain.

"This is what is inside my head?" asked Cluny.

"Inside my head too. And in all those whisperers upstairs."

"So they're all the rage. . ." Cluny hadn't really believed until that moment in the thing Godshawk had hidden in her. Hadn't believed that something so powerful could be so small. The machines of the Arkhangelsk were all big, and the more powerful they were the bigger they had to be. It seemed impossible that her whole life had been derailed by something not much larger than a teardrop. She looked at it for a moment with her eyes shining, and then flung it on the floor and stamped on it. She ground it under her boot heel. She squashed it like a silverfish and kicked it into a corner.

"I'm sorry," Fever said. She stood behind Cluny and put her arms around her and nuzzled her face in her thick hair and felt guilty at how much she loved the sunlight-in-beechwoods autumn smell of her. "I've brought you here for nothing. I don't understand any of this."

"I do," said Cluny. "I understand that these dreams of mine are just recordings, not visions from the Ancestors. And I've learned something here. Something about the old world and its ways. All their *science*. All their *knowledge*. . ."

"Cluny-my-sister!" came Marten's voice, from the room above. A moment later they heard what had alarmed him. They had left the hatch on to the roof open to let in fresh air, and through it now there came a sound Fever had hoped not to hear again. The cry of nightwights on the hunting trail.

In the evening sunlight they stood together on the roof, and as the shadows lengthened across the hillsides they started to see movements there as the hunters crept out of their hiding places. As the sun dipped behind the western hills more and more of the 'wights emerged, until at least thirty of them were visible around the base of the pyramid. They seemed to have overcome their awe of it, and a knot of them gathered at the corner where the opening was, listening as one of their feathered priests harangued them. Fever wondered if he was telling them that they had a duty to clear out the interlopers who had invaded their sacred place. Or maybe he was just saying, "Dinner's up."

Either way, things looked bleak. Marten and Cluny had dragged the heaviest pieces of furniture they could move over the entrance below, but if they could drag them there then the nightwights could shove them aside. She thought of that tower on Thursday Island where she and Arlo had managed to hold off the Oktopous Cartel's foot soldiers; but only for a while, and those men had not been half so savage or so numerous as the nightwights. She decided that she should avoid towers in future.

Now, in the twilight, the bravest of the nightwights were running at the pyramid and trying to race up its sloping walls. They were able to climb no more than a few yards before sliding back, but it was helping to rouse the others to a frenzy. *If only there were some way to communicate with them*, Fever thought. They were not animals, after all; they were able to plan and organize, as they had quickly proved by surrounding the pyramid on all sides. She felt a queasy guilt about the one she'd shot now that she knew he'd been her distant cousin. . .

Marten took his sister's hand. Fever wondered what would become of Raven's alliance if Cluny died. Perhaps he would not be able to hold it together without his prophetess. *So London will be safe*, she thought, but that was no comfort. She wanted London *and* Cluny to be safe.

So she left them and ran down the stairs again, thinking, *It cannot work*, and then, *It doesn't matter; there is nothing to lose*. The pyramid was full of dull booms and clangs – the sounds of nightwights who had crept into the entryway and were beating at the Morvish barricade from below with stones and spear-butts. Fever ran through the dim rooms, pocketing likely-looking objects. Savages liked objects, she thought. Even if they killed her, their squabbles over the things she took them might distract them for a while from Marten and Cluny.

She ran back up the stairs to the roof. Cluny turned as she emerged and said, "Fever-my-sister. . ." seeing something wild in her eyes.

Fever did not stop to explain. She went past Cluny and vaulted the low wall at the roof's edge, careering down the western face of the pyramid as if it was a drop-slide at Summertown fair. The steep slope was as slippery as glass. No wonder the nightwights could not climb it, she thought, trying to slow her hurtling descent with her boot heels, friction scorching the heels of her hands. She saw the nightwights below her, scattering and staring. Then she landed with a thump in the heather at the wall's foot and they were all around her.

"Fever!" Cluny was shouting, behind her and far above, and it sounded like the cry of a bird, plaintive and distant.

She stood up, the pyramid behind her, the nightwights in a loose half-circle all around. It was hard to tell in that dying light, but she thought some of the nightwights were those same ones who had stood staring at her before she jumped out of their lair the day before. *If you shaved and bathed and dressed them*, she thought, *they would look just like un-speckled Scriven.*

"I am like you," she said, trying not to her let voice shake, trying not to let her nose wrinkle at the stink of them. "I am one of you. You can see it. Look at my face. We are the same, you and I."

She didn't know if they could understand, but it seemed important to keep talking. "I wish my mother could have seen you," she said. "Wavey thought she was the last of her kind, but she wasn't. You are children of the Scrivener too..."

The nightwights gaped at her. The ones who had ventured into the tunnel were spilling out, coming to join their friends. Quickly, Fever reached into her pockets and took out the things she'd found inside the tower. "Gifts," she said. She held them out to the most elaborately befeathered of the 'wights, who backed away as if the things might bite. She set them down in the heather and they came closer, wary, looking to see what this strange young woman had brought them from inside their holy place. A surgeon's knife, brighter and sharper than any blade they'd seen. A silver dish. A white mug emblazoned with the words *Scrivener Institute*.

There was a muttering from the nightwights. Up on the pyramid's top Cluny and Marten were silent. A breeze ruffled the heather.

The nightwights hung back, but one, a boy not much older than Marten, came forward and gingerly picked up the mug. His eyes met Fever's. What did he see? Someone nightwight-like yet not a nightwight; someone who had been inside Skrevanastuut, and brought out these offerings, and spoken the name of the Scrivener. Perhaps, around their smoky fires in their burrows beneath the hills, his kind kept alive the memory of the first ones who had come from the pyramid, and he thought that she was one of them returned.

Whatever he saw, whatever he thought, this nightwight no longer seemed to view her as a meal. He grunted something and knelt down in front of her in the heather. Around him, slowly, all the others did the same, while Fever stood there nursing the friction burns on her hands and feeling silly, a messenger from the gods with no message to deliver.

A braying trumpet-call echoed from the hillsides, making her start. The nightwights seemed startled too. The sound came again. One turned and pointed south, shouting something.

Up out of a rocky defile there big shapes were moving. A trunk rose against the twilight and another trumpet-call battered at the walls of the pyramid. *Wild mammoths?* Fever wondered. But there were things on their backs, and as she strained her eyes to be sure of it a dazzling light appeared, sweeping across the weed-grown walls of Skrevanastuut to pin both her and the frightened nightwights in its beam. They hid their eyes and shrieked. Some fell on their faces and seemed to be trying to burrow into the ground as the mammoths came closer and more lamps were turned on. Gunfire crackled. Shot nightwights spun and fell. Fever dropped in the heather and curled as small as she could. Out from among the mammoths men came striding, blades gleaming, pistols spurting flame.

"It's Father!" shouted Marten, up on top of the pyramid. "He's brought help! We're saved!"

Beams from the mammoth-mounted lamps-o'-war raked across the heather, finding and blinding fugitive nightwights for the warriors to shoot down. Their pistols were empty now; they waded into the knots of terrified 'wights with swords and axes, slashing and hewing. A bolt thrower twanged in a mammoth's howdah. Above the screams of the dying nightwights a man was shouting, "Cluny? Cluny Morvish?"

Then the sounds of battle were gone. The Arkhangelsk warriors called out jokes to one another as they moved among the dead. Someone grabbed Fever by her coat and rolled her over and raised a hatchet above her and then stopped when he saw that she was not a nightwight. He started hauling her sideways towards the tunnel mouth, from which Cluny and Marten were scrambling to meet their rescuers. "Let me go!" Fever protested, but he just hollered at his comrades that she was his, until Cluny saw what was happening and shouted, "She's not to be harmed! She's not to be hurt!" and another man pulled Fever's captor off her, growling, "Do as the girl says!"

Fever rose shivering to her knees. Marten ran past her shouting the names of Lump and Carpet, leaping across the heather to greet the mammoths, who waited patiently behind the larger war-beasts. Men busied themselves lopping off nightwight heads to carry home to the *Kometsvansen* as trophies. The Scrivener Institute mug lay in the heather with its handle broken off. Close by in a clump of bracken a young nightwight hunter cowered, wounded, and shivering so hard that even the ferns around him shook. For a long moment Fever stared into his huge, scared eyes. Then she looked deliberately away. She did not want to draw attention to him.

A lean figure came uphill through the dusk, the tip of his staff pecking the earth in front of him. It had taken

Nintendo Tharp days to winkle the truth of Cluny's disappearance out of her foolish old father, but when he learned it, he had set out at once. He could not let the Vessel of the Ancestors endanger herself on some fool's errand to a haunted pyramid. "We were following your trail upriver when we found your mammoths wandering," he said, watching Cluny with his hard, bright eyes. "We saw your smoke this morning and came as fast as we could."

"Well," added another man, the blond-bearded warrior in leather armour who'd knocked down Fever's captor, "we made sure that it was twilight when we got here, so the nightwights would be in the open and we could make a slaughter of them!" He took off a dead 'wight's head with two blows of his sword and knotted it to his belt by its long hair. Fever risked a glance behind her at the ferns. The boy who had been hiding there was gone. The broken mug had vanished, too.

"We start back before dawn," Tharp said. "The Great Carn's heart-fortress has turned south. The march on London is beginning." He looked up at the pyramid. "What of this thing? Is there treasure inside?"

Cluny looked at Fever, and Fever had the feeling that a huge distance was opening between them. Tharp and his men were claiming Cluny back.

"It is a place of evil," said Cluny at last. "Burn it."

"Cluny!" Fever said.

"They were insane, those people of the old days," said

263

Cluny Morvish, looking down at her. "They were slaves to their own cleverness, just like you Londoners. Those Stalker-things up there are *still* slaves, remembering and remembering, without choice, or hope. Fire will free them. Burn it."

"But Cluny, they knew so much, and we shall again. I am not wise enough to understand this, but if I could bring my father here, or some of the other Engineers. . ."

Cluny bent down beside her. She said, "Fever-my-sister, I *do* understand it. You showed me; you brought me here; you made me see that these visions of mine are just the workings of an old machine. That's why we must roll on London and destroy it, you see. Because if we don't, you Londoners will resurrect all sorts of other bad old engines from the long-ago. Those old Ancients that you think so much of, they brought the Downsizing upon themselves. They left the world in ruins. This new world that we've made is better than theirs. Oh, Fever-my-sister, in a world of machines, people can't be free."

One of Tharp's men gagged Fever with a rag before she could argue. He bound her hands, and she was dragged away like a bundle while Cluny shouted, "She mustn't be harmed or assaulted. She has done no wrong. She is my sister." They heaved her up into a creaking wicker howdah, and through its weave she watched the nervous men take brush and burning torches into the tunnel beneath the pyramid. As the mammoth carried her away downhill, she looked back and saw the white smoke pouring from its apex; the smoke of lost knowledge, freckled with little glowing, dancing scraps just like the ones which had once risen from Godshawk's Head, except that these were not only the ash of ancient paper but flakes of the parchment flesh of all those age-old Stalkers.

She thought about that nightwight boy, the one who had survived. She thought about him fleeing back alone across the cold hills to his burrow. She hoped that he would get there safely. She wished that she was with him. She had more in common with the nightwights than with the Morvish.

PART THREE

26

PACKING UP

Those past few weeks in London had been busy ones. London had always been busy, of course, and busier still since Quercus took charge, but now the news from the north had raised things to a rare old pitch. Whole factories were on the move. The mills and foundries which had built the new city were being shifted aboard it; the cranes hoisted plastic-smelting vats and huge, egg-shaped steel-converters into place aboard the Base Tier, while land-barges and gangs of men piled cargo in the Gut. Cattle and sheep from the outlying farms were herded in as well, to be kept in dark, cramped, stinking pens which had sprung up between the supporting pillars.

The entire Guild of Engineers had relocated aboard the new city now. The Engineerium on Ludgate Hill had been demolished, and then all the buildings round it, the destruction spreading swiftly down the slopes. This time the pleas and complaints of the rich householders cut no ice with Quercus. Some of them moved aboard the new city too, although the big new homes they'd planned to build there weren't ready yet. Some ended up in Tent Town. Some loaded what they still possessed on wagons and took off for new lives in Hamsterdam and Paris, calling down curses on Quercus and his schemes.

The common people laughed and jeered, glad to see the rich cut down to size at last. "Good old Quercus!" they said, in the taverns of Tent Town. "That's shown them!" But they were uneasy. There were stories going round that Quercus was preparing to move London. Everybody knew of someone, some mechanic or site foreman, who had been ordered to move aboard the new city with his family. "But it can't move yet," they told each other. "That can't be right. It isn't finished. It'll be a right old squeeze, trying to fit us all aboard before those next two tiers go up." They fretted about the new threat from the north, and offered up uneasy prayers, but there was no one left to answer them; all London's old temples had been taken down, their timber and metal stored in the Great Under Tier.

From camps and vehicle parks outside the city bounds soldiers set off in long marching columns and squadrons of landships to shore up Quercus's defences in the Fuel Country. From the heights of the new city the Movement's gunners kept a constant watch, and the big naval guns swung on their turn-tables, so that it was hard to tell whether they were pointed at the hills from which Raven and his friends would come or at the restless, grumbling folk of Tent Town.

*

On the night Tharp's mammoths reached Skrevanastuut, Charley Shallow was stomping homeward through the mud beside London's starboard tracks. The city's wheels towered up on his right like cliffs, and the overhanging skirts of Base Tier kept him sheltered from the drizzle. He'd been supervising some last minute work on the exhaust chimneys at the city's stern, and he could have found his way back across Base Tier and up the elevators, but the place was so crowded with all these new people being moved aboard that he'd decided it would be easier to walk round to the front.

He'd been kept busy since his promotion. He had always imagined that the life of a full-fledged Engineer would consist of important meetings and posh dinners, but the meetings he had been to so far were dingy affairs, conducted by harried-looking men in grimy corners of the Engine District, and there were no dinners at all; he was lucky if he had time to cram in a pie or a sandwich on his way from one job to the next. Dr Crumb worked Charley as hard as he worked himself, summoning him at all hours, saying in a flat voice, "Copy this," or "Deliver that," sending him off to make checks on fuel-lines, exhaust ducts, torsion bars, tracks, wheels, drive sprockets... Never a "please" or a "thank you" or a "sorry for getting you out of bed at three in the black morning, Dr Shallow". Still called him Charley, too, which rankled. The other Engineers joked that Crumb's heart had broken when he heard the news about his wife and child, so he'd made a new one for himself all out of clockwork. They felt sorry for him in their way, but Charley had come to hate him.

Of course, he was glad of the importance which his new job brought him. Coldharbour and the other apprentices looked at him with real awe now. He had the sort of power he could only have dreamed of a few months before. But it was not in Charley's nature to enjoy his dreams once they came true. He was already dreaming new and better ones.

He turned across the city's bows, and was just striding towards the busy boarding ramps which would take him up into the Gut when a voice out of the wet twilight shouted, "Charley!"

It was a girl's voice, and as she came forward, all blurred by the rain and the dying light he got the sudden, horrible notion that this was Gwen Natsworthy's ghost, come to take her revenge on him. But when she got closer he could see that she was wide enough to make two Gwens, and when she pulled the hood of her cloak down it turned out that she was Milly Floater, the girl he used to walk out with before his luck improved.

Oddly enough, Charley felt pleased to see her. After those weeks of worry and hard work it was good to have her plain round face smile up at him again, and to remember times when he'd been free to wander round Tent Town with her, taking in shows and circuses. He still looked quickly behind him to make sure that nobody he knew could see him talking to her. "Hullo, Milly," he said.

"Hullo, Charley," said Milly shyly, pushing a strand of damp hair off her face while her eyes went up and down him, taking in his smart new clothes and the red Engineer's badge on his lapel. "Cor, look at you!"

"I gone up in the world, Moll," Charley said, and it felt good to slip back into his Ditch Street voice for once. He jerked his head at the new city. "I live up there now. The new Engineerium, right in the middle of Tier One, next to Quercus's own gaff. Assistant to the Chief Engineer himself, that's me. He depends on me."

"I heard," said Milly. "My dad saw your name in the news-sheets; they said you'd uncovered a plot and all sorts. You're an important man now, Charley. That's what I wanted to talk to you about."

Charley felt his mood start to sour. Of course, she'd not just stopped to pass the time of day. She wanted something.

"They're saying there's a list," said Milly. "People in Tent Town, I mean. Everyone knows there's not going to be room on that thing for all of us. Some people are saying there's lists being made of who gets to go and who stays behind. You know anything about that, Charley?"

"I ain't heard nothing about no list," Charley said. "You know how rumours run round Tent Town. Specially at a time like this."

"'Cos they're saying it's going to be essential workers

only, Charley," Milly blurted. "And my dad and mum and me and the little ones, we ain't essential, are we, not anyhow you look at it? So I was wondering if you could get our names on the list, Charley. 'Cos otherwise I'm scared we'll all get left behind, and St Kylie only knows what'll befall us then!"

"I ain't heard no talk of anyone getting left behind," said Charley warily. "Wouldn't be fair, would it? Everyone's equal in the new London."

She reached out suddenly and took his hands in hers; brought her face close to his. "Charley, you know that ain't true," she said. "Just look at the size of the new city, and then look at all the people in the old one, and you know it ain't true. I won't ask no more of you after this; I won't pester you for nothing, I promise; I know you probably got much finer girls than me up on that Tier One of yours. But just please get me and Dad and Mum and the nippers on that city when it goes. I wrote you out their names and everything. Please, Charley."

She pushed a scrunched-up bit of paper into his hand and he untwisted it and saw the names of her family written there in her round, childish hand, with little smiley faces instead of dots above the "i"s. It made him feel tall, standing there with her looking up at him in that pleading way. So he'd become the sort of man that people begged things from. Tall, and kind-hearted, but still one of the people, not some stuck-up cloot like the rest of the Engineers; he still remembered his roots. He thought about kissing Milly, but settled for patting her head instead, as if she were a dog. "I'll do it," he said. "I'll make sure. If there is such a list, you'll all be on it."

She was nearly pretty when she smiled. "Thanks, Charley!" she said. "Promise?"

"My word's my bond," he said.

"What's that mean?"

"It means I promise."

He really did mean it, too. It gave him a warm glow somewhere under the breast pocket of his wet white coat as he left her and went striding up the ramps. How grateful they'd be to him, those Floaters! They'd spread word of his kindness through all their neighbourhood once the new city was rolling: "That Dr Shallow, he's all right; he's not like the other toffs. . ."

But it wasn't a feeling that lasted. While he was waiting for the elevator to take him to Tier One he started to wonder whether Milly would keep her promise to him. Would she really stay away from him once she was aboard? *'Course she won't, Charley.* She'd always be looking him up, asking for something or other: work for her dad, bigger quarters, better rations. She probably still fancied him; still hoped he'd ask her out again, the silly cow.

And when the packed elevator was carrying him upwards, he started thinking how, if even Milly Floater had heard about Crumb's list, word of it must be all over Tent Town. He imagined them all out there, getting worried, getting angry. *If this new city's going to move,* he thought, *it had better move soon.*

The elevator reached its stop with an uneasy shudder. As he pushed his way out he dropped a little scrunched-up piece of paper into the used-tickets bin beside the door.

27

PHOSPHOROUS FINGERS

The Morvish rode through the dark until dawn came to meet them over the lowlands. These men drove their mammoths hard, lashing them with long whips when they dawdled, and when one stumbled in the night and fell they shot it, divided its crew and cargo among the other beasts and went on.

Fever, tumbled about on the howdah floor like a package in a hamper, slipped several times into thin sleep and bad dreams and woke at last to find daylight above her. A thin, end-of-summer snow was falling, and the mammoths were coming down a last dismal slope into the ruins of Aberdeen. The town had been abandoned before Fever was born, when the snouts of winter's glaciers started snuffling at its northern walls, but sometimes in summer nomad bands would pitch their tents there, and search the empty houses for things people had forgotten to take with them when they left.

There was a scatter of tents and campavans to the south of the town, and a Morvish landship was waiting there for

Tharp. While it was warming its engines, Fever's captors dumped her on the wet ground beside it and loosened the ropes on her wrists just enough for her to eat the grey and gluey porridge that they gave her. She wanted to speak to Cluny, but Cluny was busy in the headman's tent, and from the shouts and angry cheering that emerged Fever guessed that she was telling her vision of London again. She had been swept back into her role as prophetess; the spark and symbol of the nomads' rage.

Wistfully, Fever recalled her dream of staying in the hills with Cluny. It might even have been possible, if the nightwights could be reasoned with. And she knew they *could* be. That was the only treasure she had brought away from Skrevanastuut; the knowledge that the nightwights were her relatives, and she was not quite the last thing of her kind after all. *They could learn. I could teach them. The Scriven race could thrive again. . .*

But there was no way back, and the only nightwights within earshot of her now were the dead heads which Tharp's men were untying from their mammoths' harnesses and impaling on the prow-spikes of their landship. They set their standard there too: the red mammoth skull with its trailing horse-tails. Finally they dragged Fever up the boarding-ramp and slung her in a storage locker.

A few men left the party there, taking the weary mammoths back along the longshore to join the Morvish herds and the women and children in the *Kometsvansen*. Lump and Carpet went with them, and so did Marten. He wasn't pleased to go. "I should come with you to the war," he told Cluny. "I'm old enough to fight."

"And if you fall, Marten-my-brother, what then for the Morvish?" asked Cluny. "If things go badly in the south for us you will be Carn of our clan, and you will have fighting a-plenty to do."

"Cluny, please," he begged her. "You can tell Tharp the Ancestors want it. Let me come. I don't want to hide in the *Kometsvansen* with the women and the babies."

Tears in his blue eyes. Cluny wanted to hug him but dared not, for fear she'd hurt his spiky, twelve-year-old pride. She watched him climb up on Lump's back; watched him ride off behind Carpet and the other mammoths, wondered if she'd ever see him again. As she turned away a vision of London slammed into her, blasting in off the dry sea like a squall. She went down on her knees, and Tharp took her arm and helped her rise, leading her to his waiting landship.

In the locker where they had stuffed Fever there was a blanket and a bucket. Sometimes, if she was lucky, someone would come to empty the bucket and give her water and a little food. The only light was that which seeped in through a chink in the planking of the outer wall. For a while Fever thought about trying to widen that chink until it was big enough to escape through, but when she peeked out through it she saw there was no point; there was nowhere to run to out there and nowhere to hide. The landship was moving south across the old seabed, skirting shallow lakes, creeping through bogs on roads marked only by lines of wooden posts. It passed a line of armoured mammoths, then a convoy of clattering battle-trucks and a huge-wheeled, slave-powered landship stencilled with the markings of the Suomi. War horns howled, dinning across the flatlands. Beacon-smoke smudged the horizons.

She passed three days like that, and three bad nights; hungry, uncomfortable, frightened of the men who sometimes opened the locker door to leer in and pass comment on her, although they seemed awed enough by Cluny and the Ancestors not to touch her.

She did not see Cluny, and at first that made her glad. *You stupid, superstitious, smelly Morvish barbarian*, she thought, glaring at the ceiling of her prison as if it was Cluny herself. *No wonder the world is full of ignorance, when there are fools like you in it to set fire to all the wisdom of the Ancients.* But she could not stay angry at Cluny for long, not even in ceiling form. The other memories of her were too sweet. Anyway, Cluny had been right; what they had found at Skrevanastuut proved that the Ancients had been just as irrational as modern men, except that they'd waged their wars with far worse weapons. It was as painful to think about them as it was to think of Wavey, or Arlo, or others she had lost. Only in her memories of Cluny was there comfort. "I miss you," she said to the ceiling. "I love you."

*

By the fourth day the plains were dark with vehicles and lines of men and mammoths, all moving south. Tharp's landship cut south-easterly across the line of their march. It passed columns of Suomi dragging their primitive war-cars on mammoth-drawn sleds. It passed lines of fuel bowsers and supply wagons, then big white landships with carved upperworks; some pushing south with chimneys snorting steam, some broken down with their crews making hasty repairs. Tharp talked with their commanders, who pointed him south. Somewhere in the haze ahead, Raven's Jotungard and the Great Carn's heart-fortress were rolling side-by-side, the spearhead of this land-armada.

Tharp made them give him fuel and water, and headed on. "The Vessel of the Ancestors must be aboard the Great Carn's fort when we reach London," he told Cluny. "Without you, the Ancestors may not grant us victory in battle. Who knows what offence you have already caused them, taking off into the wilds like that?"

Cluny said, "What is to become of Fever Crumb?"

The technomancer's flinty eyes gleamed suspiciously. He had never liked that London girl. He could not fathom why Cluny wanted to protect her. He would have killed her already if Cluny had not kept telling him that the Ancestors wanted her alive. He said, "She is Rufus Raven's concern. The Ancestors cannot object to us handing her over to her rightful lord. Let Raven decide if he will keep her safe or send her to join her mother."

"You know what he will do!" said Cluny hotly. "You cannot let him have her! I forbid it!"

"You *forbid* it?" No one had ever spoken to Tharp like that; no one. "*You* forbid it?" The ways of the Ancestors were strange to him; of all the Arkhangelsk they might have chosen for their vessel, why had they picked this headstrong, infuriating girl?

They stopped to rest the engines for a while, but they were moving again before dawn, while landships and campavans rolled by on every side. "The north has woken!" shouted passing soldiers, cheering Cluny Morvish when Tharp made her stand up on the landship's prow with the banner and the gaping nightwight heads. "The north is on the move!" Away to the east, high towers of smoke were rising above the dried-out sea, marking places where battles were breaking out around the Movement's oil wells.

By sundown the engines were labouring again and Tharp called a rest while he prayed to the Repair Spirits. The ground shook as forts and landships rumbled by. A few stopped, recognizing Tharp's standard; their commanders came aboard, asking shyly if the Vessel of the Ancestors would bless them. They knelt before Cluny while she placed her hand on their heads and Tharp danced round her, chanting apps and words of power.

She thought, *It is all nonsense. The Ancestors have never touched my mind.* She kept thinking of the silver machines which Fever Crumb had shown her at Skrevanastuut. She kept thinking of the one in her own brain. She said gruffly to each man, "Go with our Ancestors' blessings."

Later, when Cluny was asleep, another barge pulled up alongside, and its master came aboard looking for Tharp. He was not seeking a blessing. He was no warrior, just a showman whose circus had been rattling around the north for a few weeks, entertaining the nomads as they mustered for their drive on London. His name was Borglum.

He stood in Tharp's cramped little cabin and looked up sceptically at the Technomancer. He said, "I've been hearing you got a Londonish girl here somewhere."

"Fever Crumb," the Technomancer said. "A nasty, sneaking creature; half Scriven."

"Last of her kind, I heard tell," said Borglum. "That makes her valuable to a man in my line of business."

"How valuable?"

"I have a purse of gold I'd give you for her."

Tharp considered. In his mind's eye the gold shone yellow as butter. "The girl would come to no harm?" he asked.

"Not unless you count having to perform for her living *harm*," said Borglum. "Not unless you count having to dress up in costume and go out in front of hard staring eyes and hear people say, 'Look at that nasty misshape' *harm*." He'd rightly guessed how Tharp felt about his prisoner, and knew he would be more likely to part with her if he thought she was going to a life of misery and humiliation. "And of course," he added, "there's always the chance of accidents in the ring. Most of my misshapes end up spiked on something pointy eventually. But that's their fault for getting careless; I ain't exactly *harming* 'em."

"Show me the gold," said Tharp.

When they came to wake Fever they didn't tell her she'd been sold. She didn't know what was happening as they dragged her away from Tharp's landship, through the light of the fires his men had lit to keep passing vehicles from running into it in the dark. She didn't recognize the *Knuckle Sandwich*, squatting in pointy silhouette against the glow of burning oil wells on the far horizon. Didn't even recognize Borglum and Quatch when they came out to take her from the Arkhangelsk. It seemed a million years since she had seen them; in that lost era before Wavey's death, before Cluny or Skrevanastuut. She had almost forgotten that she'd ever been a traveller with the Carnival of Knives.

And then she was inside, and the hatches were slamming shut, and as the old barge chugged and shuddered into motion they all came round her, Quatch and Borglum and Lucy the lobster-girl, Lady Midnight, Stick, all touching her, patting her, helping her to their warm cabin and saying, "You poor thing!" and "We're so sorry!", saying, "Your poor mother," and, "We thought you were dead. . ."

*

Borglum had arrived at Hill 60 the day after Fever left, and found the whole camp sizzling with gory stories about what had happened to Wavey Godshawk and her daughter.

"Is it true?" he'd asked, shoving his way into a meeting of Rufus Raven and his captains.

Raven nodded. The others exchanged sly glances. They'd all heard how little Borglum had once been in love with Wavey. Love was comical in a dwarf. They looked forward to seeing what he'd do.

"Where is she?" said Borglum. "Me an' my people, we'd care to give her burial. . ."

"Ash," said Raven, with a wave of his hand. "We burned her."

"Ash?" said Borglum. He found it hard to believe his Duchess was just gone. He'd feared the worst, but he'd expected at least a body. "A pyre, was it? Like burning dead leaves on a bonfire? Oh, that weren't the Scriven way. She'd not have liked that."

Raven said, "I could have given her to the Suomi, who'd have carved flutes from her bones and used her skin to make their battle drums. You think she'd have preferred that?"

Borglum shrugged. "Maybe. She always wanted to be musical."

Raven and his captains chortled. When Borglum pulled out a spotted handkerchief that could have served him as a bed-sheet and used it to wipe away a tear, they laughed still louder. Raven told him that he should stay at Hill 60, where the gathering forces of the north would be glad of entertainment. Borglum agreed. Later, almost idly, he would ask what had become of Wavey's girl, and be told she too was dead. He would look over the crag where she was said to have fallen, while the crossbowmen boasted, "A proper pincushion we made of her!"

"But a man in my business soon gets to know that you don't believe someone's dead till you've seen the corpse," said Borglum, sitting by Fever's side while the *Knuckle Sandwich* roared southward through the night. "Enough people saw your poor mum dead that I had to believe them, but not one had seen you, dear, so I reckoned you might be among the living yet. We hung round Hill 60, and we rolled around the north a bit, and we kept our ears to the ground, and we heard bits o' this, and bits o' that, and eventually we caught you up, and here you are."

"Thank you," said Fever.

"Never thank me," Borglum said. "You should hate me, rather. But for me and my talk o' the north, your mum would be breathing still, happy in London with that Crumb of hers. It was me brought her to this end, and don't I know it? And the only thing I could do to make amends, the small and single thing, was to find you living and keep you safe. That's the one thing the Duchess would have wanted."

"Well, there is that other thing, too," said Lady Midnight. She was sitting next to Fever with an arm about her shoulders, doing her best to be motherly.

"Oh yeah!" said Borglum. "I was forgettin' that. Stick, go up and check how we're doing, will you? We should be coming up on Jotungard soon."

"Jotungard?" said Fever with a start. She wondered suddenly if she could trust Borglum. "That's Raven's fort! Shouldn't we keep away from it?"

"Don't worry," said Borglum. He jumped down from his chair and started rolling up his sleeves. "We're just going to trundle alongside for a while. Master Raven won't mind. We're welcome aboard Jotungard any time. Why, just yesterday we went aboard and gave a special show for Raven and his captains and their ladies. I left something behind, though, so I need to sort it. You'd better help me."

"She's tired, Borglum," said Quatch. "She needs rest."

"She can rest all she likes when we're out of this river of steel," said Borglum, "but first there's something she needs to be part of. She'll regret it always if she ain't. You come with me, Fever dearie. We got something to do that'll please our poor Duchess, wherever she might be."

Fever didn't understand. She was tired and frightened and bruised from all those days in lockers and mammoth baskets, and she could not fathom what he wanted of her.

"It's the one *other* thing she would have wanted, see," said Borglum kindly. "You safe, that would have been first on her list, and don't you never doubt it. But second, and in quite large letters, underlined, she'd have put *Revenge*."

*

"Even clever men like Raven make mistakes," he explained, guiding Fever through the *Sandwich*'s smoky innards. "He sees a little chap like me and he can't quite bring himself to believe that I've got the same sized heart as him, and that I cared for your mother as much as ever he cared about anything. If I stood six foot tall he'd have said to himself, 'That Borglum, he's a danger. He was fond of the Duchess and I done her in, so now I can't never trust him, and I'd best get rid of him, too.' But 'cos I'm short he thinks I don't feel things the way full sized fellows do."

He came to his cabin door and swung it open; held it for Fever to step through. In the middle of the cabin squatted the paper boy machine. The light of a hanging lantern swayed and shimmered over its brass scrollwork and the plastic handles of its levers.

"Trouble is," said Borglum, flicking switches on its control panel, "my legs are too short to reach the pedals. So I thought you could do that, with those long Scriven shanks of yours, while I handle the murdering."

Jotungard and the Arkhangelsk heart-fortress were lumbering side by side across the plains, with lookouts stationed to keep watch and make sure neither pulled ahead of the other. This was the deal that Raven and the Great Carn had worked out; they would reach London at the same time, and share equally in the spoils. The great vehicles could move at barely more than walking pace, but around them the strongest and speediest of their landships rolled, and now and then, at prearranged coordinates, a few would break off and race away to assault a settlement or oil well whose garrison was still thought loyal to Quercus.

With all the coming and going in the vanguard, no one noticed the *Knuckle Sandwich* when it swerved down out of the north-west and came alongside Jotungard. The men in the *Sandwich*'s wheelhouse matched their course and speed with the huge castle; Stick, on lookout duty, shouted down a ventilator, "We're in position, boss!" All through the barge the carnival 'shapes crossed their fingers and offered up prayers to fierce and warlike gods. Borglum had told them all his plan and given all the choice to stay safe out of it, and a few had stayed behind in the north, but most had opted to come with him; they mourned the Duchess, and meant to see Raven suffer for what he'd done.

In his cabin, Borglum peered into the machine's flickery grey screen and waited for a picture to appear. "Yesterday, when we did our command performance for his Raven-ness, we left a little gift aboard his castle. One of your mother's paper boys slid in behind a tapestry down on the bottom deck. Now, if all this joggling and jolting don't break the signal up too much, I mean to wake it and send it 'bout its work. I'll teach Rufus Raven not to turn his back upon the little man."

Fever sat on the machine's saddle, pedalling quickly. She felt a dark thrill which she tried to calm, telling herself that Engineers did not approve of revenge.

"Just killing Raven, that would be the obvious thing," said Borglum. "Sneak the paper boy into his cabin while he's sleepin'; slit his throat with one almighty paper-cut. But I'm a showman, Fever. I'm an artist. Small of stature, but I think BIG. Kill Raven? That would be lettin' him off lightly. I'm going to kill him, and his people, and his castle, and his dreams, and any hope he ever had of winning himself a place in history with his treachery and grand alliances. A hundred years from now they'll worship old Quercus like a god, but mention Raven and they'll say, 'Who's he?'"

He thumped the side of the machine and a picture flickered and steadied on the screen. Just blackness, but when he worked the control levers the blackness slid aside, and a grainy, ghostly, grey-and-white image of a lamplit corridor appeared.

On Jotungard the paper boy slid sideways from behind the tapestry where Borglum had hidden it the day before. It wasn't a pale white cut-out, like the paper boys that Fever had once fought. The carnival crew had painted it with dark brown paint, and combed a pale grain through it with the tines of a fork before it dried. It looked like wood. In the dingy light of Jotungard's under deck it could pass for part of the wall until it moved.

It moved now, obeying the orders that came flicking into its electric brain from the machine in Borglum's cabin. It scuttled along the corridor on the edges of its paper feet, and stopped still and all but invisible against a wall as a pair of the Movement's red-robed technomancers ambled by.

"Where are you sending it?" asked Fever, peering over Borglum's head at the image on the screen as he started it on its way again. "Raven's cabins are on the upper decks, near the heart-chamber. . ."

"Never mind them," said Borglum.

"It would be wrong to harm anyone but Raven," Fever said nervously. "They were not responsible for what happened to Wavey."

"Keep pedallin'," Borglum growled. "Or go an' fetch someone else to pedal for me if you're feeling too high-minded. This is a *war* that's starting here. Who do you want to win? Your dad and his friends in London, or these barbarians with their murdering ways and their grubby, stupid prophetess?"

"Cluny Morvish isn't grubby," said Fever. "Well. . . She isn't stupid."

"Friend of yours now, is she?" Borglum asked.

"She's. . . Yes."

"Then the best thing you can do for her is end this war now, before she gets herself killed."

"What was that?" asked Fever, seeing white words drift across the screen.

It was a sign, bolted to the corridor wall, and Borglum's paper boy had just stalked past it. It said, *Powder Magazine: No Naked Flames Beyond This Point*. There was a drawing of an explosion underneath, for the benefit of crewmen who couldn't read.

A guard stood outside the magazine's iron-bound door,

but it is hard to guard a door when you know there are no enemies within a hundred miles. The guard was thinking about the girl he'd left at Hill 60, and when he finally realized that the paper boy was not just a shifting shadow on the passage wall he did not know what it was, or what to do. He raised his crossbow and put a quarrel through it. It came on with a small hole torn in it, the quarrel quivering in the planking of the wall behind. The scared guard dropped his bow and drew his sword, but Borglum had grown good at running paper boys during the shows he'd put on those past few weeks, and he crumpled it and spun it past the guard's feet and stood it up and smoothed it flat again. It slid like bad news through the tiny crack between the door and its frame.

Inside the magazine, in the wan, swaying light of the electric lamps, Raven's chief gunner and his mates looked up from the gunpowder they were scooping into pannikins, the big brass-bound shells they were easing off their racks.

Ever the showman, Borglum made the paper boy take a little bow as he turned it to face them.

Out in the corridor the guard began to toll a handbell.

Up in the heart-chamber, Raven looked up from the reports he had been reading. His wife put down her knitting.

Fever, legs aching now, kept pedalling. Sometimes, later, she would wonder if she should have stopped.

The paper boy held up its hands. Each finger was

painted with a greenish thimble of phosphorous sesquisulfide and potassium chlorate. It reached out both paper arms and dragged its fingers over the rough planking of the walls. The phosphorous blobs flared into flame, fierce and white and shaped like ears of corn, blinding the paper boy's electric eyes, bleaching the screen in Borglum's cabin white.

"Get us clear!" yelled Borglum.

"Get us clear!" boomed Quatch, stationed outside his door.

"Get us clear!" shouted Stick, up in the lookout.

The *Knuckle Sandwich* swerved away from Jotungard's skirts, plunging across the path of another fortress, speeding into the darkness ahead of the armada. Misshapes crowded to the portholes. Borglum scrambled from his cabin and up a companionway on to the spiny roof. Fever went after him. The forts were falling swiftly astern; signal lanterns flashing as they asked each other who was commanding that scruffy barge that had just broken ranks. Sleet blew past on the wind.

"Nothing's happening," said Stick.

"Wait," said Borglum. "Wait."

The light came first, breaking like sunrise from the base of Jotungard. The light; and then the noise; the thunder rolling across the plain, past the speeding *Sandwich* and on into the lands beyond. Amid the thunder Jotungard was seen to lift, and slew, and twist, and then it was not a castle at all but a jigsaw of black fragments all parting company with one another, pushing outwards on one red spreading rose of an explosion after another as the powder magazine set off the boilers and the boilers set off the fuel store, and the neighbouring vehicles veered and braked and some ran themselves right under the wheels of the Arkhangelsk heart-fortress in their efforts to avoid the axles and hubs and sponsons and shards of upperwork and armour which were coming down now all around.

And on the *Knuckle Sandwich*, under the thunder and the engines' roar, there was an awed and respectful quiet among the watchers. But Borglum stood at the stern rail with his clothes flapping in the breeze and raised a flask of brandy that he'd taken from his pocket; held it up gleaming in the fires of Jotungard.

"You sleep sound now, Wavey dear," he said.

28

MOVING ON

Charley woke to the sound of thunder. When he was a nipper he'd been afraid of storms, and he sat up now in his bed confused and panicky, waiting for the lightning.

But it wasn't really thunder. 'Course not. It was London's engines warming up. The vibrations shivered through him; the springs of his bedstead sang; the glass on his bedside table jittered and sloshed, and the pens in their pot on his tiny desk all trilled together like crickets. The whole room was a-shudder, and his neighbours must have woken too, because he could hear no snoring coming through the walls.

It took Charley about three blinks, about three beats of his heart to understand what was happening. Then he was up, groping for his clothes, thinking, *This is it!* He dressed, laced his shoes, and blundered out of the room, pulling on his new white coat as he went. In the passage outside he met dozens of other Engineers all doing likewise. They went down the stairways of the building in a white tide. "Is it another test?" Charley heard one man ask, and a second answered, "Can't be; not at this hour. This is real."

Out they went into the patchy glare of the electric lamps on B:19 Street (which they all called Geargate). "Look!" said someone, pointing to the street's end and the darkness beyond the tier's edge there, and they looked, and saw far-off hills thrown suddenly into black silhouette by the pale flashes leaping up the northern sky.

"Lightning?"

"Guns."

"Far off, though."

"Not far enough."

"To your stations!" a senior Guildsman was bellowing. "To your stations! Dr Shallow, Dr Crumb is asking for you. . ."

. . .while out in Tent Town the common folk of London were scrambling from their beds, stumbling in darkness or in lantern light to their tents' doors, staring at their new city, which lit the earth around its wheels with the glow of furnaces and sent up streamers of steam and smoke against the stars.

"Is it another test?"

"Maybe the Arkhangelsk are coming. . ."

"Quercus is leaving!"

"He can't be. Not without us. . ."

Nervous-looking squads of coppertops moved from street to street, collecting the last of the workers whose names appeared on Dr Crumb's list. "Report aboard the new city at once. There's an emergency. Yes, bring your family. Quickly." The plumes of smoke that striped the sky were thicker now. The ground seemed to jump to the rhythm of the engines. Milly came to the doorway of her family's shack and looked out across her city, lit now by the torches of the crowd as well as by the lamps and furnaces of the new London. "They are leaving without us!" said her dad, out in the street. He looked back at her quickly with wide, frightened eyes. Behind her in the shack her baby sister started to wail.

She ran outside to join him. "It will be all right," she said. "Charley's got us on that list. He *promised...*"

Her father didn't seem to be listening. He shook his head, said disbelievingly, "The new city ain't ready! It can't move yet!"

Milly could not quite believe it either, despite the rumours she had heard. It was too terrible to believe; she only wished she had not been born into such times as these. She could sense that there would be paintings made about this night one day, and stories told, and great songs sung, for hundreds of years, long after she was dead. She wished she could be one of them future people listening to the stories, instead of herself, stood helpless and afraid here at the start of things.

"It's all right," she said again. "They'll come and fetch us aboard. Charley promised..."

Sure enough there were men shouting in the neighbouring street; the white coat of an Engineer and the gleaming cap-badges of coppertops glimpsed between the tents, shouting names: "Maltby: quickly; bring your family. Aaronson; where is the Aaronsons' tent?"

Milly stuck her head in through the hut door, into the wailing of the baby, the sleepy questions of her brothers. "Get ready!" she shouted. "Pack some stuff! We're going aboard the new city. . ."

As Charley hurried into the control room Dr Crumb turned towards him, and the reflections of electric lamps slipped across the lenses of his icy little spectacles. "News from the north, Charley. Quercus says that we must leave now; tonight."

Thank the gods for that, thought Charley, who had not much fancied waiting for the traitor Raven and his savage allies to arrive.

"You'll stay with me," Dr Crumb was saying. "I may need a runner to take messages to the outer sectors. . ."

All around him, lesser Engineers were eyeing their gauges as pressure built in London's engines. A man ran up to report a problem in one of the fuel feeds and Dr Crumb turned to consider it, forgetting Charley. The rising rumble of the engines filled the caverns of Base Tier, and now for the first time Charley felt the city stir, edging forward just an inch as the wheels slithered in London clay.

"Those poor devils outside," muttered an apprentice.

Charley wondered for a moment who he meant. He'd forgotten his promise to Milly Floater long ago.

*

Outside again, pushing past her father, hopping guy-ropes, running between the tents to pluck at the sleeve of that Engineer. She'd half hoped it might be Charley himself, but it was an older man, looking down his nose at her as she blurted, "Please, sir, my family and me are on the list. Floater's the name. You'll see us there. Dr Shallow put us there himself. . ."

The Aaronsons hurried past, carrying their belongings in sacks and suitcases, chivvied towards the new city's boarding stairs by scared-looking coppertops. The Engineer glanced down at his list and shook his head. "No Floaters here." Turning away now. "Dyce? William Dyce?"

"Please!" shouted Milly, grabbing at him again, but a policeman shoved her aside. She fell, and by the time she was on her feet again the Engineer and his bodyguard were hidden from her by a hedge of other people, all demanding to know what was happening, or shouting out reasons why they must be allowed aboard the new city. "Please!" Milly screamed. "We are on the list! Charley promised!"

Now, in the sullen red light that seeped from the Engine District, the lucky ones could be seen climbing the stairways into the new city. Those left behind, the untrained labourers and shopkeepers and keepers of canvas pubs whom Dr Crumb had deemed worthless, all looked on in growing fright. The engine smoke drifting past them stank of betrayal. They had trusted Quercus. They had paid him the taxes he asked of them, and most had believed the promises he gave them in return. Now, in the dark, in the cold, they were learning the most important rule of politics: the government was not their friend.

From Clerkenwell and old St Kylie the first angry shouts arose. Torches were kindled; people surged to the stairways. As the coppertops hurried the last of their charges up into the city bricks and bottles began to fall on them. Caught in the crowd's tide, Milly was swept away from her family. She broke free and tried to scurry home along a side-street between rows of empty tents, but a strange barricade blocked her way. She stood and stared at it for half a minute before she realized what it was. Dead horses were heaped up there. There had been a stable in that street, and someone had brought all the horses out and shot them and just left them lying there. Milly put a hand up to her mouth. She'd liked those horses. She used to bring her little brothers and sisters down to pat their noses sometimes and feed them apples. Now their blood was soaking through the soles of her shoes. "Who'd do such things?" she said, and a man running past her paused and shouted, "It was the coppertops, of course. They're shooting all the horses. Mammoths too. If we had horses we could keep up with their new city, and they don't want that!"

That was when it finally became real to Milly. She turned back towards the city. The crowds were boiling around the feet of the stairways. Some men were climbing the tracks; others had scrambled up to the towering doors of the Gut and were trying to force them open. Through the din of the engines Milly heard the crack of rifles, and she didn't think it was just horses they were shooting any more. Then the engines roared louder still, drowning out the shots. The city shivered. Its wheels began to turn. The giant tracks slithered against wet earth, then found a purchase, inching forward over the aprons of rubble that had been packed in front of them.

The voice of the crowds rose in a despairing wail. The guards on the stairways were overwhelmed as people began to swarm up them: men in nightshirts wielding picks and spanners, frightened children, babies held up above their mother's heads in baskets like tiny boatmen on a violent sea. But the stairways were shivering; twisting; wrenched sideways as the city moved. At their heads, the Lord Mayor's men swung axes, cutting them free. One fell and then another, crashing down into the shadows between those huge wheels. On the city's edge a crane collapsed, tugged from its footings. Then another and another; one by one their legs buckled under them and they knelt down like weary giraffes and then pitched forward, a ripple spreading outward through the crowds as people under them fought to escape.

A few people, mostly men, had managed to struggle up on to the city's skirts and could be seen there battling with the Lord Mayor's soldiers, but by now most had given up all hope of getting aboard. Pushing away from the city, they left a circle of clear ground around it as it revved its

301

engines and began to turn, spewing smoke and sparks and smuts over the masses now fighting to escape its wheels.

Poor Milly, caught in the midst of them again, found herself jostled and shouted at and elbowed, knocked to her knees and nearly trampled flat. Women were shrieking and men were cursing and tents were blazing into flame, and the last cranes crashed down in ruin as the new city tore free of them. The tracks on the southern side kept rolling forward; those on the north went into reverse. The city turned laboriously, like a gigantic baby shuffling round on its bottom. It was not turning south, as everyone had expected. Slowly, slowly, it turned its back on Tent Town, and the engine's roar increased. Huge sections of scaffolding up on the unfinished higher tiers collapsed, spilling from its stern in an avalanche of timber as it began to crawl away.

Some people followed it, still hoping that somehow they might fight their way aboard. Some ran the other way. Some, like Milly, just knelt staring at the deep watery wounds where it had stood, and the wheel ruts stretching black across the rubble-fields, ploughing through the lower slopes of Ludgate Hill. She watched the new city pull away, moving faster now, dwindling slowly towards the flickers of white lightning in the far north-east.

"You're a dirty liar, Charley Shallow!" she shouted at it. But there was so much other shouting going on that no one heard her.

*

302

Dr Crumb, feeling a little dizzy from the heat and all the sleepless nights he'd spent preparing for this one, walked out of the control chamber and through the roaring Engine District. Everything seemed to be running smoothly, although he sensed a slight sluggishness in the larboard engines; the outer banks of tracks on that side were moving slower than the rest, and every few minutes the steersmen had to make a slight adjustment to the city's course. He would have to look into that. But not quite yet.

He kept walking till he reached the city's after-edge, from where he could look back upon the place that it had left behind. A mass of moving things covered the earth back there, their struggles lit fitfully by burning tents and the pinpoint flames of torches. He could make out no faces, no individuals, and he found that he felt no more pity for them than he would feel for protozoa swarming on a microscope slide. A cool and rational pride awoke in him as he recognized that he had finally achieved what he had set out to long ago. He had left all feeling behind him, along with those useless people and their useless tents. He had at last become a man of reason: a new man for a new age.

29

TOASTED SANDWICH

In spite of everything, in spite of the wild racketing and rocking and the steady fear, Fever fell asleep, dreaming uneasily, waking now and then just long enough to stop herself from being hurled out of her borrowed bunk when the *Knuckle Sandwich* rattled across some particularly rough bit of terrain. Big as it was, the carnival barge sometimes seemed to become airborne as it sped over the hummocks of the former seabed. The lookouts on the stern had reported no signs of pursuit, but Borglum would take no chances. "We just killed their chief and smashed their strongest fort," he growled. "That's liable to annoy."

She slept deeply. Once she woke and looked out of the porthole by her bunk and saw nothing but the night and the mist and the roadside bushes lit by the flare from Borglum's furnaces. She dropped her head into the pillow, into the smell of Lady Midnight's perfume (for the blind fighter had lent Fever her cabin), and slept again, and woke to hear voices bellowing somewhere above her head.

"Lights astern!"

She was awake all at once. She scrambled into the main cabin, where most of the others were crowded at the windows. Quatch turned his kindly, hairy face to her and said, "We ain't too worried yet, miss. We have the auxiliary engine running. They may not catch us."

"What if they do?" asked Fever.

Lady Midnight looked at her with those startling white eyes. "If they want to stop us then they'll have to board us, and once they board, their shooting instruments won't do them no good."

"And you have your Stalker. . ." said Fever.

"Not really, miss," the Knave of Knives put in. "Your mum fixed him so he will not kill, to avoid unfortunate accidents in the ring. . ."

"Besides which," said Quatch, "he is the auxiliary engine, you see. There is a treadmill down below, and he runs in it."

"Don't you fear, Miss Fever," Lady Midnight said. "We don't need old Ironsides to defend us. We are the Carnival of *Knives*."

Stick, face pressed to the window glass, raised his voice above the rest. "Those lights are getting *closer*. . ."

Should you ever wish to discombobulate a land-armada, there are few better ways to do it than by blowing up its admiral's traction castle. In the centuries that followed, historians of the Traction Era would refer to "Borglum's Gambit" and waste a lot of ink and paper bickering about whether the destruction of Jotungard had been the first real battle of the Northern War, or whether that honour belonged to the fighting that broke out around Three Dry Ships a few hours later. They all agreed on the facts, however. Jotungard had exploded, killing almost everyone on board and damaging many of the vehicles bunched around it, most of which had been Raven's. In that moment the leadership of the armada passed from Raven and his captains to the Great Carn of Arkhangelsk. Lit by the gaudy, dying-down fires of the wreckage of Jotungard his huge fortress pulled over and gathered its lesser forts about it as the Carns went aboard to hear how the battle-line was being rearranged.

While they debated, Raven's surviving captains wondered what to do. Many turned their forts and landships quietly aside, figuring that with Jotungard gone there was no way this northern rabble could outfight Quercus. Others, who feared Quercus less or had loved Raven better, set about avenging him. Their heavy landships could not catch the unarmoured *Knuckle Sandwich*, but they sent a squadron of monowheels south, with armed campavans to provide support, and orders to take or destroy the carnival barge.

Cluny Morvish heard the howl of the departing 'wheels as Tharp led her through the firelight and the chaos to present her at the rear hatch of the Great Carn's fort. There were Stalkers on guard there; gifts from Raven to the Great Carn, for the Arkhangelsk had no Stalkers of their own.

They had orders to let no one pass, for everyone was afraid that there might be plots afoot to sabotage this fortress too, but when their mortal officers saw the girl waiting there with Tharp on their doorstep they cuffed the resurrected men aside and welcomed her in, asking meekly for her blessing as they led her up the stairways to the Carn.

All Cluny could see were the red fingers of firelight that poked in through every arrow-slit and gun port. *This is a real war*, she thought, *and I have started it.* But she had not *chosen* to start it; it had all been done by the machine in her head. She had no more control over her life, it seemed, than those Stalkers on sentry-go outside the Great Carn's door. She wished her friend Fever could have been there to help her think it all through. Or was it just the old man's memories in her head that had made Fever Crumb seem such pleasant company?

Anyway, Fever was lost now; sold by Tharp to passing showmen. Cluny had screamed at him when he told her. She would have punched his smug old face if some of his men had not held her back. She had threatened to open the spigot on his stupid hat and boil him. She wished she had now, but a vision of London had come and the fight had gone out of her. Fever was lost, and there was nothing for her to do but follow Tharp meekly up the heart-fort's winding stairs.

The Great Carn's council-chamber was packed with men. Carved dragon heads snarled from the hammer-beams. More of Raven's Stalkers stood guard around the walls. Cluny's father was there and she wanted him to hug her, but such was her dignity now that he dared not touch her, or even smile. Tharp pushed her past him, towards the Great Carn and his advisors, towards their spread-out maps and plans of war, taking Cluny with him, leading her into the destiny that she could not escape.

The monowheels swept southward, leaping ditches like rolled hoops, the heavier campavans clattering behind them. Searchlights swept the ground ahead, fingering the deep, fresh wheel-marks Borglum's barge had left.

"Well," said Borglum, watching through his telescope as the gap between them and the *Knuckle Sandwich* slowly thinned. "I thought we'd make for London, but scratch that. Those bloggers will be on us in a half hour. Anywhere closer we can aim for, Master Fenster?"

The *Sandwich*'s steersman looked doubtful. He drew a finger southward down a chart which he'd pinned to the wheelhouse wall. "There's fighting going on all over, boss. You seen those gun-lights flashing on the clouds?" He knew a thing or two of battles, Fenster did; he'd driven stompers for the Oster-Rus before an anti-misshape Tsar seized power and took objection to his wide, six-fingered hands. "If I was Quercus," he said, "I'd aim to make a stand here; where the road crosses this here ridge. We should find soldiers there who're loyal to London."

"How far?"

"An hour, maybe."

"Let's go then. I'll tell everyone to look lively. Them as can fight: to the hatchways."

Fever thought that she was one of them as could fight. "I can handle a firearm," she said, recalling the hard thump of Cluny's arquebus when she gunned that nightwight down, and hoping the *Knuckle Sandwich*'s gunroom held something a bit less primitive; Bugharin rifles, maybe. But it turned out that the *Knuckle Sandwich* didn't *have* a gunroom. "Blades is all we use," said Stick, as he and Fever hurried to the armoury. "Who'd pay to watch gunplay? There's no artistry in guns."

He got that straight from Master Borglum, Fever thought, and maybe it was true. By that time shot from the long swivel cannon on the campavans was starting to clatter against the *Sandwich*'s hull, and it didn't sound very artistic. She went down into the oven of the under-deck, where the Stalker was running tirelessly on his treadmill and everyone else was helping to shovel wood and sea-coal into the furnaces and trying to keep out of the way of the jets of steam which kept squealing from the boilers' safety valves. It was backbreaking work, down there in the heat and the furnace-light. Within minutes sweat had plastered Fever's hair across her eyes and soaked through the armpits of her clothes in dark half-moons, but at least amid the thrashing of the pistons she could not hear the shot pecking at the barge's stern. *If we can just keep going*, she thought, trying to estimate the relative speeds of barges, campavans, monowheels, *if we can just keep moving, perhaps they'll give up. . .*

Above decks the mist was thinning. The moon appeared: the Scrivener's Moon; near full, shining on swift campavans and blazing silver on the rims of monowheels. It glittered on the points of the first grappling hook that the pursuers flung, and Borglum himself saw it and went scrambling along the upperworks to hack it free before the men who'd thrown it could climb out of their campavan and swarm aboard. They opened up on him with a panpipe-gun mounted on the campavan's roof, but he was too small a target and he scuttled back into the wheelhouse unharmed. On either side now the pursuers were pulling forward, racing along beside his good old barge.

"Faster!" he yelled at his steersman.

Master Fenster shook his head. He was amazed that the old ship was still going *this* fast.

"Then we must lighten her!" yelled Borglum.

Fever, lost in a waking dream of heat and work below decks, heard them calling her name, and the names of all those others who weren't essential to the engines' running. Then she was upstairs again, and they were tearing the *Knuckle Sandwich* apart, grabbing everything that was not bolted down, unbolting all the things that were, slinging anything that would burn downstairs to feed the furnaces and lugging the rest to the side hatches, where the waiting defenders helped to hurl it out into the rushing dark. An impertinent monowheel came dashing alongside with a man leaning from its hub-cabin to shoot a musket at them, but Stick hit him in the face with a well-aimed plaster statuette from the Temple of All-Knowing Poskitt at Kjork. The gunman pitched backwards, his pilot lost control and the monowheel veered away and fell on its side among the gorse bushes.

The rest hung back for a while after that, but as Fever helped the crew shove more of their belongings through the hatch she sometimes heard the crack of musketry, and sensed things whirring past like wasps. When she went into Lady Midnight's cabin to pull apart the bunk she'd just been napping on she found the outer wall pierced all over, like lacework, all the furniture and hangings shredded, spent carronade balls rolling around like marbles on the deck. She had lost all sense of how much time had passed since the chase began. It seemed like seconds; it seemed like days. Back in the corridor she saw herself reflected in an ornate mirror that somebody passed to her. A soot-blacked face with wide, white, frightened eyes, striped where streams of sweat had washed the smuts away. If Wavey could have seen her she'd have said, "Oh, Fever, what have you done to yourself?" That made her start to laugh as she dragged the mirror towards the hatch, but she stopped quickly, because she had blundered into the middle of a battle.

One of the campavans had finally drawn close enough to the *Sandwich*'s starboard quarter for men to leap the gap. They had landed unnoticed, and scrambled quickly along the barge's side to reach the hatch. One of them had pistolled the Knave of Knives before he could slam it shut, but their other shots had all missed – it was no easy thing to aim a gun with the barge bucketing beneath them like a maddened mammoth – and now that they were through the hatchway there was no time to reload; it was sword against sword, and Borglum's fighters were well-used to swords. Fever cowered behind the mirror until it was over; till Lady Midnight ran the last man through and kicked his body from the hatchway. Others slammed the hatch shut as she turned away, touching her blood-stained cardigan. "Don't suppose that will *ever* wash out," she said, mock-rueful, trying to raise a laugh. She had not realized yet that the Knave was dead. The others gathered round him where he lay. Fever left her mirror propped against a bulkhead and edged away, leaving them to their grief. She could hear the crash of axes as the crew below broke up the last of the furniture and started on the decking. She wondered if they would have agreed to Borglum's plan if they had known what it would cost them.

The next assault came on the other side of the barge, but it was bungled; two men fell beneath the wheels as they jumped across; the rest were beaten off by Quatch before they could make it through the hatchway. The campavans and 'wheels fell back again, grouping astern.

"Look! They've had enough!" crowed Stick, his voice echoing through the empty spaces where cabins used to be. He could not see what the pursuers could. From beneath the *Knuckle Sandwich* long pennants of fire were licking at the ground. The speeding barge now trailed a train of sparks and oily smoke.

The first Fever knew of it was when the brakes went on, a sudden juddering that was somehow different from all the juddering that had gone before. "Abandon ship!" hollered Borglum, dropping down through the trapdoor from the smashed wheelhouse. "Fire! Fire!" people were shouting, scrambling up the companionways from the engine room, the flames behind them casting their jerky, misshape shadows up the smoke. Someone was trapped down there, shrieking. In the confusion, some of the 'shapes thought it was another attack and ran this way and that with weapons ready, blocking the corridors. "Abandon ship!" Fever shouted. "Or we'll be blown as high as Raven. . ."

But there wasn't enough fuel left aboard the *Sandwich* for a real explosion. The barge just burned, wrapping itself in flame as the survivors of the carnival jumped from the hatches and hurried into the firelit scrub. Looking back, Fever glimpsed the Carnival's Stalker for a moment, still mindlessly working his treadmill as the walls collapsed around him, a runner in a wheel of fire. Sparks danced. Beyond the flames, the monowheels rolled to and fro, their engines moaning, a shot ringing out from time to time.

"Poor old barge," said Master Fenster, pulling off his hat.

"Poor *Sandwich*," said Lucy, and her face was bright with tears in the flame-light.

313

"Toasted," said Stick, with his arm around her.

"We're done for now," said Lady Midnight. "They'll hunt us down one by one. They've already got the Knave and Webfinger Joe."

"No," said Borglum. He wasn't watching the blaze or the monowheels; he'd turned to look southward instead. "The *Sandwich* brought us far enough. Look."

Fever turned. There in the moonlight a mile away a long ridge rose, whale-backed and somehow familiar. It was Dryships Hill, where she had once sat looking at the fires of the far-off Fuel Country. Just as she realized that, the lights of big vehicles appeared over its crest: one, two, three landships, and their guns went off with stabs of flame and puffs of moonlit smoke, and shells began to fall close to the monowheels, scattering them, drowning out the shrill howl of their engines as they fled.

"Hands up, hands up, all of you," Borglum was saying. "We haven't escaped from that lot just to get ourselves splattered by the other side." He had his short arms up above his head, and Fever copied him, and so did all the others, and they stood there with their backs to the heat of their burning barge as the infantry of London came hurrying down the scarp.

"Miss Crumb? We had heard that you were... I am glad to find it is not true. You came from the north?"

Fever knew this man; his curly hair and honest, northern face. She remembered Wavey pointing him out to her across the heads of dancers in the Great Under

Tier at Quercus's ball all those months ago. Captain Andringa.

"Have you seen anything of the traitor's fortresses?" he asked, turning from her to Stick and Stick to Lady Midnight, but they were all too shocked by the night's events to answer. He said, "I was sent out by Quercus to find them."

"Well, you'd better hurry back to Quercus then," said Borglum. "'Cos they're coming to find you. I sorted out Raven for you – don't thank me, it was my pleasure – but I reckon every scrap 'o' armour Arkhangelsk possesses is still hammering across that seabed. You'd better run home to London, and take us with you if you please."

Andringa's men were jogging past him, kneeling among the gorse, shooting after the withdrawing monowheels. He looked sideways, left and right along the slope of the hill, at the black hulks of Three Dry Ships on their reef of outbuildings. Around his landships on the ridge Stalkers were moving, their green eyes shining. "No," he said. "We won't be running. We shall hold them here."

"Hold them?" said Fever. "There are hundreds! Landships, forts, Stalkers. . ."

"Hold them?" scoffed Borglum. "What's to stop them just going round you?"

"There are marshes east and west of here," said Andringa. "Unless they want to go far out of their way then they must cross this hill. Besides, the Arkhangelsk are warriors. They always point their vehicles towards the sound of the guns. The flames from your barge will call them like a beacon."

Between the charred ribs of the *Knuckle Sandwich* the fires were dying down. Beyond them, along the black horizon, other lights were showing now, as the vanguard of the northern armada came hull-up. Andringa studied them, nodded. "We will hold them here for as long as we can. We can buy the Lord Mayor some time, at least."

"Time? Time for what?" Borglum complained.

"To get London away," said Andringa, as if it were obvious. "Your father has been busy, Miss Crumb. The engines are complete. Quercus is moving the city."

30

AT THREE DRY SHIPS

I t wasn't hard to see why the crew of the *Knuckle Sandwich* had not noticed Three Dry Ships until they were almost upon it. Not a light showed in the windows of the beached hulks, nor in the low huddle of buildings round about them. The townlet was deserted, its people fled before the coming storm.

"And that's what we should do too," Stick said, as he and Fever and the rest went to shelter inside the largest of the old ships. They looked into the empty cabins that were shops and homes now; all showed signs that their owners had departed in a hurry. A ginger cat mewled at them, looking up jealously from the half-eaten remains of some family's forgotten supper. "We should run, I reckon," Stick said. "Leave these London soldier boys to fight their battle."

"Stick, how can we?" Lucy said, holding tight to his hand with her pincer. "We're too tired. We need to rest."

"No good runnin'," Borglum said. "There's no vehicles nor animals left in this dump."

"We could go on foot, and hide in the marshes," Stick suggested.

"Very likely we could, Master Stickle," said the dwarf. "And very likely Arkies on foot will come and hunt us there if they win this fight. Anyway, I'm a trifle short to go wading about in sloughs. No, we'll wait and see what happens. Maybe Andringa really can hold these northern nanas off. If he don't, we'll prevail on him to find a space for us aboard one of his landships when he goes running back to Quercus. Till then, we might as well stop here. At least there's *beds*."

So they lay themselves down on beds abandoned by the folk of Three Dry Ships and there they slept, or tried to. Their dreams were bad, and several times that night Fever was woken by the sound of cannon fire, far off, but never far enough.

The third time she woke the sky outside was growing pale. She knew that she could sleep no more without knowing what was happening, so she rose and pulled on her boots (she had slept in all her other clothes) and climbed silent stairways to the old ship's deck. There, between the chicken-coops and the clothes lines of forgotten washing, Andringa and a dozen other Movement captains stood talking together on the sterncastle, passing a telescope between them. More London landships had arrived in the night and were parked all over the slope of the hill behind the town.

One of the men saw Fever come up out of the stairway. "What's she doing here?" she heard him say.

Captain Andringa told him, "Miss Crumb and her friends have done more already in this war than you," and beckoned her forward. "Miss Crumb!" he said as she reached him. "I was hoping we might spare a barge to carry you home, but it seems we shall have need of them all today. . ."

He pointed to the north. There, on the rolling land where the *Knuckle Sandwich* still smouldered, strange shapes had appeared. Neat-edged plantations of young trees, Fever thought at first, and wondered how she had not noticed them before. Then she started to see movements among them, and men on horses cantering from one to another, and she realized that each of those bristling squares and oblongs was a unit of men: soldiers standing motionless with their pikes and long, north-country muskets pointed at the sky. Between them in the mist waited squadrons of campavans and the big hard shapes of landships, grey as outcrop stone in the dawn. Far behind them she could just make out still larger shapes: the traction castles of the Arkhangelsk Carns, gathered about the Great Carn's heart-fort. They were being held back ready for the moment when their smaller, faster moving comrades shattered the Londoners' defensive line. *Which one is Cluny on?* Fever wondered. *What is she doing, now, at this instant?*

"We'll be hard pressed," said the man who had complained about Fever when she came on deck.

"We held them at Hill 60," said Andringa.

"Our *Stalkers* held them," said another man. "They have Stalkers of their own now, thanks to Raven."

"We'll hold them just the same."

Borglum came clambering up the same stair Fever had used. "What, you lot still here?" he asked in mock surprise when he saw Andringa and the other men. He stood on tiptoe to peep over the parapet. The sun was rising above the eastern fog-banks now. The banners of Arkhangelsk showed their bright colours. "Oho!" he said. "How long till the fun starts?"

"You and your people will be safe here, Master Borglum," promised Andringa. "You are well behind our lines."

"Are we?" said Borglum. "That could change. Lines move, Captain, but these old hulks won't. If the tide comes in they'll be overwhelmed, and the tide's coming all right; a tide of steel."

"Then we must dam it, Master Borglum," said Andringa calmly.

From one of the northern landships a cannon boomed. Fever saw the puff of smoke drifting away, and heard the shot go whirring overhead.

"Get your people under cover," said Andringa to Borglum, and to his comrades, "Gentlemen, we must rejoin our units. . ."

He had to shout the last few words, for all along the northern line guns were going off, red-gold muzzle-flashes stabbing out of a spreading cloud of smoke. The shells passed above Three Dry Ships with a sound like geese on the wing and burst among the dug-in landships on the slopes of Dryships Hill.

"They're softening us up ready for an attack," said Borglum cheerfully. "It won't last long. Those northern nanas don't like shooting matches; they'd sooner get to close quarters." He shoved Fever ahead of him, back down the stairs, and she was glad to go; the air outside was buzzing with shot. But down at ground level the misshapes were arranging breakfast, sitting out the barrage together as if it was any ordinary storm. With them she felt safer; she even managed to eat a couple of the pancakes which Quatch rustled up, although she had thought she had no appetite at all.

The dry ship shuddered. From somewhere on the decks above came a huge crash, followed by the lesser sounds of debris falling. Dust drizzled down between the planks of the roof, settling on the pancakes like cinnamon.

"They found our range, I see," said Borglum.

"Took 'em long enough, the amateurs," grumbled Master Fenster.

Roundshot hammered the old hull with a sound like drumbeats.

"Don't fret," called Borglum, above the racket. "Won't last much longer. We'd best be ready."

"What for?" asked Lady Midnight, and her voice was suddenly too loud, for the bombardment had stopped.

They all ran to the stairs and up on to the roof, where

the washing still hung unharmed. Fever crowded with the others to the old ship's gunwale. Behind the veils of brownish smoke which shrouded Three Dry Ships, engines were roaring and huge shapes moved: Andringa's landships were rolling through the town and heading out across the old seabed to meet the enemy. Behind them jogged squads of infantry, and the sunlight breaking through the smoke-clouds lit glints on the bayonets of their Bugharin rifles like little silver flames. In front strode squads of Stalkers, some with their claws unsheathed, others revving the engines of their battle-strimmers, their heads swinging from side to side as they searched the smoke for northerners. Officers ran ahead of them, bright swords upraised, shouting them on. Their banners blew sideways on the morning breeze, and as the breeze strengthened the smoke was drawn aside like a curtain and through the last rags and frayings of it Fever saw the Arkhangelsk vanguard rolling south.

"Now the ball begins," said Borglum.

A line of Arkhangelsk landships was advancing to meet the Londoners. Behind it, the big fortresses had finally crept into range and started firing their cannon, but none of their shots reached Three Dry Ships. They burst instead among the London landships, trying to knock out a few before the two lines met. Already Andringa's Stalkers had broken into a run. One group of them reached the bows of an Arkhangelsk ship and went swarming up its steep sides like insects, burrowing in through gun-ports and hawse-holes, or scrambling all the way up to attack the gunners on the open upper deck. That landship skewed aside, losing speed, but the rest came on, and within a few minutes they met the London ships, and the two lines disappeared again, engulfed in a spitting grey-white fog pierced through and through with flame.

"There are so many of them!" Fever said.

There were at least two Arkhangelsk ships for every Londoner, and the Arkhangelsk were bigger, with three or four decks and huge turrets jutting from their flanks, stubbled with cannon-barrels. But the London ships were faster, and tougher, and their guns fired more quickly, while on their upper decks sharpshooters kept up a steady crackle of rifle fire, cutting down any Arkhangelsk who dared show their faces over the parapets of their ships.

"Just like Hill 60," said Borglum, who'd watched that battle from a distance, too. "Maybe this Andringa *can* hold them..."

In early afternoon Tharp came to fetch Cluny Morvish from the chamber they had given her. "What's happening?" she asked him, as she trailed after him down the winding stairways of the heart-fortress. "We are not making another assault, surely?"

Half a dozen times that day Tharp had made her go and stand among the blowing banners up on the heart-fort's forward bastion, where the men could see her as they readied themselves to charge into the wall of smoke and noise that hung in front of that long hill to southward. "They will fight better knowing that the Vessel of the Ancestors is watching them," the old man had promised, while the war horns brayed and the drums thrummed and the attack-ships revved their engines. But each time the survivors had come back beaten; shot-holed vehicles dragging themselves along like escapees from a scrapyard; the wounded men draped on their upperworks like broken dolls.

"Are we losing?" she asked Tharp, hurrying along with no idea where he was taking her.

"The Movement are strong," the old man said. "They have stronger forts and better guns. But we shall break their line. . ."

Cluny shuddered. London kept rising in her mind, driving all the other thoughts into the corners. In the wilds, with Fever Crumb, she had thought that she was learning to cope with the visions, but now they seemed worse than ever.

"The Great Carn has ordered an all-out attack," Tharp was saying. "We will advance with our whole force; forts, warriors, mammoths. And you shall lead us."

"Me?"

"Your presence will show our warriors that the Ancestors are still with us. Some are beginning to doubt it."

I'm not surprised, thought Cluny. *I doubt it myself*. She dared not say that to the Technomancer, and so she said instead, "What if I'm killed? What will that show them?"

"The Ancestors will not allow that," Tharp said. "You will ride on the Great Carn's own war-mammoth, and

I shall be with you, chanting apps of power which will make the bullets of the southerners turn to mist before they touch you. Not only that; the Great Carn has given you a bodyguard. Here. We have gained something at least from this flirtation with Raven."

The room he led her into was long and low; an afterthought of a room squeezed in between two of the fortress's engines and hot as June. Cluny had seen enough now of the Movement to know that the two men who waited there in their red robes were Raven's technomancers. One of their Stalkers waited with them, armoured and faceless, unmoving except for the faintly flickering glow of the green lamps which were his eyes. Words that Cluny could not read were stencilled on his chest and shoulder pads and across his massive, metal brow. She looked at his big hands and thought of the blades that were housed inside them. He was a veteran, his armour scarred with dents and scratches, and she thought, *This might be the very one that killed my brother. . .*

"He will protect you," promised Tharp, sensing her unease. "These technomancers of the Movement have sung strong apps to him; they have told him that his only purpose is to do your bidding and to keep you safe."

Cluny was not certain what she was supposed to say. "Thank you," she told the men in red. She said it to the Stalker too, but he only looked at her.

Tharp said, "They call him Master Shrike."

*

At first the battle had been terrifying. Soon it began to drag. On Dryships Hill even the birds grew used to the noise and began to sing again; Fever could hear them whenever there was a pause in the firing, and see them flitting between the gorse bushes. Now and then the ground jerked as another landship blew up. For the most part it seemed to be the northerners who were suffering; Fever could count twenty of their ships wrecked and burning for only a few of London's. One had kept moving long after its crew were dead; a massive, self-propelled pyre which lumbered through the battle and ploughed into the sheds at the outskirts of the town before its engines finally gave out. Through its smoke she watched Suomi infantry pushing forward behind shield-walls on the eastern flank. High screens of armoured timber, mounted on wheels and propelled at walking pace by crude steam engines, the shield-walls had worked well against terrified snowmad tribesmen, but London's guns punched through them as if they were wet cardboard, and the Suomi fled.

But Andringa had no reserves, and when one of his landships was captured or destroyed it left a gap in his line, while the ships his enemies lost were replaced by others pushing in from the north. Nor could the Londoner's armour protect them from the northern Stalkers, which climbed in through their gun-ports to slaughter their crews, while from the gun-ports of some Arkhangelsk ships long whips of lightning struck down their own

Stalkers, crackling like frost as they wrapped around the iron men. And some of the ships in the northern line were Raven's, as fast and strong as anything from London, and when one of those rolled forward a long, terrible duel began, with no predicting which ship would win.

In mid-afternoon, with the sun glaring through the smoke like a red-hot penny, the line broke and the remnants of the London fleet came crawling backwards to Three Dry Ships, the surviving infantry and Stalkers running between them.

"That's it," said Borglum. He started to shoo his people away from the old ship's side, herding them towards the stair-head. "Come on. Show's over. We got to get ourselves aboard one of those things and pray it's faster than anything the Arkies have got."

"Are they running?" asked Fever, running herself as she followed him down the stairs again.

"All the way to the sea, if they've got any sense," said Lady Midnight, coming down behind.

But Andringa and his men must have had no sense at all, or else they thought there was no point in running from the Arkhangelsk. As the misshapes neared the bottom of the stairs they found themselves shouldered aside by soldiers coming up; soldiers with blackened faces and wide, shocked eyes, Bugharins in their hands and a reek of powder-smoke about them. Lucy shrieked, imagining that they were Arkhangelsk, but they were Andringa's men, come to make a stand in Three Dry Ships.

Outside, as Borglum led his people through the miserable streets and up the hill, men were everywhere, dragging barricades across the gaps between sheds and cottages, setting up a demi-cannon on a tripod. The reversing landships scrabbled up the hill and into positions on its terraces. None went further than halfway up, or showed any sign of running back to London, let alone carrying hitchhikers when it went.

"What now then?" asked Master Fenster.

"Keep going," said Borglum. "We can at least get this hill between us and whatever unpleasantness happens here. . ."

War horns were sounding as Fever and the others followed him uphill between the waiting ships. The slope was steep, and after the first thirty feet she stopped and paused for breath and looked back, just in time to see the northerners' vanguard break from the smoke. Arkhangelsk infantry were milling between the oncoming vehicles, and dozens fell as the men who'd stationed themselves in Three Dry Ships opened fire. The landships on the hillside around her began to fire too. The Arkhangelsk ships faltered. Already a couple were in flames, but the northern foot-warriors kept coming, hard men in mail and wolfskin, much like the Morvishmen she'd met, fearless and keen for glory. Their battle cries rose above the noise of guns and engines as they charged into the little town, piling through windows and shot-holes into the old hulk where Fever and her friends had sheltered. Others swung past the town and started up the hill, driving Andringa's men before them, letting off arquebuses and crossbows as they came. Master Fenster, running ahead of her, suddenly turned round and dropped his gun and fell. Fever tripped over him and someone stumbled over her, and a shell bursting further up the slope blinded her with its spray of dirt. By the time she crawled back to where Master Fenster lay he was dead.

She looked for Borglum and the others. There was only smoke, and the gaudy leaping light of a burning landship a little way off along the hill. Half the hillside seemed to have been blown into the sky and was pattering down in pieces all around. From below came the shouting voices of the warriors. She scrambled up and started running blindly, tripping on dead men and scattered packs. It sounded as if the sea was finally returning to Three Dry Ships; roaring down from the north in a storm-wave like the one that had once swamped Thursday Island and orphaned Arlo.

Someone grabbed her, but it was only Quatch, dragging her down into the doubtful shelter of a barricade made from empty crates and a broken door. Borglum crouched there too, and Lady Midnight. The dwarf said, "You want ter watch yourself, scamperin' about in that Arkie coat; one of our brave boys'll put a bullet in you."

"Where are the others?' she asked.

"Dunno," said Borglum. He was loading a Bugharin he'd found somewhere, glaring out over the barricade into the smoke. "Everybody's runnin' this way and that. It's all gone pear-shaped."

"Master Fenster's dead," she said.

"Stalkers!" someone shouted, further down the hill.

Out of the drifts of smoke below they came, ghostly at first and then suddenly solid. A glint of gunlight on raised blades; the beams of green eyes slicing the smoke. The cry went up all along the London lines: "Stalkers!" A fortress a little way downhill was overrun, the Stalkers swarming over it like ants, men leaping from upper decks to escape them. From somewhere to the left a squad of Andringa's Stalkers came hurrying slantwise across the slope of the hill. Battle-strimmers revved and snarled and for a moment it seemed they would drive their rivals back, but the mortal warriors of the north poured past them, leaving the Stalkers to fight each other. Through a tear in the smoke Fever glimpsed what looked like mossy boulders moving, and before she could say anything the mammoths were upon them.

These were not amiable mammoths like Carpet and Lump; these had been bred for size and fierceness, and armoured so heavily that they looked more like machines than animals. On their trunks and forelegs were long segmented sleeves of iron, rivets winking in the firelight. Their heads were hidden in spiked guards, their wayward tusks were tipped with sharpened steel, and they were half mad with terror and fury. Swinging their big heads from side to side they crashed through the knots of defenders, crushing anyone who stood before them, snatching up in their trunks those who tried to flee and flinging them away into the smoke.

"Borglum!" Fever shouted. "We have to run!"

"Run from them hairy bloggers?" Borglum shouted back. "Not likely. If they're chucking mammoths at us then Andringa's lads must really have mucked up their landships. We'll win this yet." He raised his gun, taking aim at the biggest mammoth he could see, a monster of a mammoth that had just appeared out of the smoke, galloping westward along the face of the hill. In its howdah a red mammoth skull had been mounted on a tall staff, fluttering with pennants. A Stalker stood there, and two armoured Arkhangelsk, and a man who waved his thin arms high above his silly hat, and another figure, slighter, all in white, with a cloud of rusty hair blown back. . .

Fever shoved Borglum's rifle sideways just as it went off.

"What are you playing at, Fever Crumb?" he asked, reaching for a fresh bullet. "Whose side you on?"

"I know her, that girl," said Fever. "That's Cluny Morvish." Even there, in that awful place, it felt good just to be saying Cluny's name.

"That's right," Borglum said, more gently. "You're fond of her."

Fever nodded, and for a moment, as their eyes met, she thought he understood. Then something hummed past her like a hornet and punched him backwards.

331

"Borglum! Borglum!" Lady Midnight shouted as he fell against her. A mammoth – not Cluny's but another, still larger – was thundering up the slope towards their barricade, and men its howdah were firing guns down at them as it came. Without thinking, Fever reached for the rifle which Borglum had dropped. Without thinking, she pulled the bolt back, raised it to her shoulder, stood to take a better aim. As long as she didn't think, her body knew exactly what to do; Godshawk had hunted mammoths and fought in battles of his own, and his memories were in her muscles and her nerves. She let him take charge for a moment as she squinted through the rifle's sights, ignoring Quatch bellowing at her to get down, ignoring Lady Midnight's wails of "Borglum!"

There was a little eyehole in the mammoth's armour, with a little, bright, mad eye glinting out. Fever squeezed the trigger carefully and put a bullet through it, and felt an elation that was not her own as the beast reared up screaming, flailing at the air with its spiked forelegs, its hind feet trampling the marksmen who tumbled from its back. *I must make sure to get its tusks,* she thought, watching it crash down. *What a trophy they will make!* The thought was Godshawk's, not her own, so she stuffed it down into the cellar of her mind and shut a door upon it and ran to where Lady Midnight cradled Borglum. He was shuddering, shuddering, but when he saw Fever bend over him he went still, smiled, said, "Duchess? That you? They told me you was. . ."

"Oh, Master Borglum," she said, kneeling down beside him, but he was not there any more, and Lady Midnight, weeping, laid him down and said, "We must leave..."

Light broke over them. An Arkhangelsk war-lamp was raking its beam through the smoke to dazzle the defenders and show the attackers what they were attacking. Out of the light came Stalkers, looking like black spiky cut-outs with their edges all nibbled away by the glare. Fever felt their green gaze brush her face as Lady Midnight caught her by one arm and pulled her away. "Come on, dearest, we must go now, or join poor Borglum in the Sunless Country..."

A Stalker kicked through the barricade. Quatch turned back to meet it; grabbed it by its metal face and wrenched its head off in a spray of nasty fluids. Its flailing body twisted free and killed him with a random swipe of its claws, dropping him on top of Borglum while Fever and Lady Midnight scurried up the hill. The neat lines of the battle had all gone now; there was fighting everywhere they looked: mammoths, landships, Stalkers, warriors, Andringa's soldiers, an unexploded shell bounding downhill like a barrel. There was a steady roaring sound, no longer the noise of individual guns, just one long, dreadful din.

"Now you must guide me, Fever, dear," shouted Lady Midnight. "This ain't no Carnival of Knives and my eyes ain't much good to me with all these fires and such to dazzle them."

So Fever took her hand and they went together between blazing landships, past London Stalkers who had been re-killed and stood burning like man-shaped braziers. They reached the summit, but as they started down the far side they found battle in front of them too. Northerners had got round behind the hill somehow, moving on foot in small and silent groups between the thorn-bushes while the defenders were all busy with the main assault. A huge Suomi cut down a London officer just ahead of Fever and then turned to lunge at her, but there were no fires behind him, so he showed up bright to Lady Midnight, who found a dagger in her belt and flung it into his throat. He fell with a gurgle, and as they went past him they saw that the man he'd left on the ground was Captain Andringa, struggling to rise while a widening red stain soaked through his tunic. Lady Midnight stopped and heaved him up; swung him over her shoulders and went on stooped beneath his weight, ignoring his commands to go on and save herself. "He's such a nice captain," she said to Fever. "We can't just leave him here to die or be lost." She was determined to save someone from the battle, even if all her friends were gone.

"You can't carry him all the way to London," Fever warned. Carnival fighter or not, the big woman was already straining beneath Andringa's weight, but she just gritted her teeth and went on down the hill, and as Fever went after her the smoke around them flared golden, for the afternoon sun had dipped below the edge of the pall that hung above the battlefield, and its light glittered on the bogs and culverts of the southward plains.

They pressed on, while men ran past them, throwing away packs and rifles as they went, fleeing before the northerners' advance. From behind came the hoarse trumpeting of mammoths, the clang of Suomi war-bells, the ramshackle clatter of the northern landships heaving themselves to the hill's crest, shunting aside the ships which had stood so long against them. Lady Midnight panted, stumbling; Andringa groaned and bled; Fever wondered uselessly if there was some way they could share his weight. The light grew, and the smoke thinned, and the mist of evening hung above the drainage ditches and the brown, autumnal fields, and there, beyond the fields, above the mist. . .

What was *that* thing? What *was* it?

Other fugitives nearby had seen it too; Fever could tell by the way their heads went back, and the wonder that woke in their weary faces as they looked up and up. And she realized that the thunderous low growl she had been hearing for some minutes now was not the noise of the battle behind her but was coming from that monstrous shape as it tore its way out of the fog-banks in the south.

It was the sound of engines.

London had arrived.

31

BATTLE'S END

London had arrived. Through a night and a day it had clawed its way northward, while the people huddled on its deck plates and the Engineers who controlled it slowly grew used to the idea that their city moved. Its speed on that first journey averaged just under ten miles per hour. It shed its tracks with maddening regularity, and several times an engine failed, but the city just halted to make repairs and then rolled on its way again, grinding the New North Road to grit beneath it. Behind the fog and the drifting smoke of battle, nobody at Three Dry Ships had noticed its approach. Through all the thunder of the guns, no one had heard it. *The Future,* Quercus would say later, *is something that sneaks up on us while we are busy doing other things.*

Fever let her eyes rove over it, finding familiar structures beneath the ugly new fortifications. There was the stairway they called Cat's Creep, rising up the central axis through the unfinished tiers. There was the platform where she'd stood with Dr Crumb on the day she first went aboard. . .

"What is it?" asked Lady Midnight, gazing at it with her white eyes. "It's *hot*. . ."

"It's come a long way," said Fever. "It's London."

"See?" said the carnival woman, reaching up to pat Captain Andringa. "I told you we'd get you there."

Behind them, northern forts and battlewagons coming over the crest of Dryships Hill slowed in confusion as their crews made out the thing that waited for them. Fever imagined them frantically checking their charts, trying to identify this misplaced mountain. *People aren't used to this*, she thought. Even she, she discovered, had never *really* believed that London could move: her head had grasped it, but her heart had not. Yet here it was, and although she understood the principles by which its wheels turned and its engines worked, she was as astonished by it as everyone else. *None of us is used to geography that moves. . .*

But they would have to get used to it, because here it was, a hundred miles from its birthplace and moving still, rolling carefully and cautiously towards her. Its bows broke free of the drifting mist. The serrated doors of the Great Under Tier looked so like the snout of a hungry dragon that she remembered Cluny and thought, *This is Cluny's vision. This is Godshawk's dream, made real.*

The northern landships on the hilltop began to fire. Fever ducked instinctively, but the shots were pitched high over her head, tearing splinters from the palisades that ringed each of London's tiers. At once, big guns aboard the city started to reply: ship's guns, whose shells fell thick among the clustered vehicles on the ridge. Some were mounted so high on the skeletal girders of the upper tiers that they could shoot right over the hill at the nomad forts and castles behind it. And all the time the city kept on rolling. It showed no sign of slowing in the marshes; its huge tracks sank down through the mire and mud to grip bedrock beneath. At its stern, exhaust stacks hawked up thunderheads of smoke. Uprooted trees were wedged between the teeth of its tracks. The ground throbbed like a drum-skin. The horizon trembled. It was still a mile or two off, but it was moving quickly, and Fever noticed that the men around her were moving too, running back to Dryships Hill as if they thought they would be safe there.

Fever started to go with them, edging backwards, unable to drag her eyes away from London. It was hard to fight the instinct that told her to get away from something so big and powerful. No wonder Cluny had been terrified when it rolled into her dreams. Cluny had more imagination than Fever; she had understood better the heft of the new city; its predator strength. It was all that she could do to stop herself from turning and running.

Lady Midnight called out, "Don't you think we ought to try to get aboard?"

"They won't let us," said Fever, looking at the little ant-like figures on the city's skirts. "They'll think we're northerners, they'll shoot us down."

"I've been called a lot of things, but never a northerner,"

338

said Lady Midnight scornfully. "Besides, we've Captain A. You'll vouch for us won't you, Captain A?"

Captain A said nothing, but she set off anyway. Fever followed, and noticed that others were going in the same direction; soldiers from London, forgotten by their enemies, were hurrying across the city's path towards the outer tracks, where iron stairways reached down almost to the ground. One of them was waving something – a tattered banner, torn from its pole – and from a sandbagged gun-nest at the top of those stairs men waved back, and readied a long metal ladder to let them climb aboard.

Fever started to run. The wet ground shuddered under her as London neared; the water in the puddles danced. Lady Midnight staggered, cursing. The city was slowing, probably wanting to make sure it had knocked out all the northern forts before it crawled into the range of their cannons. As it slowed, men came down the stairs and fitted their ladder into brackets that stuck from the bottom step and slid it down until its lowest rung was inches from the ground. The foremost of the fleeing soldiers grabbed it and started to climb.

"Wait! Wait for us!" gasped Fever, running, though reason told her that she could not be heard above the racket of London's wheels and engines.

Half the soldiers were aboard now; the man with the banner waved it triumphantly as he reached the top of the stairs.

Fever fell, sprawling on her face in a soft and slimy patch of bog. By the time she had crawled out and wiped the mud from her eyes the last of the soldiers was climbing the ladder.

"Wait!" she shouted, running, lungs straining, throat burning. "Wait!"

The men on the city helped the last climber aboard and prepared to raise their ladder.

"Wait!"

One saw her and pointed. The others noticed her. They left the ladder there. The city was moving not much faster than a brisk walking pace, and as Fever and Lady Midnight scrambled across the band of disturbed earth near to the outermost track, the dangling ladder came to meet her, its bottom rungs whisking through the long grass, like a ladder to heaven in a fairy tale. A man came down it, seized hold of Andringa and started to heave him up; Lady Midnight followed, pushing from below. Fever was the last aboard; she grabbed the ladder, climbed a few rungs, and could go no further. In the end they hauled it up with her clinging to it like a shipwrecked sailor to a piece of wreckage. They helped her off at the top, but doubtfully. She lay beside Lady Midnight and heard them say, "These two ain't ours. They look like misshapes. Old Crumb won't have put their sort on his list."

Andringa was sprawled nearby, looking about as dead as anyone Fever had ever seen, but he heard too, and opened his eyes. "Sergeant," he said, "this lady is under my protection, and the other is Fever Crumb. She is Dr Crumb's own daughter, come home from the wilds, and she will certainly, certainly be on his list. . ."

Thank St Kylie, Charley thought, as London finally began to slow. All night and all day the place had been quaking like a jelly. He had lost count of the number of bruises he had from banging into walls, or having things bang into him. Wherever he went in the Engine District, staggering like a drunk across its tilting pavements, things had been falling from shelves, or cascading out of cupboards which swung open suddenly as the city lurched. People had been warned to stow stuff safely, but things had been forgotten in the rush, and nobody had quite imagined how rough London's first ride would be. *A ship on a stormy sea would feel like this*, he thought, *and sailors learn to cope, don't they?* But he had never been on a ship, or seen the sea. He had spent the whole night concentrating on just not being sick, and when the battle started and the huge, reverberating booms of the guns came quivering through the fabric of the city, he found himself wishing bitterly that the Underground had won and stopped the thing from ever being built.

Feeling sullen and sleep-deprived, he edged along the crowded pavements behind his master. Dr Crumb seemed to think that sleep and comfort were like hair; affectations which good Engineers should do without. All night he had been busy, and now that the city was almost at its destination he had chosen not to rest but to come down and check all the buttresses and bracings on Base Tier, in case the recoil from those huge guns up above was putting too much stress on them. *All well and good*, thought Charley, glaring at his back, *but why does he have to drag me with him?* He choked on the hot and stinking air, kicking his way through huddles of miserable people who had come aboard in a hurry before the city moved and had not yet been assigned quarters of their own.

They had checked three of the big iron braces without finding any sign of cracks or warping, and Dr Crumb was just preparing to check a fourth when a man came shouting, "Oi! Dr Crumb!" It was one of Quercus's coppertops, the badge on his shako glinting in the Base Tier gloom.

"What is it, constable?" asked Dr Crumb. "Is there an emergency? Nothing structural, I hope?"

"No, no, sir, no," the policeman said. "It is only . . . we have your daughter aboard, sir."

Charley grabbed a handrail to steady himself, and hoped the coppertop would think it was just the lurching of the pavement which made him sway and blanch. Fever Crumb? Here? *Alive* and *here*?

"My daughter is dead," said Dr Crumb.

"I can't help that, sir," said the man. "She came aboard with a foreign misshape woman and Captain Andringa. He swore she's Miss Fever Crumb. But he's been took to the infirmary now, and we can't let her go topside unless we're quite sure of it."

Charley was sure of it. It would be just like his luck. *Is she completely indestructible?* he wondered bitterly. So it had all been for nothing; Fever was back despite his best efforts. Dr Crumb would not want Charley any more.

He followed Dr Crumb and the coppertop along the walkways which bridged the Great Under Tier and down a stair into one of the side-crofts. A ragtag crowd of battered soldiery had gathered there, barely recognizable as the same brave fellows who had left London to defend the northern approaches. The smoke from London's engines still lingered under the high iron roof, but through vents and grilles the evening light came in. Under one such vent, where the air was freshest, a young woman waited.

"Well, sir," asked the coppertop, in a confidential way. "Is that her?"

"It... It looks a little like her," Dr Crumb admitted.

"It's her," said Charley. He was shocked at Fever's appearance too. Would hardly have known her, if it weren't for those mismatched eyes of hers, which widened slightly as they lit on Dr Crumb. Her prim white coat was gone, replaced by northern clothes so dirty that they looked as if she'd taken them off a dead she-tramp in a muddy ditch. Her greasy hair trailed almost to her shoulders. Her face was altered too; gaunt, bruised, empty-looking. In the hollow of her throat hung a nomad amulet; wires and circuitry and little bones.

Motioning to the policeman to remain where he was, Dr Crumb went over to her. Charley, assuming the gesture

343

had not applied to him, went too. Her mouth twitched. She was trying to smile, but after the long trauma of capture and chase and battle she could not quite remember how. Charley didn't know that, though. He just thought, *Still the same frosty little bitch, then.*

Dr Crumb stopped and stood swaying a few feet from the girl. If he felt anything at all he did not let it show.

He said, "I was told you were killed, Fever."

"That was not true."

"Clearly. But your mother. . .?"

"Wavey is dead."

"Ah."

"She was very brave. She fought and fought but in the end there was a Stalker and it . . . and she. . ."

"Quite," said Dr Crumb.

Fever was weeping before she could stop herself. She reached for him but he stepped back in alarm and she was left there with her arms outstretched, tears dripping from her chin.

"I'm sorry," she said. She wiped at her face with the cuffs of her tunic. She tried to laugh, forgetting that Dr Crumb was just as unsettled by laughter as by tears. "I have been too long among the nomads," she said.

"Yes," agreed Dr Crumb, and his eyes went to the talisman around her neck.

Charley Shallow, looking on, felt the first stirrings of hope for himself. This wasn't going the way he'd expected; nor the way Fever had expected, neither. It was

344

like Crumb had armoured himself so thickly against all feeling when he'd thought she was dead that he couldn't feel anything now she was alive again.

"Father," said Fever, in a small, experimental way. She had never called him that before. Watching his reaction, she realized that she never would again.

"You should rest, Fever," said Dr Crumb. "You are emotional. It is to be expected, perhaps. Rest will help you to overcome your weakness."

She nodded meekly.

"You will excuse me. There is much to do." He turned to leave, hesitated, turned back. "Please remove that trinket. That thing around your neck. It looks most irrational."

Fever put her fingers to the charm. "It is only jewellery. A friend . . . my friend . . . Cluny Morvish gave it to me. It was her present to me. . . It is all I have left of her."

Dr Crumb frowned still harder. "Cluny Morvish? You surprise me, Fever. Is she not the witch, the priestess who led this mad crusade?"

Fever hung her head, knowing she could not explain.

"Charley," said Dr Crumb, "take Fever to the Engineerium. Find her some quarters and some clean clothes. Soap and water, too; she is in a most insanitary state. Whatever she needs. . ." He glanced at Fever again, but would not meet her eyes. "You will excuse me, Fever. There is so much to be done. . ."

Walking away, he looked as rough as he had on the day he heard she'd died. Charley watched him go. In his head, little green plans were shoving their noses up into the light like February snowdrops. He turned to Fever, smiled his brightest smile. "Dr Crumb is terrible busy, Miss Crumb," he said, shouting over the steady booming of the city's guns, reaching out to steady her as the deck lurched. "Come on; let's get you to the Engineerium."

The long guns of London had hammered the heart-fortress, smashing its upperworks, silencing its cannon before they could land a shot upon the city. Most of the landships and the smaller forts were already destroyed, ground under London's tracks as it drove its huge weight through the crest of Dryships Hill. The rest were in flight, scudding northward like clouds before a gale.

Cluny did not know how, but she was still alive, still in the armoured howdah of her war-mammoth, which had carried her back from the hill with the rest of the Arkhangelsk forces when the city appeared. From the lee of the shattered heart-fortress, through the smoke of its burning, she looked up at her city of dreams. She was not so scared of it now that it was real. All around her people were screaming, running, hiding their eyes, falling face down on the shaking ground as if a god had appeared in front of them. Her mammoth's rider had hidden his face in its russet topknot. But she was calm, as if her nightmares had all been preparing her for this. The new London did not look nearly so grand or shiny as it had inside her head. In the effort of dragging it out of Godshawk's imaginings

346

and into real life it had lost some essential beauty. What were all those bits of timber doing, nailed up all round it like the fences of some savage pound? It kept its jaws tight shut, and the guns flashed and thundered on its shoulders.

Behind her in the howdah Tharp was gibbering, "All is lost! We must fly!"

"No," Cluny heard herself say. Her voice was high and clear amid the din. The rider looked back at her from the mammoth's neck, his face grey with terror, eyes wide behind his goggles. Only the Stalker she'd been given as a bodyguard seemed as calm as she was, watching her impassively from his station at the rear of the howdah. "No," she said again, and she raised her voice as loud as she could in the hope that the men on other mammoths and the battered landships round about her might listen. "We can fight this thing. It's only a machine. If we ride in between its tracks and get beneath it and aim our guns up at its under-workings we can break it and stop it, and when it is stopped we can climb aboard it. When we meet them hand-to-hand upon its decks the warriors of London will be no match for the warriors of Arkhangelsk. . ."

She broke off; her voice was hoarse from shouting above the racket of the battle. A scant mile away, the new city butted towards her, shoving a bow-wave of torn earth before it. Around her men were shouting, relaying what she'd said to other men. Her father's landship *Fury* was swinging round, gunning its engines, black puff-balls of smoke popping from its smokestack like a string of pompoms tugged from a conjurer's hat. She saw Carn Morvish standing on its open gun-deck, his sword in his hand, his face turned to her. Mammoths bellowed, struggling against the riders who struggled to turn their heads towards that oncoming terror.

"You crazy witch!" screamed Tharp, grabbing at her from behind with his thin hands. "What are you doing?"

"We can't outrun it," said Cluny. "We must fight it."

"You're mad!" the technomancer shouted. He raised his staff to strike at her, but the Stalker Shrike reached coolly forward, lifted him by the collar of his robes and flung him out of the howdah. Cluny saw his indignant face gawp at her; heard his shriek, going down. She peeked over the howdah's edge and saw him scrambling away through mud and mammoth-dung, and that was the last sight she ever had of him. Then she climbed out of the howdah herself, ripped the skirts from the stupid dress he'd made her wear, and clambered bare-legged to where the frightened rider sat.

"Get off," she said. "Run home, if you want to."

The man looked at her dumbly. She shoved him sideways and he went half-tumbling and half-scrambling down the mammoth's side while she settled herself in his place, reaching forward to brush the arch of a hairy ear with her hand, making soothing noises as the creature stamped and fretted.

London was a half-mile away. Its gunners had lost interest in the heart-fort and the Arkhangelsk lurking in its lee; they were training their weapons on the fleeing forts and landships further north.

She drew the rider's musket from its scabbard on the mammoth's neck. She looked back. Shrike had come to the front of the howdah, gripping the handles of the swivel gun that was mounted there. Cluny raised the musket in one hand and took a firm grip of the mammoth's topknot with the other. She felt she should shout some war cry. What would Doran-her-brother have shouted when he led his men against the Movement's Stalkers at Hill 60? It didn't matter. Nobody would have heard her anyway, and before she had even lowered her hand they were all surging forward. A few dozen mammoths, a handful of landships, a campavan or two, a lone monowheel, skeins of men on foot with tattered banners; all that remained of the grand alliance of the north hurled in a last, desperate rage against the city of the future.

They had halved the distance between themselves and London before anyone aboard the city even noticed them. They had halved it again before the gunners up there could bring their guns to bear. The warriors howled; the guns of the landships boomed and stuttered; from the forward turret of the *Fury* a Tesla gun played its icy lightning across London's tracks in the hope that something which destroyed Stalkers would work on mobile cities, too. Clinging to her mammoth's neck, ducking under the shots which the Stalker behind her kept pumping at the rolling tracks ahead, Cluny thought wildly, *We will win! We're too*

*small for them to even see! That's why my dream came, so that
I could stop this thing. . .*

Then the shells from London's guns were falling all
around her; sudden trees with twisting fiery trunks and
spreading canopies of chalky smoke. Bodies cartwheeled;
debris tumbled; mammoths screamed, reared, fell, ran
riderless. She saw the *Fury* hit, the stern-part where her
father stood blown into pieces, the severed bows slewing
round helpless in the path of London. Then some shard
of shell or wreckage went through her mammoth's skull
and splashed its brains over her and it was falling, down
on its knees and forward into the grass with its tusks
snapping and Cluny somersaulting off its head. The Tesla
gun aboard the *Fury* was still firing wildly, scattering its
lightning everywhere, and she turned to the Stalker as he
rose from the mammoth's wreck and shouted, "Master
Shrike, watch out!", and then the lightning touched her
and her mind filled with cold white fire.

It was Shrike who saved her. He had been ordered to
keep her safe, and so he did. He strode through the last
sputterings of the lightning to where she grovelled blindly
in the grass, and lifted her, and carried her out of London's
path. There, amid dead men and shattered landships, he
laid her down, and looked at her. As far as he could tell,
she was asleep. She reminded him of something, but he
could not say what; the dying Tesla gun had brushed him
too; his consciousness faded in and out. For an instant he
half-remembered who he was, and a murderous red rage

rose up in him because of what had been done to him. He bared his claws and killed a band of northerners as they came fleeing past. His anger at the living was so fierce that he turned on Cluny and would have killed her too, but he stopped himself; he stopped himself, and took a banner from one of the men he'd murdered and spread it over her, tucking her in as if she were a sleeping child. Then, before the rage could come on him again, he left her there, and walked away; away through the smoke; away through the wreckage and the vast traffic jam of fleeing forts and landships tangled in their own supply train; away into silence and the legends of the defeated north.

32

HUNGRY CITY

At sundown Quercus walked out on to an observation balcony high above the doors of the Great Under Tier. The city's guns were silent by then except for the faint, steady tick as their barrels cooled. The routed nomads had finally passed out of their range into the low grey haze to the north. The Lord Mayor leaned on the balcony rail, looking down at the heaps of carcasses and wrecked machines which marked the place where that last northern charge had collapsed in front of London like a spent wave.

Dr Crumb joined him there. The smoke of wrecked landships twirled up past them; the bitter scent of the burnt hair of mammoths. Dr Crumb had meant to tell the Lord Mayor that Fever had returned, but now that he had the chance he found that he did not know how to start. Having her back was as great a shock as losing her. That witch-doctor's amulet around her neck... He feared that during her adventures she had let go of reason and sought comfort in prayers and magic. He hoped that rest and safety would restore her, so that she could work at his side again, quietly and calmly, as she had when she was younger. If not, there could be no place for her in London. London needed only useful people; there could be no exceptions. . .

"We have captured her," said Quercus suddenly, startling him. "The Arkhangelsk witch; the maid who sparked this madness. Cluny Morvish. Some of our men found her on the field."

"What will become of her?" asked Dr Crumb.

"She must die, of course. And let's hope her death will be an end of it." Quercus was always glum after a battle. He had struggled long and hard to build this unstoppable city. Now that he had seen what it could achieve, he was not entirely sure that it had been the right thing to do. "They were brave," he said, "Raven and his allies."

"They were irrational," said Dr Crumb. "It was inevitable that London would defeat them."

"It was a waste," said Quercus.

He was thinking of the waste of lives, but Dr Crumb, who had been eyeing the landships and the smoking ruins of the northern forts, misunderstood.

"Nothing need be wasted, Lord Mayor," he said. "Look: there on the battlefield are all the raw materials we need to strengthen the city and complete the building of the upper tiers. I shall organize work-gangs to go out and begin breaking up those vehicles and salvaging their fuel. London is very low on fuel, and there must be tonnes of coal in their bunkers; gallons of oil. Iron and timber, too. We have room for it all in the Great Under Tier."

He smiled, pleased with the neatness of his idea. "Do you know, when Dr Stayling first told me of your plan to motorize London, I thought it was absurd. I remember telling him that if London moved then other cities would follow suit, and only the fastest would survive. 'A sort of municipal Darwinism', I remember calling it. I had not realized till now how right I was.

"This new London is like a mighty predator, introduced into a world where previously walled cities and these nomad castles were the pinnacle of evolution. But we are stronger and more intelligent than them, and so, just as in nature, we shall prey on them, and we shall *eat* them; their fuel will go into our holds, their fabric will become part of London. Even their people, if they have useful skills, could be brought aboard. We will absorb their strength, and it will strengthen us."

"But what if someone else builds something faster and stronger?" asked Quercus, thinking of the latest rumours from Paris.

"We must out-evolve them, Lord Mayor," said Dr Crumb. "We must grow more quickly than they do. It should not be hard. We have a head start."

He gripped the handrail and leaned forward, looking out across the battlefield, imagining the uses to which all that iron and timber and even mammoth-bone could be put.

He said, "I have sometimes reprimanded people, in the past, for referring to the under-tier as the 'Gut'. Yet, in a sense, they are correct to do so. The Great Under Tier *is* London's gut, through which nutrients will be absorbed into our city. Those doors at the front are London's mouthparts. Open them, Quercus. Let the city eat."

Fever waited in the small room which Charley Shallow had shown her to. She bathed at the washstand, and dressed in the clothes he'd found for her: black trousers, a crisp, grey shirt, a new white coat. She tied her hair back, but she could not bring herself to take off Cluny's talisman. The feeling that she had had all through the battle, that numb certainty that she might die at any second, refused to leave her, even though reason told her she was safe.

I'm home, she thought, but it meant nothing. She could feel the city shuddering and shifting, and hear the girders groan. The guns had fallen silent hours ago, but there were other noises; deep trembling booms, long creaks and clashes. Also, someone was knocking at her door. She stood up, trying to tidy herself, hoping it would be her father, but when she called "Come in," it was Charley Shallow who opened the door. She tried to pretend that she was pleased to see him. He had been kind to her. Kinder than Dr Crumb.

"What is happening?" she asked. "These noises. . . Are we still moving?"

"Oh no, Miss Crumb," said Charley. "We are stopped for the night. London is eating. It's your dad's idea. They've heaved the Gut doors wide open, and some wreckage from the battle is being dragged inside. Raw materials, you see. So that the building work can go on."

Fever stared at him. *It will devour us all*, Cluny had said. She had understood the future far better than Fever. The city trembled, and she trembled with it.

"My father?" she asked. "Can I see him?"

"He's very busy, Miss Crumb," said Charley sorrowfully. "Not to be disturbed." Secretly, he was pleased to see tears shining in her eyes again. The more tears the better, as far as he was concerned. The more irrational she seemed, the less Dr Crumb would want to do with her, and the more he would rely on Charley Shallow.

"You was asking about that Cluny Morvish girl?" he said. "Well, it turns out she's all right. . ."

"Oh, I'm so. . ." Fever started to say, and then saw how glum and owlish Charley looked.

"She's a prisoner. Picked up off the battlefield."

"Is she wounded?"

"I don't know."

"What will happen to her?"

"Execution," said Charley. "That's what I've heard. Tomorrow, before London gets moving again."

He saw what that did to Fever. The way her hand went up to clutch that nomad charm she still wore. So she had a heart after all, and it looked like it was breaking. Relishing the pain it caused her, he went on, "Raven's dead, and all them northish Carns, so your Miss Morvish is the last leader of the alliance left. Quercus means to make an example of her, and get rid of her in case the Arkies who got away rally to her again."

"But she wouldn't want them to!" said Fever. "I can vouch for her. She won't! I'll promise!"

Charley shook his head. "Quercus won't listen," he said. "He's a nomad himself, remember? They see it as weakness, men like him, to let their enemies live. He'll have his people cut her throat in the morning; splash her blood on London's tracks to keep his old gods happy."

Some huge hammer seemed to be pounding, down in the city's depths, but it was only Fever's heart. "He can't," she said. "He can't!"

"Try telling him that," said Charley. He turned towards the door. Then, glancing back at her as if the idea had just occurred to him, he said, "At least . . . I suppose he might listen to your father. Quercus has a lot of respect for your father. . ."

The sudden opening of the office door blasted Dr Crumb's papers everywhere. Startled from his calculations, he snatched at the sheets as they whirled around his head. His ink-pot went over, drenching the efficiency reports from the larboard engines. Before he could reach for a cloth to mop them with, Fever was shoving the whole mess aside, leaning across his desk to scream at him.

"You must not let him do it! It's barbaric! It's irrational! We have to stop him! It isn't her fault! She thought she was having visions! It is one of Godshawk's machines, just like the one he put in me. . ."

"What?" gasped Dr Crumb, picking up lists and diagrams, trying desperately to put them back in order. "Fever, control your feelings! Remember the exercises I taught you to control your feelings! I have found them most useful these past weeks. . ."

But Fever was shouting at him again: more gabble; more emotion. Dr Crumb felt emotions of his own rise in response: pity; horror; disgust. That filthy technomancer's trash was still around her neck, and her thoughts seemed disordered; he could not grasp what it was she was trying to tell him.

Charley Shallow, entering the office behind her, explained. "It is this Cluny Morvish person, Dr Crumb. Miss Fever seems to be *attached* to her. She was most upset to learn that Quercus means to execute her."

"It is irrational!" shouted Fever.

"It is certainly most unpleasant," Dr Crumb agreed, mastering himself and speaking calmly in the hope of calming her. "But it is not irrational. Alive, the Morvish girl would always be a threat to London. Our city seems strong, but it is vulnerable at present. She cannot be allowed to live. She is only one individual, Fever. Individuals do not matter. Have I not always taught you so? They are expendable. The greater good. . ."

"What about *me*?" asked Fever, cutting across him, her voice all scratchy with emotion. "Do *I* matter? Am *I* expendable?"

And what was he to say? He could not lie to her. "We are *all* expendable, Fever. . ."

She made the strangest noise then; a harsh screeching cry, like the call of a bird. She was gone; the door swinging shut behind her, then wrenched open again as Charley Shallow hurried after her.

"You matter to *me*, Fever," said Dr Crumb, hopelessly, and much too late. But there was nobody to hear him.

She ran down the stairways of the Engineerium, through the lobby, out into the street that wasn't really a street, just a wide corridor, full of engine-stink and passers-by who glanced curiously at her tear-streaked face and went on, filled with worries of their own. What would Wavey have done, she thought, if someone she loved had been imprisoned, awaiting execution? What would Godshawk have done? His memories stirred in the lees of her mind; her body tensed; her hands made fists, remembering how he had gripped swords, knives, how he had struck men down in battles with the Parisians and cutting-out expeditions against pirates in the Western Archipelago. *He* would not have left Cluny Morvish in a cell; he would have done something, no matter how reckless and irrational; he would have rescued Cluny from the Londoners just as Cluny had rescued her brother from the nightwights' lair.

But how could Fever hope to mount a rescue, alone against the whole of London?

A touch on her shoulder. Charley Shallow had followed her out of the Engineerium. He was pressing something into her hand and she looked down and saw that it was his Engineer's badge; the little red enamel cogwheel he had taken from his coat lapel. She looked up into his face, not understanding.

"Engineer's badge gets you into most places in this city, Miss Crumb," he said gently. "They're keeping your friend in one of the landship hangars off the Gut if you want to talk to her."

"Why?" asked Fever. "There's a prison, isn't there?"

Charley shrugged. "We're overcrowded, and we left all our criminals behind. The prison's been reassigned as workers' housing. And there's plenty of empty hangars now, what with all our landships smashed. They're holding your friend in number 14."

Fever watched him speak. She wondered what was going on behind those dark, clever eyes. She had a feeling that he knew just what was going on behind hers; her feelings for Cluny, all of it.

"Why are you telling me?" she asked.

"You want to help her get away, don't you?" said Charley. "And I want to help you. You helped me once. Remember? That day me and Bagman came after you in the Brick Marsh. You helped me out of that sinkhole when you could just have run and left me there to drown. You didn't have to do that. I'm indebted. Indebted to you, Miss Crumb. And I always pay my debts."

He took her arm, steering her along the street, away from the Engineerium, leaning his head close to hers and speaking quickly and softly. "There are guards on that hangar, but not many, and they'll not stop you going in, what with you being an Engineer, and a Crumb to boot. It's getting out again with your friend that will be the difficulty. There's only the one door; no windows or anything you can slip her out through. But I reckon I can fool the guards into leaving. I'll give it a minute or two after you go in and then run up to them with a story of trouble on the other side of the Gut."

Fever shook her head. A moment before she had been racking her brains for a reckless scheme; now that she had been given one she could only see its flaws. "What if they won't all go? Anyway, the door will be locked. . ."

"Not locked," said Charley. "Bolted. I checked. You leave the guards to me. Once they're out of the way I'll undo the bolts and let you and Miss Morvish out. It's chaos down in the Gut tonight. No one will notice you if you stick to the shadows. You can get her to one of the side exits."

Fever looked at him, mumbling her thanks again. There was concern for her in his eyes; in his pleasant smile. He had nothing to gain by helping her, and no reason to lie. She should be glad to have him on her side. So why did Godshawk's memories, grumbling again in that substrate of her brain, keep reminding her of heels he'd known, and tricksters?

She ignored them and said meekly, "Thank you. Thank you, Charley Shallow."

33

THE SCRIVENER'S MOON

She went on alone, leaving Charley to follow. The elevators were all out of order so she went down the Cat's Creep stairs, down into the bustle and confusion of Base Tier. At the stairs' foot she stopped, shut her eyes, and tried to calm herself, remembering the way to the Gut. She knew that when she got there she would have to talk her way past Cluny's guards, and she was not sure how; she was a dreadful actress, a wretched liar. How would she make them believe her? How would she stop her ears turning red?

She would trust Godshawk's memories, she decided. *They are like a book you can take down whenever you want*, Wavey had said, but that wasn't quite right. They were more like coins on the floor of a dark pool, dimly shining. If she needed to, perhaps she could ignore her own thoughts and reach down into the pool and take out the ones she needed, just as she had that afternoon when her shot brought down the mammoth. She did not know how to spring people from prisons, but Godshawk did. For the first time his memories started to seem like a good thing. They were as much a part of her as the science she'd learned from Dr Crumb or the feelings that Arlo and Cluny had forced her to accept, or the love of danger and excitement she had inherited from Wavey, which made her heart race nervously and deliciously as she started across Base Tier.

The streets were full of people; huddled sleepers camped among their belongings on the pavements, workers hurrying from one repair job to the next, people moving aimlessly, making their way towards the city's edge in search of air that did not smell like hot stoves. Fever shouldered her way through them, glancing back from time to time to make sure that Charley Shallow was still following.

In the Great Under Tier there was chaos, just as he had promised. The huge vault was as packed with people as it had been the last time she was there, on the night of the Lord Mayor's ball. But the doors were open to the night, and instead of dancers and musicians there were salvage gangs heaving wrecked landships and shards of shattered forts up Dr Steepleton's loading ramps, breaking them apart with saws and welding gear. Outside, torches flared in the dwindling ruins of the Great Carn's heart-fort as that too was rendered down, and lines of men, like worker ants, dragged its fragments into London.

She fought her way past the work-gangs, the heaps of salvage, the shouting foremen; past Hangar 10, Hangar

12, and there ahead of her was 14, the big white number stencilled on its tight-shut doors and a space of calm around it; three soldiers standing guard. She stopped and looked at it and wondered again what to do, until a helpful salvageman noticed her there and said, "They're keeping that nomad prophet girl locked up in that one, ready for killing in the morning."

Fever looked over her shoulder. There was Charley Shallow, watching her from the shadows beside a stack of landship wheels. He nodded encouragingly, and she knew that she should feel glad to have him on her side, but she didn't; some unreasonable part of her still didn't trust him. She squared her shoulders, took a deep breath and strode towards Hangar 14.

The guards pulled themselves to attention when they saw her coming. "I am here to see the prisoner," she shouted, above the huge noise of the work going on behind her. "Orders from Dr Crumb."

They looked doubtful, but they could all see the badge she wore. The sergeant in charge of them said, "I'll have to come in with you, Miss . . . I mean, Doctor. . ."

"I will go alone," said Fever, with a quick, contemptuous glance, feeling Godshawk's easy arrogance lifting her chin and stiffening her spine. "She knows secrets. My father told me to speak with her alone."

"That's Dr Crumb's girl," said one of the other men.

"Five minutes, then," the sergeant said. He did not want trouble with Dr Crumb; everyone knew that it was Dr

Crumb who decided who stayed in London and who was left behind. "I'll have to shut you in there with her, miss. Orders. But don't worry; she can't hurt you."

He undid the heavy bolts and swung the door open; swung it shut and bolted it again as soon as Fever had stepped through. It was dim in the hangar; a greasy dimness lit by one weak lamp on the high rafters. A big space that felt small after the Great Under Tier. Last time she had looked into one of these hangars it had seemed cramped and crowded, with two landships parked there side by side. Now it was empty; just tall racks and shelves around the walls stacked with tools and spares; the floor sloping gently to a large drain in the centre that let the water out when the landships were hosed down. Cluny sat hunched against the far wall. They had roped her wrists together and tied her feet to a ring-bolt in the floor, but she raised her head as Fever went towards her. Fever smiled reassuringly, but Cluny did not look reassured. She struggled to rise, frightened, making ready to defend herself; making fists of her bound hands. Fever caught them, held them, hushed her. "Cluny, it's me."

"Fever? You're all right!"

How she had missed that rolling northern voice! "Yes," she said, "I'm all-rrrright."

"Are you making fun of my accent, London girl?"

"I wouldn't d-rrream of it!" said Fever. She knelt down, kissing Cluny's fingers, looking into her poor, bruised, beloved face; into the vast dark pools of her eyes.

Only then did she realize that Cluny was blind.

"It's gone, Fever," said Cluny. "Godshawk, or the Ancestors, or whatever it was. I was touched by the fire from a Tesla gun, and the dreams are gone. I can't see London or the lanterns or any of it any more."

"Can you see anything at all?" asked Fever, thinking in panic, *How can she get away if she cannot see?*

"Nothing," said Cluny.

I will have to go with her, Fever thought, and then realized that that was what she had really meant to do all along. She would not stand watching while Cluny went away from her into the dark, as Arlo had. She would not make the wrong choice again. Of course she would go with her.

Cluny said, "Is this how it was for you, when the magnetic gun went off?"

Fever shook her head and then remembered that Cluny couldn't see her. "No. There was a bright flash, and I passed out for a short time, but after that. . ." She wondered if the device in Cluny's head had been wired somehow to her optic nerve or the vision centres of her brain. She wondered if the pulse from the Tesla gun had scorched her retinas and without mechanimalculae to help repair her she was taking longer to recover her vision than Fever had. "It will be all right," she promised. "You'll see again; you'll see again; in a day or two, a week. . ."

Cluny made the wry little smile that Fever loved. "They're going to kill me in the morning, did they not tell you? Anyway, what is there now to look at, except London,

367

and I've seen enough of that. It's nice to have a chance *not* to see it, for a change. What are you doing?"

Fever had found a hacksaw among the tool racks and was busy cutting the cords on her wrists. "You have to leave."

"Fever, there are guards outside."

"I know," said Fever. "There is someone who will help us. . ." How long had she been in the hangar? A minute? Two? Outside, Charley Shallow would be sending the guards away. In a moment he would undo the bolts and it would be time to go. *Don't trust him*, warned the Godshawk part of her.

She turned, checking the hangar for windows or air vents, but the walls behind the storage racks were blank, just as Charley had said. She had to trust him. There was no other way out, was there?

From behind the stack of landship wheels Charley had watched Fever go into the hangar. He had watched the guard shut the door behind her. He waited, watching, until three minutes had crawled by. He wanted to give her plenty of time to untie the Morvish girl. He wanted to make certain that she was caught red-handed. He wanted her to be dragged back to her father weeping and disgraced. He could already hear himself saying, "I'm sorry to tell you that Miss Crumb was taken helping her nomad friend escape, sir. . ."

When he was sure she had had long enough he ran

to the hangar, shouting, "Stop her! The Crumb girl! She's here to help the prisoner escape! She's got no right! Quickly! She stole my badge!"

The guards sprang up, alarmed, confused, reaching for their rifles. The sergeant was already at the door, the big bolts rattling back. He swung it wide; guns were levelled; the light from welding gear in the Gut sputtered and flashed into the oily dark.

The oily, *empty* dark. The cords that Fever had cut from Cluny's wrists and ankles lay on the deck like a nest of slow-worms. There was no sign of Cluny or Fever, not even when the men brought lanterns in.

"Witchcraft!" whispered one of them.

"Those northerners have powerful technomancy," said another.

"Shut up and look for them, you useless cloots!" yelled Charley, striding into the hangar, his eyes going over the bags and crates and toolboxes on the shelves. None was big enough to conceal an Engineer or a nomad prophetess. He turned, baffled, and the drain cover in the middle of the floor shifted with a small metallic grunt under his foot. He looked down. He stooped and tried it. It lifted easily. "Look, sir!" said one of the guards, and there in the shadows under the shelves lay the four bolts which had held it in place and the socket-wrench which Fever Crumb had used to undo them.

Charley threw the cover aside and stared at the black hole that she had squeezed down. He felt offended that she hadn't trusted him, and puzzled as to why. What now? Go down there after her? He didn't fancy that; anyway, those drains were a real maze. But they must all come out somewhere eventually, down beneath the central tracks. . .

He turned to the shocked and frightened guards. "There's still time to catch them. Come on!"

The shaft led down into a larger sewer; a broad iron tube that snaked along London's underbelly. Through gratings in its roof every few yards water was splattering: water from the ruptured tanks of all those damaged elevators, finding its way out through the new city's drainage systems. Light came down too; not much, but just enough for Fever to see the way ahead as she waded along, leading Cluny by one hand.

"You were right about London," she said. "You were right about all of it. I'm coming with you. We must find your people and the *Kometsvansen*."

Cluny said, "Carn-Morvish-my-father is dead. Marten-my-brother will be Carn now. But how can he protect the people, with all our landships and war-mammoths gone? We shall be at the mercy of small empires, and land pirates, and London. . ."

"Not if you go west, into the hills," said Fever. "Get to the country round Skrevanastuut. We saw good land there, didn't we? Where others will not follow, because they fear the nightwights."

"But we fear the nightwights too!" said Cluny.

"They are just people," said Fever. "I talked to them, remember? I should like to talk to them again. . ."

They waded on a little further, through the downpours from a few more drains, and Cluny said, "If I tell him to, I think Carn-Marten-my-brother will lead the Morvish there. And I think he will be needing a technomancer. Will you be our technomancer, Fever Crumb?"

"I'll be whatever you want me to," said Fever.

The sewer sloped gently towards London's stern, and every forty or fifty yards there was an opening in the floor down which the water gurgled into the darkness between the city's tracks.

"We must jump now," said Fever, when they reached one. "Just like when we left the nightwight lair."

"How far down?" asked Cluny.

"Sometimes you just have to *jump*, remember?"

She guided Cluny to the edge, let her jump, waited a moment, then jumped after her. A long drop. A soft landing, her new white coat drenched in mud. All around her in the dark the huge, tracked wheel-units towered. All around her drips came down, pouring from London's drains and underbelly like rain out of an iron sky. She helped Cluny up and took her hand again and they made their way towards the city's edge, slithering through ditches that its tracks had carved, scrambling up the banked earth between them, until at last they emerged from the shadows and a silver light fell on them.

It was the Scrivener's Moon, hanging full and fat

above the battlefield. It was shockingly bright, and it cast long shadows, and it showed them up clearly to Charley Shallow, who had come out through the hangar doors and was now hurrying through the mud outside the city, keeping watch for them.

It was just their movement that he saw, for their clothes were the same colour as the mud around them. He glanced at the men who followed him, but they were all looking into the shadows under London; they'd not seen. He darted back and snatched a pistol from the sergeant, pointing into the darkness between the nearest banks of tracks. "In there! I thought I saw something move. . ."

Because he wanted to confront Fever Crumb alone. Then, whatever happened, there would only be his word for it. It would have been sweet to go and tell Dr Crumb she'd been arrested, but sweeter still to tell him she'd been shot down trying to resist. There would never be any danger then of Crumb forgiving her. Nor any danger to Charley now, since the girl was unarmed and would not be expecting him. He hefted the gun in his hand, remembering how he'd chased her through the Brick Marsh with Bagman. He'd failed that time; let the old Skinner down. Tonight he was going to make up for that.

He waited until his companions had all gone hurrying into the gloom beneath the city, then turned and ran the other way, straining his eyes in the moonlight for those two fleeing figures.

*

They moved away from London, and the going grew easier, here where the earth had not been torn by the city's weight. Crowds of men were busy down around the open jaws, smashing up wrecks and dragging salvage up the ramps, but here there was only the moonlight and the marsh grass blowing. They turned north, following causeways and winding marshmen's paths.

After a mile or so they reached a patch of dryer ground; a low rise topped with thorn trees, where a burned-out northern landship stood with moonbeams poking through the shot-holes in its hull. Fever paused and looked back. There London lay, immense, rumbling, pricked with window-lights, the smoke of its chimneys smeared across the moon. She imagined how it would grow in the years that were to come; gorging itself on the wreckage of the towns and land-fleets it would conquer, eating on the move, putting up new buildings and new levels as it dragged itself across the earth, never stopping now; five tiers, six, seven. It would be difficult; it would be near impossible; there would be crises and disasters, but her poor, foolish father would make it work. She imagined the machines that the Engineers would soon devise to make the catching and dismantling of its prey easier. The doors of the Gut would be widened and strengthened until they were truly jaws, and they would yawn and snatch and crunch year after year, feeding a hunger that would never end. . .

And she would not be part of it.

She turned away, ready to move on, but as she reached for Cluny's hand a voice called out, "Well! Won't your dad be disappointed when I tell him about all this set-to? He thought you was *so* rational."

Charley Shallow had come up the side of the rise, hidden by that wrecked landship and all the lacy shadows of the trees. He came towards her like a ghost in his white coat, raising the moon-shiny pistol, pulling back its hammer with a creak and a click. Fever backed away from Cluny, and watched the way the gun's mouth followed her. She was surprised that he was there, but not particularly surprised that he was pointing a gun at her again. She had never really believed that he had changed. She scanned the moonlit marsh behind him, trying to see if he'd brought others with him.

"Don't worry," he said. "We're all alone. I got separated from the others somehow. That's what I'll tell your dad, miss, when I get back to London. That's what I'll tell them all. How you attacked me; you and your blind barbarian girlfriend. What else could I do but shoot? Not that old Crumb will care too much. He never wanted you back. You weren't *supposed* to come back, don't you see? Quercus half suspected Raven was planning something, so he let you and your mum go north just to see what happened. Why send human beings into danger when you can send a couple of Dapplejacks? You were his canary down a coalmine. You were the finger he held up to test which way the wind was blowing."

He'd not really thought of that before, but as he said it he realized that there was probably some truth in it. It hurt Fever, anyway, and he enjoyed hurting her, here in the last seconds of her life. "It was a relief to Dr Crumb when you were gone," he said. "'It's so *quiet* without them, Charley,' that's what he said to me. He doesn't need you any more. Not now he's got me. He'll be *glad* you're dead again."

"Fever, who is he?" asked Cluny.

"This is Charley Shallow," said Fever. "The one I told you about. The one who was going to help us."

"He does not *sound* very helpful. . ."

"What tipped you off?" asked Charley, still watching Fever. "How did you work out I'd set you up?"

"Just a feeling," Fever said.

"Funny," he said. "I didn't think your lot went in for them." He went closer to her. Not too close, for you could never trust a Scriven, but he did not want to miss, because the pistol was an old-fashioned one and he had only one shot. He glanced at Cluny as he passed her, but her wide, unseeing eyes told him she was no threat. "Don't worry for yourself, Miss Morvish," he told her. "I'll not hurt *you*. There's an executioner in London waiting to do that, and I'll make sure you get back there to keep your appointment with him."

But Cluny could hear him even if she couldn't see. His words told her where he was, and as soon as he was past she threw herself at him from behind, snatching at the gun. They crashed down together; the pistol dropped;

Fever lunged for it. Charley grabbed her ankles and she fell hard and struggled away from him, running her hands through the grass where she thought the gun had fallen. Charley tried to crawl after her, but Cluny had her hands around his throat and her whole weight on top of him. None of them shouted or spoke; there was no sound except their breathing; the scuffles of their movements, a few strangled grunts from Charley. Fever's hand closed on something in the grass, but it was just a rotten branch. She saw metal glint in the moonlight and went scrabbling for it. Charley kneed Cluny hard in the belly, flung her off him and jumped up panting. Reaching into his coat he pulled out the Skinner's knife and turned, looking for Fever. He found her standing a few feet away, pointing his own pistol at him.

They both remembered the last time they had faced each other like this, across that pool in Godshawk's ragged garden. Back then, Charley had hesitated; now, Fever did not. Before he could lunge at her with the knife she carefully pulled the trigger.

It was the final shot of the Battle of Three Dry Ships, and as the clap of it rolled away across the marshes Charley gave a little whimper of surprise and disappointment. He dropped his blade and put a hand up to his head and stumbled away, knees buckling, folding into the grass. Smouldering scraps of wadding settled round him where he lay, glowed there for a moment like little orange eyes, and went out.

"Fever?" shouted Cluny, not knowing who'd shot who. "Fever?"

"I'm here," Fever said.

"Is he dead?"

"I think so," said Fever.

Charley lay on his side in the grass. She could see the blood spreading across his face like a black hand. Then one of his feet shifted, a little secret movement. Was he only stunned? Or just playing dead, like a child pretending to be asleep? She dropped the empty gun and stooped to pluck his knife out of a tussock, thinking that she should go and finish him, but not wanting to. She felt no guilt about shooting him: that had been rational; he had been a threat. He posed no danger now. She looked at the knife in her hand and read the Skinners' motto branded on its haft.

"Was that why you wanted to trap me, Charley Shallow?" she called out. "Still that same old hatred, after all these years?"

Charley didn't answer. Maybe he *was* dead. She decided that she didn't care. She turned and threw the knife as far as she could, and heard the splash as it fell into a mere.

Charley heard it too. He let out a shivery breath into the wet grass. For a moment he'd been sure she was going to come and stick him with Bagman's knife. Even without it, he didn't fancy the idea of fighting her any more, not her and that nomad wildcat together. Blood was running thickly down the side of his face from where the pistol-ball had clipped his forehead. He did not think the wound was bad, but it was starting to hurt, and coloured shards of light danced behind his closed eyes. For a moment he felt angry at what Fever Crumb had done to him, full of pity for himself and ashamed at the thought of creeping back to London covered in blood and having to admit that he had failed. But his mind kept working, despite the pain, sly and busy as a fox. He quickly saw a better way.

I tried to stop them, Dr Crumb, but Miss Crumb shot me. . . That's what he'd say. *I didn't want to hurt her. I asked her to come quietly but she snatched the pistol from me. . .*

No, Charley Shallow was no failure. He was a brave lad who had only tried to do his duty. He was a wounded hero, and the scar on his brow would be his badge of honour. No one could doubt his loyalty to the new London now he had spilled his blood for it. Maybe the only thing he could have done for himself that was better than shooting Fever Crumb was letting *her* shoot *him. Turn again, Charley*, he thought, and opened one careful eye to watch as Fever walked away from him to where the blind girl knelt. *Turn again Charley; Lord Mayor of London.*

Fever helped Cluny to her feet and they stood there for a moment, holding each other, Cluny still trembling a little.

Fever forgot Charley Shallow. She kissed Cluny's brow, her cheek. "My mammoth-girl," she said, and might have kissed her mouth, except that Cluny drew back in surprise.

"Is this you, Fever?" she asked. "You are not thinking that you're Godshawk again?"

"Oh, I'm me," said Fever. "I think I'm more me than I have ever been."

Cluny did not seem quite certain what she felt about that. She paused, smiled shyly, frowned, and then said, "When that gun went off – I saw the flash."

"You're sure?" asked Fever. She took Cluny's head between her hands, pushing the hair out of her eyes, tilting her face so the moonlight fell upon it. "Can you see anything else?"

"There is a light," said Cluny. "A white light. Is it someone coming?"

Fever laughed. She forgot Charley Shallow. She stuffed the gun into her belt, guessing that even an empty gun might be useful on the road north. "It is the moon," she said, taking Cluny's hand again. "It is only the Scrivener's Moon."

EPILOGUE

That winter was bad. By the time spring crept among the hills there were few men of the People left. That was how Midge came to be made chief. He had never wanted to be anything more than a hunter, but now he was the strongest in the tribe, so it was right that he should lead. He was the only one who had returned from the god-place; he wore a star-shaped scar on his shoulder where one of the mammoth-men's fire-tubes had spat at him, and he carried with him the White Lady's gift, the cup with red signs on it. He had told the People his story, over and again, all through the cold months; how she had come down from the god-place to speak strange words to him and give him the cup. Although she and her companions had fought so fiercely against the People, she had tried to stop the mammoth-men from killing them, and she had saved Midge's life. The shamans said she had been a powerful spirit; a goddess maybe; if Midge had her favour it was right that he be chief.

In the month of Long Light old lame Jek came back one

day from a hunting trip with the news that strangers had come to the valley under the Oakwall; mammoth-folk with tents and herds and things the People had no name for. That was bad, because Oakwall was only a half-day's walk from the caves where the People lived. If the mammoth-folk settled at Oakwall, even for just one summer, then they might find the People, and come hunting them with lights and fire-tubes. Midge thought hard about it. He prayed with his hands wrapped around the White Lady's cup. Then he gathered his few hunters, and they set off for Oakwall to see the strangers for themselves.

They travelled by night and laid up under a rock when the sun came. As the day faded they crept out on to the crags above the valley. The sky was golden, but the sun was old and low and far-off in the west and it no longer hurt Midge's eyes. He heard voices close by. Motioning to his hunters to stay hidden, he wriggled forward on his belly until the valley opened below him like a green bowl, the lake in its bottom still holding the light of the sky, the Oakwall beyond it rearing up in shadow, a high, fissured cliff all cloaked and whispering with twisty trees. There were caves in that cliff where another tribe had lived once. They had died of a sickness long ago and the People did not go there for fear of ghosts.

The newcomers seemed unafraid of ghosts. Tents and big square things Midge did not know a word for were scattered all along the lake shore, and herds of animals were grazing there. Midge started to count the mammoth-folk he could see, but they were too many. Women, children, boys, but not many men. They must have had a bad winter too, he thought, in whatever land they'd come from.

Nearby, water went roaring down between the crags in a channel it had carved for itself through the rock. There a few of the mammoth-folk had gathered, all busy about something in the stream. Theirs were the voices he had heard. They had chosen a strange place to fish. Midge slid through the bracken like an adder to a place where he could look down on the strangers and see what they were doing.

Well, he could see, but he couldn't understand. Two boys were waist-deep in the water, just where it flowed fastest through the steepest and narrowest part of the channel. They were wedging in place there a thing made of metal, a kind of wheel, which started to turn as the water hit it, flicking sharp shards of sunset light into Midge's eyes. The wheel's fat axle stretched across the stream to rest on either bank, and things like ropes or snakes led out of it into a humming wooden box. Two young women waited by the box. One was crouched down, fumbling with the ropey-snaky things, and the other, the dark-haired one, was trying to help, but Midge could tell by the way she moved that something was wrong with her eyes. He thought how rich these mammoth-folk must be to have let her live. Then, as he studied her face, it began to seem to him that she was the one who had been at the god-place the previous summer. One of those boys in the stream, the fair one, he had been there too. And the other young woman, the one who was laughing at something which the half-sighted one had just said. . .

He must have flinched when he recognized her, because she stopped laughing and looked up at him, and even from that distance he knew her odd-coloured eyes and her face which was so almost-like the faces of the People. It was his White Lady – looking whiter than ever now, for her hair was tied back off her strange face, and instead of the brown clothes of the mammoth-men's women she wore a coat of white that fluttered in the wind, so bright it hurt Midge's eyes.

She jumped the stream and stood on the near bank, looking up at where Midge lay. He didn't think that she could see him, but she knew that he was there. The boys had scrambled out of the stream, groping for the weapons which lay beside their strewn clothes, but she made a gesture and they did not pick the weapons up. The other young woman called out to her, "Be careful!" but she did not look back.

"Hello!" she called. "Don't be afraid. My name is Fever. I think we've met before."

Midge trembled, and let go his spear, and stood up so that she could see him. There was no point trying to hide from a goddess. He called to the others and saw them from the corners of his eyes as they stood up too, laying down their spears.

Fever Crumb's eyes swept over them and then returned to Midge; those big, serious eyes of hers, one grey, one brown. She smoothed her coat, and touched the amulet around her neck. Smiling, she came towards him through the bracken, holding out her hands.

ACKNOWLEDGEMENTS

Toiling away down in the engine rooms of the World of Mortal Engines are a lot of people without whom the whole thing would grind to a horrible, shuddering halt. They include my editors Marion Lloyd, Alice Swan and Jessica White, Alyx Price and her team in publicity, and everybody else at Scholastic; my agent, Philippa Milnes-Smith; Karl Barwe Paul for the *Kometsvansen*; my military advisor and ideas testing range Jeremy Levett, and the Legend that is Kjartan Poskitt. Thank you all.

DISCOVER THE SECRETS
OF ANNA FANG'S PAST IN

NIGHT
FLIGHTS

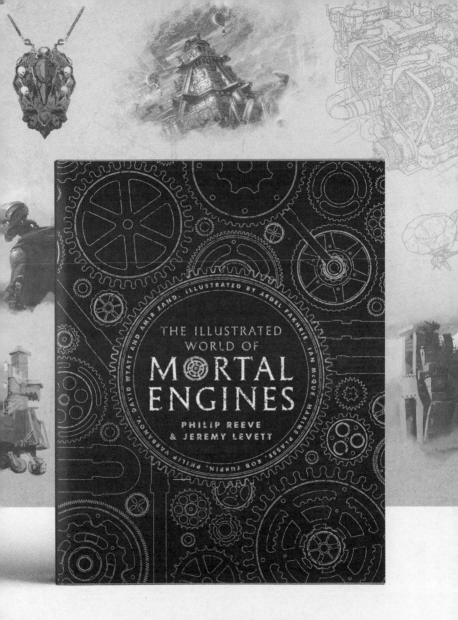

THE ILLUSTRATED
WORLD OF
**MORTAL
ENGINES**

PHILIP REEVE
& JEREMY LEVETT

DAVID WYATT AND AMIR ZAND. ILLUSTRATED BY AFDEL FAKHRIE, IAN McQUE, MAXIME PLASSE, PHILIP VARBANOV. ROB TURPIN, PHILIP VARBANOV.

A FULL-COLOUR ILLUSTRATED
GUIDE TO THE WORLD PHILIP
REEVE HAS CREATED ACROSS
FIFTEEN YEARS AND
EIGHT BOOKS.

Philip Reeve was born in Brighton in 1966. He worked in a bookshop for many years before becoming an illustrator and then an author. His debut novel, *Mortal Engines*, the first in the award-winning epic series, was an instant bestseller and won the Smarties Gold Award. The Mortal Engines Quartet and its three subsequent prequels cemented his place as one of Britain's best-loved authors. In 2008 he won the CILIP Carnegie Medal with *Here Lies Arthur*.

His recent works include the Railhead trilogy and a series of books for younger children, co-written and illustrated by Sarah McIntyre. A movie version of *Mortal Engines* was released in 2018. He lives with his wife and son on Dartmoor.

WWW.PHILIP-REEVE.COM